WMD ONE: TRIPLE PLAY

A WMD Directorate Novel

MAVERICK LEE

ISBN-13: 978-0692670361

Printed in the United States of America

This book is dedicated to those individuals who fight to prevent the use of Weapons of Mass Destruction (WMD) anywhere in the world.

TABLE OF CONTENTS

PROLOGUE

The huge army supply warehouse was filled with at least seventy-five men pointing large caliber machine guns at each other. The Chechen, Colonel Umarov, eyed the Iranian, Amir Abbasi, warily. "Give me my money now," Umarov demanded.

"Give me my merchandise then," Amir demanded in return.

Colonel Umarov motioned to a few of his men, who wheeled a small wooden crate into the middle of the warehouse. Amir similarly motioned to a few of his comrades, who placed fifty large black duffle bags on the row of tables next to the Colonel.

It took twenty Chechens over one and a half hours to count and test the money. The Chechens did not want to be swindled, so they meticulously examined every stack of US$100 bills, testing a sample of each of them using ultraviolet light and chemicals to ensure that they weren't counterfeit. The bills were all real. The total count in the duffle bags was a cool $100 million.

Meanwhile, during the time that the Chechens were examining the money, Amir's men had opened and were inspecting the small, lead composite-lined crate. Inside was a military-style backpack, clearly of Russian origin, with various plastic and metallic parts protruding out of it. The Iranians also did not want to be swindled, so they carefully scrutinized the backpack, testing it with various instruments that they had brought along with them. The backpack itself contained a basic keyboard and screen, so they turned the screen on and tested all of the backpack's components. A background hiss and telltale clicks emanated from the Iranians' Geiger counters all during this time, indicating the appropriate presence of ionizing radiation. Like the cash, the backpack too was real. It was a special Russian GRU variant of an "RA-115" army tactical field weapon – in layman's terms, a Weapon of Mass Destruction (WMD), in this case a 2 kiloton nuclear bomb.

   Allahu akbar (God is the greatest), thought Amir to himself. *Now we can take the fight to the Americans.*

PART I

"Eternal vigilance is the price of liberty."
-Attributed to Wendell Phillips

CHAPTER 1

Nogales is a city that straddles both the United States and Mexico. It is the largest international border town in Arizona. On the US side, the population only numbers about 20,000, but on the Sonora, Mexico side, there are over ten times as many people – for a total of about a quarter of a million people overall. With that many people, you can easily remain hidden in Sonora, Mexico. And that is what Amir's group wanted. Their guide was José Acevedas, a Sonoran by birth. José was a member of the Ciudad gang. The gang specialized in smuggling illegal aliens and drugs across the border. American movies always depict illegal aliens running across deserted roads and hills in the dead of the night, through holes in border fences that have been cut by their handlers. Of course, that is how a few illegal aliens and drug runners do manage to get through. But a much larger number of illegal aliens and drugs also pass into the United States at night, or even in broad daylight, through a series of tunnels that connect the countries in border towns like Nogales.

Since the mid-1990s, US and Mexican law enforcement authorities have discovered scores of tunnels that span the US-Mexico border. The tunnel that José would use was in a nondescript Mexican apartment building in between the streets Internacional and Calle Del Rey, about 150 feet away from the border. The other end of the tunnel ended in a warehouse on East Delaware Street, approximately 550 feet away from the border, on the US side. The tunnel had been designed to move both people and drugs into the US, while also allowing guns and cash to get into Mexico. Ironically, this tunnel had been found previously by US Customs and the DEA after a joint drug interdiction program. The tunnel, as a result, had been sealed up two years ago. Logistical reasons, however, prevented the authorities from completely filling in all the tunnels that they found. First, it was too expensive to do this for all of the tunnels. Second, in many cases, the effort could have precipitated cave-ins. So instead, US Customs and the DEA had resorted to sealing only the entrances and exits to the tunnels. Now the US governmental agencies were not stupid; they had sealed the ends of the tunnels very carefully, and had placed monitoring devices on the seals, with alarms that would be set off if the seals were broken. But there were hundreds of tunnels along the US-Mexico border and the US government simply could not monitor all of them. José's gang had cleverly tunneled into this tunnel from a close, but different, location under the Sonoran apartment building, thereby negating the alarms. Indeed, their side tunnel exit ended up only thirty-five feet away from the original tunnel exit. The Border Patrol, itself a part of US Customs, couldn't alarm every part of the tunnel. José's gang took advantage of this fact.

Moreover, José's gang had thwarted the ground radar that the Border Patrol used to ferret out human and drug smuggling. The Ciudad gang conducted their activities solely during the daylight hours. Because of budget cuts and manpower constraints, it was impossible for the Border Patrol to use ground-penetrating radar 24 hours per day. Instead, they had to concentrate their efforts at night, which was generally the right call. Ninety percent of the drugs and people moved at night.

But José's gang succeeded by not doing what was considered normal and customary. The gang realized that the best approach for them was to "hide" in broad daylight. They had a special deal with the owners of the warehouse, themselves

Mexican nationals, who used the facility to store the perfectly legal electronics components that eventually got shipped to Mexico for further work by the *maquiladoras* that dotted the town.

Therefore, during the noon hour of a cold and blustery Friday in the last half of December, four people entered the Calle del Rey apartment building. One was José. The other three looked of indeterminate national origin. They all wore worker's coveralls that identified them as janitorial workers of the Highpoint Electronics Warehouse on the American side. Amir was the leader of the three. Javad Mazdani was the finance guy, and the most fanatically devout. Karim Shirazi was the technical expert in the group. Karim got to wheel or help carry the crate that contained the RA-115 backpack. The backpack remained in fairly good shape, only a little beat up after its travels from Chechnya. The nuke had been through thirteen countries since leaving the Chechnyan army barracks warehouse about two months ago. The RA-115 had remained almost in pristine condition because it had remained in its lead composite-lined crate, although it had been jostled around a bit.

Wheeling around, or sometimes helping to carry the crate, though, wasn't easy on Karim. The backpack alone weighed a shade above forty pounds, and when you included the lead composite-lined crate, the combined weight was over a hundred and fifty pounds. Forty pounds was not a light load by any means for the nuke itself. It was way less than previous versions of the RA-115, however, which were not only heavier but larger too.

"Ándele, Ándele," José muttered to them, making the universal hand signal for the group to hurry up.

While Amir, Javad and Karim barely understood even basic Spanish, they unmistakably understood the need for speed here. The threesome quickened their pace. José led them through the apartment lobby rapidly, and the group quickly descended to the basement level. They got to the storage closet and José produced the key to open the door. José only needed a short time to unscrew the large wall panel inside the storage closet. The group crawled through the open panel and into the tunnel. José replaced the wall panel after the last of them had gotten through, and after they had lowered the crate into the tunnel via a pulley and rope system.

The tunnel itself was dark, dusty and full of spider webs. *The explorers opening the Egyptian pyramids must have felt the same way,* Karim thought to himself, *when they found the secret passage to the tombs of the pharaohs.* The air in the tunnel smelled musty as well, as though the tunnel had not been used for years. In fact, this tunnel had been used only about thirteen months ago by José himself to move about 200 kilos of high-quality cocaine into Arizona. José's gang had avoided using this tunnel since then until now, so as to avoid falling into a predictable pattern, where bystanders might begin to recognize them. Instead, José and the Ciudad gang alternated using one of the other fifteen tunnels that the gang had as primary or backup ways into Arizona.

As the trio slowly moved down the dark tunnel, the passage narrowed slightly as they slowly and quietly moved closer to the US border. It was about 12:15pm in the afternoon and there was a fair amount of noise right outside the tunnel. The group could hear the regular apartment noises of Mexican housewives making their lunches, washing their laundry and carrying out their other daily afternoon household chores. They could also hear the muffled sounds of the numerous shopkeepers on Internacional Avenue hawking their wares to the tourists shopping for trinkets to take back home.

Despite these background noises, the group proceeded very quietly so as not to attract attention. While the tunnel was about five feet high so that they didn't have to crawl, nonetheless it was still slow going, walking stooped over, especially with Karim wheeling his heavy load bent over in an awkward position. If they had made any loud noises, it might attract undue attention and alert someone to their presence. So they were careful. Careful and slow. Karim was perspiring heavily from having to drag the crate over the uneven tunnel ground, so much so that the armpits of his janitorial coveralls were drenched in sweat.

By 12:57pm, the group had reached the warehouse on East Delaware Street, and after some additional effort, had managed to get through the wall panel of a large storage closet in the warehouse. Karim slumped down wearily on the floor, motioning to José that he needed to rest. His partners Javad and Amir only had to carry regular daypacks, nowhere near as difficult as Karim's load. Since Javad was the finance guy, his backpack contained thick wads of used twenty and one hundred dollar bills. This cash would allow them to survive in the United States until they had completed their mission. While they rested, the group ate a quick lunch of burritos and horchata that José's gang had previously hidden in the storage closet.

Karim, Amir and Javad ate and drank together in silence, each of them ruminating quietly about all of the trials and tribulations they had undergone to get here. They had survived a few close calls getting out of Chechnya, and the trio had almost died in a terrifying boat ride across the Atlantic, where they each had gotten violently seasick and had suffered from dysentery-like symptoms. But they had all made it.

"We need to focus now," Karim admonished his friends in Farsi. "Is Hossein ready to pick us up?"

"He better be," replied Amir. "I just spoke with him yesterday to confirm our schedule. He said that he had the van and that he would meet us here at 5pm."

"Then we must hide the crate again until 5pm," Karim noted to the other two. Karim moved over to a large mobile garbage bin with wheels, and opened up the false bottom. The trio carefully lifted the crate containing the nuclear backpack into that bottom; afterwards, Karim told Javad and Amir to put in their packs as well. Next, Karim cut some foam elements to fill up the empty space remaining so that the false bottom fit snugly after it was placed back on the garbage bin. The trio then took turns placing trash on top of that false bottom. Voila, they had now created the illusion of a three-quarters-full garbage bin.

José provided the threesome with some brooms and other janitorial equipment, and the group spent the next three or four hours moving around the factory floor, emptying trash cans into various garbage bins and otherwise living the life of a warehouse janitor. It was exhausting. When 5pm rolled around, Amir's arms ached, Karim's back was killing him, and Javad desperately needed a nap. But at least they only needed to do this for one day. Being a real janitor was amazingly tough work.

Since it was quitting time, they went to the loading dock at the back of the warehouse, emptying out the trash in their bin into an industrial trash container. Hossein was late, really late. The group grew edgy as they waited for Hossein, none more so than Javad who was cursing Hossein in a low voice the whole time. Most of the Highpoint warehouse workers had already left by 5:30pm, so they tried to look inconspicuous, sitting there on the steps of the loading dock, with a 2 kiloton nuclear weapon only five feet away from them.

At 6:18pm, a large white van glided into the loading dock area and squeaked to a halt next to the group. The van had Nevada plates, very few other discernible markings, and seemed to run a little low on its suspension. It rode low because of all of the lead composite plates in the cargo area weighing down the car. Hossein got out of the driver's side door, with Javad immediately tearing into him.

"Where have you been?" exploded Javad. "You're over an hour late!"

"I can't believe you!" yelled Karim.

"We need to get out of here now," Amir said, speaking in a low and even voice, "without making a scene. We can argue later."

José stood there with his hands crossed, mildly amused at these outbursts, but saying nothing. José had seen too many drug traffickers bickering among themselves for him to say anything or to otherwise get involved. He might get beat up or killed. José just wanted to get paid and to get out of there, back to the Sonora, Mexico side.

The lead composite-lined crate with the RA-115 backpack went into yet another lead composite-lined hideaway compartment, this time within the raised floorboards of the van. Javad then pulled out three stacks of $100 bills to finish paying off José. Javad had argued forcefully that they should kill José as they were leaving, but Amir, as the group's leader, had vetoed the idea. Amir reasoned that killing José would have potentially attracted too much attention from the police. It also would have resulted in José's gang looking for retribution. Amir's team needed to stay under the radar for approximately two more weeks – after that, it wouldn't matter as their job would be done.

"Big brother," Hossein said to Amir in perfect English, "I know that you are mad at me. And I know that I have been late to things almost all of my life, starting from when we were just little kids growing up. But I have always come through in the end."

Amir just shook his head and replied. "You are just like Uncle Mehdi. Always with the excuses. Always not doing what you are supposed to do. I'm used to it. Not going to get into an argument with you now; we need to get going immediately." They had a long drive in front of them to get to Nevada.

CHAPTER 2

"Bright Red. Coordinates 39.45 degrees north, 119.74 degrees west. Vector 121."

"Copy that, Birdmaster. We are verifying Bright Red via fly-by."

The FBI's Weapons of Mass Destruction Directorate was in control of this operation. The WMD Directorate had access to the Department of Defense's state-of-the-art military satellite radiation sensors, which had picked up the telltale signal of plutonium at the coordinates. After the signal had been detected, Don Llewes, the head of the Nuclear Emergency Support Team (NEST), which was the key nuclear scientific and technical assistance group supporting the WMD Directorate, had scrambled its eight-person Lincoln Diamond Nuclear Radiological Advisory Team (NRAT) to the area.

The plutonium signal had emanated from an area just southeast of the main Reno airport. Two reconnaissance members of the NRAT had taken NEST's King Air B-200 aircraft from Nellis Air Force Base in Las Vegas to perform the first low and slow fly-by runs. The aircraft had ultra-sensitive radiation detection equipment, which would allow the NRAT to confirm the satellite imagery.

After the confirmation, NEST protocol was that the NRAT would scramble a Bell 412 helicopter and two "Hot Spot Mobile" trucks to the area to pinpoint the exact type of radiation, together with its precise location, down to the nearest meter. Within one hour of the satellite warning, the King Air aircraft had in fact provided the needed confirmation. As a result, the remaining four members of Lincoln Diamond, together with two other members of the NEST logistical team and their trucks, were ensconced in a modified C-130J Super Hercules military transport plane on the way to Reno-Tahoe International Airport.

Katherine "K2" Kung felt the adrenaline rush as the transport plane took off. This was her first mission as the Lincoln Diamond NRAT leader, and K2 was proud of her team: she felt that they were ready for anything. Katherine was a thirty-one year old wunderkind, with a bachelor's degree and a PhD in physics, both from Stanford. She had worked a few years at the Lawrence Livermore National Laboratory (LLNL) in Northern California, as a nuclear weapons simulation scientist, but then she got interested in ensuring nuclear deterrence, so she started working for NEST. K2 was still based in Livermore at LLNL, as most of the NEST scientists in the NRAT were either based at LLNL or at Los Alamos National Laboratory (LANL) in New Mexico. It was a very incestuous relationship among the NEST personnel and the regular LLNL and LANL lab staffs because of how specialized the nuclear physics field was. Often, NEST scientists were given regular LLNL and LANL lab jobs as cover, to hide their affiliation with NEST.

Today, the FAA had given Lincoln Diamond a flight designation of FLYMASTER, meaning that they had priority over all other aircraft in the adjacent airspace or on the ground. Every other aircraft would just have to get out of their way. This was better than being in first-class on a commercial jetliner. It was more like having a special FASTPASS at Disneyland that allowed you to cut into the front of every line. No waiting for them.

The low whirring of the blades of the Bell 412 chopper came on the airwaves as the co-pilot radioed in his finding. They had zeroed in on the radiation source: it was triple-confirmed now as plutonium, and the signal was steady, if not particularly strong. Even though the chopper had the latest sound-deadening technology, much like the MH-60 Black Hawk stealth helicopters that were used in the raid to get Osama bin Laden, the chopper pilot and co-pilot didn't want to get too close to their target for fear that they would be discovered. The plutonium signal was coming from an industrial warehouse about three and a half miles southeast of the Reno-Tahoe International Airport.

With the triple-confirmation, Don Llewes made the NEST procedural call: "Implementing augmentation protocol. Lincoln Diamond Augmentation Team is live. Code for the operation is Snow Falcon."

"Roger that, Birdmaster," Katherine replied.

The Lincoln Diamond Augmentation Team consisted of thirty-one people, including the NRAT. The augmented team constituted a full complement of nuclear weapons specialists, as well as some additional logistic personnel. "K2, you have operational control of all NEST assets on the ground. FBI Special Agent in Charge Smithline is running Snow Falcon overall. Report to me as well for all technical issues."

"Roger, Birdmaster. Understood. We will be on-site in fifty minutes." The other 21 team members would be arriving by different methods, mostly other airplanes and helicopters, but the entire team would all be there within two hours. The C-130J Super Hercules cargo plane glided down the tarmac and came to a rest near an air freight hangar at the side of the Reno-Tahoe airport that the FBI had commandeered. The Super Hercules was huge, and had replaced the C-141 Starlifters that NEST had previously used because of that increased capacity. Three FBI agents were stationed there already and were waiting for the NEST team to disembark.

Two NEST trucks rolled smoothly out the back of the military cargo transport plane. Immediately, NEST logistical team members began to finish plastering the trucks with the logos of the main electric power company for Reno. These logistical specialists could make the trucks look like utility trucks for the electric, water, cable or phone companies of any of the top thirty or so cities in the United States. They had authentic paint color panels and logos, even down to realistic numbering codes and license plates for the trucks. The logistics team members worked quickly. Next to them, four NRAT members began to fiddle with the nuclear weapon detection equipment, making sure that they weren't adversely affected by the flight, before reloading the pieces into the truck.

Three FBI agents watched the NEST team at work with detached amusement. Some of the equipment looked like it came out of a Star Wars movie set. There was even a piece of equipment that looked like a big flamethrower attached to a large set of tanks. This device could be wheeled around or worn like a bulky backpack. One of the younger FBI agents nudged his compatriot, pointing out K2.

"Wow, not bad. Pretty hot, considering she's one of them NEST geeks. She's probably just started over there. I'm going to go over and see if I can score some points." He ambled over to K2, who was busy reviewing her checklist and tweaking a handheld gamma radiation detector.

"Hi there, ma'am. I'm Kyle Adams, local Reno FBI. We're here to escort NEST to the Snow Falcon command center. It's only a couple of miles away from the Bright Red site. Can you tell me who is leading NEST here on the ground?" Kyle pointed to one of the older NEST guys. "We heard that his nickname is K2. Is it this guy?" He moved forward, closer to K2, trying to act natural.

K2 looked up from what she was doing, quizzically regarding the junior G-man. "No, it's not," she smiled sweetly at Kyle, "I'm K2, Katherine Kung, and I'm in charge here. And of the entire Lincoln Diamond Augmentation Team."

"And there's a strike out," muttered Sam Chalkias in a low voice. Sam was the FBI compatriot to whom Kyle had been previously talking. "Sorry about that, ma'am; Kyle here is pretty new here. The only women he knows are his mom and sisters. Well, maybe a few casino blackjack dealers too." Kyle's face turned bright crimson. "We need an estimated time for departure," Sam continued. "We'll split up in the trucks with you to support the deployment. Since we're locals, we can show the drivers the best route. SAIC Smithline wants you, K2, to come with me and set up shop in the command center first."

Before K2 could answer Sam, another NEST member started talking. "Hey, K2, we are checked out and good to go on the gamma, neutron and long-range alpha detectors," reported K2's chief technical officer, Ben Yang. Ben was a lanky thirty-nine year old, with a PhD from Caltech in nuclear physics. The assistant technical chief, Sri Srikanth, also a PhD from Caltech and in the same graduating class as Ben Yang, echoed the sentiment.

"Backup foamer is good," Sri noted, "but as you know, the primary one is still sometimes screwy. Running the diagnostics on it. Nothing concrete so far." The FBI agents looked to K2 for guidance as to when they would be ready to go.

"OK then," K2 nodded, "we'll be ready to roll in five minutes. We'll re-run the tests for the primary foamer on the fly."

Five minutes later, the group drove out of the air freight hangar into a crisp December morning. While there was no snow on the ground yet this year, the forecast was for very heavy snow within the next ten days. It was about eight degrees Fahrenheit, with a slight wind. Low clouds littered the Reno sky, and it brought about a somber feeling to the day, perfectly appropriate in light of the situation. K2 rode in the passenger seat of a black Suburban with Sam, invisible through the tinted and bulletproof windows. The two utility trucks followed closely behind the Suburban as they entered onto the airport access road. The caravan quickly moved through the Reno streets in the heavily industrial part of town. There was a little bit of traffic in the area, but it was not that bad since this was the weekend. At least they could avoid fighting the regular morning commute.

Sam drove the Suburban to the command center, which was only about two miles away from the Bright Red warehouse in a different warehouse zone. After the FBI had made a few calls to AT&T, a functional command center had been quickly assembled. The command center contained a number of dedicated high-bandwidth telephone and internet lines, attached to a local telephone central office box, to handle the special command computer and wired and wireless communications equipment that the FBI needed to run the operation. The command center technicians were surrounded by a maze of wiring and power cords tied to computer equipment. The whole setup looked like what a "command center" should look like. In the back of the warehouse stood huge backup power generators, together with a bunch of wireless signal amplifiers, all of high-level quality and all with military-grade encryption. This was top-notch stuff. The place resembled a US military command post more than anything else, and in fact that is what it really was.

That was mostly because about 99% of the FBI's nuclear counterterrorism team came from the US military, often from various Special Forces units. So they generally all knew each other, or knew of each other, from their military experiences. Thus, they had a similar mindset that translated into how they operated the unit. FBI Special Agent in Charge (SAIC) David Smithline was no exception. Only thirty-two years old, David already had commanded an Army 1st Special Forces Operational Detachment-Delta unit, commonly known as Delta Force. He had participated in over eighteen classified military operations, mostly in Afghanistan and Iraq. Originally from Raleigh, North Carolina, and a graduate of nearby Duke University, like his father and grandfather before him, David exuded the charm of a Southern gentleman, had the intellectual firepower befitting a magna cum laude graduate of the Duke history department, and exhibited the athletic prowess resulting from being a collegiate wrestler. A solid combination.

There were ten other FBI agents at the command center already, mostly communication specialists, with five more on the way. The center was operational, but perhaps only 75% fully ready to go, so there was a hustle and bustle about the place as the agents worked to get the command center fully "battlefield-ready." Sam had parked the Suburban and guided K2 into the command post.

"David," Sam said, "here's Katherine Kung from NEST."

"Thanks Sam. Hey K2," David remarked, "congrats on the promotion. Hope Duane is enjoying his retirement. Ben and Sri at the Bright Red site yet? Give me the summary."

"Hi David. Ben and Sri are setting up," K2 reported. "Here's what we've got so far, most of which you know already from Don: plutonium-239 is confirmed. Signature looks Russian in origin, very likely from the ADE-2 reactor in Zheleznogorsk, which was shut down in early 2010. Ben is in 'Hot Spot One' truck, and will park here, just outside the back gate of the Bright Red warehouse." K2 pointed to the location on the huge map of the warehouse area that the FBI had printed out of the Bright Red site from satellite imagery. "Sri is in 'Hot Spot Two' near the front of Bright Red, but needs to be more over here," K2 pointed to a different spot on the map, "since this is where the utility box is located. We have to make it look like they're fixing something. We're doing further technical analysis to figure out the exact amount of plutonium. It's a lot, we can't tell exactly, but a significant amount of plutonium-239. Definitely not good. Based on what we know so far, the call is that it's an IND, but we can't be sure yet. It could be a regular nuclear bomb."

Jack Smith, from the Defense Intelligence Agency (DIA) spoke up. "OK, we don't have good intel on the bad guys here. Chatter from a few signal intercepts and some linguistic analysis indicates that the men are from various Middle Eastern countries: The leader probably is from Al Qaeda, but there could be some folks from Hezbollah, and maybe even some from the Iranian Al Qods Force. These guys are teaming up more these days. We don't know how they got the plutonium into the country, maybe through Canada or Mexico, but I would bet on Mexico since this is the Southwest. These guys are all well-trained by Al Qaeda near as we can tell. They're also pretty well-organized, which makes us think that this was planned out for at least three years. Some serious money went into this operation, probably financed through Al Qaeda or Islamic Jihad in Yemen."

"Okay. Jim, given what Jack just said, what's the initial recommendation?"

Jim was Jim Broussard, David's friend even way back in his early Delta Force days, and a proud member of the Army's 52nd Ordnance Group based out of Fort Campbell, Kentucky. Jim ran the Explosive Ordnance Disposal (EOD) unit that was designated as the Army partner of the FBI's nuclear counterterrorism unit. The EOD was responsible for figuring out how to neutralize nuclear weapons, whether they were full-fledged nuclear weapons, improvised nuclear devices (INDs) or "dirty" bombs, more generally called radiological dispersion devices (RDDs).

Jim pointed to a digital printout of the interior floor plan of the warehouse that the FBI had taken from an electronic database of Reno real estate records. "We will need two of your guys to do recon first, David. We need to be sure that this interior floor plan is up-to-date. If the plutonium-239 is in this office part of the warehouse here," Jim motioned towards the upper center of the floor plan, "then, we take two 30mm cannon Humvees and place them here and here. From the satellite imagery, looks like the plutonium is stored in a box within a closet off the main office, which helps because it is in an enclosed space. According to your techs, infrared heat signatures show seventeen terrorists: five guarding the perimeter (including one perched on the warehouse roof), ten scattered in various parts of the warehouse, and two in the office where the plutonium is."

"Can we get a pipe and hose to the closet for the foamers?" K2 asked.

"Just what I was thinking," Jim said. "We take a hose and stick it down the air vent here. Then we pipe it into the closet over there. After that, we flood that closet just before we enter to try to capture the IND with Mark's ground troops. But we also enter with our Humvees just in case we can't retrieve the bomb before they try to activate it, in which case we blast the IND apart with the 30mm cannons that I was talking about. The Humvees will be in quadrant X4 and quadrant B7."

Now it was Mark Childress's turn to speak up. Mark was the leader of the twenty FBI ground troops who would try to capture the IND or nuke before it could be activated. "I've got ten guys who will storm the front door, led by Artie M, and ten guys, led by Paul Antam, for the back door. They will start taking out the twelve terrorists as fast as they can. It will be dicey. At least five of the terrorists inside will probably be awake and armed. And one of the two in the office will likely be awake, or awaken quickly, so he could try to detonate the IND before we can secure it. We believe that it's fairly likely that we will have to blast the IND to smithereens rather than just seize it."

K2 piped in, "We will have eight members of the Lincoln Diamond Augmentation Team who will be in hazmat suits ready to check out the plutonium radiation levels if we have to blast it. They'll be standing by to get inserted after the firefight is over."

"All right," David spoke up, "work with the subteams and plan it out with my tactical ops group. Meanwhile, K2, keep me informed about any new information about the nuclear materials." And so the teams gathered together for the tough part of planning the intricate operation, trying to anticipate the various contingencies that could occur.

The command center was abuzz with activity for the next two hours, as they went back and forth planning various scenarios and contingency plans. At the end of that time, Ben stopped by to report in to K2.

"Just what we thought, K2. We have a reading consistent with a significant amount of plutonium-239. 99.99% certainty that is from the ADE-2 reactor. We uplinked our own copy of the floor plan, and can double-confirm that the plutonium is in a closet in quadrant E3. Foamers would be an excellent choice. They would dampen any radiation spread from the 30mm cannons, and just one foamer would cover the closet, which we estimate at a volume of, let's see, 10 feet by 5 feet by 11 feet, equals about 550 cubic feet. Each foamer is rated to cover 800 cubic feet, so we have a lot of leeway there with just one foamer. Infrared shows only one bad guy on the roof, so the FBI tactical team will have to take that terrorist out, and then rope down to the closet to get to the air vent. Shouldn't be too much of a problem."

"Yeah, right, Ben," K2 replied. "Heard that before. It's always what we don't know that bothers me."

Day had turned into night in Reno and the bright lights of the downtown casinos dominated the nighttime sky. The five terrorists guarding the outside of the warehouse were bundled up in thick jackets to protect themselves against the frigid temperature. As with all guards, they grew more and more tired as the day had progressed. Boredom had started to affect the guards, and they seemed more intent in staying warm than in serving as lookouts. Even so, the terrorists had an established routine for switching watch duties, rotating every eight hours.

The FBI believed that they had a good sense of the operation: fifteen of the terrorists were the muscle of the group, arrayed into three groups of five, likely serving eight hour shifts each, with an additional two terrorist leaders being the brains and responsible for the IND. One of these two was probably the technical lead and the other the overall group leader.

Since there were only two entrances into the warehouse - the main front door and the back loading dock area - it was easy to understand why the terrorist leaders would station two men each at the front and back. The lone terrorist lookout guard on the roof was an extra security precaution. That individual, if not taken care of, could sound the alarm and thwart the whole plan.

The main scenario plan was coming together nicely. The FBI would place a number of snipers on the roofs of adjoining warehouses. These sharpshooters would be positioned so that they could simultaneously take out the five terrorists guarding the perimeter. While these terrorist lookouts had radios, they didn't use them except for check-ins about an hour before each shift change. The FBI communications guys had been analyzing the radio chatter among the terrorists and could jam the radio signals at those frequencies anyway at the right moment just in case. The twenty man FBI assault team would quickly move into place by foot after the snipers had taken out the terrorists.

The team had argued a bit about the best timing to go in. David was adamant about going in sometime around the midpoint of the midnight to 8am shift. That would be a time that the guards would be really tired, and when many of the other guards (and hopefully the leaders) would likely be sound asleep. The lack of light would be helpful too as only they would have night vision equipment, while the terrorists would be in the dark. K2 noted that her team would need at least 20 minutes to set up and deploy the foamer through the air vent and into the closet. And that was only once the foamer was in place on the warehouse roof; there was the not so small matter of figuring out how to get the foamer on the roof in the first place. The team quickly reached a consensus on this. They would use a special stealth version of the MH-60 Black Hawk helicopter to quietly transport a foamer (and the backup) for that task. Ben and Sri would be on point for this job.

3:30 am (known in military jargon as 0330 hours or just 0330) Pacific Time (PT) was agreed to as the initial go time. It was only about six hours away, and they had lots of preparatory work to do in that period of time. For crack teams like the FBI and NEST people, this was when they thrived. They were all adrenaline junkies and the rush from the stress of meeting a known deadline kept them going and focused on the task at hand.

Ben and Sri had the toughest technical jobs. The primary foamer was still finicky, and they didn't know why. The foam itself seemed not to like the cold, as it was clumping. The NEST techs had drained the tank and were figuring out the best refilling methodology.

"What's the deal with this thing?" Sri complained. "It's jamming all the time. The foam should be like whipped cream here, and it's coming out like small moon rocks, or sometimes even not coming out."

"Yeah, the foamer was stored in a warm environment, within specs, but at the high range of the temperature specification," Ben replied. "Looks like the foam doesn't like these big temperature swings. I've got a call into Jindar at the manufacturer, and he's looking into the development notebooks to see if he's got any solutions."

"I'm not holding out much hope on that, buddy. We've got, like," Sri looked at his watch, "five to six hours max before go time."

"Yeah I know. But what else do you want me to do about it? I've slowly cranked down the temperature in the reservoir tank filler. Every thirty minutes, it'll drop another five degrees. I figure by about 2am or so, we can begin to refill the tank from the reservoir and avoid the clumps."

"How about the backup tank?" Sri wondered.

"It's testing fine for now, as you know. So don't jinx us. Maybe the temperature gradient's only one of the factors; maybe there's also something mechanical going on here in the pump. I can't figure it out, though, because the diagnostics were checking out on both of the tanks earlier."

K2 had wandered by and made eye contact with Ben and Sri. To her unspoken "are we good?" stare, they gave her the universal shrug stating "we're trying, just leave us alone." K2 knew better than to interfere; Ben and Sri would let her know if they needed help or if something was really wrong.

Jim's team was in a different cluster in the warehouse. If snatching the bomb didn't work, they were tactically thinking about how to best blast the hell out of the IND after the foam was in place. Luckily, they had a fixed, non-moving target at which to aim. That helped a lot. 30mm cannons, though, are rather big, and hard to get in the right position in a city warehouse environment. Essentially, Jim's team had three separate Humvee vehicles with 30mm cannons mounted on the top. These single-barreled cannons were computer-controlled and could fire at an alarmingly fast rate of about 300 rounds per minute, although the modified Humvees themselves could only carry about 60 rounds per vehicle. While most of these cannons were used on Black Hawk helicopters, EOD had about half of the custom Humvee ground vehicle versions that the US Army maintained with respect to these lethal weapons.

As noted previously, Jim had already had a plan of action for the 30mm cannons. And David had to agree that it was a solid plan. The essential elements of the Humvee deployment were simple: one Humvee (Cannon 1) would drive through the front door, and one (Cannon 2) would drive through the rear door. The vehicles would be positioned inside the warehouse at particular areas where they had an unobstructed view of the office area where the closet was located. If the ground troops couldn't get to the IND first, then the two Humvees would open fire. The third Humvee (Cannon 3) would be held in reserve just in case the first two didn't get the job finished. The EOD team also had a few Black Hawk helicopters with 30mm cannons at their disposal, but they too would be held in reserve for now. The helicopters were deemed inappropriate for this stealth operation because they wouldn't be able to get a good shot from outside the warehouse.

"Who's driving Cannon 1, Rick or Steve?" David asked Jim.

"Rick's on Cannon 1 and Steve's got Cannon 2," Jim said. "Mark is still recovering from his arm injury, so Joe's got Cannon 3. Checked out the semi-autonomous driving software too and it's installed."

David arched his eyebrows at Jim.

"I know; I know, David. The software's been improved something like 100% from the test runs where it failed pretty badly. We were thinking only a month ago of just totally ripping out the software. As you know, if any driver gets hurt, by having the software, we can still theoretically drive and shoot for him from central control here. Really, David, this version of the software is way better than the previous version. However, nothing substitutes for these guys' experience – that's why they're primary - at least this way, we think we've got some relatively reliable secondary support in place."

"I'll believe it when I see it," David replied. David Smithline was no technophobe; he understood the value of computers in warfare. But he still didn't quite trust fully-automated technology, and felt, quite rightly he thought, that when split-second decisions needed to be made, nothing substituted for in-the–field human decisions and human ingenuity. David especially believed in the need for local human control with respect to many vehicles, whether they be fighter jets or Humvees. The Army and the Air Force had been moving to drones for all types of vehicles: aircraft, helicopters, tanks, boats and jeeps, anything that moved. Control from afar, the military seemed to be saying, saved lives. But David knew that, sometimes, a soldier needed to be there in person to be effective, rather than operating a joystick from thousands of miles away. Seeing, feeling and sensing the relevant parts of the battlefield environment was something that even the most sophisticated cameras and sound equipment couldn't yet replicate.

Like NEST, EOD had its own scientists and technicians that kept their equipment running smoothly. Diagnostic testing on the Humvees had revealed no gun problems or pump problems, unlike the case with the NEST foamers. Instead, EOD had discovered that they had a more "low-tech" problem – the Cannon 2 Humvee had a simple, old-fashioned malfunctioning timing belt. The timing belt just could not be made to work right. So the EOD automobile techs were busy switching out the belt, checking the transmission and the rest of the vehicle, and of course double-checking the 30mm cannon gun mountings and ammunition.

It was now 0130 hours PT and the teams were working harder and faster than ever.

The sniper team was composed of twelve of the best sharpshooters that the FBI had, split into three groups of four people each. Because someone at the FBI had a wicked sense of nuclear humor, their call tags were Glow 1, Glow 2 and Glow 3. Glow 1 was responsible for taking out the rooftop terrorist, together with helping NEST with the foamers. Glow 2 would take out the terrorists in the front, while Glow 3 would take out the terrorists in the back. David felt more at home with the snipers than any other members of the team because of his Delta Force background; these guys felt like brothers-in-arms. Guys like these had saved David's butt countless times in his Delta Force days, when operations got hot and nasty really quickly, despite all of the pre-planning. David always felt that his snipers were the most reliable part of his team.

Richie Gutierrez ran Glow 1. While David knew most of the sharpshooters, David was friendliest with Richie since they had served in Afghanistan together in the same unit for five operations. Richie was like David's kid brother. Richie was a five foot eight inch tall, lanky twenty-five year old from a small town in Georgia, and he was the consummate prankster. He was the comedian that everyone loved, always with a perfect wisecrack, and a leader who knew how to relieve people's tension by keeping things light. Richie always told people that David was a good guy even though he was a "Northerner," because of course in the Deep South, North was a relative term, and North Carolina was like a "border state" to Richie.

Glow 1 team would operate by having two of its members take out the rooftop terrorist from the roof of a different warehouse. Because they wanted to account for different locations of where the rooftop terrorist might be standing when the operation started, Richie stationed two of them, Ronnie Williams and Billy Howe, on top of different buildings so that at least one would likely have a good angle for shooting. Richie and the fourth member of Glow 1, Johnny Guisewhite or "Johnny G" as everyone called him, would go on the Black Hawk helicopter with Ben and Sri and help with the foamer.

Johnny G could be considered the exact opposite of Richie. Not in terms of effectiveness, but in terms of personality. Where Richie was always the life of the party, full of jokes and making fun of everything and everybody, Johnny G was about as serious as they came. Almost like a straight man to Richie's comedian personality, Johnny was Bud Abbott or Dean Martin to Richie's Lou Costello or Jerry Lewis. Their best routine was often when Richie had the guys rolling in the aisles and Johnny G would just say "I don't get it. Was that supposed to be funny?" which would make the guys laugh twice as loudly.

The time was now 0155 PT.

"All right," Ben said, "let's fill the primary foamer tank."

"Roger that, Ben," Sri replied. He started fiddling with some knobs and twisted the filling hose from the reservoir into the opening of the backup tank.

"What's the temp now?"

"Well, the reservoir is now reading 9.5 degrees Fahrenheit."

"Not bad. The outside air is holding around 8 to 9 degrees, so it's pretty close. Better than the 20 to 25 degree difference we had before."

"Yeah, Jindar thinks that the lab notes imply that we're good if we can make sure that the temp difference is not greater than 5 degrees."

"Was that from a calculation or was that from a SWAG?"

"Nothing 'scientific' about this 'wild-assed guess', Ben. Jindar's real tired as he's been up for the last 20 hours, the last 10 of which was trying to figure this thing out. It's like 4:56am in the East Coast where he is."

"Yeah, our lives suck too, Sri. At least he's getting double overtime over there, unlike us, so tell him to pretend to have a formula that we can use."

"I love it, Ben, when you go all scientific method on me," Sri joked. "Ready to go?"

"Unless you got a bad feeling, let's do it."

So Sri turned the knob on the reservoir and the aerogel foam started to flow into the backup tank. The two men shuffled around nervously as the foam sputtered a bit, but there was no clogging and the backup tank continued to fill up with the foam.

Ben and Sri beamed like little kids in a candy store. After a quick fist bump between the two, they loaded the main and backup foamers and themselves into one of the FBI vans for transportation to the Black Hawk helicopter. Richie and Johnny G also got into the van with their Heckler and Koch MP7A1 submachine guns and various other firearms. While the other two members of Glow 1 would take out the rooftop terrorist,

Richie and Johnny G needed to be ready for any contingency that could happen.

K2 came on over the encrypted radio headset. "We good, Ben and Sri?"

"Yup, good to go," they both chimed in simultaneously. "Well, good as could be expected sitting next to these guys with machine guns," Ben added. It was only a 10 minute drive to the Black Hawk and Richie was cracking jokes most of the way.

"OK, E(ye)-in-steins," (that was Richie's name for Ben and Sri), "let's go over the plan again. We take this 'shaving cream' here," pointing to the foamer tanks, "and pipe it down to these terr-or-ists after Johnny G rappels down to the office from the roof. Estimating it will take Spiderman here," pointing at Johnny G, "about three to five minutes to get down to the office partition and get the hose in position, and another twelve minutes to get enough shaving cream into the bomb closet."

"That's about it," Ben shrugged. "Remember, you've got to verify that the IND is in the closet with this wristwatch radiation detector before sticking in the hose. Our guys out in the Hot Spot mobile truck will also continue to monitor things, so they will give you a heads up if the bomb signature has changed, which would mean they probably moved it."

"We've got the foamer tank machinery placed solidly on these sound-deadening racks. We'll lower them gently on the roof softer than a baby's butt," Richie promised. "I'll assume that you E(ye)-in-steins have truly fixed the foam jamming problem."

Ben and Sri just showed Richie their crossed fingers. Richie rolled his eyes at this.

It was now 0300 hours and each of the teams were fully operational and ready. The next 30 minutes felt like an eternity to K2, but David just calmly went over every element of the plan again. His training automatically kicked in to help him deal with the moment, keeping him calm and collected.

The command center was abuzz with activity as each of the units checked in again, verifying their ready status. The clock read 0323; the Black Hawk helicopter was in the air. The sniper teams had checked and re-checked their rifles and scopes, and were locked onto their targets.

"T minus 30 seconds," David intoned as the time neared 0330. His reminder was a mere formality as each of the team members had synchronized their watches down to the second. The snipers chimed in per the protocol:

"Glow 1 ready."

"Glow 2 ready."

"Glow 3 ready."

At exactly 0330, five well-aimed shots took out the five terrorist lookout guards immediately and nearly simultaneously. The command center's monitors glowed with the infrared visuals of the terrorists falling down where they had stood only moments before. Of the fifteen remaining terrorists inside the warehouse, the infrared images showed only four of them were vertical and moving around; the rest were in horizontal positions, presumably sound asleep. The ones that were moving appeared to have no idea that their comrades outside had been taken out. The operation was going pretty smoothly so far.

"Black Hawk moving," the command center tech told David and K2. "Forty-five seconds to rooftop."

The chopper whirred quietly through the crisp Reno morning air. It wasn't totally silent of course, but for their purposes it would suffice, as most of the terrorists inside were sleeping and the helicopter wasn't going to get that close to the roof. The helicopter hovered about thirty yards above the warehouse roof and slowly winched down two foamer machines that sat atop well-designed sound-deadening racks. Ben, Sri, Johnny G and Richie had gone down with the payload, which was indeed softly deposited onto the warehouse roof as smooth as a baby's bottom.

Interestingly, in a bit of clever engineering, the power for the machines had been built directly into the racks, dense battery packs that could keep the foamers going for three or four times longer than needed. With the foamers delivered safely on the roof, the four NEST/FBI teammates quickly got to work.

"Diagnostics check on primary and backup," Sri noted. "Final results in two minutes."

Ben replied, "OK, got it. Screwing the hose on now." Ben unwound a portion of the hose apparatus and locked it into the foamer intake system.

At the same time, Johnny G, dressed all in black and with camouflage black on his face and other exposed skin, took the other end of the hose and began stealthily walking towards what they called insertion point alpha, a utility door that allowed access to the inside of the warehouse from the roof. The door opened up onto a catwalk of sorts, and Johnny G had a thin black rope connected to his belt by an electronic release mechanism that would allow him to glide down to the ceiling of the office area where the plutonium IND was located. Richie and Johnny G descended onto the catwalk and Johnny connected one end of the rope to the catwalk. Richie was also dressed all in black; they looked like a pair of ninjas in a Japanese martial arts movie.

"Ready?" Richie mouthed quietly into this mouthpiece microphone.

"Ready," Johnny G replied equally quietly.

"OK, move down slowly. Talk to me or tug on the line if there is anything wrong. I'll talk or tug if I see or hear anything wrong."

Johnny G slung himself over the catwalk and pushed a button on his belt. The rope began to slowly unwind and he further descended down towards the office ceiling. As he went slowly downwards, he could hear the snores of some of the terrorists below. That was fortunate as it would hide some of the sounds he was making in his descent.

"Stop!" Richie whispered just as Johnny G was about halfway down. Richie gave a firm tug on the rope. He had noticed that one of the terrorists who was awake was moving to go to the bathroom. Johnny G dangled motionlessly in the air while a hundred feet away someone was shuffling off to the toilet holding a small flashlight, moving with the quick gait of a person with a single-minded urgency to relieve himself. "He's gone. You can start moving again."

"Thanks Richie," Johnny G whispered as he started again to inch down onto the top of the office. He oriented himself toward the back corner part of the office where the closet was located, and gingerly stepped onto the ceiling of the office closet. Slowly he moved towards an air grate that had been cut into the ceiling. This would be the opening that would allow them to put the foam into the closet. He checked his watch and confirmed that a plutonium signal was emanating from the area below – the plutonium IND or other nuclear device had not been moved from the closet.

While it was a reasonably tight fit, Johnny G was able to snake the hose down into the closet through the air vent, a grate and pipe contraption. He heard the toilet flush and shoved the hose down even further into the opening, the noise masked by the flushing noise. Then he had to be motionless as the terrorist ambled out of the bathroom and slowly made his way back to the bed where he had been sleeping.

Two other terrorists were seated at a table pretty far from the office. These two were playing cards, talking in low voices and smoking cigarettes together. Probably they were guys on the next shift who couldn't sleep anymore and were just passing time before their shift duty. The other two terrorists who were awake were even farther away from the office, aimlessly walking around and talking to each other, arguing about something meaningless.

The time was now 0347. The moment of truth had come; the Glow 1 team would now try to foam the closet. At Richie's verbal signal, Ben flipped the switch and the primary foamer whirred to life. The gentle whoosh of aerogel foam started its long journey from the roof to the closet, again not totally silent, but good as could be expected. The sound level was that of a person's exhaling sound when blowing bubbles. The terrorists had installed a bunch of space heaters in the warehouse so that they wouldn't freeze to death at night; the noise from these units helped to mask the foamer machine sound.

Most importantly, the foamer seemed to be working. Johnny G could see that the foam was continuing to spread out all over the closet, covering the plutonium IND, together with the rest of the items in the closet. The foamer didn't jam as Ben and Sri had feared. Success!

Gradually, the shelves and cabinets in the closet got covered with the thick white foam. The foamer device was working perfectly. Within five minutes the entire bottom half of the closet was encased in the foam. You couldn't even see anything else in the bottom half of the closet any longer. Excellent coverage. His mission accomplished, Johnny G would wait on the office ceiling for further instructions.

It was now 0350. Richie scrambled up ninja-like from the catwalk back through the opening, and exited onto the warehouse rooftop where Ben and Sri had been waiting.

"Piece of cake," Richie smiled. "You E(ye)-in-steins are good for something after all. Let's get you guys out of here so that we muscle guys can do our part." Richie helped place the two NEST scientists into a harness so that they could get winched up to the Black Hawk. Scientists were useless in a military firefight. Richie and Johnny G would stay to help with the logistics of storming the warehouse. When the NEST scientists had been secured back inside the helicopter, they had radioed their success to SAIC Smithline. David gave the go-ahead to get the ground troops in full ready position.

The ground troops were prepared and raring to go. In fact, as soon as the Glow teams had taken out the terrorist guards at 3:30pm, the ground troops had already been moving fast into position. Ten of them had amassed at the front entrance and another ten at the back entrance. The three Humvees, their engines off, had also been pushed slowly into place near the front and back entrances. Infrared sensors now showed that only four of the remaining terrorists were awake – the two that were still talking and smoking at a table, and the third and fourth, who were now, troublingly, walking around together near the entrance to the office. Crucially, the leaders still seemed to be asleep in the office.

It was 0352 in the morning. David and the central command team announced the next stage of the operation.

"T minus one minute. Two bogeys up at quadrant B8 for strike team alpha. Neutralize in stealth, and control zone B where the other three are sleeping."

"Roger that, central. Alpha confirming."

"Strike team beta, three bogeys are in zone T still. Neutralize in zone T1 and T3."

"Affirmative, central. Beta confirming."

"Glow 1 leader takes out walker at quadrant M5."

"Glow 1 leader confirming. Roger and locked in, central," Richie whispered from the catwalk.

"Glow 1 trailer takes out the other walker at quadrant M6."

"Glow 1 trailer confirming, central," Johnny G intoned softly.

The tricky part would be dealing with the two leaders who were ostensibly asleep in the office. The leaders had to be neutralized before they could activate the IND or whatever it was. That was why the Snow Falcon team had gone to all of the trouble with the foamer. If these two awoke before they were neutralized, they might immediately try to detonate the bomb and ruin all of these carefully laid plans. The foamer was some added insurance in that regard, but they had to prevent the activation of the bomb in the first place. The NEST technical team had estimated that it would take at least a minute or two for the terrorist leaders to try to activate the plutonium IND.

"T minus thirty seconds." The adrenaline was really pumping now, but the team was experienced and disciplined enough to keep it under control.

"T minus ten seconds." The teams tensed: strike teams alpha and beta nodded to each other and readjusted their hold on their weapons.

"Snow Falcon Go," David whispered from command central. The strike teams quickly opened the front and back doors to the warehouse simultaneously and flooded into the building stealthily, fanning out to accomplish their assigned tasks.

Suppressed fire echoed through the warehouse, little rat-a-tat-tat popping sounds, like popcorn kernels going off in an air popper.

The operation was going like clockwork. All of the initially targeted terrorists were down or controlled within forty-five seconds. Unfortunately, one of the sleeping terrorist guards had gotten up and had fired off a machine gun blast before he could be stopped. The blast had awoken the rest of the terrorists, including the two leaders in the office, and the infrared showed them scurrying around inside the office.

"Crap," David muttered under this breath. They had predicted that this would happen, but David was hoping that they didn't have to activate this part of the plan.

"Cannons go!"

"Dammit!" Johnny G exclaimed. He was still on top of the office closet roof. "Time to get out of here." He pushed a button on his belt and an electric motor began to whir as he began to quickly rise up to the catwalk. Richie was also pulling him up manually to assist in hastening his ascent.

Some members of strike teams alpha and beta, in the meantime, were opening the warehouse bay doors at the front and the back of the warehouse to allow the Humvees to enter unimpeded. Cannons 1, 2 and 3 roared to life and drove into the warehouse and into their pre-designated quadrants.

The rest of the strike team now had control of the entire warehouse except for the office area. The two leaders were holed up in the office and one was shooting at them with an AK-47. The strike team was laying down return fire from multiple directions. The infrared sensors showed that one of the terrorists was squatting down in the closet, probably trying to activate the start code for the plutonium device.

"Code red!" shouted David. "Code red! Cannons 1 and 2 are greenlighted."

The scene in the warehouse was chaotic as the ground troops stopped firing and scattered for cover.

"Move out alpha and beta!" Mark Childress cried out. "Artie back to the front and Paul to the back." The strike team men started hauling butt. Up top, Richie had lugged Johnny G over the top of the guardrail to the catwalk and the two Glow 1 teammates were heading up to the roof out of harm's way.

Beep-beep-beep-beep-beep. Cannon 1 was locked onto the target. "Cannon 1 synced," Rick said.

"Cannon 2 synced," Steve confirmed. Rick pressed his firing button and shot off six 30mm cannon shots in a burst from Cannon 1. Steve immediately followed by shooting off an additional six 30mm cannon rounds from Cannon 2. The explosion would have been deafening had the strike team not been wearing special earplugs and headsets that minimized the noise. The closet was obliterated along with, hopefully, the plutonium IND. Lots of foam, and lots of bits and pieces of the closet, were now strewn everywhere on the floor of the warehouse.

The two terrorist leaders in the office came walking out with their hands held high in surrender, as eight NEST technicians in hazmat suits ran past them and began to turn on their diagnostic equipment to figure out radiation levels. The foam was supposed to stay encased around the plutonium and prevent substantial leakage of radioactivity. It seemed like it was working as the hazmat suited guys were giving people the thumbs-up signal.

The two terrorist leaders had just about reached the Cannon 1 Humvee. "Nice shooting Rick," one of the terrorists said to the Cannon 1 driver, taking off his special earplugs. "You too, Steve," the other terrorist leader shouted to the Cannon 2 driver, after removing his special earplugs as well.

David Smithline got on the intercom and gave the signal to his staff to turn on all of the lights in the warehouse. "Simulation is complete," David stated. "Good job, ladies and gentlemen. Operation Snow Falcon is done. Let's wrap it up."

K2 exhaled deeply as she tore off her headset. "Nice work, NEST team, especially you guys, Ben and Sri."

The lights came on in the Reno warehouse where the simulation had taken place. The tired and sweaty members comprising strike teams alpha and beta began stripping off their black assault uniforms and started stacking their machine guns and clips of blank ammunition back into various equipment bins lying around the warehouse.

While it was the end of the simulation exercise for most participants, for the leaders it was just the beginning. Now they would have to commence the arduous process of analyzing and re-analyzing their actions to see where they could improve their performance. The WMD Directorate needed to conduct training exercises periodically in order to keep their teams in shape and to find a set of best practices or protocols for various situations. That way they could have a host of playbooks ready for the most probable situations, although of course there were always those who wanted a playbook for every conceivable event. That was essentially the FBI's "old guard" method of preparation. David, however, had vehemently resisted that kind of thinking, which he regarded as dangerous and short-sighted.

As the survivor of numerous firefights in Afghanistan, David knew that, most of the time, playbooks simply got thrown out of the window after the first shot was fired. Now some combat operations went by the textbook. Maybe about 20% of the operations fit that description, but they were far and away the exception rather than the rule. The real world was too fluid and dynamic, and the best military operatives, like Delta Force, the Navy SEALS and similar organizations, were trained to be flexible and able to adapt to new unplanned-for conditions.

The simulation leaders had a little over a week to prepare a comprehensive report and then present it to a special subcommittee meeting of the Department of Homeland Security (DHS), in coordination with the Homeland Security Council (HSC) component of the National Security Staff (NSS), the National Counterterrorism Center (NCTC), the Department of Defense (DoD), and NEST's parent organization, the National Nuclear Security Administration (NNSA) of the Department of Energy (DoE), along with the rest of the alphabet soup of government names. No rest for the weary.

"See you in Washington, DC," K2 said to David. "That's where the real radioactivity is, politically."

"Agreed," David replied. "Let's see how DC responds to these nuclear terrorism simulation results."

CHAPTER 3

"Aren't these results just bullshit? The simulation looked pretty rigged in favor of success to me." This was Jonathan Proxmeier speaking, the key aide to the Homeland Security Advisor (HSA), Pat Jorgensen, who ran the HSC. Proxmeier was attending on behalf of the HSA today because Jorgensen had to meet with the President on another matter.

OK, David thought to himself, *so this is how it's going to play today at the HSC.* "What do you mean Jonathan?" David replied smoothly. Don Llewes, the head of NEST, and Marcia Brown, the FBI Executive Associate Director for the National Security Branch, and acting head of the WMD Directorate, were rolling their eyes during this exchange. Proxmeier hated NEST and the FBI, and was always trying to make the two organizations look bad, even incompetent if he could. Marcia had told David privately that Proxmeier probably hated the FBI because his brother got rejected by the FBI Academy a few years ago. She didn't know why Proxmeier hated NEST. Maybe it was guilt by association with the FBI.

"Well, for example, the command center here was set up with all of the equipment and everything in place like within one hour of when the "crisis" happened, and it was located right where you need it, only five minutes away from the simulation zone. How realistic is that?"

"Somewhat fair point there, Jonathan," David admitted.

"Damn right," Proxmeier snorted.

David held up his hand to indicate that he hadn't finished talking. "But none of the team, including me, had notice of the exact time of the exercise, so that was a fair test. However, as to your point, for budget reasons, the command center site had to be known in advance, and the simulation designers needed to have AT&T give us a place that was close by and, for the most part, pre-hooked up. It saved us about $550,000. So when we called AT&T for a location, the simulation designers had already worked out a deal with them where 80 percent of the command center wiring was already pretty much ready to go, and all we needed to do was to plug in some stuff. Granted, that's a little unrealistic. But in a real emergency, we can use one of the regional command centers that have been already set up, although then we wouldn't have the advantage of proximity to the target site, and we wouldn't have the luxury of allowing all of the players, including the ground troops, to have face-to-face meetings and planning sessions with the command center staff. That face-to-face interaction is enormously helpful, and that is the potentially unrealistic and unfair situation that I think you're talking about."

"Among other things, David," Proxmeier said as sarcastically as he could.

"Look Jonathan," Marcia interrupted, "it's a simulation. The command center component is only one part of the simulation. For this trial, we were mostly concentrating on three other elements:" Marcia started ticking them off with her fingers, "(1) the state of interagency cooperation, primarily among the FBI, NEST and DoD; (2) the FBI's ability to mount a seek and destroy mission for a rogue IND; and (3) whether the NEST's new aerogel foam would work."

"And, as you'll see on page fourteen of the report," David continued, "re (1) we did pretty good. Katherine Kung of the Nuclear Emergency Support Team, Jim Broussard of the Army's Explosive Ordnance Disposal unit, and I compared notes and found that, while we had a few miscommunications among our staffers during the simulated crisis, we were operating at about," David looked down at the page, "94% efficiency or so according to the auditors."

"That's because you all happened to know each other from before," Jonathan relentlessly continued. "I see on page 27, for example, you note that Broussard and you had worked on a lot of field operations in Afghanistan together seven years ago or so. And Kung and you had done a field exercise together two years ago."

"But that's the point, right? Knowing people in advance, and how they think, helps us; it's a good thing. And not just among the leaders. It's especially helps our junior team members bond, as they don't work together normally since we're all in different organizations and locations. Most of the new folks had never even met more than 10% of the rest of the Snow Falcon team before the simulation. Now they have all met each other and the NEST technical leads, Ben and Sri, have worked real-time with my FBI sharpshooters and the strike teams. No substitute for interpersonal experience if, god forbid, there's a real crisis. Ratchets up everyone's efficiency numbers."

"It just seems too convenient that everything worked out so well."

"Actually, I think that you're right there," David smiled disarmingly, "but for the wrong reasons."

"Wait a second…," Jonathan flushed.

"No, let me tell you what I mean, Jonathan," David continued. "Lots of things went right that day, but it was too convenient as you say, in too many ways."

"So you're agreeing with me."

"No, not really." Jonathan just looked exasperated now. David went on, "What I mean is that it was too convenient, not because we knew each other, not because we had the command center conveniently located and wired up for us, not because we executed a good military plan, but instead because things were too," David paused trying to think of the right words, "... too ... straightforward in the simulation. We weren't forced to think outside the box too much. The scenario was too linear, and we didn't have to make a lot of hard decisions."

"So the bottom line is that the simulation failed," Jonathan declared triumphantly. "I think that SAIC Smithline has just said something like that, except in a roundabout way."

"Actually, to be clear, I'm saying that the simulation was a success. We did meet each of our main objectives, (1), (2) and (3). And, particularly under (3), we did force the NEST techies to think outside the box when the foam started clumping. So it wasn't too linear for them."

K2 jumped in at that. "That was the most valuable part of the Snow Falcon simulation to me. We showed that the aerogel foam worked in real-world conditions, after we fixed the clumping problem. It was an unexpected bonus that we learned about the temperature gradient problem through the simulation. We completely had no clue before that the gradient mattered to foam performance, with the product specs drawn up the way they were. Even today, the developers can't fully explain mathematically why there was a clumping issue. But the NEST team, mostly Ben and Sri, together with a few of the manufacturer's tech people, figured out how to make it work on the fly within hours, under extreme time pressure. It could have been something else, a different problem completely. Ben and Sri just passed an important test, getting experience learning how to solve hard problems as they come up. We logged the temperature gradient issue, of course, and we'll have a working protocol for that from now on."

"But while NEST got challenged by the sim," David went on, "the rest of the team wasn't challenged so much. So the simulation results weren't a fail," David looked right at Jonathan as he was saying this, "but I am saying that I think that the simulation design needs to be beefed up a bit for the military guys. That's my overall report assessment, most of which is set forth on pages 37 and 38."

Admiral Lakerloff, a representative of the Navy, spoke up. "I know what you mean, David. But it's hard to do these simulation designs. And they don't always correlate well with the real-world. My SEAL team boys who do best in the sims usually do the best in the field. They are the SEALS after all. But, David, think about Hunter Grisholm from Seal Team Six. I think you two did a special op in Tora Bora." David nodded and smiled as he recalled his buddy Hunter. "Hunter was one of the worst performers in the world in our simulations, but my best field guy ever."

"Yeah, but that's Hunter," David shook his head fondly. "He's the exception that proves the rule. I think that, maybe subconsciously, he purposefully botches at least half of the simulations just to screw with the instructors' heads. Name anybody else who fits that profile." Lakerloff shrugged. "So for the rest of us mere mortals, simulations raise the floor level of our performance. I get it that good simulations are hard to design. We do a few tabletop ones that stretch our brains a bit. However, maybe we should get a bunch of Delta and SEAL instructors to do a full-fledged clusterf--- of a field operation like only they can do. Have us all running around with our hair on fire. That'll rattle the teams enough to bond and think together to get us to the next level."

"Or fail miserably," Proxmeier said.

"And then fail better," David shrugged, "until we get it right. After all, it's only the fate of the entire country at stake."

They sparred some more about the Snow Falcon assessment report. Politically, Proxmeier wanted the report to get in a few digs at the FBI Quantico instructors' failure to design a great scenario. Marcia refused to go along with this, and wanted the report to stress the fact that the simulation results were a success. David really didn't give a crap about all of this report-writing, which ultimately just gave him a monumental headache: he just wanted his team to get better, and get better significantly, through these simulations.

But committees and subcommittees exist mainly to produce reports (that is their primary function after all), so K2 and David were resigned to the fact that they would have to play the game through to the end. The final report therefore contained somewhat meaningless sentences like "Deployment of field resources generally met established criteria, but additional research and development would be required in the future to optimize the field scenario." and "The current exercise showed certain capabilities that could be enhanced by additional scenario parameters." David was adamant about including one concept, and after a half-hour of arguing over the precise wording, it came out in the report as: "Future exercises should be designed to place additional emphasis on non-linear solutions."

All of the participants left the meeting exhausted and vaguely dissatisfied, which many subcommittee members counted as a win. Not Proxmeier, however; he left pissed. Don, Marcia, David and K2 needed to decompress so they all went to the hotel bar at the Hyatt hotel near Dulles Airport, where K2 was staying while in town.

"Proxmeier is such an a-hole," Marcia vented as she sat down at their booth.

"Grade A," Don agreed. "But I have to say that he does keep us honest. The four of us sometimes get into groupthink mode. David, do you think Lakerloff is going to go to bat for us and get us some simulation help from his SEAL buddies?"

"Maybe. But the SEALs are really busy these days out in the field. We're not going to be priority one, when they've got a dozen real-life ops to plan."

"How about Delta help?"

"Same thing. My guess is that we can legitimately plan on some assistance on and off over the next one or two years for a sim that would happen maybe three or four years from now."

"Three or four years from now? That's an eternity. I guess I should take that as excellent news, from my personal perspective. I'll be retired by then, like Duane. K2 can deal with this mess after she takes my job."

"Thanks Don, you dinosaur," K2 joked. "You're not going to get off that easily. First of all, who says that we're going to let you retire that quickly, or that I'm taking your job when you do go? Even if you are retired and I'm running the show, I'll make sure to run the next simulation right next to your favorite flyfishing place in Montana."

"Yeah," Marcia continued, "we'll have an F-16 do a fly-by right when you're casting a line."

"And we'll follow it up with a nighttime raid on your cabin with a couple of helicopters shooting 30mm cannons at you," David continued. "How's that for non-linear?"

They had to drink to that scenario, so they did, and spent the next half hour chatting, eating and drinking, and not necessarily in that order. Then it was Don's time to go, as he needed to be up early the next morning for a meeting with the Energy Secretary. Marcia too said her goodbyes as she needed to meet with FBI Director Ronald Edelman at 0800 hours Eastern Time (ET) sharp to discuss the results of today's meeting.

David and K2 sat together, nursing their drinks. Both of them were half-buzzed from the drinking and the good conversation. They were also on a high from stress relief after finishing the painful subcommittee meeting. David found himself staring at K2. He had always wondered whether K2 had a boyfriend, but could never bring himself to ask her directly because he didn't want to hear the wrong answer. David usually wasn't that way with most women; if anything, he was known as being a little too direct. In K2's case, however, they had only really talked at length about work or work-related activities. David did know a few personal things about K2's background. For example, he knew that she was born and raised in the San Francisco Bay Area, and because she had attended Stanford, she really could be considered a true Northern California girl. Even now, by being based at LLNL, she was only a short one hour drive away from San Francisco. David also vaguely remembered that K2 had told him that she had a sister living in New York City, and a brother who was somewhere in Asia, Hong Kong maybe? K2 also loved to play tennis, and loved to go skiing in Tahoe. But other than a few other minor tidbits -- like she really loved the music group Imagine Dragons -- that was about it in terms of the personal information that David knew about K2.

"So, umm, when are you going back to the Bay Area again?" David asked.

"Well, you know Don. After he meets with the Energy Secretary tomorrow morning, he wants to have one more set of follow-up sessions with some of the NEST team out of Joint Base Andrews. So I'm scheduled to stay another three days and then head on back home on Christmas Day." K2 flipped her hair back tiredly. "What's your schedule?"

"I have the same case of the "boss is busting my butt" syndrome that you got. Marcia wants to set the agenda with Director Edelman at 8am on Christmas Eve, of all days, so I'm not invited at the front end. Can't have me throwing a wrench in the clean storyline that Marcia wants to paint. I have to come in at 10am for an hour and a half to do a dog-and-pony show on some of the "details" stuff. Then I get to go fly to see my parents in North Carolina on Christmas Day. Only a day and a half at home, though. I have to go to Quantico for some mandatory training classes that have to be completed by the end of the year. I had to cancel previously scheduled training sessions because of real work, of course, but now I have to go or Marcia will kill me."

"Any vacations?"

"What's that?" They both laughed. "Well, if I had my way, I would have flown back to North Carolina at least a few days ago, so that I could see them for at least a week. My mom is a stickler for getting the family together no matter what for at least three or four days during the Christmas season. I've only missed eight or nine Christmases ever, and that was mostly because I was in Afghanistan or the like. She gave me a pass on those Christmases."

"Hey, my mom's that way too. I've only missed three Christmases, and usually I'm able to be there a whole week.

Generally, the clan all try to fly back to San Francisco and eat a big home-cooked dinner together."

"It's turducken for us – a big, messy glob of turkey, chicken and duck all stuffed together."

"Ooh, sounds intriguing."

David thought K2 was the one who was intriguing, but didn't say anything about that, and instead just appreciated the moment of being together. K2 stood about five feet seven inches, with gorgeously long black hair, and the most beautiful eyes that David had ever seen in a woman. David had never subscribed to the formula that beauty times brains equals a constant, and K2 was living proof that it wasn't true. Most importantly to David, K2 wore just a bare minimum of makeup. David hated it when women would plaster their faces with a lot of cosmetics, totally preferring the natural beauty look that K2 had.

Tonight, K2 was wearing a white silk blouse with a navy blue jacket and skirt combination that accentuated her shapely figure. David shook his head; he shouldn't be staring at her that long. He was a little lonely these days, and way overworked; he hadn't been dating anyone seriously for something like a year.

"Hello? Earth calling David."

"Huh?"

"I was asking whether you were going to be able to go golfing with your dad over New Year's weekend this year. I think you told me before that was also one of your big holiday traditions, and then you spaced out on me."

"Sorry about that. Just tired, I guess," David tried to cover for himself. "Umm, what did you ask again? I was thinking about something else."

K2 laughed. "You really can't keep on reliving the sim, and how to improve your team. You former Delta guys have got to let it go sometimes – the team did well enough for now, David."

"Right," David shook himself out of it, "You're right, I know. I know what you mean, K2, uh, Katherine. The team ..." Now he was just discombobulated.

"Look," Katherine chided, "you're obviously tired; you're just rambling now. I'm just rambling now too. We're way too exhausted. I have to do some work tonight and then get up to drive to Andrews by 9:15am. Can't believe that tomorrow is December 23rd already! We'll catch up some more tomorrow or the next day before I leave for the San Francisco Bay Area. Have a good night," K2 said, giving David a little hug as she got up to leave. It felt great to have Katherine touching him. She smelled great too, like walking through the Duke Forest on a spring day in Durham, North Carolina.

"You too, have a good night," David said, hugging her back.

Katherine waved as she left the bar. It almost came across as a wistful wave, as K2 was lonely too. Although K2 didn't know about David's dating situation, they were pretty much alike; Katherine also hadn't dated anyone seriously for about a year. Like David, mostly it was because she didn't really have the time for a serious relationship, since she was so busy and was traveling so much. Both of them didn't feel that they could be super serious about dating right now at this moment in their lives - or was that just a cop-out? Each of their immediately prior relationships ended (and they weren't even very serious relationships) because their dates told them that they couldn't take it anymore. Even when physically there, their dates complained that they weren't mentally there for them. David's and K2's brains were always thinking about some work project.

In addition, their dates complained that David and K2 weren't even able to be around physically on a regular basis. Something would always seem to come up: an emergency training session, an unplanned meeting with some government agency, a personnel crisis, etc. Something would always take them away on the special weekend when they had promised their dates six months in advance that they would be there.

Of course, neither of them could rightfully complain too much; this lifestyle was their personal choice. They were highly successful and dedicated professionals who knew what they were getting themselves into. Katherine, however, had always questioned why it had to be an either-or choice of a good career or a good family life. Society would be better off recognizing that it was in everybody's self-interest to allow people to have both. David and K2 knew that theirs was a high-quality problem anyway; they were fortunate enough to be able to choose to have a good job. Some folks were relegated to work hard in a bad job, and they were still not able to have a good family life. Both K2's and David's great-grandfathers fit that description perfectly. So stop feeling sorry for yourself, Katherine admonished herself, and either do something about it, or just accept it.

Katherine had actually heard that David didn't have a current serious girlfriend. One of the female FBI communications staff members, Julie Mansville, had mentioned it in passing about six months ago, mainly because Julie herself had wanted to date David. Julie had asked if Katherine knew David well enough to help Julie in getting that date. K2 had mumbled something about not knowing David that well to help, but said that, if Julie wanted, K2 could ask David about it anyway. Julie had never followed up, so the issue just went away.

That had led Katherine to think about David Smithline as a potential date for herself. K2 thought that they would make a cute couple; certainly they didn't feel awkward in each other's company. K2 always admired David's quiet confidence. He was a doer, not just a talker, and he was a friendly and fun guy to be around to boot. Not to mention that he was a great hugger; K2 could get really used to those hugs.

Serendipitously, David and K2 were both thinking of the other at the same time when they were brushing their teeth. However, by the time that they were ready for bed, they had both reverted to thinking more about their respective meetings the next day, planning what they were going to say and do. Old habits die hard indeed. Then, for tonight at least, both David and Katherine would just fall asleep within ten minutes of their heads hitting their pillows, not thinking about work or each other, or anything else for that matter, as they drifted into a deep, dreamless slumber.

Katherine woke up to the shrill ringing of her hotel telephone. *Ugghh*, she thought, *I hate these wake-up calls.* Picking up the phone to make it stop, she just couldn't bring herself to get up right there and then, so she flopped back onto the bed for an extra fifteen minutes of rest. That was when her secondary alarm, her cell phone alarm, began to blare and K2 was resigned to actually having to get up and start her day.

Changing quickly, K2 left her room, shoveled in the free continental breakfast offered at the hotel, and got into her rental car to drive to Andrews. It was only a forty-five to fifty minute drive from her hotel to Joint Base Andrews (which was formed by the merger of Andrews Air Force Base and Naval Air Facility

Washington) with medium traffic, so K2 was able to easily make it there with time to spare. Her meeting with Don didn't start until 11am, so she had an extra hour.

She spent the time catching up with some East Coast members of the NEST family. There was John Van Dyke, the leader of the Roosevelt Diamond Augmentation Team. Roosevelt Diamond covered all of the Eastern seaboard and then some. John was of Duane Mandel's generation of old-timers, full of amazing institutional knowledge and wisdom, but unfortunately was about to retire because he was getting a little old and he had been diagnosed with cancer. Ben and Sri were also here, teaching some other NEST members about their findings with respect to the foamer. Walter Van de Wiel, one of K2's classmates from Stanford, also was puttering around the lab, making adjustments to a next generation gamma radiation detector.

Katherine shot the breeze with all of them for a while, and finally went over to the conference room where Don would hold a meeting for the next four hours to go over the simulation results. Sometimes she wondered if it would have been better for her to stay on the technical side rather than the management side. Ben and Sri had passed up numerous opportunities to go over to the "dark side," as they put it, and were having infinitely more fun doing their cutting-edge work in applied physics. Being stuck in a long-term management position frankly would have driven each of them crazy; they were just not suited for that kind of work.

But Katherine was wired differently. While she couldn't say that she loved the management meetings, K2 actually enjoyed the challenge of managing people and projects, and she was good at it. Unlike Ben or Sri, or Sabrina McAllister, the newest technical superstar, a PhD from the University of Chicago, K2 didn't live for the science alone. Importantly, however, with her degrees, her technical work experience, and her personality, she had the credibility, intellectual firepower, and likeability to run the team. To a person, each member of the Lincoln Diamond Augmentation Team respected and trusted her management and technical judgment. That couldn't be said of everyone. NEST had tried an experiment some six years ago of hiring a senior management leader without the requisite technical background and skills and it proved to be a disaster. The team simply did not respect that manager, and the team could never gel together. The griping and dissatisfaction kept on growing until it reached a boiling point, when Don Llewes lured Duane Mandel out of his first retirement to restore order.

The participants were gathering in the conference room for the meeting. After settling down a bit, Don began the meeting by congratulating everyone on a job well done. Operation Snow Falcon was considered a resounding success from the NEST perspective. The Secretary of Energy was pleased, and there were going to be commendation letters in everyone's personnel file with respect to the operation.

Next, Ben and Sri provided a blow-by-blow account of the primary foamer's jamming problem. The participants gave the two a standing ovation after they were done. Ben and Sri performed some mock bows, and were generally having a good time hamming it up to the loud applause. Next, they got serious and gave a presentation on how to further tweak the aerogel foam formula to prevent the jamming from happening in the first place. The foam research team had identified a few surfactants that could be added to potentially alleviate the temperature gradient problem. For the next fifteen minutes,

Sabrina McAllister and her team presented on the physical chemistry of these surfactants and why some recent data results from the nearby University of Maryland's spectroscopic ellipsometer favored the addition of these particular ingredients.

Equations for the complex reflectance of the aerogel foam system soon littered the whiteboard in the conference room as the team debated over the merits of the results. These models were pretty tricky to interpret, and the team quickly decided that a significantly larger set of data measurement points were needed to fully model the system accurately. Don agreed to a three month period to develop this data and begin testing what they were calling at present "version 5.3" of the aerogel foam.

This part of the meeting only took an hour and a half. Afterwards, while Ben and Sri and half of the NEST team got to leave, Don and K2 had to remain to review the other components of the simulation. For example, the two of them had to document in detail the NEST logistics efforts; this work took a few hours and they only finished after working through lunch. While NEST would receive an overall "A+" for the Snow Falcon simulation, Don and K2 had noticed that a few members of the logistics team were late by about a half hour to Reno because they had thought their backups were on call at that time and not them.

When these two NEST members were paged, therefore, they had simply called in and told the program operator that their backups were on duty this week and that there was a scheduling screw-up. The operator had dutifully logged this. It made sense, since there had been a whole series of changes on the call list for these few weeks. So the operator had called the backups who agreed that the schedule had been changed, but for the following week, not this week. That led to a paging again of the original members and by the time things were fully straightened out, almost a full half hour had passed. This kind of thing happened infrequently, but Don and K2 made the logistics teammates go through the entire communications protocol all over again, just to ensure that this wouldn't happen again in the future. The program operator was told that, if there was a real emergency, he should just override any protests of any specific team member, and just go with who was on duty according to the roster document. They could argue and sort out any mistakes later; if someone got double duty unfairly, it could be made up to them.

This was all common sense, of course, but these were the kinds of human resources issues that they just had to get right in case of an emergency. Conversely, common sense or not, these were always the issues which were tough to get right in any sufficiently large organization.

The rest of the logistics effort had gone very well. The logistics team had gotten the decals exactly right for the power company logos and the stickers on the "Hot Spot Mobile" trucks. The equipment in the Hot Spot trucks had performed perfectly in assessing the radiation signature of the mock plutonium. The handheld mobile radiation detectors had also worked well, although they were going to need to switch to the newer version in the next few months, just like with the aerogel foam. Unlike the case with the foam, however, this was a planned upgrade, three years in the making. The new unit purportedly would be smaller, about the size of four Apple iPad tablets stacked together, would be slightly more sensitive, and, this was the key element, would have significantly lower power consumption. These detectors could work almost fifty percent longer before needing to be recharged.

Finally, after the logistics review had occurred, Don and K2 had to go through a financial gap analysis for NEST for the next year. While the Secretary of Energy had promised Don that NEST's funding would stay the same for the next fiscal year, Don needed to figure out how to stretch the NEST budget to accommodate some unexpected issues that they had identified.

For example, the new radiation detectors were set forth as a line item in this year's October 1 through September 30 fiscal budget. The problem was that the detector improvement program had a cost overrun of twenty percent. That would normally be fine, since they had a contingency factor built in, but this was a cost overrun of twenty percent beyond the contingency factor. That overage amount had a ripple effect through the rest of the budget, and sent Don and Katherine scrambling to figure out how to solve the expense problem.

Non-financial issues also existed. The software for the NEST servers that were supposed to permit real-time coordination within the group of all technical data and computational analysis of the radiation signatures was full of glitches. It was proving hard to fix, as the original program was mostly based on 1970s code. While the software worked a vast majority of the time, sometimes the software just failed. Compounding the problem was the fact that the software was complex enough that, sometimes, no one could truly figure out exactly why it failed.

There were upcoming personnel gaps too. John Van Dyke, the Roosevelt Diamond NRAT leader, was sixty-two years old, and had Stage 2 lymphoma, a blood cancer. John was going through chemotherapy treatment even now; the expectation was that he would need to retire sometime in the next three to six months. Don could not figure out who could replace him. John's heir apparent, a lanky forty year old originally from the University of Illinois Champaign-Urbana, had been lured away from NEST by a private company offering double the salary about a month ago. Everything had been thrown out of whack by that unexpected departure. The Roosevelt Diamond Augmentation Team was a little chaotic right now.

These were the headaches that Don and K2 and the senior management team faced day-to-day, but to their credit, NEST just soldiered on and did the best they could. Like the Navy SEALs, their informal motto was "The Only Easy Day Was Yesterday."

It was 6:30pm when Don and K2 called it a day. They would resume talking about the budget and personnel matters the next day at 9am. That next day would be a light day, though, and they were scheduled to finish by 4pm. Don had called Marcia, and after consulting with David and K2, the four had agreed to have drinks and an early dinner together at the historic Old Ebbitt Grill near the White House around 5pm tomorrow. This way they could finish early, since K2 had to fly out really early on Christmas Day morning.

K2 was excited to be able to see David again, and she drove back to her hotel in good spirits. She had eaten a leftover sandwich from lunch as dinner, but really just wanted to use the hotel fitness center to get some exercise in before turning in that night. She was just settling in to watch some local news, when her high school friend Cynthia happened to call her to catch up on things. Cynthia was the mother of two little kids already, and was always trying to figure out what Katherine was doing so that, as Cynthia said, she could live vicariously through K2's exciting life as a single woman.

"Yeah, real exciting," Katherine told Cynthia, "I am by myself in a hotel room in DC. Tomorrow, I have an action-packed agenda consisting of a government budget meeting." K2 wasn't allowed to tell anyone exactly what she did, so Cynthia thought that K2 just worked as a nuclear scientist department manager at the Livermore lab doing some unspecified kind of fusion research. Inevitably, their discussion would turn to men, and Cynthia always joked that K2 must be getting seduced all of the time by hot Russian KGB agents seeking the latest information about our nuclear fusion program. K2 assured Cynthia that she was only getting seduced at most three times per week, and that only half of them were really good looking, suave James Bond-like guys. They laughed at this, as they always did, but Cynthia would, inevitably, segue neatly into asking about Katherine's real love life.

That was where K2 repeated herself to Cynthia: "What part of 'I am by myself in a hotel room in DC' do you not understand?" *Uh-oh*, thought K2, *here it comes*. And Cynthia would oblige.

"You know," Cynthia said, "since you're by yourself, if you are really looking, I have this one guy who might be perfect for you." Whereupon, like always, Cynthia would go into all sorts of details about this guy who was a friend of a girlfriend of hers, and she heard that he is blah, blah, blah. Whereupon, like always, K2 would promise to Cynthia that she would think about it whenever she had the time, which was hardly ever, blah, blah, blah.

In the distant past, Katherine had actually gone out with two of Cynthia's suggested dates, but the dates proved too awkward and K2 had figured out that part of the problem was that Cynthia's idea of a perfect date for her wasn't consistent with her own ideas of a perfect date. Cynthia had this view that because K2 had a government paycheck, that she would want someone who was really rich and make her comfortable financially.

Therefore, Cynthia's dates for K2 were an assortment of investment bankers or hedge fund types who really didn't mesh well with K2's personality. Not that she had anything against these people, but she didn't have anything really to talk about with them either. One of her private equity fund dates kept on boasting about the "special carried interest" definition that their lawyers were able to import into their last fund as if Katherine had a clue as to what that meant.

Apparently it meant a lot to him because it constituted the entire subject matter of their coffee get-together, as it was clear that the guy was incredulous that the fund got these terms. It was fine to K2 that her dates were interested in money, but they also had to be interested in other stuff too. At least talk at length about your family and friends, sports, and, preferably to K2, some science, along with your latest business adventures.

After Cynthia and K2 had finished this particular conversation, K2 realized that she had been mentally comparing all of Cynthia's dates to SAIC David Smithline, and they had all been coming up deficient. *Something to keep filed for future reference*, she told herself, as she got in bed.

Unlike K2, David Smithline was in a foul mood almost all afternoon. The morning meeting with FBI Director Edelman had gone fine, but now David had to do his annual personnel ratings for his team. He just wanted to give them all top ratings. Human resources, however, was onto his tactics, and demanded that he give at least a few of his people less than top marks.

David already had won the battle not to have to place his people on any kind of even soft "curve," taking his case all of the way up to the FBI Director. When he was with Delta Force, the very eliteness of the unit allowed David to avoid using any curves whatsoever. Delta was already the best of the best – what was the meaning of a curve in that instance? But the FBI special nuclear counterterrorism unit, part of the WMD Directorate, would not get that pass because they simply didn't have any significant operations under their belt as a group, like the Delta Force units had in spades. As a result, they were only somewhat protected, and they were way more subject to this bureaucratic mumbo jumbo. Yes, they were elite, but there was some talk about cutting their budgets because they hadn't proved that they were needed. Proxmeier, in particular, thought that they could do with only three-quarters of the people they had. Proxmeier had wanted to take the monies that would be saved by axing one-fourth of David's team and funnel it over to the TSA, so that more airport screeners could be hired to reduce airport waiting times. This pissed off David no end, and was one of the key causes of his foul mood. David felt that anyone who he gave less than top marks to would be automatically scrutinized and would be transferred out of the elite counterterrorism unit. Moreover, David knew that he would not necessarily be able to ensure that this person could get into a similar elite unit befitting the quality level of the individual. David felt personally responsible for these folks and he would be damned if he wouldn't fight for each and every one of them.

When Marcia had called him in the early evening and told him about the plan for a foursome dinner with Don and K2, David's mood had brightened considerably. He attacked the pile of personnel rating documents with a new zest, eager to get them done and out of the way. David had managed to finesse a few of the so-called "less than top marks," David called them his A-minuses, to his satisfaction. It was 8:30pm when he finished and began to head home. All he had to do tomorrow was to attend an annual management training class on new legal compliance matters, finish some other paperwork, and then he could head out to dinner by 4pm so that he could beat the traffic and get to downtown DC by tomorrow at 5pm. Things were looking up.

Or so it seemed until David's beeper and cell phone simultaneously started squawking at 4:45am the next morning. Disbelievingly, David stared at the beeper screen bleary-eyed. *You gotta be kidding me*, he thought to himself, *this is supposed to be one of my easy days. Is this just a sick joke?* He dutifully called in to the service number, and the operator assured him that there was no mistake; David was supposed to report to the war room in Building Five at Joint Base Andrews in one hour, much less if he could manage it. This was a priority code alpha alert.

A priority code alpha alert was the highest level of alert that the FBI's special nuclear counterterrorism unit had in place. It meant drop everything, and do exactly what you are told to do. No excuses whatsoever, not even if it's your wedding day, the day of your child's birth, or the day of your father's funeral. So David quickly dressed and drove like a bat out of hell to Andrews.

CHAPTER 4

When David got there, he went to the special conference center "war room," where the rest of the FBI, NEST, and DoD senior management team was gathering. Lots of bleary-eyed people were getting their coffee fix. Pretty much the same senior management members from the simulation were in attendance: Don and K2 from NEST, FBI Associate Executive Director Marcia Brown, Mark Childress (David's tactical ground troops leader), Jim Broussard from the Army's EOD group and Jack Smith from the DIA. This time, however, HSA Pat Jorgensen, who was the President's chief counterterrorism advisor, was there in person, along with the Chairman of the Joint Chiefs of Staff, General Bill McTighe, and Marcia's boss, FBI Director Ron Edelman. Even Louis Branden, the Vice President himself, was present, sitting in for the President who was attending the G7 conference in Asia. The President had already been partially briefed; and would attend the tail end of the meeting by video after a G7 dinner. This meeting in fact would be considered a full emergency session of the HSC. Finally, in the back of the war room were a couple of Jack's DIA colleagues, one of whom who was not introduced by name. Instead, this gentleman was just introduced as D-1.

Vice President Branden called the meeting to order exactly at 0545 hours ET and asked Pat to provide the details. Pat's voice was somber and deadly serious. "Ladies and gentlemen, I regret to inform you that we have credible evidence that there is a 35% chance that a nuclear bomb has been successfully smuggled into the United States." Murmurs and whispers reverberated throughout the war room, but the Vice President stopped them with a wave of his hand, and continued.

"It goes without saying that we have to find it before it can be detonated. Jack's team at DIA will tell you what they know. This intel came from them and we considered it validated this morning at 4am. This is D-37;" the Vice President pointed at the screen and an image of a Middle Eastern man with his face and voice distorted electronically showed up, "please tell your story."

D-37 cleared his throat and spoke up in heavily accented English: "I am deep cover DIA, stationed in Marseilles, where I am calling from now. I am working as a Hezbollah trainer with the Al Qods Force of Iran, which is as you know part of the Iranian Revolutionary Guard Corps. It's essentially Iran's version of our Special Forces. In Marseilles, Al Qods provides aid and services for Al Qaeda, Hezbollah and Hamas, together with some training for these groups' operatives. Three weeks ago, this man," D-1 showed a picture of Amir on the screen, "came through Marseilles. More on him later. He had a crate with Russian-Cyrillic markings on it. It came from Chechnya based on the other crate markings. Inside the crate we think was possibly this," he now showed a picture of the Russian army tactical field weapon, "a GRU variant of the RA-115 nuke." Murmurs started up again throughout the war room, including audible words like "Holy shit!," "How is this possible?," "No way!" and similar exclamations of disbelief.

Jack Smith broke into the conversation. "Not that we think that it is the Russians directly behind this threat. As far back as 1997, the retired former Russian General Alexander Lebed told the US Congress that 84 out of 132 suitcase-sized nuclear weapons were missing from the Russian arsenal. Later, he amended that to say that there were probably about 100 of out 250 nukes that were missing. Lebed noted that these nukes were mostly 'RA-115' weapons, although the Russian Ministry of

Atomic Energy and various other Russian governmental authorities have vigorously denied that any such RA-115 or similar nuclear weapons have ever existed. From our intel, we know that the Russians managed to secure most of those first-generation RA-115 weapons in the early 2000s. However, there have been recent third- and fourth-generation RA-115s developed by the Russians, including those by its largest foreign intelligence agency, the GRU. We understand that about 10 to 15 of these nuclear weapons, mostly of the backpack variety, are also unaccounted for in the Russian arsenal. Background chatter suggests that a GRU-variant of the RA-115 somehow may have gotten over to Chechnya and put up for auction to the highest bidder. We think that a splinter cell of Al Qods, led by Mohammed Rahimi, may have purchased it." Jack waved off a few questions from the group. "Rahimi may not even be acting on behalf of Al Qods generally, or with the blessings of the ruling ayatollahs. We think that Iran wouldn't be so crazy as to set off a nuke against us, as we would immediately retaliate. However, maybe they think that since it is a Russian nuke that it would be untraceable back to them. Anyway, hold your questions on the provenance of the nuke. D-37, please go on with the story."

D-37 continued, "So after I tried to find out more about the crate, to no avail, I reported its existence to my handler, and we sent some pictures of it to DIA, but I didn't know and didn't see what was inside the crate. The reason we think it was a RA-115 nuke is what D-65 will discuss."

The screen shot split in half, and D-65's face and voice, similarly distorted electronically, popped up on the left half of the screen, while D-37 occupied the right half. D-65 began to talk: "I am deep cover DIA in Venezuela, working for one of the main gangs in the country. The gang, called Supremo, does a lot of trade with the Middle East extremist groups like Al Qods, Al Qaeda, Hamas, and Hezbollah. The Russian crate had been put aboard a freighter from Marseilles, and via a few other ships, somehow ended up at La Guaira, the main Venezuelan port, which is located north of Caracas. Supremo runs approximately one-third of the illicit La Guaira trade, mostly arms and drugs. Sometimes we handle special shipments, like the crate. We have about a thousand different items on the DIA watch list it seems, but somehow I immediately remembered the crate from D-37's posting. As a result, I paid attention to where it was going. When the crate was stored in a nearby port warehouse, this same man," again the picture of Amir was flashed on the screen, "came by to inspect it. He had shooed everyone away when he opened the crate, but I was on the second floor office of the warehouse with my DIA binoculars, and managed to snap a few shots of a corner of the open crate and of the man. As you can see," D-65 now put the picture on the screen, "the object inside the crate kind of looks like a part of a backpack. It certainly isn't absolutely clear in the picture what is there, and it isn't absolutely clear that it is a backpack. Moreover, I was only able to pass the thumb drive containing the pictures to my handler after a full week had passed; we had a big gang operation and I couldn't get away. Obviously, I would have dropped everything had I known it might be a RA-115 nuke, but I had no idea. I thought that there was some fancy new high power rifle inside a backpack, not that the whole backpack itself was the weapon."

Jack Smith then took the lead. "Then we wasted another week," Jack admitted. "The handler is supposed to upload each of the files to the DIA server on a regular basis, no more than one day after receipt from any agent. And he generally does that.

He gets about 30 thumb drives a month, and manages to get at least fifty percent of them uploaded within a day or so. This time, the handler's only daughter was sick in the hospital, and his wife was away on another DIA assignment, so it took four days for him to upload it. Then we got a bit of luck. We've obviously got some amazing software. The MAESTRO and MAGIC software programs can do feature comparison mapping; luckily, a new improved version of MAESTRO had come online in the past few weeks. While only a part of the inside of the crate was visible, the new version of MAESTRO told us that there was a 6% likelihood that the item in the crate was a GRU variant of the RA-115 nuke. The old MAESTRO version would have given it a 4% likelihood estimate."

"Holy crap!" exclaimed Don. "That was cutting it close."

"I know, I know," Jack continued. To address the puzzled looks of a few of the participants who had not been through this kind of review before, Jack said, "We have a protocol for flagging items in the DIA database for further review. Do you know how many terabytes of data we collect every month? It's freaking mindboggling. And do you know how many false alarms of WMDs we get every month?"

"8,327 for this last month and 7,325 for the month before," Don replied to this rhetorical question. "And that's only if you're counting items that are above the 5% threshold."

"Right," Jack continued. "So DIA, NSA, NEST and a few of the other players developed a cutoff point of a 5% likelihood estimate. If the probability was viewed as 5% or greater, then a human would do further review. We had the cutoff at 1% right after 9/11, but the software sucked then, and there were something like 390,000 hits we had to look at every month. Drove us all f-ing crazy. The current number is making us crazy enough, but at least it's still pretty easy to knock out most of these alleged "hits." It's the whole "false positive" versus "false negative" problem in statistics; where should you draw the line? The math whizzes worked it out with the powers that be, and the protocol now is set at 5%. In addition, the NEST special analysis group only gets involved when the likelihood estimate is greater than 15%."

"At a 15% cutoff, we still get about two dozen serious domestic incidents to look at every month," Don noted. "Thank God that they all have turned out to be nothing so far. Let's all hope and pray that this turns out to be nothing too."

"Believe me; I am hoping and praying too," Jack said. "But we have never gotten an estimate number as high as 35% before domestically. As many of you remember, we had a 35% likelihood estimate called out when NEST had to scramble out to Eastern Europe for Project Fab-Tab. Of course, that was a real "dirty" bomb, a RDD that we had to take care of. SEAL Team Six and some of our foreign special forces friends did that job. To be fair, there were a small number of 35% cases outside the US that turned out to be false alarms too, so you never know. D-65, please continue."

"So now it's Day 12 after I first snapped the picture in the warehouse. DIA Mexico got a tagline on a DEA drug bust in Nogales. Guy named José Acevedas. José wouldn't turn on his Ciudad gang buddies. However, he had some information for DEA that he thought would be interesting in exchange for leniency. He said that he had been paid double the standard drug rates to smuggle three guys who he personally thought looked Middle Eastern through to the US. One of the guys was carrying a big heavy backpack. José assumed it was probably full of cocaine. The backpack tagline in the DEA report filed yesterday morning triggered a DIA analyst at Joint Base Anacostia-Bolling to take a further look, in light of the MAESTRO hit."

"Like I said," Jack broke in, "we got a little lucky. We tested José for background radiation last night. It wasn't definitive, but possibly consistent with a Russian backpack nuke. D-65 was yanked out of deep cover immediately and flown by a special jet over to Nogales immediately to corroborate."

D-65 noted, "I am still here in Nogales to help figure things out, especially since I partly grew up in Mexico as part of a gang myself, and know some Mexican slang. Enough so that I can be pretty useful. In fact, it so happens that I know a few of José's compadres, and others by reputation, so José opened up a bit to me. I talked to him until 0400 hours local time this morning and we got the following information: (a) José took the Middle Easterners, including this guy, Amir Abbasi, through to the US side six days ago; ...." All of the participants at the meeting groaned. Six full days ago! That was terrible news. "(b) the white van, José thinks it had Nevada plates, that they got into was driven by another Middle Easterner, Hossein Abbasi, Amir's brother; and (c) José has a general idea of what Amir's partners look like. He worked with one of our sketch artists and he turned out some pictures of them for us, including Hossein, who José saw briefly, but obviously saw less than the other partners, since Hossein only showed up as the driver at the end."

"Tell us about Amir and his partners," David requested.

Jack Smith said, "That was next on the agenda. Amir Abbasi is from a family of prominent businessmen in the Pahlavi dynasty from 1925-79. After the Shah fell, the family had to scramble to prove their loyalty to the clerics. The clerics, including Ayatollah Khomeini, really didn't trust the Abbasi family, but they still needed businessmen like them to help run the country, help keep the oil flowing, and help ensure the country was supplied with products. Religion alone doesn't pay the bills. D-1 will give you all the details."

D-1 came from the back and moved over to the lectern at the front of the room to present. "I am part of DIA's special services branch. I am charged with basically coordinating everything we know and think about Iran. Admittedly, the greater part of our intel is just a patchwork of reasonable guesswork and half-corroborated gossip. We synthesize it all, especially the pronouncements of the mullahs, and most of the time it is messy as hell. Let's start with the facts we do know for sure: Amir Abbasi," Amir's picture came on screen again, "was born in Tehran in the early 1970s, and continues to be a Tehran resident. We believe he is the oldest son in the family, and probably was 4 or 5 years old during the 1979 revolution. Yousef Abbasi is Amir's father, and Yousef had a family of four kids: Amir, then a daughter Farah, then another son who died, and then the youngest child, Hossein." D-1 put up a family tree of the Abbasi family on the screen. "The Abbasi family, as Jack said, was mostly a bunch of prominent businessmen pre-Shah downfall. Rich, but not stinking rich. Not one of the top 5 families, but maybe one of the top 250 families in the country, to give you a flavor as to our best guess. One branch of the Abbasi family, Amir's uncle Omid, was heavily involved with the nationalized oil and gas industry in the mid-1990s when some of the original powerhouses got purged and/or executed by the ayatollahs in 1990-91. You really didn't want to be too powerful a businessman then, because the clerics would just take you and your family out, since you were perceived as a threat. Yousef was heavily involved in the food industry, and probably pissed off the new Supreme Leader, Ali Khamenei, in the early 1990s, or he just got perceived as a threat himself. Yousef wasn't executed; instead, he was jailed for having moderate "reformist" views we think, from 1990-95. Only Amir's uncle Omid's status was able to keep Yousef's kids and their families-- Amir, plus his wife and two kids, Farah, who has five kids and married into another oil and gas family, and his brother Hossein - alive and out of jail. Yousef is in his mid-70s and is still puttering around from what we hear, bitter at his treatment, but smart enough to keep his mouth shut. DIA thinks that Amir and Hossein must have "volunteered" for this terrorist mission in order to protect the Abbasi extended clan. That is a total wild guess since we don't know that much about Amir and Hossein. For all we know, they could be true believers of the cause. We do know that they both studied agricultural business at Tehran University and speak English and French fluently. In fact, Hossein was born in the United States on one of his dad's business trips. As a US citizen, he lives mostly in the United States, helping to run his dad's food company, Global Consolidated Foods, Inc., which is technically headquartered in Switzerland and technically still controlled by the dad through a number of shell companies. There is a food processing subsidiary, GCF Euro Brands, located in Los Angeles, which Hossein has worked for over the past decade. We say that the parent Global Consolidated Foods is technically controlled by Yousef, because after he was jailed, DIA believes that the clan at one point had to 'voluntarily' relinquish control over the parent entity to the government extremists."

"Al Qods?" HSA Jorgensen asked.

"Maybe," replied Jack. "As the equivalent of our CIA and Special Forces units rolled into one, Al Qods is tasked with all foreign activities sanctioned by the ayatollahs. But, as I said before, there are different factions within Al Qods, and we believe that Rahimi is acting alone as a rogue operative not under the control of the Iranian government. Here are the facts as we know them: the Al Qods senior director that the French had made a double agent in late 2010 had no knowledge of Yousef or Hossein being part of Al Qods. That same senior director said that Rahimi had pissed off the ayatollahs and maybe even had been booted out of the organization. So who knows what's really going on, but it isn't good. Rahimi may still be running some Al Qods operatives who think that Rahimi is still a powerful insider within Al Qods."

"They're going to try to nuke LA then?" the HSA questioned. "We got Hossein tracked?"

"Well, that's the thing," Jack continued. "We have initiated all-out surveillance on GCF Euro Brands, surveillance on Hossein's LA apartment, and surveillance on his cell phone and credit cards. Unfortunately, he has gone totally off the grid."

"Christ!" the Vice President and the HSA muttered simultaneously. "Give me some good news. What's the plan?" the Vice President asked.

"We're monitoring all of Hossein's known associates and locations that he has frequented in the past few years, based on discussions and wiretaps of those known associates. DIA and FBI had a file on him, but because Yousef was jailed, we figured that he was one of the good guys, more on our side than anything else. The extended Abbasi clan has a number of folks who migrated over to the United States; they are mostly trained as doctors and other professionals, not suspicious at all. Mostly they are good American citizens, some of whom settled in LA and some in the East Coast, mostly New York. We are trying to talk to all of the extended family and friends, and we're using a whole bunch of tricks to get them to talk to us – standard stuff about maybe they're getting an tax refund or an inheritance or something like that. The closest family and friends, and business associates, are getting the most coverage, but we will have a hell of a time covering all of them in LA alone."

"Anywhere else we should be looking?" the HSA chimed in.

"Since the van had Nevada plates, we also have teams in Las Vegas and Reno combing the area. Do you know how many white vans with Nevada plates there are in the whole state? Thousands, way too freaking many to run down at this point. Reno is a long shot – why would a terrorist nuke Reno? – although it would be quite ironic in light of Operation Snow Falcon. If the target is Nevada, we are concentrating on Vegas because at least there we think that there could be some symbolic thing going on, nuking from their point of view, the "infidel's ultimate city of sin," or something like that. Maybe that makes some sense to them, especially if done on New Year's Eve. Pure conjecture. I am still leaning towards LA, though, from a population impact perspective."

"Other cities?" asked the HSA.

"Well, we've thought about San Francisco, Phoenix, Los Alamos, Denver, a whole slew of scenarios. We even are thinking about the 'what if the plan is that the bomb gets driven to the East Coast' scenario, and thinking about how a bomb could get to DC or New York. We're looking at that in detail, and have got resources against those possibilities. Our focus now, however, is: (1) Los Angeles, and (2) Las Vegas. We're thinking New Year's Eve as the date that make the most sense, since that's when a lot of people will be celebrating together, particularly in Las Vegas, Los Angeles, and of course, New York, where they do the countdown on TV."

"That only gives us a week before they are going to set off the bomb," said the Vice President.

"Look, we don't even know whether the bomb might just be set off today, or tomorrow on Christmas Day. Christmas Day would be a pretty significant date as well, don't you think? It's 0618 in the morning, and we have had a priority code alpha in place since 0445 hours. The President has moved the country into DEFCON 3 status, the same status that we had after 9/11. It's only been about an hour and a half. This morning at 0800 Eastern Time we are going to mobilize a hell of a lot of people, and there are going to be a lot of questions. We have to avoid widespread panic. We're debating on showing Amir's picture on national TV, but that's a Presidential call when he gets videoed into this meeting, right after the G7 dinner among all of the heads of state. We are so far advising against going fully public for now. We are also against, at this time, issuing an 'Imminent' threat under the National Terrorism Advisory System until the subjective threat assessment goes above 50%. As you know, the NTAS has never been fully activated at the highest level since it was instituted in 2011. Remember two years ago, we had activated it at the 'Elevated' level as you remember, in Operation Full Shield, and mobilized a ton of people and nothing happened. We got killed in the press for that one. We are initially recommending a similar 'Elevated' full alert, again with local police and National Guard involved. Local eyes and ears everywhere. We'll base it off of some different information, so as not to alert these Iranians that we may be on to them. We'll say that we are on alert because of some Al Qaeda airliner threat that we know about, which has the advantage of being true, but we've assessed that threat at only a 0.3% likelihood estimate."

"The press is going to crucify us if a nuclear bomb goes off before we find it, and they learn that we didn't do a full announcement of what we knew at the time."

"That's why I'm saying it's the President's call. But we feel that a full 'Imminent' NTAS announcement works against us and basically heightens the probability that the terrorists set off the bomb now, if a bomb even exists. Remember that 35% is high, but it's not even that close to 50%. Do we want to start a nationwide panic for nothing? And, if there is a bomb, the DIA analysis group thinks we've got a significantly better chance to find it if we don't announce now, and just monitor for a few days. We can go the NTAS 'Imminent' route on the morning of Christmas Day if we get new information or some other information breaks. Even with an 'Elevated' status, if it turns out that nothing happens, we are still going to get hit for crying wolf too often. That is why we are getting everyone's opinion aired out here before the President joins. What does everyone else think?"

Vice President Branden spoke. "Pat, what's your assessment of what we should communicate?"

"Mr. Vice President, this could be a damned-if-we-do announce, damned-if-we-don't situation. But I have to agree with the DIA here. It's the morning of December 24th. Let's see what happens over the course of the day. If we get some more information verifying the existence of a nuclear backpack, we can announce specific details this evening or tomorrow morning on the 25th. Meanwhile, we pull out all the stops. And I mean all the stops."

"Ron?"

"Marcia and I both concur on behalf of the FBI that we go all out, with no public dissemination for the moment, other than the NTAS 'Elevated' status using the Al-Qaeda misdirect. Mr. Vice President, we're mobilizing just about every agent on the force starting at 0700 Eastern Time. As you know, we have a Joint Counterterrorism Task Force, the JCTF, set up with the states and localities, so we are activating the phone tree at the same time. It's all coordinated of course with the NCTC in McLean, Virginia."

"Bill?"

"The Joint Chiefs are going to support the search. The National Guard Bureau has told us that we can mobilize about 25 brigades to help out in the effort. That's about 80,000-100,000 people that can supplement the FBI and the local police. Of course, they're not really trained in counterterrorism, so most of their work will be helping out to patrol critical infrastructure and helping out on needed roadblocks and the like. Since we're also on the JCTF, we've got some coordination here. As you know, the HSA has full operational command here over the overall JCTF. NEST is in command of the scientific and technical search operations. If we find the terrorists, and need to mount an operation to capture or disable it, then of course FBI is in command. SAIC Smithline knows a lot of the Delta and SEAL boys, so we can always provide additional military support as needed – he'll let us know what he needs."

For the next thirty-eight minutes, before the President of the United States was scheduled to join the meeting, the participants began to plan for the next few days. Joint Base Andrews would continue to be the hub for the JCTF for the particular operation, liaising with the NCTC. The NEST team would be based out of Nellis Air Force Base in Las Vegas, where a great deal of their technical equipment and people were located anyway. FBI SAIC Smithline would also have a command center at Nellis as well as one at the FBI headquarters in Los Angeles, which was located in Westwood, near UCLA. This would be no drill, like Operation Snow Falcon. Instead, they would use the pre-wired command center infrastructure already in place at Nellis and Westwood, and they would not need AT&T help to get it set up. All of the state-of-the-art equipment was long ago put into place. Smithline and K2 would leave immediately after the presidential briefing and executive instructions.

As the members were continuing to plan out the operation, now dubbed Operation Safety Screen, the President of the United States abruptly came on the video screen a full fifteen minutes early. "What the hell is going on, Louis?" President Ryan Besselman yelled into the phone. "How is it possible that a nuke got into the US? I thought that we had ways to prevent that very kind of thing from happening." President Besselman took a deep breath, to control his seething anger. "All right, no blame game for now. I made an excuse to get out of tonight's G7 dinner as early as diplomatically possible. Give me the latest, Pat."

"Mr. President," HSA Jorgensen said as calmly as he could, given the circumstances, "we have Operation Safety Screen in play. Since you are in Europe already, we respectfully suggest that it is a perfect opportunity and excuse for you to stay out of DC so that we don't have you and the Vice President in the same vicinity. Of course, you are running the show, and we are here to brief you on the situation." So Jorgensen and the others took President Besselman through the briefing, bringing him up to speed on what the other participants already knew, and what they had aligned to as a recommendation on the communications plan.

"You realize that it's all on me if a nuke goes off and we didn't tell people the details regarding what we may have suspected?" the President complained. "David, what do you think?"

"Respectfully, Mr. President, it's your call, but the press is the last thing I'm worried about now," Smithline replied. "We have got to maximize our chance to find and stop this weapon from detonating if it in fact has been smuggled into the United States already."

"I know, I know," the President sighed. "This is not going to happen on our watch, ladies and gentlemen. The United States, no, actually the entire world, would be changed forever."

Not on our watch, and not ever, agreed the group. Don Llewes assured the President, "We'll find and disarm this nuke. Give us the time."

The HSA prodded the President. "We'll need a decision as to our strategy, Mr. President. We need to activate now, find Amir Abbasi and his crew, and disable the nuke."

"I feel like I have no choice. I hereby approve the team's plan," the President reluctantly replied. "Pat, you're in control of the JCTF. You have until 1830 hours Pacific time tonight," the President continued, "and then we'll reassess whether to inform the public. If there is a nuke, take it out before it goes off please."

"Yes sir, Mr. President."

And so the biggest manhunt, or perhaps more accurately "object hunt," in the history of the United States of America began on December 24th at 0700 hours ET as part of the JCTF's Operation Safety Screen.

CHAPTER 5

In Los Angeles, the JCTF was secretly surveilling about fifty of Hossein's closest family, friends, and business associates. Not a single one of them, however, was meeting up with, calling, or otherwise contacting Hossein. Massive numbers of new radiation detectors were being placed all around Los Angeles, Las Vegas, and other prime target cities, although many of these cities already had a significant number of radiation detectors in place. While there were a number of false alarms (for example, a shipment of medical devices had set off a few alarms in a warehouse district in East LA), nothing real was registering.

The Operation Safety Screen personnel were working hard. It was particularly frustrating because they were all so overworked already, and now they were working even more extra time so near to Christmas. But they plodded on, confident in the importance of their duties and looking for the one break that would allow them to find Hossein and the nuke.

"Yes, ma'am. That's A-(like apple)-b-(like boy)-b-(like boy)–a–(like apple)-s-(like snow)-i-(like inside). Any records of credit card usage in the last few days?" asked FBI agent Kyle Adams. Kyle had been tasked the thankless job of trying to follow up on the very remote possibility that the Abbasis could be tracked through their financial transactions. Even Kyle thought that this was a longshot; surely no terrorist group would use anything other than cash during the critical part of its operations? The FBI had gotten a warrant to go through the Abbasi corporate and personal bank transactions as well over the past few months to see if they could detect suspicious transactions to see where they were located. Nothing had turned up in their investigations so far.

A few of Jack Smith's DIA personnel had teamed up with some LA-based FBI staff to more efficiently reach out to Hossein's extended family and friends. Hossein's secretary in LA (Hossein's official title at GCF Euro Brands was Vice President of Strategic Business Development) had told a DIA agent posing as a potential GCF customer that Hossein was unreachable until the new year as he was driving around the Southwest on vacation with friends. Unfortunately, Hossein had left strict instructions not to be disturbed. The secretary instead noted that another Vice President, Mr. Afir, the VP of Sales, would be glad to return the call. Similarly, when the FBI had left a message with Hossein's work phone asking for a reply to an IRS inquiry, the call also had not yet been returned. The FBI also had gotten a FISA court order to tap Hossein's cell phone as well, but that phone had not been used, and in fact was turned off completely and was untraceable. The FBI suspected that Hossein had bought a different, disposable cell phone and had turned off his normal cell phone.

The US government had mobilized over 12,000 people (including the National Guard) in the Los Angeles and Las Vegas metropolitan areas to conduct roadblocks and various search operations, all under the pretext that they were looking for potential Al Qaeda terrorists who were trying to replicate 9/11. In order not to tip off Amir and Hossein that they had specific information about LA and Las Vegas, mobilizations had also occurred in New York City, Boston, Washington, DC, San Francisco and Chicago. Because the mobilization was so widespread and so indiscriminate, and only a relatively few people knew about the RA-115 situation, the media so far had covered the story in a perfunctory way, treating the actions as merely precautionary. It had helped that the nation had gone through the smaller Operation Full Shield mobilization about two years ago and nothing had happened. In fact, the media had played the story as the typical overreaction by Washington to a threat that probably didn't exist, much to the delight of the Safety Screen team. Of course, they had had a hand surreptitiously in persuading the media to run with this story angle, but you never knew what the independent press would do in the US.

It was now 1800 hours PT on December 24th. Nothing material had been learned about Amir or Hossein's whereabouts. Everyone was tired and on edge.

David and K2 had flown to Nellis AFB in Las Vegas following the meeting, after barely having time to pack some clothes and toiletries. The two of them had been jointly setting up the command center for the past few hours. Even though the Nellis "war room" ostensibly was a ready-to-operate regional operations command, there were still a fair number of tweaks necessary to make it work right for this particular operation. Mostly, it involved adding another two huge banks of computer screens to provide live feeds of the huge National Guard operations that were going on across the West Coast. Most of the NEST technical staff and EOD people had been shuttled to the Los Angeles vicinity. A host of reconnaissance flights had already occurred with the King Air aircraft and a phalanx of about 16 helicopters marked to look like LA Police Department choppers. The flights had yielded twenty-seven false positive hits in Los Angeles and twelve in Las Vegas, but nothing material had surfaced. The RA-115 nuke was not findable.

David believed that the "people" part of the operation was their best hope. Surely one of Hossein's family or friends knew where Hossein was and would spill the beans.

At 1830 PT, the check-in meeting started.

"Give me some good news," Vice President Branden implored.

"Wish we could," replied the HSA and Marcia Brown simultaneously. "Please provide the details on the LA situation, David," Marcia continued.

"Well, like Pat and Marcia just said, no good news yet. We've been moving fast today in LA on four or five fronts. First, we have fifteen strategically located checkpoints at various key highway arteries, airports and ports in the LA metropolitan area. Obviously, since we have the info that a van is involved, we are thinking that the highway arteries are the key. However, to be consistent with the media story, we wanted to have checkpoints at the airports and ports as well. Second, we've been doing lots of flyovers with planes and helicopters, all with our state-of the-art radiation detection equipment. Third, we've got serious 24x7 surveillance around all of Hossein's known hangouts, together with all other Abbasi-related locations. Fourth, we have had people reach out to Hossein's known acquaintances, including work colleagues, family and friends. Fifth, we've got people doing technical intelligence gathering: reviewing bank records, phone logs, email accounts, and the like. We've just gotten FISA court approval to activate DCS1001, where we can now intercept and review in real-time almost 99% of all phone, email and internet traffic going into and out of LA. For these fourth and fifth categories, we really need more time to see if anything pans out. Give us another 24 hours and we'll fill you in again."

"And the other cities?"

"Again, nothing to report," the HSA replied. "We've got slightly lesser but similar efforts going on in Las Vegas, San

Francisco, Washington, DC, New York City, Boston and Chicago. We even have a small group in Denver and Dallas. Nothing to report here either, for now," Jorgensen looked at David and K2 to confirm this and they nodded their heads in corroboration, "but as David said, give us another 24 hours. Of course, tomorrow is Christmas, so who knows what the hell will happen. Our recommendation is to keep going and not do a public announcement."

"Understood and agreed." Vice President Branden looked at Katherine from his screen, "How about NEST technical resources support? Do you have everything you need?"

"Yes, Mr. Vice President. I'd say that we're at about 80% readiness now. By close of the day tomorrow, I think we'll be up to 95%, and 99% by Dec 26th. The sensitivity of the equipment is being cranked up, which is why we're getting all of the false positives. But better safe than sorry."

The President came on the call after another ten minutes, and the team briefed him assiduously. Like the Vice President, the President trusted the team and agreed with the recommendation not to go public just yet. The meeting ended promptly at 1930 PT, although no one left satisfied. Afterwards, plans were refined and everyone agreed to check in again periodically over the next 24 hours, but the large group meeting would happen again from 1830 to 1930 hours PT tomorrow.

The sun rose uneventfully on Christmas Day, December 25th, just like it had for every other day. While the JCTF Safety Screen team was exhausted, they knew that they could not let up now. In fact, if anything, the team went into overdrive mode and FBI agents throughout the country were methodically and doggedly going through their surveillance and search protocols, looking for any sign of Amir or Hossein Abbasi.

One FBI contingent concentrated on the Nuri family. Karim Nuri was a partner of Yousef when they had first opened their LA subsidiary, which had branched out past the original fruit canning operation long ago. The Nuri clan were relatives of the Abbasi family, and were second generation Angelenos; a large segment of the Nuri family tree had gone into medicine just like their Abbasi cousins. There were a slew of doctors and dentists named "Nuri" in the LA Yellow Pages, ranging from orthopedic surgeons to pediatricians to orthodontists. Many of these Nuri medical professionals were second cousins to Amir and Hossein.

There were seventeen individual Nuris that the FBI team had on their list to check off. Using a variety of different techniques, the FBI team had managed to speak to only thirteen of them by 1700 PT, mainly because it was Christmas Day. None of them were able to shed any light on where Hossein or Amir might be.

David and K2 were frantically preparing for the 1830 PT call, despite the fact that there really wasn't anything new to say. They just had to report on what they had done, and what was left to do. David had been coordinating some of the National Guard units in tandem with a colleague of Bill McTighe's, as well as trying to work with his own FBI units in their search for Hossein. Concurrently, K2 was scrambling around herself coordinating some additional air sweeps, mostly in LA and Las Vegas. Nothing had panned out so far. By 1815 PT, they took a little break to compare notes. "What a day, K2. Quiet, yet hectic internally. It's like we're in the eye of a hurricane. Thanks for the report. I read it and agree with your conclusions. By the way, what did your parents say when you told them you couldn't come home for Christmas?" David asked.

"They were really mad, of course, in the beginning, especially my mother," K2 responded, "but you know moms. By the end, she was just feeling sorrier for me than for herself when I told her I had to work today and tomorrow. She really questioned why the government would have us working on Christmas Day. I told her we weren't really working that hard today, a little white lie, but that the reason I couldn't come home was that we had to have some important meetings on Monday and I just couldn't get away. How about you?"

"Yeah, my mom is more philosophical about these things. I've missed enough Christmases where she was just resigned to my not coming this year. I think that I could tell, though, that she was a little more hurt this year, since I had insisted to them earlier that I was really sure that I could come. I just hate doing this to mom."

"Tell me about it," K2 replied. "Oh, yeah, I'm the same way. Hey, you know, I don't even think we had time today to say 'Merry Christmas' to each other yet. So 'Merry Christmas' to you," she said, giving David a little hug.

"Merry Christmas to you too," David replied, giving K2 a hug back. "I'm glad at least I get to spend Christmas with some friends like you, although the circumstances suck," David said a little awkwardly before recovering. "OK, here's how I think we should approach the agenda," he continued, and they got back down to business.

Since there really wasn't much to report, the 1830 PT briefing that evening was short. The President and Vice President were definitely not happy that there wasn't real progress to report after two full days of searching, and reamed the team leaders out. They understood that it was Christmas Day, but said that this was no excuse; they needed answers now.

HSA Jorgensen, smarting from his being chewed out, in turn chewed out FBI Director Edelman, Edelman chewed out FBI Executive Associate Director Marcia Brown, Brown chewed out David, and the verbal abuse flowed downhill from there among the senior leadership. Things were getting more and more tense. The Vice President challenged the Safety Screen people in no uncertain terms to find the nuke by the next evening report at 1830 PT on December 26th.

However, rather than just leaving it at that, the Vice President, because of the extreme strain he was feeling from the President, rather unnecessarily blurted out a threat: heads would roll if nothing was found by the end of the day on December 27th, a mere two days ahead. Edelman and Brown offered to resign their posts first before they were relieved of command. SAIC Smithline offered the same, and a slew of other staff too, before the Vice President, realizing his blunder, starting walking back his threat. He said that he recognized that everyone was working hard and doing good work, and that he needed the entire senior team in place throughout the crisis. He apologized profusely for his blowup. Of course, that didn't make anyone feel better. Not because of the Vice President's retraction that people would be fired, they didn't care so much about that, but they were all such Type A people used to accomplishing the impossible that they felt their failure more deeply than any mere words that the Vice President had said.

The mood was bleak as the core team gathered after the Christmas Day evening report, as they just had no significant new areas to follow up on for the next day. Los Angeles was a huge area to cover, let alone the fact that they also needed to consider Las Vegas, Denver and all of the other cities. They were running out of options, and running out of time. They had all worked hard on Christmas Day and had nothing concrete to show for it. The 26th didn't figure to be much better. It would still be really difficult to follow up with people on the day after Christmas. Some people would still be hunkered down following their Christmas parties with family and friends. Most people would be out and about, as the day after Christmas of course traditionally was when people went shopping, returning or exchanging gifts opened the day before. Either way, people would not be easily available or interested in talking to the FBI.

The Safety Screen team was getting really stressed, and the anxiety level was almost palpable and growing with each passing hour. They were really dreading the 1830 PT briefing on December 26th if they didn't find anything. It would be ten times worse than that of the previous day's meeting in terms of stress and the yelling. HSA Jorgensen, FBI Director Edelman, and FBI WMD Directorate leader Brown each thought their heads were going to explode already with the dressing down they received from the Vice-President at the last meeting. To their credit, the senior officials had mostly kept their professional demeanor intact and just bore the brunt of the criticism for their junior ground troops. Everyone knew that the Vice-President was a hothead and was just venting his frustration. *At least he is not as much of a jerk as Proxmeier is*, David thought to himself.

CHAPTER 6

The day of December 26th would mostly be taken up by sifting through old approaches. While each of the Nuris by now had been contacted already one way or the other, the team was naturally conducting some follow-up meetings just to double-check. In some cases, they felt that the Nuris may have been holding something back because of the way that the original meetings had been conducted. For example, sometimes the FBI agents had been posing as estate attorneys, asking where Hossein was so that they could tell him about an inheritance windfall. These days, especially with well-educated folks, like most of the Nuris were, people could see through these ruses easily. Those contacted probably thought that the FBI agents were just salesmen, lying to get through to Hossein in order to sell him something. As relatives, they probably knew that no one in the Abbasi family had passed away recently, at least no one close to Hossein who would leave him any substantial amount of money. However, it was the holiday season and the FBI was afraid that nothing would work, as people were often just too busy with their own lives to deal or think about much else. Maybe no one in the Nuri family really knew where Hossein was at this time.

Then the Safety Screen search team caught a break. One member of the Nuri family, Banu, a dentist in Irvine, was doing emergency weekend appointments for a few of her long-time patients. At 4:30pm, she had just finished up fixing a crown on her last patient when FBI agent Mohammad Ahmadi entered her dental offices asking to speak to her. Introducing himself as a member of the Iranian-American Chamber of Commerce (IACC), the FBI agent told her that Hossein was on the short list of those who might be selected as one of ten honorees for the annual IACC dinner in the middle of January. Fortunately, Mohammad actually was an IACC member as part of his FBI cover, so his story would check if anyone did any due diligence. The potential honorees were asked for references, Mohammad explained, and Hossein had put a list of people down, including Banu. Banu flipped her hair wearily.

"Really?" she replied. "He put me down? Hossein and I see each other at holiday gatherings, but my cousin Samir is who he really hangs out with. I'm surprised that he wrote me down, especially since we got into a little tiff this past summer."

Mohammad assured Banu that Samir was also on the reference list, but that the IACC needed to interview and talk with all of the references. He also smoothly replied that the reference list was from the beginning of the year, so that may have explained why Banu was still on the list. "Can you tell me what you are most proud of Hossein doing? For example," the FBI agent pulled out a piece of paper printed from the internet, "I see here that GCF Euro Brands sponsors an annual holiday food drive, and here is Hossein from before Thanksgiving this year doling out crates of food to LA homeless shelters."

"Well, to be honest, that was a program that my father Karim demanded that the company undertake about ten years ago," Banu explained sheepishly. "My second cousin Hossein's job, as Vice President of Strategic Business Development, is to serve as one of the key public faces of the company. So of course he would be in the press releases about public service. Look, we got into an argument, but he really isn't a bad guy. I'm tired, and I need to go home now," Banu said, starting to walk out of the lobby of her office.

Mohammad doggedly pursued her. "All right, I get what you're saying. And I'm sorry for taking up your time; I just need to do this vetting, and tomorrow I need to take my son to Disneyland so I hope that you can just spare me one more minute. Look, the award is mostly to acknowledge that he's helped out the Iranian-American community in terms of business and philanthropy. You know what I mean: we need to be able to say that Hossein's been involved with expanding business and hiring people in the LA community. That he's raised the profile of Iranian-Americans in LA. That he's donated to the Iranian-American community, maybe by providing internships to some Iranian-American college students; that kind of thing. So that's what we're here to confirm."

"Well, OK, by that standard, I guess, I can confirm that he's fine," Banu said, half-absently, as she was starting the process of closing up her office. Her receptionist was putting away the last patient files of the day in the next room.

"Wow, that's a pretty guarded recommendation." Mohammad smiled as he replied to indicate that he meant no offense. "You must have gotten into some big argument with him. I know that you don't want to speak ill of your relatives, even if he's only a second cousin, and I don't expect you to, but do you mind my asking at least what your argument was generally about? Here's where I am going with this: the IACC doesn't want to pick Hossein as one of its annual honorees and then find out next month that he's a pedophile, or a drug addict who's about to go in rehab. We're all about good public relations for the Iranian community."

"No, no, nothing like that," Banu said, waving her hands emphatically. "Nothing illegal. And I shouldn't be telling you this, but as you can see, I'm not a typical Iranian woman, who sits quietly in the background. My dad wanted me to break the mold, so I did by becoming a dentist, the first female dentist in the Nuri family. As for the argument, let's just say that Hossein maybe was too "Americanized." Hossein loves the excitement of a quick buck, so he just fell into gambling by nature. Loves every type of game you could bet on – poker, craps, sports betting, horse racing – you name it, Hossein does it."

"As you said, though, it's not illegal, so why argue about it?"

"Well, it was affecting the family. His dad Yousef hates gambling with a passion, as does my father Karim. His sister Farah, who I am close to, she's like a second sister to me, also loathes gambling and can't understand why Hossein would get into it. Especially since his Uncle Mehdi lost basically his entire life savings to gambling -- you'd think that would be a lesson to Hossein. Mehdi was a prominent doctor who got addicted to poker and horse racing; thought he had a system for each and just couldn't stop. Lost his medical practice, lost his home and lost his fiancé. The perfect trifecta. So the fight really was about keeping the family happy. Farah told me that Hossein would disappear on three day "business trips" to Las Vegas, when Farah knew very well that the business part took maybe a day. And then Hossein would deny everything and get mad at us."

"Hmm, the IACC wouldn't like to honor an addict. How bad is his gambling habit?"

Banu quickly realized that she had shared too much. She replied defensively, "Well, maybe I'm being too melodramatic because of what happened to Uncle Mehdi. Uncle Mehdi IS a gambling addict; Hossein IS NOT an addict. It's not debilitating or anything. I mean, come on, he's the Vice President of a company. He maybe goes," she ran her fingers through her hair, "oh, I don't know, maybe once every month or two. It's just so frustrating because the family doesn't want him to end up like Uncle Mehdi."

"How did Uncle Mehdi end up?" Mohammad asked gently. "Sorry, can't help asking."

"He's kind of a broken man. The family doesn't really talk to him much. He lives in Vegas I think, ironically enough given his gambling addiction, in a home rented to him by my cousin Samir. Samir's a cardiologist in Las Vegas who is into real estate. Has something like a dozen rental houses there." Mohammad's ears perked up at this.

"Wow, he's like some kind of real estate king. A dozen houses is a lot."

"Yeah, that's his form of "gambling" I guess – but it's more appropriately called "investing," and Samir's pretty smart about it. He bought over half of the homes in 2010-11, after the real estate crash, so the purchases were close to the market bottom. The homes have all appreciated a fair amount over the last few years, and moreover he's got them rented out to fully cover costs. I told Hossein that he should take up real estate investing instead; it's more socially useful, and could satisfy his interest in speculating and gambling."

"What did he say about that?"

"Said that there's no thrill in real estate investing. And I can understand that. I have gambled a little bit, mostly slot machines, but I completely stopped after seeing what happened to Uncle Mehdi. Nothing provides your brain as much quick stimulation as hitting a slot machine jackpot, or bluffing and winning a big pot in poker. I get that. Real estate wins are too slow to provide that kind of instant gratification, even if they're way more likely."

"Hmmm, you've been very helpful, Dr. Nuri. So far, nothing you have said disqualifies Hossein Abbasi from being an IACC honoree this year. I actually very much appreciate your straightforwardness. In all honesty, most of these background checks are pretty cursory and nothing comes out of them. In this case, you've given us the unvarnished truth, and it still isn't problematic for us at all."

Banu paused as she had pretty much finished the lock-up procedure. She motioned over to her receptionist that she was almost ready to go; they always walked out together to their cars. She looked over at Mohammad. "No problem. In a way it's good to have talked about this with a stranger. I'm just frustrated by Hossein sometimes, and it's kind of cathartic to just talk about it."

"One final thing," Mohammad continued. "We haven't been able to find Hossein recently. We need him to, uh," Mohammad was improvising fast here, "fill out some paperwork for the annual dinner, particularly if he's going to be an honoree, which looks pretty likely as I told you. It's due before the end of the year, but Hossein doesn't seem to be answering his cell phone, and his secretary doesn't have any other forwarding number for us."

"Oh, I think I know where he is; I overheard Hossein and Samir talking about this at a previous get-together. You should talk to Samir. Whenever Hossein goes to Vegas for vacation these days, Samir lets him stay in one of his rental homes for free. They were talking about something like that for the end of this year and how they were going to try to get together for dinner at least, so I'm pretty sure that Hossein's in Vegas now."

Bingo, thought Mohammad. "Perfect. I'm not 100% sure if my colleagues were able to find Samir either on his cell to do his confirmatory interview, since it's the holidays," Mohammad continued smoothly. "Looks like we'll have to find Samir to find Hossein. Do you know how we can reach Samir for the next few days?"

They were now walking out of the office. Banu locked the door behind her and was walking away with her receptionist. "Sorry, lot harder there. Probably no cell service. He drove with his family for a vacation for the whole week or so; they are going to Bryce Canyon and Zion National Park in Utah. I don't think the IACC will be able to interview him until the first Monday after New Year's Day."

"Hmm," Mohammad mused, "that's too bad. Thanks, Dr. Nuri, you've been extremely helpful. We'll just have to figure out how to deal with this. The IACC appreciates your time and candor. You don't know how helpful you've been," he called out to the departing dentist.

Mohammad rushed back to his car and immediately phoned his supervisor to let him know what had happened. This was the first solid lead that they had gotten since Operation Safety Screen started.

The information got quickly relayed over to David Smithline at Nellis. The command team immediately sprang into action. They decided to move along multiple fronts: first, ten FBI agents were dispatched over to Bryce Canyon and Zion to try to find Samir. A separate FBI team was formed to try to piece together Samir's real estate holdings from public records so that they could try to observe each of the properties. A third FBI group was tasked with combing through Samir's financial and cell phone records to see if Samir could be located that way.

One would think that a group of dedicated professionals having the resources of the FBI would be able to completely piece together a person's business holdings or location within a matter of an hour or two. The truth, however, is that, in America, there are so many ways that an individual could hold economic interests through various entities that it is hard to immediately unravel a person's holdings. And often people cannot be located that quickly either. In Samir's case, by the time that the December 26th 1830 PT daily check-in meeting started, the FBI had found six rental homes that clearly belonged to Samir, but nothing like the dozen rental houses that Banu had suggested that Samir owned. Tax records were being combed through and double-checked, but it was becoming clearer that Samir, in all likelihood, managed a few of the rental homes for other relatives that weren't showing up. Or maybe Banu was exaggerating or mistaken about the dozen homes. Either way, David Smithline knew that they had to find out quickly where Hossein was staying. The homes that they were surveilling hadn't yielded any results yet.

"Give me some good news, for once," Vice President Branden begged at exactly 1830 PT, opening the December 26th meeting almost the same way that he opened it every day. He was speaking more evenly now, not yelling, as he had buried his anger, chastened by the reaction to yesterday's debacle. "We all really need it. I don't think any of us have slept for more than a few hours each day for the past three of four days."

"Well," the HSA started, "we've got one really solid lead that happened just recently." The Vice President's face perked up at this. Finally, this could be some good news. Jorgensen went on to relate Mohammad's meeting with Dr. Nuri at her dental office.

"Have they found Samir yet?" the Vice President demanded.

"No, not yet," David replied. "A FBI tactical force is out looking for them. We had dispatched them originally to Bryce Canyon and Zion National Parks in Utah, but re-routed them as I will explain. They should be on location within an hour or so. You see, we had gotten the FISA court to immediately approve a full tap on Samir's financial and cell phone records. Credit card review showed that Samir had rented a medium-sized RV from RVAmerica in Las Vegas last Sunday. They had reservations in Zion and Bryce this week, but with the snow there, looks like they cancelled those plans and headed towards California instead. We have a gas station receipt from 1500 PT today at a gas station in Death Valley National Park, near the Furnace Creek area. Unfortunately, we can't find an RV reservation for Samir in Death Valley tonight, whether in Furnace Creek or anywhere else; we do have one for tomorrow night in Furnace Creek. This probably happened because the Death Valley campgrounds are really popular in December and were fully booked already, since Samir was going at the last second. So Samir must just be backcountry RV camping by the side of the road or something until tomorrow."

"Won't this make it really hard to find them?" the Vice President asked.

"Maybe," David replied. "The tactical force has three choppers available to it and two Suburbans. We have a license plate for the RV. There are a lot of back roads to cover. However, we think that there's a 70% chance that we can find them tonight. Even if we can't, we figure that Samir will use his credit card sometime tomorrow morning, and we can find him that way pretty quickly. It's clear that he's not trying to hide since he is using his credit card so openly."

"Separately, we've got about a dozen agents watching the six rental houses that we know are owned by Samir," the HSA continued. "Don't forget, the real objective is to locate Hossein and the nuke. On top of that, just to be safe (after all, Banu could be lying, or Hossein could have been covering up his true location by lying to his relatives about his current whereabouts), we still have a bunch of people surveilling the LA area for Hossein."

"Anything else?" Vice President Branden asked. "It's the evening of December 26th now. Find Hossein and the nuke by the end of day tomorrow … please. By the way, which contingency plans are you thinking about using when we do find Hossein and the bomb?"

"As you know, Mr. Vice President," the HSA noted, "we've got a lot of off-the-shelf playbooks for these situations. We'll have to figure it out depending on the facts and circumstances. Everything from the full military assault to the more arcane."

"Of course," SAIC Smithline remarked, "we would prefer a subtler approach than blowing up a Las Vegas home with 30mm cannon fire from three or four Humvees, or from a Black Hawk helicopter for that matter. Unlike the Snow Falcon simulation in a warehouse zone, there are way more logistical issues in a suburban or urban neighborhood. We have a special tactical operations group consisting of FBI, NEST and EOD members thinking up some contingency plans with DIA depending on what facts and circumstances we find on the ground."

"Whatever works. Just neutralize the nuke and call it giving me a late Christmas present."

"Believe me, we're all looking at stopping the bomb as the ultimate Christmas gift, Mr. Vice President, to the American people," the HSA said.

"OK, so we check in again tomorrow. You guys go; I'll brief the President; no need to waste your time. This time we check in as soon as possible if Samir is found and we have Hossein's location."

At the same time, in a separate conference room, the WMD tactical operations group meeting was lively and getting more and more raucous. "There is no way we can guarantee that we would be able to get three Humvees in position in a suburban neighborhood." This was Jim Broussard of EOD speaking loudly. "Maximum we can guarantee would be one or two in place, assuming the house is not at the end of a cul-de-sac. If there is a cul-de-sac with an open backyard, then maybe three."

"Don't worry, Jim," Rick Columbia, leader of Cannon 1, chimed in, "even if it's only me in Cannon 1, I'll get it done."

"Not questioning your abilities, Rick," Jim said, using a more conciliatory tone, "but, let's face it, there's limited mobility in a small neighborhood. Depending on where the nuke would be stashed in the house, it could be an impossible shot. Even for you. Which means that we have to rely on our ground forces."

"What about the foamer?" Rick asked.

"Well," Ben pointed out, "once again, it would depend on where the nuke is stashed. If it's in the garage, then maybe we access the roof and foam it from there. However, if it's in a first floor closet of a two story house, there won't be any easy way to get the foamer hose into the space, if you see what I mean. And that assumes that we can get a specific location of the nuke in the first place. What if it's stashed in a radiation-shielded container? We may not be able to get a full read on where the nuke is within the house. That means, like Jim said, we just rely on a full frontal assault by our ground forces to take out all the terrorists. A couple of the troops could carry portable foamer tanks in their backpacks, I guess, but the coverage won't be that good. Maybe with the element of surprise, we can get to the nuke before they can set it off, but who knows?"

"Great, 'who knows what the hell will happen?' should be our operations motto today," groused Jim. "David and Katherine would love that. I'll tell them that when I see them after this meeting."

Rick ignored Jim's sarcasm. "So the best we got now is a full out night assault to take out all of the terrorists first before they can hit the nuke's self-destruct button. Is that right?" Rick said. "What's the destruct mechanism for a RA-115?"

Sri spoke up. "OK, if Amir really has a third generation RA-115 GRU variant, then we've got the detailed technical specs. After all, we have in our possession a few of these nukes ourselves – ahem, you'd have to ask someone way above my pay grade as to how we managed to do that." Ben just gave Sri the "don't talk about that" look, so Sri went on. "Well anyway, there are a bunch of fail-safe triggers on these things to prevent the operator detonating this thing accidentally. The Russians are not suicide bombers after all, and there is no way that Amir's group has the technical capability, in our opinion, to reprogram the software. The timer has to be set for at least a minimum of three minutes. The timer's default is six hours. Let me see," Sri looked down at a spec sheet in a notebook that he was holding, "looks like the maximum time you can set the timer for is 24 hours.

Having a timer of course allows the nuke backpack carrier the ability to get away from the blast site, although at the minimum setting of three minutes it wouldn't help much. At any time before t-minus zero, the operator can override the detonation sequence by inputting a 20-35 digit alphanumeric Cyrillic code that they would have pre-programmed previously. The three minute time minimum presumably gives the operator a few chances to do just that if necessary."

"So we can storm the home and shut off the bomb?" Rick asked excitedly. "We must have some smart NSA cryptographers who can break any code."

"Uh, well, maybe not. We have a few problems here. First, manually entering five wrong codes locks out the override mechanism for good, so we may need to take out all of the terrorists before they can purposefully lock us out of the override. Probably we can get past that one. The second problem is more technical. The first two versions of this GRU variant had a software flaw that NSA found out about, so we do have a device that can 'break the code,' as you said Rick, and shut down a 'version 1' or 'version 2' GRU RA-115 bomb. We heard that the GRU found out about the flaw about ten years ago, and executed the head software engineer who designed the code. Let's just say that the engineers who designed 'version 3' were really incentivized to not have any flaws in the software program. I'm not a software geek, so I'll let my buddy Brian here from NSA explain it better."

"Glad to Sri." Brian began, taking over the conversation. Bottom-line is that NSA so far can't find any immediately exploitable software flaws in the 'version 3' RA-115 that would allow us to stop the bomb within three minutes. We need about 40 minutes or so to break the code. Note that we don't have to worry about locking out the override since we found a tricky software redirect to solve that problem. We will have unlimited tries to override the detonation code. Ironically, there is a brand new 'version 4' of the GRU RA-115, developed a little more than a year ago, that has an intentional backdoor programmed into it so that you can defuse the nuke instantly if you have a special thumb drive. We found out about that backdoor and reverse-engineered the thumb drive. So now NSA can defuse all 'version 4' GRU RA-115s. Privately, we think that the reason for the backdoor is that GRU all of a sudden got worried about these backpack nukes getting used within Russia itself. Unfortunately, this nuke is a 'version 3' RA-115 for sure, based on the pictures, and not a 'version 4' RA-115."

"So what you're saying is that we're screwed. If the terrorists can arm the RA-115 and we can't get our hands on it with more than 40 minutes left on the timer, that is," Rick remarked glumly. "Can you go through the front-end arming process again? Maybe we can just take them out before they arm the thing in the first place?"

Jim replied, "Yeah, unfortunately, that's our best shot and it will be hard. Arming the 'version 3' RA-115 probably only takes at max a couple of minutes, maybe only one minute or so if you were really efficient. You see, while the nuke has been designed to avoid being set off accidentally, the designers also wanted to ensure that someone couldn't stop it from being relatively easily armed in the first place." He pulled out a schematic drawing of the RA-115 and put it on the whiteboard. "Now there are two modes of operation: (1) 'quick arm,' and (2) 'slow arm.' In quick arm, the nuke can be armed within a minute or two as I said. First, there's a sequence of codes to enter into the system. That's what takes most of the time. After those sequences are entered, then there's a little keyhole here where a special titanium key unique to each RA-115 is inserted and turned. After it's turned, then the operator has to press these two buttons simultaneously. As you can see, the buttons are located pretty far apart on the backpack so you can't push them together by accident. But one person can do this easily in a few seconds after the codes are entered. That's it; no additional codes to enter or anything. In 'slow arm,' designed to be used when the nuke is in transit, or for additional safety, the operator has to go through all of the steps in 'quick arm,' but then the person also has to replicate the steps again, including re-entering all of the codes again within two minutes of finishing the quick arm requirements. If the replication steps fail, then the operator has to start the arming process all over again. It's a double fail-safe approach. For our planning purposes, we have to assume that the nuke is in 'quick arm' mode, however."

"This is a pretty crappy situation, folks," Ben Yang interjected. "Wishing that this nuke is a 'version 4' and not a 'version 3' won't make it so. We've got to play the hand we are dealt. This isn't some simulation any more. If there are only a few terrorists, then we might have a reasonable shot at getting control of the nuke before it's activated. In our past tabletop scenarios, under normal conditions, we only succeed about half the time. I've always thought, 'good enough, we can't do anything about it anyway,' but now it's real, man, and it hits home hard. We may only have a 50/50 chance of preventing this nuke from taking out a lot of Las Vegas and killing maybe tens or hundreds of thousands of innocent people. It's just unacceptable. We've got to increase our odds of stopping the bomb."

Richie Gutierrez from the Glow 1 sharpshooter unit chimed in. "We know, we know. I think you're underestimating our probable success rate a bit. Even if the house is alarmed, we think we can get in without setting the alarm off. We believe that we can take out most of the terrorist guards quietly and get control of the bomb. So maybe it's 50/50 with respect to getting control of the nuke before they can even start the activation process, but I've always thought that we have a 90% chance of getting control of the nuke within a minute or two before the nuke can be activated. This is our playbook response, I think. Storm the house."

"Yeah, yeah, I get it," Sri stated, "but that timing is pretty ridiculously tight. Remember that in Snow Falcon we ended up losing our surprise element and it took some extra time to get the Humvees in place to blast the IND. Anyway, even in Snow Falcon, it took us close to two minutes alone from the time the terrorists were first trying to arm the bomb to the time that we blasted it. It would take longer to get control of it."

"Granted, but nevertheless, that's the playbook. And we actually got the Humvees to the location to blast the IND in that simulation within one minute after the firefight broke out. So here's the theory: in the worst case situation where the RA-115 is fully armed and we can't turn off the timer, we get control of the nuke within, say, two minutes and then we run it outside and foam it up. Then we take Cannon 1 and blast the hell out of the bomb, all within three minutes."

"Wow, cutting it a little close, don't you think?"

"Well, got any other bright ideas? We think that the radiation exposure from blasting the nuke would be minimal, pretty much limited to a few streets around the neighborhood."

"I'm thinking, I'm thinking," Ben chided.

"You E(ye)-in-steins better keep thinking then. FBI tactical ops so far is saying that the playbook we just went over is Plan A, and that's that. Totally willing to listen to any improvements and contingency plans you geniuses can come up with. Frankly, even Plan A will have at least eight minor variations depending on what we find out about the specific facts and circumstances on the ground. Right now, we are assuming that we don't want to use heavy firepower and just blow up the home without going in, because we can't guarantee that this approach would disarm the RA-115. Particularly if it's inside a safe hidden in a closet or something like that. Hey, if the nuke is in the garage inside a truck, then hell, maybe the plan is that we just drive the truck out of the garage before they can arm it."

"That would be easy," agreed Sri.

"Yeah, but we're not banking on that. We think that the most likely outcome is that we'll have to storm the house and take the nuke physically. If it hasn't been armed, then we're good of course. If it has been armed and we can't stop the detonation sequence, then we can try to get a clean shot from Cannon 1 or Cannon 2 to prevent it from detonating, or at least to reduce the impact of any detonation."

"How can we tell if it's armed or not?" Rick asked.

"Oh, at least there's an easy answer for that question," Jim explained. "The RA-115 has been designed to emit a soft, beeping noise every second so that the operator knows the nuke countdown timer is working and to get the hell out of there. And there's a visible timer too, that counts down the time on the front monitor panel of the nuke."

"Hmm, one to three minutes is a helluva short time to get control of a bomb after it's been armed," Rick said. "Close range terrorist firefights just take time to play out. How many people are we talking about here, Mark?"

Mark Childress, the tactical ground troops leader replied: "Well, we've got our eight sharpshooters on the roofs. For the initial insertion team, we've got the same two teams of ten troopers each led by Artie M and Paul Antam," Artie and Paul gave the group a mock salute, "that we did in Snow Falcon. Artie and Paul's Plan A playbook is to go all out and storm the house, take out all of the terrorists, and get the bomb no matter what, damned the consequences. Once the operation starts, they've been told to forget about hiding behind doorframes and the like. Forget about getting into an extended firefight with the terrorists. Instead, the teams are just supposed to keep on advancing until they get control of the nuke, do or die. Worst come to worst, we've got a backup group of twenty troopers as well. We just send wave after wave of people 'til we get the bomb."

"That's f-ing crazy!" Sri exclaimed.

"Yeah, well, welcome to my world," Artie replied. "Reminds me of my days in Marine Force Recon. We were told one time to just storm this facility and kill this guy no matter what. One idiot had the cojones to ask about the contingency plan if the facility and guy were too well guarded. The answer that came back of course was: (1) there is no such thing as "too well-guarded"; and (2) as for the contingency plan, see (1) above."

"I get it, I get it. From a FBI assault team perspective, there is only Plan A. There's no real Plan B," Ben said. "I am just saying that we really need to think of a less suicidal approach, a true Plan B doesn't get half of Artie and Paul's team killed off," he continued a little testily. "There's got to be one."

"Appreciate the thought, Ben," Artie replied, "but don't worry about the assault team. We know our job, and we don't back down. Oo-rah."

"You Marine guys are awesome, man. You've got your battle cries and your honor code; I'm glad that you are on my side. I just want you guys to actually live to fight another day. What about the exact opposite of a full frontal attack?" Ben said pensively.

"What do you mean?"

"I mean, what if we just tried to steal the bomb without the terrorists knowing about it? Or better yet, switch it with a fake nuke," Ben continued excitedly. "I remember it was a thought in one of our tabletop simulation reviews. You remember Plan Switchblade that Sri and I discussed with you guys."

"Oh yeah, I remember Switchblade," Jim said. "Yeah, it's possible. However, there are a whole bunch of things that have to be true for that to work. First, you have got to have absolutely rock-solid intel about the exact location of the nuke. Second, you have to have some way to get stealth access to the nuke. Third, you have to have good intel about the terrorists on the ground. Fourth, you got to have an exact replica of the nuke, if you're going to do a switch. I'm sure that there's a fifth, sixth and seventh thing, but that's enough for now. Last I checked, we're zero for four on the above."

"Yeah, yeah, yeah. Man, you are really a pessimist, Jim," Ben continued. "I note that if we get good intel on the home, that could take care of the first issue. And if that happens, I'll rely on you recon and special forces guys for the second and third issues. On the fourth issue, put that on Sri and me. We have already created, and have in storage, over a dozen 'fake'

RA-115 nukes. These fakes are based on real RA-115s that we have obtained via various sources that we aren't allowed to ask about. Then, based on the way that this 'version 3' RA-115 looks when you get control of it for us – it could have picked up some distinctive wear spots from all of that travel – we and a special ops stealth insertion team can do the switch, picking the bomb that looks like the closest to the real bomb, and replicating any needed wear spots as require to make it look exactly like the original. We've also found a way to replicate the keylock mechanism so that the original titanium key will work in the fake bomb."

"OK," Jim sighed, "totally agreed that you can prepare for this as Plan B. I think we're talking about a 1% chance that we can implement this, however."

"Agreed," Ben and Sri exclaimed simultaneously, each doing a fist bump with the other. Sri continued, "We're on it guys. Don't worry, we'll still spend a lot of time working with you on Plan A, as there are a few more things I want to tell the assault team about handling the RA-115. There are other methods in 'beta testing' now that we can think about using to try to disable the electronics on the bomb rather than blasting it with the 30mm cannons. They may not be ready for action yet, though, in this short a timeframe. We'll see."

And so the team went over about ten different variations of Plan A and outlined about five different variations of Plan B, discussing and arguing over each of them way into the night.

CHAPTER 7

It was after midnight in Death Valley. Three Black Hawk stealth helicopters were flying frantically throughout the park, trying to figure out where Samir's RV might be located. Each helicopter had infrared heat sensors, so they could tell where people were camping out. The helicopters would be supplemented by land vehicles which could help check out each of the RVs that the Black Hawks found that potentially could be housing Samir Nuri. That way, the Black Hawks wouldn't have to fly so close to the ground, which would have kicked up a lot of sand and dust and would have alerted Samir to their presence. The FBI had called the main Furnace Creek hotel where they eventually got to a clerk who was good friends with the owner of a local jeep rental place. The clerk eventually got the FBI search team in touch with that owner, and the government agents had been able to rent six jeeps from the guy just recently.

Thus, for the next few couple of hours, FBI search personnel would be driving all over Death Valley National Park looking for a RVAmerica recreational vehicle (there were so many of them!) with the right license plate, guided by the helicopters and the two Suburbans.

Sam Chalkias and Kyle Adams, from the Reno FBI office, were driving in one of the rentals, a white Jeep Cherokee that no longer was even remotely white as it was covered by multiple layers of Death Valley dirt and dust over the last few days.

"How far until the next RV, Sam?" Kyle yawned.

"Well, Helo 1 said that they got a heat signature reading about twenty miles up this road" replied Sam. "Consistent with two adults and two kids, so it could be Samir, his wife and his two kids."

"That's what you said the last time. And the last time before that."

"And that's what I'll continue to say. And one of these times, I'll be right, buddy," Sam smiled.

"You'll be 50 years old the next time you're right about something, Sam," Kyle said, smiling back. "Oh wait, you turn 49 this year, grandpa, right?" he teased, knowing that Sam had only just turned the big four-zero this year.

"Har-de-har-har, my ugly young friend," Sam teased back, as he recognized somewhat begrudgingly that girls found Kyle fairly attractive. "At least I'm aging well, kind of like fine wine. You've somehow managed to get a few girls to go out with you for now, but when you hit 30, man, you are going to be so ugly, you're gonna be totally screwed. The dateless wonder, we'll call you."

The friends continued their banter as they were rocketing down the road, traveling about 85 miles per hour. When they got near to where the RV was supposed to be parked, the pair slowed down their Jeep and peered around.

"Do you see anything?"

"Nope, it's just pitch black around here."

"Helo 1, we got nothing. Give us a hint – which direction?" Sam asked.

The radio crackled and hissed a bit, and they could hear the low whispers of the blades turning on the Black Hawk. "Seeker 2, you are really close. They are about 2.7 miles northwest to west of you. Do you see any service road or anything?"

"That's a negative," Sam replied. "The road's just going due west it seems. We'll drive a bit more up the road and see what we can see." They slowed down even more and squinted into the distance.

"Wait," Kyle exclaimed, "I see something ahead. It's not exactly a paved road, but there's a wide dirt road or trail here where it looks like a large number of vehicles have traveled before, because of the ruts."

"See it," Sam confirmed, turning the Jeep on to the dirt trail. "We are going off the main road, Helo 1." The Jeep bumped along the dirt and rocks, and they veered a little more northward past a few hills, which was why they probably weren't able to see the RV from the main road. All of a sudden they could see a RV parked alongside the dirt trail and Sam quickly and quietly braked about 100 yards behind the RV. "Helo 1, we have a visual and are going to check it out."

Kyle pulled out his sidearm and nodded to Sam as he exited the car. He slowly walked up the trail, proceeding quietly, listening for any sounds emanating from the RV. There really weren't any so far. Kyle checked out the license plate, which was a match to Samir's rental records from RVAmerica. Kyle walked up to the RV, where he could hear light snoring sounds coming from inside the vehicle now, with no indication that anyone was awake. The FBI agent quietly circled around the RV, double-checking to make sure that nothing was moving inside the RV.

After satisfying himself that everyone was asleep, Kyle walked back to the Jeep. "Well, Sam, it's the right car and everyone seems to be asleep. Let's call it in."

"Helo 1," Sam called, "we've got a match. RV occupants all seem to be asleep. Waiting for instructions."

"Excellent job, Seeker 2. Hold your position. It's 0206 hours PT now. We are re-routing units to your location and we'll look to rendezvous with instructions around 0300. Let us know if anything changes on the ground."

"Roger that Helo 1."

And so they waited as Seeker 1 and Seeker 4 drove like bats out of hell to get to the RV. Helo 1 and Helo 2 glided over to position as they radioed in to the Nellis command center. David and K2 gave each other the thumbs up sign when they had heard that the team had found Samir.

"How are we going to handle Samir?" Katherine asked David.

"We'll pay it by ear, but my gut says that Samir isn't in on the plan. Let's look at the facts:" David said, ticking them off with his fingers, "(1) he's a respected cardiologist, probably making around a half million a year, with at least half a dozen rental homes in Las Vegas – basically he loses the most by setting off a nuke in Las Vegas; (2) he's got what looks like a stable, good family life, a wife and a little boy and girl, and he's out RV camping with them, not exactly a typical terrorist activity; and (3) there's no indication that he's trying to hide his whereabouts. After all, he used his credit card to rent the RV and to buy gas, and he's been using this cell phone normally to call his mom. No, just doesn't feel like he's in on it. However, we have to play it like he is on it, just in case, of course."

"Radio in standard ops then for the intercept?" asked one of the command center techs.

"Yeah, the whole nine yards. Cell signal jammer so he can't call out and warn Hossein; even though where they are now, probably can't get any cell signal normally anyway. And everyone wears a bulletproof vest and helmet, etc."

"Got it chief. Where do we take them?"

"Right here at Nellis. If he is in on it, then he'll freak out that he is back near ground zero where the bomb is going off. Especially since his family will be with him."

"Let's put them in Building Six, in the two conference rooms," K2 said.

"Good idea, K2," David said, smiling at her. "We'll isolate Samir from his family, and then put some heavy-duty pressure on."

Imagine being in a deep slumber, and then woken up just before 3am by six FBI assault team members brandishing serious weaponry. Samir found out what that was like and he didn't like it one bit. Samir did think that he heard the agents screaming "FBI, FBI, keep your hands up," but at first, Samir still thought he was being kidnapped by some thugs. Truthfully, in his half-awake state, he couldn't really think straight enough to figure out what was going on. His wife, Parisa, was yelling "What's going on? Save the kids, Samir!" at the top of her lungs, and four year old Sahar was bawling loudly. Two year old Vahid probably thought that this was all just a bad dream. Vahid was thrashing around trying to get back to sleep.

Kyle got the plasticuffs on Samir and Parisa, and the agents turned on the lights in the RV. "Target secured," Kyle radioed to Helo 1.

"Roger that Seeker 2. Landing now."

"What the hell is going on?" Samir demanded. "Let my family go. Are you kidnapping me or something?"

"No sir," Kyle replied. "As we said, we are from the FBI. Can you please confirm that you are Samir Nuri of," he looked down at his paper, "512 Rampart Drive, Las Vegas, Nevada? We need to talk to you if you are Samir."

"I'm not telling you anything," Samir huffed. "I'm an American citizen with rights. Let me talk to my attorney. If you are really part of the FBI, let me see some ID as well."

"You're not under arrest sir," Sam replied. "And here's my ID," he said, flashing his badge to Samir and Parisa. "We urgently need to find the location of one Hossein Abbasi, your second cousin. Do you know where he is?"

Samir looked puzzled. "Why in the hell are you looking for Hossein?" he said. "Anyway, I'm not telling you guys anything until I talk to a lawyer."

Sam shrugged. "OK, I understand that you might be a little discombobulated as it is around 3am in the morning and we have just woken you guys up from a sound sleep. If you won't talk now, we're under instructions to take you back to Las Vegas. First, however, we need to double-check your identity." Sam looked around and saw Samir's wallet on the nightstand next to the bed. Walking over to it, he pulled out Samir's driver's license and saw that it showed a picture of Samir with the right Las Vegas address. He put the license back in the wallet and slid the wallet into Samir's back pocket. "Ma'am, do you have a purse or some essential stuff that you need to take with you for the kids? We are going on a short one hour or so helicopter ride."

Parisa had calmed down a little by now as she had seen all of the jackets on the team that clearly indicated that they were from the FBI, as well as seeing Sam's FBI badge. Clearly, these were not kidnappers at least, and her kids were not in immediate danger. Also, the fact that the FBI agent had said that Samir himself was not an arrest target helped calm her down as well. So she simply said wearily, "Let me think. My purse is over in the top drawer of that cabinet," she said, nodding over to the left, "and my diaper bag is on top of the counter."

Meanwhile, Helo 1 and Helo 2 had landed and the FBI team loaded the groups in the various helicopters, together with the gear. They had taken the plasticuffs off of Parisa at this time so that she could deal with Sahar and Vahid, but they carefully confiscated Samir and Parisa's cell phones for now, just in case.

Samir would go in Helo 1, together with Sam, Kyle and a few other agents, and the rest of Samir's family would leave in Helo 2. It was 0343 PT in the morning when they took off into the clear morning sky.

Nellis AFB was buzzing with activity even though it was not yet even 0500 PT in the morning. The lights were on throughout the facilities dotting the airbase, and you could often see people walking quickly between the buildings as they were completing various duties and being summoned to do others. David Smithline had taken a nap for an hour, just to recharge his batteries a bit, and K2 and a number of the team had done the same. The regional command center team was beat. The team was running on pure willpower alone.

As K2 had suggested, they had put Samir and his family in Building Six. In the beginning, the FBI team kept the family together in the largest conference room. Vahid had fortunately gone back to sleep, and the FBI had helped make a makeshift bed for the boy out of a medium-sized mobile electronics cart that was covered in blankets. Sahar was draped all over her mother, who was seated in one of the conference room chairs, and both looked ready to fall asleep again.

Only Samir did not look sleepy, his sleepiness outweighed by his anger. As the chief cardiologist at the UNLV Medical Center, Samir was more used to giving the orders rather than having to follow them. He stomped around the conference room, patting his sleeping son on the head and then doing the same to his daughter. He looked defiantly at Kyle, who was also seated in the room, together with two other agents. Sam entered the conference room after a few more minutes had passed, and motioned to Samir.

"OK, sir, the FBI SAIC, that's Special Agent In Charge, is going to need to speak with you now in another room. "Don't worry, your family will be here waiting for you. As I said, you are not under arrest. Rather, you are a just person of interest with respect to a certain situation that has developed."

"Can you tell me what this is about? You took my phone; can I have it back? Can I call my attorney?" asked Samir. Samir didn't have a criminal attorney, although he did have a lawyer that he used for family matters like his children's trusts and the like, and he figured that he could get a referral.

"You can discuss each of these issues with the SAIC," Sam replied. "Will you please follow me?" He motioned Samir to the door. At first, Samir thought about just saying no, that he wasn't going anywhere. But he then thought better of it and, resigned to the situation, Samir hugged his wife and followed Sam out of the room. They walked clear down to the other end of the building, and entered a slightly smaller conference room, where SAIC Smithline, Jack Smith, Jim Broussard, Mark Childress, and K2 were sitting. Two other FBI agents bearing conspicuous sidearms were also stationed just inside the door.

David had been reviewing a hastily put together file of Samir Nuri's background. David had to admit to himself that he admired Samir. Samir had worked hard, had adapted to America and clearly was an asset to his profession and his community. As a result, Samir was rightfully living the American dream. He looked like one of the good guys, for sure. David hated having to drag Samir and his family through this. But the stakes were too high. After talking with the others beforehand, David decided to play it straight-up and appeal to Samir's sense of patriotism and fair play.

"Hello, Dr. Nuri, please sit down," David started respectfully. "I am FBI Special Agent in Charge David Smithline, and this is Jack Smith, Katherine Kung, and Mark Childress, some of my governmental colleagues. Special Agent Chalkias you have already met. We regret inconveniencing you and your family ..."

"Inconveniencing?" Samir exploded. "You have got to be kidding me. You drag me and my family from a sound sleep and drag me to Las Vegas to a military base – where are we anyway? Is this Nellis Air Force Base or some secret FBI facility? Are we in Area 51 or something?"

"You're at Nellis," David replied calmly, trying to defuse Samir's anger a bit. Either Samir was a very good actor, or this was the response of an innocent man.

"Is this some kind of Middle Eastern profiling thing? Yes, yes, I am Iranian, in case you didn't know that already. Did you pick me up because you think I'm some kind of terrorist mastermind? What, I'm funding Al-Qaeda or something? And how the hell did you find me anyway? We were supposed to be at Bryce Canyon right now. What, are you like tracking me or something from my cell phone?"

"Actually, no, where you were in Death Valley has no cell signals. So we didn't find you that way," David said cryptically, without offering any other explanation. "Look, as Special Agent Chalkias mentioned, we are not really arresting you or anything. We are simply looking for Hossein Abbasi, who I believe is your second cousin."

"Yeah, Hossein is my second cousin. What do you think, that he's funding Al-Qaeda or something? Let me tell you a bit about Hossein: he loves coming to Vegas, but let's just say that normally he leaves here with a lot less money than he comes with. He's totally strapped for cash, and he's leaving it at the casinos, not with any terrorist group, believe me. Unless you're telling me the Bellagio is a front for Al-Qaeda," Samir laughed.

"No, we don't think he's funding Al-Qaeda either," David assured Samir.

"Well, then, why are you looking for him? Like I said, is this some kind of bullshit profiling thing? Just because he's Iranian, you're hassling him. He's not exactly Muslim, you know, or even religious at all for that matter -- not Muslim, not Christian, not anything. I can't ever remember him praying for anything, except maybe for hitting a slot machine jackpot. It just makes no sense to me. Maybe, and I mean maybe, if you were telling me that you were looking for his brother Amir, then it would make more sense, because at least Amir's more of a practicing Muslim."

"Huh, that's interesting that you mentioned his brother, Amir," David mused reflectively. "Do you happen to know where Amir is as well?"

"I don't believe this," Samir said in an exasperated voice. "Why are you trying to twist the words that I am saying? Are you really looking for Hossein, or are you really looking for Amir? Amir, by the way, I think is somewhere in Europe or Asia now. Sorry I can't be more specific," he added sarcastically.

"Dr. Nuri, all we are saying is that we understand from our sources that you are allowing Hossein to stay in one of your rentals. We simply would like to know which one."

"Sources, what sources? And why should I tell you? I'll repeat myself; what do you think Hossein did that's so illegal?" Samir asked.

David sighed. "Dr. Nuri, I consider myself a fairly good judge of people. Based on your record, you've done a lot for the people of Las Vegas, as a cardiologist," he looked down at Samir's profile sheet, "as a food bank donor and volunteer, and as a good father and family man, from what others have been telling me about you. So I trust you, and believe that you are a good American, who would not want innocent people hurt. Since you've been reluctant to talk to us about Hossein without understanding the situation, I am going to tell you the situation."

With this, David pulled out a number of pictures from a folder at his side. They had rehearsed together how they were going to play this. They didn't want to make Hossein and Amir look too bad at first; David needed to build up to this a bit. "We have on good intelligence that a small nuclear bomb," Samir's mouth dropped open in surprise as they had his full attention now, "this nuclear bomb," David displayed a picture of the RA-115, "has been smuggled into the United States. It was placed inside a Ford Econoline van, and was driven from Mexico to Las Vegas by this man." David now displayed the sketch artist's picture of the van driver from José Acevedo's description.

Samir's belligerence had disappeared. He sat down in the chair next to David and picked up the sketch, looking at it closely. Without any trace of sarcasm or anger in his voice now, Samir said, "Well, I guess that this kind of looks like Hossein. Just can't be, though. Hossein is the furthest thing from an extremist."

David said gently, "Hossein may not even know that there's a nuclear weapon involved. He was just the van driver as far as we can tell, transporting something that looks like a backpack. He could have just been told that they were smuggling in some documents for Iranian people who were fleeing the mullahs. Who knows? We just want to find him, and find him quick."

"Wait a second, none of this makes sense. Hossein may be a bit of a gambler, and he likes whiskey and women too, by the way, but that just makes him like most single guys in Las Vegas. How would he even know how to get in touch with nuclear terrorists in the first place? How would they find Hossein? He's the VP of Strategic Business Development in a LA food company, for god's sake."

David hesitated a bit. He looked at this team, who gave him back the look that it was up to David what to do now. Sighing to himself, David made a gut-level decision to tell Samir a bit more information. "Well, we think that Amir is involved too." David displayed the DIA's picture of Amir in Marseilles. "This was taken in Europe, and shows that Amir may have been involved in getting the nuclear bomb transported over to the US. Again, maybe Amir didn't know exactly what he was transporting. We certainly don't know all of the details, but our sources say that Amir came over with the bomb, and then loaded it into Hossein's van. Here's the picture that we have of the guy that came into the US with the bomb." David pushed forward D-65's picture of Amir now.

Now Samir was rendered speechless for a little while, as he processed all of this startling information. Samir picked up the picture of Amir, scrutinizing it even more carefully than he did Hossein's. "Now this really looks like Amir. I still don't believe, of course, that they're involved in any terrorist activity, particularly Hossein. I agree, however, that the evidence looks bad so far. There's got to be another explanation."

"So, Dr. Nuri, are you going to help us?"

Samir ran his fingers through his hair. "Of course, of course. I am a loyal American, no matter what you believe."

"We believe --" Sam started to protest, but Samir held up his hand.

"No, no, let me finish. Some of you," Samir said pointedly, looking at Sam, "look at me and think, hey, he's Iranian so he must be a terrorist killer. Well, I'm not a terrorist or a killer. And I'm proud to be an Iranian. An Iranian and an American. You know, actually, let me amend that. More important than this nationality stuff is that I believe in the sanctity of life. Especially as a doctor, I am just against any extremists that kill innocent people."

"Well said, sir," David remarked, nodding appreciatively. "Like I said, I believe that you are a good man."

"So here's the info you want: Hossein is staying at 1235 First Avenue, in Summerlin, which is basically half an hour northwest of the Las Vegas Strip. It's near the Summerlin Medical Center."

Mark Childress looked down at his notes. "This place owned by you?" he asked Samir, whispering to David, "it's not one of the homes we got our people surveilling now."

"No, it's not one of my rental properties," Samir noted. "I own ten rental homes in town," he explained to the group, "but for economies of scale, I also help manage another ten rental homes for some of my relatives. Indirectly manage is more accurate, I guess, as the day-to-day stuff is managed by a professional property manager that I hired, but I get a bigger discount with the additional 10 rental homes, since the property manager loves managing so many properties. Hossein is in my sister Reyhan's rental home; well, that's not totally accurate either. It's owned by a trust that was set up by my mother's family for Reyhan and my other sister Mina."

Mark wrote down the address, nodded to David and Jack and quickly dashed out of the room to call for a surveillance team. They would start surreptitiously watching the house now, using over three dozen agents in various shifts so as to avoid suspicion of having the same people hang around the area over a long period of time.

"I have to tell you that I still don't believe that Hossein is really involved in any of this," Samir continued. "Maybe, just maybe, I could believe that Amir would do something crazy, like giving money to someone to fight Israel. But I can't believe Amir would set off a nuclear bomb in the US. And Hossein? No way Hossein would have anything to do remotely related to terrorism at all."

"Like I said, Dr. Nuri, maybe he doesn't know what's going on really. You said that he is short on cash; maybe he's doing the pickup because they're paying him a bunch of money? That seems plausible."

"Possibly," Samir admitted. "Hossein does like to spend money and live the high life. His VP job pays well, but not nearly as much as he needs to maintain his lifestyle. He's got an amazingly nice Porsche, which I always found a little funny since I'm driving a Honda Odyssey and I've got to be a thousand times wealthier than he is. Hossein's also got timeshares in Tahoe and Aspen. He's always seems to be going out to eat at nice places. He also always seems to be hanging out with some extremely attractive women. Now it may sound like I'm jealous, but I'm really not, or at least I don't think I am. I just find it ironic that he's always asking me for money when he has all of these nice things. That said, I love him like a little brother. Maybe I'm living vicariously through him when he tells me about all of his adventures."

"So what's the deal with the free rentals?"

"It's simple; he's family. What else can I say? He used to always stay at the Wynn or the Bellagio when he came to Las Vegas on vacation, and he still stays at those hotels sometimes when he's in town on business. Sometimes he gets a free room as a comp benefit for how much he gambles I think. But for over the last, I don't know, four or five years, Hossein often has asked me whether I can put him up in an empty rental. He's stayed at one of the rentals that I manage maybe a grand total of ten or fifteen times, I guess. Something like that; I don't exactly charge him for the rental, so I don't have any lease agreements. I sometimes pick him up from the airport and lend him one of my cars too, although he mostly drives himself from LA. He told me that he didn't need a car this time, as he was driving from LA this time in his company car. It's a BMW X5 SUV."

"So this trip had been planned for a while."

"Oh yeah, for sure. We talked about this in, let's see, maybe February or something of this year? Hossein specifically wanted Reyhan's place this time. My own rentals are more, you know, like 1 to 2 year leases, so when I have let Hossein stay in one of my houses, it's usually when a long-term tenant has left and I need to fix up the place a bit before renting it out again. Reyhan's rental, on the other hand, is a short-term rental place, you know, like on the website VRBO, where you rent out a vacation home from the owner for a weekend, or by the week or so. That's because Reyhan often uses the rental for herself when she comes to Las Vegas for the winter to escape the snow in

Vancouver, or when she wants to go shopping with my wife at the Fashion Show Mall or Caesar's Forum Shoppes. So it kind of sucked for Reyhan to give the rental now to Hossein, because it's high season now and she could have rented it out for a lot of money."

"Despite this, she gave the rental to Hossein for free?"

"Yeah, Hossein kind of worked her a bit. You know, this can be my birthday and Christmas present, he said to Reyhan. So Reyhan relented and said fine, you can have it until January 4th. This was one of her best years already, I think, in terms of rental income, so she was probably feeling able to be generous. Mina wasn't even consulted, as she leaves all of the property management decisions to Reyhan."

"Why do you think that Hossein wanted Reyhan's place?"

"I'm not exactly sure. I remember that we were talking about it again in a party we had in LA over the summer. I had noted to Hossein that one of my tenants was moving out in mid-December so that he could use that home instead of Reyhan's. He had stayed in that location of mine before and liked it. Then again, he had stayed in Reyhan's place before too. Hossein insisted that he wanted to stay in Reyhan's place again this time. I think that Hossein joked that, because crime rates were going up so much, he felt safer in Reyhan's place. He said that he may bring some confidential company project documents to work on, and he liked the fact that Reyhan's place had a safe room. And ..."

David, Jack, Mark and K2 all started speaking at once, "Wait, wait, wait, hold a second, what did you say about a safe room?" they said all at once.

"Reyhan's place has a safe room," Samir started and then paused. "Oh come on," when he realized what the government agents were thinking, "you don't think that he's possibly storing a nuclear bomb there, do you?"

"Actually," Mark said, "I kind of do think that. Why does the home have a safe room anyway?"

Samir glared at Mark before he continued. "Reyhan is my 26 year old sister. She's single, has a boyfriend, but doesn't mind traveling alone to visit my wife and go shopping and the like, as I said. We always told her to just stay with us, but she often stays in her rental. My dad appreciated that she wanted to get into real estate, but was always a little worried about her traveling alone and staying by herself. So he made her buy a home that had a safe room in it. It's like a little "panic room" that you can access from the master bedroom closet. I always thought that it was a home used by the witness protection program or something, but I don't know, maybe it was just some paranoid survivalist who owned it before. Anyway, the room's locked up so that the tenants can't get into it, but a family member can go inside there to hide if he or she was being robbed. The room has a landline phone that you can use so you can call for help, and it's got food and water for a few days. Oh yeah, and it's got a little bathroom too. Reyhan mainly uses it to store some valuables, like jewelry and stuff that she doesn't want to bring back and forth from Vancouver. She keeps clothes in it too, so she doesn't have to lug around a lot of suitcases. This way, she can just bring a small carry-on along with her purse, and avoid checking in any big pieces of luggage."

"So how big is this panic room anyway?" K2 asked.

"Maybe around 12 feet by 10 feet, I guess, excluding the little bathroom. It's allegedly bulletproof. It's got some kind of metal shielding around the walls, and a door with a metal core, so bad guys can't get in too easily."

"How do you get in and out then?" K2 further inquired.

"There's a special key that you can use to open and lock it, or you can use the special keypad and punch in a 10 digit code. The door to the room is hidden behind a mirror in the closet, and the master bedroom closet has a separate regular wooden door that we lock when Reyhan's not there so that the tenants can't use that particular closet."

"Needless to say, we need to get the details of this safe room immediately," Jack remarked to the group. "Can you help us do that?"

"Sure, sure, no problem," Samir shrugged. "I think that I have the special safe room floor plan in my home office. There's also a little write-up about how the safe room works within the purchase documents. I'll have to look at my files."

Jack addressed the team, "This may make things a little tougher folks. We could lose precious seconds breaking into this room if it's really fortified well."

"I still think that you are crazy to think that Hossein's in on this. I can prove it to you if you let me. Hossein has a special cell phone that only a few members of the family and some really close friends know about," Samir explained. "It's registered to one of his sales staff, but Hossein uses it exclusively. He told us that he has it so that some former girlfriends can't track him down, and to avoid everyone ringing him all the time on his business cell phone with sales pitches."

Sam Chalkias, who had been quiet up to this time, exclaimed, "Well, I'm not sure we can let you talk to him; you might inadvertently clue him in that we're looking for him." He looked to the others for support.

David chimed in at this point, asking, "What are you proposing to ask him that makes you think that you can prove his innocence?"

"Look, if I can ask him about how his vacation is going, where he's been gambling and eating out, you'll see that all that he's there for is to have fun, not to set off a nuclear weapon. I can even ask him about what he's going to be up to for the next few days so that you can more easily track him and see that he's not a terrorist."

Mark spoke up: "We may not have the time to just let him run around and track him. What if he sets off the bomb today?"

"Now? Look, even if I believe you, it makes no sense to me. If he really wanted to set off a nuke, why wouldn't he have set it off on Christmas, as some kind of anti-Christian statement or something?" Samir replied, looking quizzically at the others. "Not that I think that he's involved anyway, but wasn't Christmas his big chance? And he's not going to do it today for sure. Let me tell you why. One of the big things that Hossein wanted to do this vacation is to play in the big MGM slot tournament championship tonight. He's been talking about it a lot. It's some special promotion, where you pay something like $2,500 to be in it. Some lucky person is guaranteed to walk away with at least $1,000,000. Does that sound like a guy who is going to set off a bomb today?"

"What about New Year's Eve then?" Mark continued.

"Well, what about December 30th, January 1st, or January 2nd, or March 20th for that matter?" Samir replied, sounding a little exasperated. "My god, I can't give you an answer for every date on the calendar."

David ran his fingers through his hair. "All right, here's what we are going to do. We're going to get a team in place and monitor things for a few hours. At the same time, we're going to prepare a script for your potential call with Hossein."

After he left Samir, Mark Childress coordinated with his ground troop team leaders, Paul A and Artie M. Together with Jim Broussard, they reviewed the present situation on the ground. 1235 First Avenue was in a subdivision of about 100 homes. The house was a relatively standard Spanish-style looking two-story tract home, with a three-car garage, and a desert-styled landscaped front yard, meaning that there were a few trees and plants embedded in a "lawn" that consisted of pebbles and a few strategically placed larger rocks.

The team needed to figure out how they were going to stage any assault without drawing attention to their presence. This was not going to be easy since there were lots of neighborhood families with children living around the rental house. Fortunately, one of the neighbors two doors down from the 1235 house was selling her home, and appeared to have already moved out of the area. Later in the morning, they were going to call the real estate agent and get access to the house. Other, finer elements of the assault plan were discussed and reviewed.

CHAPTER 8

When the sun came out early in the morning of December 27th, it weakly peeked out of a passing set of clouds. The sun was further obscured by the morning fog; it was an appropriately somber and hazy start to the day. Just like the minds of the Safety Screen team, the day was unsettled. Maybe the day would turn out to be clear and bright, maybe the opposite. The path forward was murky and difficult to see. But the team would just plow forward to the best of their ability.

By 9:30am, the FBI had gotten hold of the real estate agent selling the neighboring home, and had secured the keys to that house. The FBI agents were very careful not to tell the real estate agent what was really going on. Instead, the FBI agents had posed as gas company representatives, and had come up with a story about a potential gas leak that required them to have access to the inside of the empty house. The owner of the home was in Europe anyway and gave his approval by email, after being informed by the real estate agent regarding the request. The FBI team stressed to the agent that there wasn't any imminent danger or anything, but that some municipal workers would need to work around the empty house for at least the next few days. So this would allow a bunch of agents to get close to 1235 First Avenue without arousing suspicion.

NEST positioned a "Hot Spot Mobile" vehicle diagonally across the street from the house. This time the vehicle was disguised as a telephone company repair truck. This vehicle now had improved, very sophisticated infrared sensors, together with the most current versions of NEST's radiation detection equipment. From the infrared data, the NEST technicians inside the van had quickly ascertained that there were six people inside the home. Two of them appeared to be guards, based on the way they were stationed. It looked like they carried machine guns and had pistols. The other four were Amir, Hossein and the other two people that José Acevedas had identified to the DIA. One of the six seemed to always be present in the master bedroom area where the RA-115 was stored inside the safe room.

More importantly, this group of six people mostly stayed inside with the shades drawn. Understandably, they didn't want to draw attention to themselves. The Iranians would only venture out in limited circumstances. A little after 11:30am, the garage opened and a red BMW X5 came out, driven out of the driveway by Hossein, who was clearly by himself in the car. An unmarked FBI sedan quickly followed the BMW as it exited the neighborhood and entered one of the main Summerlin roads.

The radiation detection equipment in the van showed some trace elements of a radiation signature emanating from the home when the equipment was cranked up to its maximum limit. It was very, very faint, but the radioactivity signature from those traces was there. Ironically, the signal seemed consistent with materials from the ADE-2 reactor in Zheleznogorsk, just like the situation in the Snow Falcon simulation.

Ben had a few of the NEST technicians scrambling to figure out why their airborne detection equipment hadn't been able to find this signal previously from their air sweeps. Part of the issue was the limit of detection problem, but it also turned out that the Las Vegas air sweeps had generated what they thought were about twelve false positives. Two of those false positives were in fact from Summerlin. After a cursory review of the data, the junior technicians responsible for the screening had made the erroneous conclusion that the radiation must have come from the nuclear medicine unit at Summerlin Hospital, since the hospital was relatively nearby. The technicians were pre-disposed to believe that there was nothing there. So it looked like the situation was that a few false positives were really true positives, but the NEST team couldn't figure that out based on the data. *Wow*, thought Ben, *the organization clearly has to be better trained on this, particularly the first-line technicians initially reviewing the results.*

The equipment had placed the location of the RA-115 roughly in the location of the "safe room" that Samir had discussed. Samir had drawn a rough sketch of the layout of the home; it was a four bedroom home, with the master bedroom on the first floor. The safe room was located behind the master bedroom closet, but strategically placed near the middle of the home, not reachable from any outside walls of the house. Access would be difficult, stealth access even more so.

While Samir was helping out the Operation Safety Screen team, Hossein had stopped off at a local Iranian restaurant. There Hossein picked up his take-out orders of chelo (rice) with kebabs, cucumber salads, yogurt with mint, and other typical Iranian lunch fare. The surveillance team was able to intercept a cell phone call that Hossein had placed while waiting for his order.

"Hi Erika," Hossein said. "Miss me? I'm so excited for the slot tournament tonight! We are going to win big and then I will treat you to a mega-vacation in Europe!"

"Really? That would be wonderful! I always wanted to go to France, Hossein," Erika replied enthusiastically. "I hear Paris is so amazing!"

"It is; it is! And then tomorrow, you're coming over still from 3 to 6pm or so, right? To the 1235 First Avenue house, right? The one you went to before, last year. Good, you remember. And your friend Candy's coming too, right? The other guys in the home will be gone to pray and celebrate at the mosque because it's Mawlid then, so it'll just be Hamid and me at home."

"Yeah, yeah. It'll be me and Candy. She really likes your friend Hamid from the last time we partied together."

"We are going to have an awesome time tonight! And an awesome time tomorrow too! It's going to be fabulous. See you soon! Wait, I forgot, did your shift change again for today? When are we meeting tonight?"

"Well, Joanne is sick again, so I have to cover for her until seven thirty. So I'll just see you during the slot tournament, maybe around seven forty-five. Luckily it's so close. Don't worry; I'll find you. Bye for now." The line clicked off. The FBI communications team looked at the intercept log – Erika was Erika Garfield from her cell phone information. After about ten more minutes, Erika's profile came up from the databases. Erika was a bartender at the MGM Grand. After the FBI made a quick call, they found out that there were eleven Candys and Candaces on the MGM payroll, so the FBI agents weren't sure who she was yet. Maybe another MGM bartender, maybe a blackjack dealer, maybe part of housekeeping, or maybe someone who didn't even work at MGM. They would need to find out all of this soon.

There were now many hundreds of FBI agents in the Las Vegas area who had been pulled from Los Angeles and the other locations. This allowed the original Las Vegas team to get a little more rest as they could be relieved by the extra staff available. In order not to tip off the terrorists, National Guard units were still conducting searches as before in Los Angeles and other cities, to make it look like nothing had changed in terms of the focus area.

The great bulk of the Safety Screen operational activities, however, were now of course centered in Las Vegas, although most of those activities were not visible to the public eye. Newscasters still complained vociferously about the inconvenience of these roadblocks and other related activities. One channel in Los Angeles even had the audacity to broadcast a news segment called "Your Tax Dollars at Waste" in regard to this work. *If only they knew what was really going on*, David thought to himself; *then we wouldn't have these ridiculously pathetic PR issues to contend with.* In any event, the negative media actually gave them more cover to accomplish their real objective.

Jack Smith of the DIA had been designated as the point person to work with Samir regarding the potential telephone call with Hossein. From an intelligence standpoint, the JCTF needed to know some key pieces of information. First, did Hossein know anything about the presence of the RA-115 nuke? Second, assuming that Hossein knew about the bomb, did he know when it was going off? Third, while they were pretty sure that the nuke was in a crate within the safe room, would Hossein be able to confirm this intel? Fourth, who were the people with Hossein in the home? Fifth, how would Amir and Hossein transport the RA-115 to its intended detonation location, and where was that location?

The problem was that they couldn't ask Hossein directly about any of this. So Jack had worked with Samir and some other Safety Screen team members all morning to figure out how to indirectly get this from Hossein. Jack unfortunately was not fully aligned with David as to whether Samir could truly be trusted not to inadvertently tip off Hossein that the FBI was after him. However, it wasn't Jack's decision to make. David had gotten Brown and Edelman to support David's point of view, subject to HSA Jorgensen's final approval.

"So let's go over it again. You're going to pretend to call from where?" Jack asked Samir for what seemed like the tenth time.

"Death Valley. You'll insert some static on the line. I'll tell him about how our plans have changed, and that I may be coming back tomorrow to see how he reacts. I'll see if he is available for lunch or dinner tomorrow or the next day, or even the day after that."

"OK, good. And of course, we'll be on the line listening, with the ability to cut you off immediately if anything goes weird."

"Yes, of course," Samir said tiredly. "I get it; you don't trust me completely still, even though I let you know where Hossein is staying. I didn't have to do that, you know."

"No," admitted Jack, "and believe me, we appreciate that. Frankly, I'm beginning not to be so worried about your purposefully warning Hossein about us. As you said, you gave us his location pretty readily, and you have given us all of the details about the safe room that we need. No, now I am just worried that the tone of your voice, or the specific words that you use, are inadvertently going to make Hossein suspicious. You might give yourself away by accident. Do you normally call him on this special line?"

"Sometimes," Samir replied. "Let's put it this way; I call him on this line often enough where it won't be super-suspicious or anything."

"On your calls, do you speak in English or Farsi mostly?"

"We speak completely in English. Hossein has worked hard on getting Americanized, which again is why I think that you guys are wacko if you think he's in on this," Samir said. Jack grimaced at this inwardly; they hadn't told Samir that the super-sensitive equipment detectors in the "Hot Spot Mobile" van had pretty much confirmed that a RA-115 nuclear backpack was in the house.

It was just after noon now on December 27th. The normal evening Safety Screen briefing would be supplemented by another call, with a more limited audience, at 1300 hours in light of the new situation. In that earlier meeting, David had strenuously argued for allowing Samir to call Hossein, and after the pros and cons were discussed at length with Jorgensen, Edelman, Brown, Jack Smith, K2, Jim and some other senior leaders, David had convinced the entire group that their best bet was to go forward with the call. It might help the Safety Screen team figure out where they stood and give them actionable information. The HSA then noted that he would inform the President and Vice-President about what they were planning to do, but that the call to Hossein was greenlighted.

This approval was relayed to the rest of the applicable team members, and the call occurred at 1345 hours, just as Samir was getting to the gas station for a fill-up.

"Hi Hossein," Samir said through some static. "Sorry for the bad reception. I am in the middle of the desert here. My battery's low too, so I may lose you pretty soon one way or the other. Just wanted to talk to you, cousin."

"Hey Samir," Hossein said excitedly, "always great to talk to you. I'm in your lovely hometown of Vegas. How's Bryce and Zion? You know I've been to Vegas about 30 times and never made it out to Bryce or Zion ever before."

"We never made it either. We're not at Bryce or Zion. There's really bad weather in Utah. Believe it or not, there's snow on the ground in both places. So Parisa made some calls and we're in Death Valley now."

"Death Valley? Wow, you're in California instead of Utah? Cool, I hear that it's really pretty in Death Valley in the winter since it's not so hot. You know what? I've actually never been to Death Valley either. You know me; I head straight to the casinos when I'm driving from LA. How're the kids liking Death Valley? You must show me some pictures of Vahid and Sahar playing in the middle of the desert. You're still coming back on January 3rd, right?"

"Nope. We couldn't get reservations here in Death Valley for that long since it was so last minute. We're thinking of coming back home tomorrow. Either that or going to Disneyland."

Hossein's voice became noticeably more agitated. "Hey Samir, you work too hard, you know, to miss out on your vacation. You must promise me that you will go to Disneyland for the whole week, my cousin. Don't change your return date." Jack frantically waved his arms around to get Samir's attention and pointed to a question on the piece of paper where they had rehearsed contingent questions.

Samir looked down at the paper and gave Jack the "I got this; I got this" look. Samir continued with the conversation: "Hey, what's your problem, cousin? You know how Parisa and I think that Disneyland is ridiculously overpriced at this time of year. We called and they told us it's going to cost like $600 a night for a room; we never pay that kind of money unless I'm getting reimbursed for it."

"Well, I'll pay for it. No worries; it'll be on me. Your whole Disneyland vacation."

Jack could now tell that Samir was now getting agitated himself. He gave Samir the "calm down now" look. Samir spit out his next words to Hossein: "Oooh, big spender. Weren't you the one just asking me for money a few months ago? Since when have you offered me free money before?"

Luckily, Hossein mistook Samir's anger as sarcasm about Hossein's historical habits as a freeloader. "Come on, I'm serious, Samir. You know I had a bad run of luck at the slots and the tables back then. Well, I'm happy to report that one of my business deals, the biggest one, came through and I'm going to get an extra $300,000 in bonus money from GCF this year. It wipes out most of my debt and gives me a little play money. And you're my favorite cousin, man. I love you like a brother," Hossein continued emotionally. "Look, I know how much I owe you, brother. You've really helped me out, over the past few years especially. So let me treat you. I insist that you go to Disneyland. You just can't come back to Vegas early."

"A brother, huh?" Samir replied sarcastically. Jack glared at Samir. Samir got the message. He sullenly turned back to the phone and continued the conversation in a less sarcastic tone. "Hey, nice of you to offer, man. Thanks, I accept. Parisa and the kids will appreciate it. I appreciate it." Jack waved his arms around some more and pointed to a different part of the paper. "But, um, Parisa, uh, still wants to come home a little early to get Sahar ready for pre-school. So we'll probably come back the night of January first."

"Evening of New Year's Day? That's OK, man. Just ring in the New Year in LA, dear brother. Like I said, you deserve the rest."

More pointing by Jack to the paper. Samir went on, "So can you do dinner with us on that night?"

"Uh, I'm actually heading back to Los Angeles before then. Looks like I will have missed you this time around. We'll get together in LA or next time I'm in Vegas."

Samir plowed on with the questions. "Hey, this $300,000 in bonus money. You always complain to me that Yousef and Amir are such tightwads on bonuses. How do you know you're going to get it?"

"No, no, Samir. I know I always complain about GCF and the way the family runs it. But this time it's good. Amir's actually in the US now, and has already given me half of the bonus money up front."

"Lucky man. Maybe your luck is changing," Samir said, a little bitterly, Hossein thought. "How's Reyhan's house?"

"Oh, the place is just like I remembered it. Thanks for offering me your place, but, you know the bonus? I'm storing the paperwork for the big deal related to the bonus in the safe room, so that way I know I don't have to worry about someone stealing it. It gives me piece of mind that I'll get the second half of the bonus."

"Yeah, Hossein, I get it." Samir's mind was spinning now, a little out of control. Jack could see it in Samir's face. "You know what Hossein, ...," Samir started, and Jack quickly hit the "end call" button on the phone. Hossein looked at his phone. Jack was already texting Hossein the message "sorry bad signal - battery almost out too. talk later" on Samir's phone. Hossein just shrugged and continued filling up his gas tank. *Crisis averted*, Hossein thought, *thank Allah that Samir's family is not coming home early.*

"That bastard!!!" Samir exploded. "He was going to ruin me, basically blow up all that I worked for over the past fifteen years. My practice, my rental properties, all would be worth nothing after a nuke explodes in Las Vegas. That whole freaking Abbasi family is nuts! Curse those people! The Nuri family is done with the lot of them! I'm going to tear Hossein's heart and lungs out and feed them to him!" Samir stopped, buried his head in his hands, visibly shaken by what had just transpired.

Jack empathized with Samir. He motioned over to one of his colleagues, who would gently escort Samir back to his wife and kids after he got it back together a little bit. Jack quickly ran down the hall to the main Operation Safety Screen tactical ops room. They would have to decide what to do with this newfound information.

With all of this new intelligence from the intercepted call by Hossein to Erika, and from Samir's call to Hossein, Ben and Sri argued vociferously now for Switchblade, the potential Plan B. The nuke wouldn't be set off until New Year's Eve. Before that, on December 28th when only two of the eight terrorists would be in the house, they could sneak in undetected and switch out the nuke while the two men were distracted by the two women. Even Jim Broussard was warming up to the idea of using Plan B over Plan A now. In particular, Plan B avoided the logistical problems with placement of the Humvees around the neighborhood. Artie M and Paul also thought that Plan B was feasible but, worst come to worst, were still preparing for the full frontal assault, if Plan B got derailed. There was a growing feeling that Switchblade was viable. The FBI tactical ops team worked out some ideas and passed it along to David and K2, who were persuaded. An option that had seemed only 1% likely a few hours before now became their number one option.

At the regular 1830 PT briefing that evening, the President and Vice President both participated in the meeting as they were told that there was a major decision to be made. The Safety Screen team knew that, ultimately, no matter what Plan A or Plan B they had thought about, the President or Vice President would need to approve the final plan.

"What do we have, Pat?" President Besselman demanded immediately.

"Sir, we believe that we have solid information that the terrorists have a nuclear bomb in a rental home in northwest Las Vegas. We know the address of the home and we have a strike force nearby. The solid information includes specific technical confirmation that the bomb is there by one of our high-quality radiation detection machines."

"Yes!" the President and Vice President exulted. "So we're going to storm the place in an hour and take it out, I assume" the President continued. "I will gladly greenlight any assault plan that you, Bill, Ron and Marcia are aligned on. This is GREAT news. Thank you all. We did it; you did it." The President sounded relieved.

"Uh, Mr. President, it's not that simple," the HSA said delicately. "It appears that the nuke is in some kind of a safe room, like a 'panic room' kind of structure within the rental home."

"Well, take the freaking nuke out of the safe room. We're the United States of America, goddamn it, the most technologically advanced country in the history of mankind! We've got the firepower, right Ron, right Bill? Just let me know what you need and I'll approve it immediately. Let's go!"

FBI Director Ron Edelman cleared his throat. "Yes sir, we have a detailed assault plan. When we run the scenarios, if we go in now, this afternoon, or tonight, we think that we have about a 70-80% chance of success, sir. However, if we wait until tomorrow, sir, we think that we will have a 95-98% chance of success. SAIC Smithline will explain the details."

David took the cue in stride and explained the situation quickly. "Mr. President, Dr. Samir Nuri, who as you recall from the previous briefing is Hossein Abbasi's second cousin, has been instrumental in helping us find the terrorists. Today, he has also been instrumental in helping us learn that the terrorists are going to set off the RA-115 nuke on New Year's Eve, probably somewhere near the Strip for maximum effect. There will probably be around 300,000 to 500,000 people on the Strip at that time, counting the workers and other staff inside the casinos and the like."

"My God! What a catastrophe that would be!" the President said emphatically. "But who cares about what's happening on New Year's Eve? It's only December 27th now. New Year's Eve is four days away. Let's take out the nuke immediately. What if they change their plans and set it off today?"

"I'm not suggesting that we cut it that close, Mr. President. But we think "go time" should be tomorrow, something a little less than 24 hours from now, for a few reasons. The first reason is this: our primary "A team" is exhausted. They are running on empty. We think that banking some sleep would significantly increase their performance level. Not that we won't have a full secondary "A team" on full alert until then and ready to storm the house if necessary, just in case."

"We finally know where the nuke is, and you want me to wait a day. You've got to be kidding me! Let me hear your other reasons. Pat, Bill, Ron and Marcia, you really OK with this?"

Pat, Bill, Ron and Marcia nodded their assent, and signaled David to continue. "The second reason is this:" David continued. "We intercepted one of Hossein's calls. Tomorrow is Mawlid, the Prophet Mohammad's birthday on the Iranian calendar, and four of the six terrorists appear to be going out of the home to a local mosque to celebrate the holiday in the late afternoon. That means that only two terrorists will be left to guard the nuke. Much easier to take out the nuke in that situation."

"Hmm," the President mused, "go on. That's pretty compelling."

"Third, we think that we can find out information about the whole network of terrorists if we switch out the nuke for a fake one. So the plan is not a full-out assault, but a stealth ops called, appropriately enough, Plan Switchblade." After David initially related the plan, both the President and Vice President gave David a "you gotta be kidding me look" so David held up his hands as he continued, "I know, I know, kind of 'Mission Impossible' like, but this is not a movie. Just hear me out. The NEST guys have ginned up some fake RA-115 nukes. They are made from real but deactivated RA-115s that we have in storage. NEST had previously prepared these fakes in case something like a Plan Switchblade was possible; we think this is one of those situations. We keep the 'full assault plan' as an immediately available backup option in any case, so I'm not suggesting that we are not preparing for an assault. The JCTF group, however, now thinks that, since there's only two terrorists to deal with, we can potentially create some diversion and insert a fake nuke in the safe room. We don't have the plan fully baked yet, since there are a lot of variables involved. But again, we are asking for you to approve Switchblade if we feel that it is possible. If the game-time decision is that we don't think we can make it work, then we do a full-scale assault. Should Switchblade work, after we switch the nuke out then, because there's no danger, we just wait around for the terrorists to try to explode a non-working RA-115. When the nuke doesn't work on New Year's Eve, or whenever they plan to use it, the terrorists are going to be really pissed. They're going to call or email their colleagues back in the Middle East and then we're going to find out who the hell sold them the real RA-115, because those colleagues are going to go after them with guns blazing for selling them a dud bomb. Worst come to worst, we just have a bunch of bad guys trying to kill other bad guys. Best case, we can fully trace the way these terrorists got a nuke to prevent it from happening again in the future."

"Not bad," the President admitted, "but what aren't you telling me? What's the risk of this plan compared to say going in now?"

"Sir, the main risks we think are these: first, as you said yourself, they move to set off the bomb now or tonight and we have only our secondary 'A team' rather than our primary 'A team' ready to take it out. Second, there is a risk that our intel is wrong, or the yet-to-be-fully planned diversion doesn't work. In that situation, it's possible that we lose, say, 10 or 20 seconds in trying to deactivate the nuke compared to a full frontal assault. Katherine Kung and the NEST folks tell me that, if the terrorists can arm the nuke, that we probably only have three minutes to blast it. I sincerely doubt it, but it is possible that ten or twenty seconds may make a material difference if we really screw up Switchblade."

"Anyone at all on the team have any qualms about Switchblade?" the President demanded. "Tell me now. Pat, Bill, Ron, Marcia, Katherine, you are all 100% aligned with this plan, right? And don't give me any bullshit about how this is the best plan we can find so far with our time constraints, and that it's a Presidential decision. No copouts. If any of you have one iota of doubt, or there's some fact or assumption about this Switchblade plan that's bothering you, you tell me straight up right now. Louis, you got any thoughts here?"

Vice President Branden sighed, "Mr. President, we are going to get crucified in the history books if we wait and the nuclear bomb goes off today. Let's just go now. 70%, 80%, 95%, who know what the hell the right numbers are? Those are just estimates. We know the location of the nuke now; let's do it now. The Switchblade diversion isn't even fully planned out."

"I thought you'd say that, Louis. You're such a politico. I love you, but you've been in politics all of your life. I was fortunate enough to be a general in the United States Army, and I dare say that I have learned that it is sometimes best not to rush into battle. And certainly not to rush in for fear of any history book second-guessing." Vice President Branden was a little miffed at being called out like this, but he bit his tongue and didn't say anything. "Let's break up the decision into parts," the President continued. "The first decision is go today, or go tomorrow. While I was originally assuming, like Louis, 'why the hell would we wait a day?,' the team has put forth some compelling reasons why we should wait. So, as I've said before, unless someone has another assumption or fact that someone's holding back on," Pat, Bill, Ron, Marcia, Katherine, David and the rest of the participants on the call emphatically shook their heads no, "then I agree with the team that we go tomorrow. The second decision, which quite frankly is a little harder for me, is whether to go full out assault, or go try a switch and, if that fails, then go full out assault. That seems like a tactical decision to me. David, when I was a two-star major general, I remember your briefing me after one of your successful operations. I was impressed by your character, your intelligence, and more importantly, your preparedness. You exuded trust then, so I trust you now. You earned it. I think a lot of the job of the President is figuring out the right people to trust, and then just getting the hell out of the way. I'm not going to micromanage your team. So your team's switchout plan - Plan Switchblade - is approved if you think that you can do it. You go get it done, son, either way. Safety Screen team, thank you for all of the hard work, but the hardest part's yet to come."

"Thank you Mr. President. We will get it done," David nodded.

Ron, Marcia and Pat joined in, "Mr. President, we will not let you or the American people down." The President and Vice President signed off the videoconference call, and the Safety Screen team had their answer. Plan Switchblade was on. Now they just needed to figure out the minor detail of how to best accomplish the switch, if possible. The full-out assault was still the contingency, but David was confident that the team could make the switch successfully.

CHAPTER 9

The first thing they had to do was to figure out how to plan for the diversion. Everyone agreed it would be pretty hard for an operative to sneak into the safe room without being detected. Hossein and/or Hamid would probably be in or near the master bedroom, especially since they were entertaining the ladies and getting back to the master bedroom was probably a goal of theirs. Breaking into the safe room from outside the home was out of the question. It would be too noisy, and the point was to do the switch without leaving any signs that they had done so. Samir had given the Safety Screen team the keys to the back door, and two copies of the special key to the safe room, together with the ten digit code as well. An operative could get in stealthily if there was a diversion.

The team had quickly come to the realization that Switchblade would only work if Hossein and Hamid were somehow incapacitated. Maybe the two would be passed out after drinking; maybe they could be drugged. Drugging Hossein and Hamid carefully seemed to be the best approach. The follow-up question was whether the team had to enlist the help of Erika and/or Candy to help accomplish this.

Rick Columbia and Jim Broussard certainly assumed that insider assistance was necessary for Switchblade to work. It would be too hard to coordinate the diversion without Erika and/or Candy's help. And they thought that getting that insider help was not likely. As a result, Rick and Jim were now far less enthusiastic about Switchblade compared to before; they started concentrating on planning the full-out assault plan contingency.

Jack Smith, perhaps because he was more used to stealth ops, was a little more sanguine about the possibility of

Switchblade working. He agreed with Rick and Jim, though, that they would need Erika and/or Candy's help on this to make the plan work successfully. David and Jack had profiled Erika some more, and it turned out that one of Erika's high school friends was Leticia Gonzales, who happened to work in Las Vegas as a FBI forensic accountant. She was somewhat involved in Safety Screen. She had helped figure out what real estate Samir had owned, but she was not part of the main Safety Screen team. Leticia was not even fully "under the tent," i.e., in the know that a nuclear bomb was potentially in Las Vegas. Leticia was only told that Samir was a person of interest in a general domestic terrorist case. They would actually have to disclose to her some elements of what they knew in order to have her convince Erika to help them.

"So let me get this straight, Jack," David said, "your idea is to bring Erika in tonight after the slot tournament, use Leticia to establish trust, and then tell her about Hossein and Hamid and see if she will help us out. Why not now?"

"Well, Erika's got two meetings with Hossein, one tonight and one tomorrow afternoon. We have no idea whether she's game to help us or not. We don't need to tip Hossein off early because we are still going to need part of tonight to fully develop our assault plan with the primary 'A team' folks."

"Candy's a wild card; we are still not 100% sure who she is. So my call is to leave her out of this."

"I'm with you on that one, David. Too many variables. If Erika will work with us, we keep Candy in the dark. We can drug her too. We've got a great drug that I'm sure you know about – the field calls it Ro – as in Rohypnol, but it has a much better safety and efficacy profile. Ro has a much shorter duration than Rohypnol, so that's why it's called Ro - get the joke? Ro can be put in the food and drink that Erika would supply to the party. We can rig up some cameras to, so that we can know the lay of the land in the home better for our stealth operatives to go in."

"Wow, I'm a little uncomfortable drugging people here if we don't have to," David replied. "However, the Presidential executive order we have does spell out expressly that we are authorized to do just about anything we need to in the name of stopping a nuclear bomb."

"Your call. I'm obviously way less squeamish about these kinds of things than you are. We can always just go full out assault, but we'll just be taking other kinds of risks in my view."

"Yeah, I know that for sure. I'll get over my qualms; I've heard about Ro, and it is safe and effective according to our FBI medical personnel. How much time are you estimating to switch the nuke?"

David looked at K2 for this answer. "Well, that depends," K2 said, acknowledging some uncertainty here. "Here's what we got so far. Assuming that Erika can drug the whole party, including herself, somewhere between 1510 and 1515 hours, then the drug will take something like thirty to forty-five minutes to kick in. We'll have from around 1600 hours to say 1700 hours, to be safe, to do the switch. Ben and Sri are on point as the technical experts, so they'll be going in with the stealth team. It could take five minutes to do the switch, or maybe the whole hour."

Sri provided more detail. "Mostly the time will depend on whether we already have a pretty exact match for the real RA-115 or not, and whether we have to do any major touch-ups to the fake. Replicating the lock is pretty easy; we've got a machine that can do this fast. Ben and I have currently ginned up a dozen fakes in various states of wear. We'll pick the closest one, and then improvise from there. The rest of the time will be taken up by trying to look at the scene and, if necessary, replace or modify any ancillary device, like a Geiger counter or the like, that could give away that there's a fake."

"There are a few other technical things that we'll need to make sure about," Ben added, "including permanently disabling the real nuke, but that's the gist of it. We would like you to calibrate the dose of the drug so that they wake up around 1715 or 1730 hours, giving us an extra fifteen to thirty minute cushion for us, and also for them to clean up and have Erika and Candy leave before the other six terrorists are scheduled to return."

Switchblade would all depend on Erika, although Erika didn't even know it yet. Erika Garfield was a happy-go-lucky twenty-five year old bartender, originally from Missoula, Montana, who in her four years in Vegas had already seen it all, but had not grown cynical or anything. She had just let it all wash over her. Her patrons loved that about her personality, that free spirit. Erika was as popular with her hometown regulars as the tourists. Hossein had met Erika about a year and a half ago during a business conference, was instantly smitten, and had taken her out on a number of dinner dates and business parties, especially during the conferences sponsored by the food associations that GCF belonged to.

While not technically his "girlfriend," Hossein played the field too much for that, Erika was one of Hossein's favorite friends to hang around with. Erika, in turn, loved how nicely that Hossein treated her. Hossein was always the gentlemen, unlike some previous guys that Erika had dated. *And quite frankly*, she thought to herself, *the sex was pretty good too.* Hossein had even fulfilled one of Erika's childhood dreams of going to Disneyland and enjoying a "princess" experience. Erika had even met Samir briefly a few months ago; they had done breakfast together one time when Hossein was just finishing up a long set of business meetings over the previous few days. That Hossein was willing to introduce her to his extended family made Erika feel special. When Erika was in a pensive mood, she often thought that this was an indication that maybe, just maybe, their relationship could get to the next level.

The only thing that Erika didn't like about Hossein was that he could be overly fixated on money. But that was like a lot of guys, and so Erika just chalked it up to the Y chromosome. As far as Erika could see, Hossein was too rich already to be so focused on money. Erika always told Hossein to just relax and enjoy life more.

There hadn't been much business in the bar as it was a weekday afternoon. But Erika had promised to cover for Joanne, who was out sick with either the flu or a bad cold. A few tourists had stopped by here and there, but the real drinking of course wouldn't start until much later that night.

She had whiled away her afternoon shift, sometimes even trading a few texts with Hossein. Hossein was in a really good mood these past few days. Most of his texts were about how excited he was to be seeing her tonight and tomorrow. His other texts related to the slot tournament that Hossein had a premonition that he was going to win.

Erika was under no such delusions. As a Vegas resident, she had seen too often guys who thought they were on an unstoppable roll. Guys that thought that they were due to win because they had just gotten some impossibly bad beat in poker. Guys that thought they had invented some system that couldn't lose. You name it, Erika had heard it before, and the only constant was that these guys never won. And even the one guy that Erika knew that had hit a big jackpot, a little over $500,000, somehow, incomprehensibly to Erika, had ended up in debt over $50,000 by the end of that same month. If you could believe that. It made no sense, but there it was: even the winners were losers.

At 7:42pm, Erika quickly took off to the slot tournament location, texting Hossein that she was on the way. Hossein quickly texted back that she should take her time and that they should meet at the MGM buffet line instead: Hossein had already lost; he was out of the tournament.

"What happened, Hossein?" Erika said, after giving Hossein a little hug and kiss when they found each other in the buffet line.

"Oh, it was bad from the get-go, Erika," Hossein lamented. "I didn't even hit a winner on any of my first twenty spins. All my wins after that were small ones too, so it just kind of deteriorated from there. What really pissed me off was that the grandma sitting next to me couldn't lose. And I was thinking of taking that machine, but she beat me to it when I was thinking about it."

"Oh, it's OK, Hossein, you have to let some other people win sometimes," she said playfully. "Didn't you tell me you just got some big work bonus? So what if you didn't win big tonight; let's celebrate some."

"Hey, I gotta be back home by midnight or my brother will be pissed at me," Hossein replied. "So what do you say we blow this joint and get some takeout?"

"You're on," Erika smiled back at him. "Let's go back to my place." And so they did, secretly followed by about a dozen FBI agents. Erika's apartment was not in as nice an area as Hossein's rental home; it was much closer to the Strip. The complex sat in a somewhat seedy, rundown neighborhood and was misnamed "The Vegas Paradise Arms." They had ordered Chinese food, mostly chow mein noodles, and had brought the delectable meal to Erika's combination living and dining room, where Hossein had popped open a nice bottle of wine that he had previously purchased. The FBI had already managed to bug her place and were listening in to their conversation.

"Wow, this is high-end Cabernet," Erika noted and she sipped the 2011 Cakebread vintage that Hossein had poured. "A little too nice for this Peking beef, but I'm not complaining."

"Yeah, well, we're celebrating, remember?" Hossein winked at Erika, as he moved in for a deep kiss and embrace. They knew each other's bodies so well by now that they fell into a pleasant and easy lovemaking rhythm as they slipped out of their clothes. The two had moved to Erika's bed. After they finished their lovemaking, Erika and Hossein just cuddled a bit, finally resting in a spooning position.

"So isn't this better than sitting in a smoky slot machine tournament?" Erika said teasingly.

"You may have something there," Hossein replied easily. "Wow, it's not even 10pm. Let's talk a bit about tomorrow."

"What do you want me to bring? I can bring some of the Oban you've got stashed over here," Erika said, referring to the case of whiskey that Hossein had placed in Erika's home so that Amir wouldn't find out about it.

"Nice. Great idea," Hossein spoke approvingly. "Just bring one bottle, though. You know that Hamid, bless his soul, doesn't really drink. So bring him that yogurt drink that you've got in the fridge for me. He loves it twice as much as I do. Hamid's funny. He doesn't really practice religion, he's a nominal Muslim, but he was brought up in it enough so that he still doesn't drink or gamble or anything. Sex he goes for, though, so Candy and Hamid are perfect for each other."

"When am I going to see you after tomorrow?"

Hossein looked away. "Well, as I told you, Amir is a bit of a slave driver. This is why I'm sneaking you in for tomorrow; I didn't realize we were going to be able to have so much fun tonight as well." He smiled at Erika, stroking her hair absently. "I still have to drive back to LA on New Year's Eve, if you can believe it." He looked at Erika. "There's a stupid party that GCF is co-sponsoring with some business partners on New Year's Day, and I have to represent the company. I'll miss you, though. I'll see you next time I'm in town, probably over President's Day weekend."

"Okay, but that's like a month and a half from now. Maybe you can come by earlier than that," Erika said invitingly.

"We'll see," Hossein replied noncommittally. "We'll see what happens."

Hossein left at about 10:30pm, waving to Erika as she stood silhouetted in the doorway of her apartment. Hossein had had a pretty satisfying week, even if he didn't win any money in the slot tournament. Hossein whistled to himself as he drove away, thinking to himself how lucky he was that he had another satisfying day coming up tomorrow.

Three minutes after Hossein left, the FBI had Leticia Gonzalez call Erika on her cell phone. Erika had just been getting ready to take a shower when she heard her cell phone ring. Thinking that it might be Hossein, Erika scrambled nude out of the bathroom and picked up the phone.

"Oh, it's you, Leticia. What are you calling me so late for? My god, when was the last time we spoke, two months ago.

Nothing's wrong with you is it? Is there an emergency? Are you OK?"

"I'm fine, Erika. Sorry to be calling you so late, but we really need to talk. OK?"

"Uh, OK I guess," Erika replied. "Whatever you need."

Erika was just too nice a person, David thought as he and a number of other senior Safety Screen leaders were listening in on the call. People who were too nice tended to get hurt, unfortunately. "So go ahead, talk," Erika continued.

"I mean in person. Can I come over and talk to you now?"

"It's like 10:30, wait," Erika stole a look at her clock, "no, it's 10:35pm. Come on, can't this wait until tomorrow?" Erika pleaded to her friend. "I'm really tired, and I have to take a shower. You said there's no emergency."

"I didn't say that, Erika. I just said that I was all right. That doesn't mean that there's no emergency."

"What does that mean, Leticia?"

"Look, let's just talk in person. I'm actually in the parking lot downstairs from your apartment."

"What?!?" Erika exclaimed.

"I'll explain when I see you. I'm coming up now. It'll be me knocking in a few minutes," Leticia finished as she hung up.

Erika was getting a little angry now, as she quickly put on some clothes. Leticia was a friend, but not like her best friend or anything. Leticia was really overstepping the boundaries here.

The knock came in only one minute, which surprised Erika a bit. *This really must be some emergency*, she thought to herself. Peering into the eyehole of the door, she confirmed that it was Leticia out there. "Leticia?" she called out, just to be sure.

"Yeah, it's me Erika. Open up."

When Erika opened the door, however, it wasn't just Leticia who greeted her. A few other men wearing suits came out of the shadows flashing their FBI badges. Erika gasped and fell back away from the door as Leticia and the men came in. "What's going on Leticia?" she said alarmed. "I didn't do anything wrong."

"No, no, don't worry, Erika," Leticia reassured her. "These are my colleagues from the FBI. They asked me to call you so that they could talk to you in person. We have a bit of an emergency, and it might be the case that only you can help us out."

Erika shook her head disbelievingly. "I'm a bartender, as you know, Leticia. How can I be the only one who can help the FBI? I have no idea what you are talking about."

Leticia and three other FBI agents entered Erika's apartment and Leticia closed the door behind them. "Can we sit?" Leticia asked.

"Sure." Erika sat on one of her kitchen chairs, and motioned for the FBI agents to sit on the sofa or any of the other kitchen chairs.

"Erika, do you know this man?" Leticia said, as she showed a picture of Hossein that was taken by the FBI at the gas station this morning.

"Oh no, not Hossein," Erika wailed. "He just left my place. I had a bad feeling that you were going to ask me about him. What did he do? Embezzle some money? Rob a bank or something? You told me that bank robbers are a big part of your cases, Leticia."

"Hi, Erika. I am Special Agent in Charge David Smithline. I am sorry that we have to meet so late tonight and under such circumstances. I'll get to the point quickly. We have strong evidence that Hossein Abbasi is involved with a terrorist group that may explode a bomb in Las Vegas," David said, as the team had decided not to freak Erika out by telling her that the bomb was in fact a nuclear weapon, "although he's not the bomber himself."

Erika's mouth gaped open in surprise. "You're kidding me. Hossein's not Al Qaeda; he's Iranian. There must be some mistake. Hossein taught me the details about how much the Islamic sects are different. Kind of like Catholics and Protestants. He said that the Al Qaeda terrorists were mostly Sunni Muslims, from Saudi Arabia and the like. Iranians are Shi'a Muslims, and while we don't like Iran now, Shi'as are not the same as Sunnis. Hossein's not even a practicing Muslim. He's here in the United States now, he told me, because his family was supporting the Shah way back before 1979 when the Iranians were our friends."

"Hossein's given you good information about the religious situation," David explained delicately. "And we're not saying he's a bomber, Erika. It's just that it looks like Hossein's helping out some bad people, and he's the main lead for us to stop from setting off the bomb. And while it's not Al Qaeda, it may be Al Qods, the Iranian secret police and spy agency all rolled into one, although we don't even know if they are involved. Whoever's behind this, we just want to stop them. Maybe Hossein doesn't even know there's a bomb involved."

"Well, I still can't believe any of this involves Hossein," Erika said in a defensive tone. "And what does this have to do with me?"

"We understand that you will be seeing Hossein and his colleague Hamid at 3pm tomorrow, ..." David started to say.

"What?" Erika cried out, realizing that this could only mean that the FBI had been wiretapping her conversations. "How do you know this? You've been listening in to our conversations?" she accused Leticia. "For how long has this been going on?"

"Calm down," Leticia said to her friend, "it's only been recently, today as a matter of fact, that the FBI realized that Hossein may be, however inadvertently, helping these terrorists out. So they got approval for a wiretap just today on his cell phone." David decided not to correct Leticia's ignorance that the JCTF had in fact been looking for Hossein for longer than that. Leticia looked over to David for support. Leticia continued talking to her friend: "Look, I myself have just been told about this today. But it's pretty compelling, Erika. Hossein is sneaking you and your girlfriend in when most of his other, uh, I guess we'll just call them colleagues for now, are going to be celebrating the birthday of the Prophet Mohammad. So this is the perfect time for the FBI to take a look around the home and completely bug it. They'll even install hidden video cameras. That's all they want to do, I swear. David here told me that they would only install surveillance equipment and maybe deactivate any bombs if they find any." David definitely decided not to add anything to Leticia's statements here, which were technically accurate, but of course didn't give the full story.

"You're not going to even arrest Hossein?"

"Well, no, not at this time. As we told you, we don't even know the full extent of his involvement. And the video cameras we will install are all court approved. See, here's the warrant – it's called a FISA warrant - for wiretapping and electronic surveillance." She showed Erika the paper. "We simply need to get into the home and try to figure out what's going on. We need to know if there are any bombs there, or bomb-making equipment. This is to prevent people from getting hurt. Remember, we think most of this stuff is being done not by Hossein directly, but by Hossein's colleagues."

"This is pretty weird, you know," Erika decided. "I guess I understand why you want to bug and video the whole house. But it's very secret agent-like. I feel like I'm in a James Bond movie or something."

"You don't have to do this if you don't want."

"I know, I know." Erika smoothed her hair back with a sweep of her hand. She sighed. "OK, I'll do it, I'll do it. But only if you tell me later whether Hossein truly knows about and is involved with the bombing plot. I need to know whether he's just a dupe or whether he's really in on it all."

"Agreed," David said immediately, although he was afraid that he knew the answer pretty much already.

"What do I need to do?"

David interjected, "Here's the play. And thanks again Erika; you don't know what this means to the team. You don't really need to do anything different from what you would have normally done if we didn't talk to you tonight. That's the beauty of this. We will rig you up with some small hidden cameras so that you can let us see what is going on in the home. Then we are going to put something in the drinks that you are going to give Hossein, Hamid, Candy and yourself. These drugs are not harmful, and will only cause you to feel drowsy and go to sleep for about an hour. Once we see from the cameras that you are asleep, we'll come in and install the cameras and the like, and also check for bombs, deactivating anything that we find. After you all wake up, then you just leave. That's it."

"Really, that's it?"

"Yup, and we will help keep you safe after that as well," Leticia said. "I guarantee that. It's what I demanded from this team," she said, pointing to the other agents, "before I agreed to talk to you this way." The two friends hugged, and Erika sniffled a bit. This was coming way too fast for Erika and she was so confused. Erika felt that she had lost a little of her free spiritedness tonight, and she didn't like it one bit. She felt a small bit of cynicism take root in her body. That cynicism had never been present before.

"I have to tell you that I still can't believe any of this. Has Hossein been lying to me all along? Am I just the most gullible person alive? I never thought Hossein was a choir boy, but you know, only just a little too money hungry. And how about his cousin Samir? My radar had him pegged for sure as a good guy – is he a terrorist too? I don't even know if I can trust my gut anymore."

David assured Erika, "Don't beat yourself up. Your gut is just fine. Samir is one of the good guys; in fact, he's the one who allowed us to find Hossein. Think how hard it was for him: Hossein is a relative of his and he is helping us. Don't let anyone paint all Iranians, or any group of people or religion, as bad or good. It's the individual that counts. You're a good individual; I know that and appreciate it."

Erika nodded, somewhat mollified by David's assurances. David left Leticia and another agent with Erika, returning to Nellis to work out the remaining parts of the plan. Tomorrow would be busy, but the senior leaders would all get to bed by 0300 so that they could get up refreshed by 1100 hours the next morning. The primary assault team would similarly get a good night of rest tonight. They would have to be on top of their game tomorrow. It would be no simulation this time; this was the real thing.

CHAPTER 10

David and K2 had almost identical dreams that night; they both felt that they were alone floating along in a cloud looking down at an earth that was just waking up to a new day. The birds were chirping and flitting around, and a light breeze was moving the cloud gently along. Then a more violent wind took hold, blowing them towards the earth faster and faster until they could see that they were nearing an intersection in Las Vegas. Finally, inexplicably, each of them were on the ground running past the intersection towards a home, 1235 First Avenue, of course, as part of the FBI assault team. Each of them were with their teammates now, running into the home towards the safe room. One of their teammates opened the safe room door and they were all in, but something was weird. They had set off some alarm, and their ears were filled with the incessant beep, beep, beeping of that alarm. Each woke with a start to the sound of their clock alarms blaring at them. It was 1100 hours on the dot.

Most of the primary assault team had slept in the home two doors down from the target house. To avoid detection, the Safety Screen team would engage in an elaborate choreographed plan, successfully placing a number of snipers up on the rooftops of a few select and adjacent homes. A different utility truck, this one a cable company vehicle instead of a telephone truck, would be placed down the other end of the street with scads of monitoring and radiation equipment. A large U-Haul truck would also be parked in front of the home two doors down to make it looks like someone was moving in. This U-Haul would contain one of the Humvee teams, namely Cannon 1 with Rick Columbia.

The team became more anxious as the go time of 1500 hours approached. Ben, Sri and Johnny G were dressed in cable company repairmen uniforms and were practicing loading and unloading their mobile carts full of the replacement RA-115s.

"Hey, Hossein, we are about to leave now," his brother Amir called out in Farsi. "Remember, brother, you are not allowed to leave here when we are gone."

"Yes, yes, I promise brother."

"By the memory of our dear grandmother Parizad?"

"Indeed, by the memory of Parizad, I swear that I will stay in this home." Amir looked Hossein deeply in the eyes and confirmed his seriousness.

"I believe you, brother. We are almost done here. I am proud of you, which is why I let you have last night to do whatever you wanted. We are only three days away! So close, and yet so far. We will only be gone for three hours, and will be back for dinner. You shouldn't have any issues."

"Will you go now already?" Hossein said in an exasperated voice, tossing Amir the keys to his BMW X5 SUV. "It's the middle of the afternoon; nothing will happen in the next few hours. Hamid and I will be home the entire time."

Javad, Karim and Abdul gestured to Amir impatiently. "Hossein's right," Javad said, "we should go now so that we can pay the proper respects to the Prophet, and then we can come home earlier." So the four Mawlid celebrators piled into the SUV and opened the garage.

"The bogeys are on the move, central," reported Mark Childress from inside the cable company vehicle. "Infrared confirms four bogeys moving, repeat, four bogeys moving. Two remaining bogeys inside the house." Hossein peered out from one of the closed drapes to confirm that the van had left and quickly texted Erika, asking where she was. Erika texted back that they were only a few minutes away now. She tried to be nonchalant about her reply, but luckily it was by text, as her stomach was in knots already. She practiced a few deep breaths to calm herself down. Fortunately, Candy was driving and concentrating too hard on the road to notice Erika's nervousness.

Candy pulled up to the curb in front of 1235 First Avenue, and jumped out of her beaten-down, old Toyota Celica excitedly. She liked Hamid, who exuded a kind of fiery exoticism that turned her on. Candy practically ran up the walk towards the front door, with a snack bag in her hand. Erika took another deep breath, picked up the bag containing the drinks, and followed Candy to the door.

Hossein had spied them from the inside as soon as they had stopped, and had opened the front door by the time they got there. He was beaming in expectation of the fun that they would have together. Hamid, if possible, was even more excited, anticipating his reunion with Candy; his memory recalled the fantastic time that they had together the previous encounter. Candy practically jumped into Hamid's waiting arms, and Hamid's face was suffused with joy as he took in Candy's scent and almost palpable heat. Erika tried to replicate Candy's excitement, quickly hugging and kissing Hossein suggestively after he had closed the door.

Per the FBI's instructions, Erika had placed her purse containing a small video camera facing the family room so that the agents could see what was going on. She would place a separate makeup bag into the master bedroom for the same purpose. Another camera was hidden in the food bag that would allow the agents to see what was going on in the kitchen.

"No, no, no glasses," Hossein said, as he took a swig of Oban directly from the bottle. "You remember what I told you about my brother Amir; he disapproves of my drinking alcohol. We'll keep the glasses clean and drink straight from the bottle, and then you can take the bottle away."

Hamid had barely disengaged himself from Candy when Erika shoved his favorite yogurt drink in his face. "Drink up, Hamid," Erika coaxed. "You'll need your energy in the next hour," she winked at him. Hamid blushed a bit and took a deep swig of the drink, then another, and then another, finishing the drink and letting out a little belch. The four of them started laughing good-naturedly. "Wow," said Erika, "you really are loading up your energy. Watch out, Candy," she smiled, handing Candy her favorite fruit-infused wine cooler. Erika said, "You too, Candy. Drink up, I got you your favorite stuff."

Mimicking Hamid, Candy took three massive swigs of the drink, and then finished it by the fourth swig. No belch, but she pulled Hamid over to the couch and began to undress him seductively. The two were at it quickly. Erika looked at Hossein and smiled. Hossein took another two sips from the whiskey bottle, feeling the gentle burn run down his throat followed by the immediate warm and tingly sensation that he loved so much about drinking Oban.

Erika had downed half a wine cooler herself, and then she held her hand out for Hossein's bottle. After he had passed it to her, she took a few sips and then poured a little of the whiskey down her shirt and winked at Hossein. Hossein lost no time in taking the hint. Taking back the bottle, he downed another gulp before putting it on the table, signaling to Erika to go into the master bedroom. Erika followed Hossein down the hall; taking her makeup bag with her into the master bedroom, she placed it on the nightstand facing the bed. Hossein and Erika began where they had left off in Erika's apartment the night before, Hossein inhaling and then tasting the Oban that Erika had poured on herself with his hungry tongue and then lips.

"All right, I think that we can agree that Erika isn't self-conscious about being filmed," Jack said as the team, somewhat embarrassed, watched the show being played out on the video camera.

"At least she's playing her part well. I don't think that Hossein has a clue that she is helping us," Marcia added from the comlink in her office in Washington, DC.

"Yeah, that's true, but we may have a little problem here," Jack said. "Uh, Erika may be playing her role too well. We told her to get Hamid to drink at least half of the yogurt concoction, but he drank just about all of it really quickly. I think that Hamid is going to be knocked out for a bit longer than we had hoped."

"How much longer?" David worriedly asked.

"Hmm, it's 1515 hours now. We think that he's going to be out like a light starting in about thirty minutes. So that's around 1545. However, instead of being asleep for one hour, with the amount and speed that he downed the drink, my techs are thinking he's going to be out maybe two or two and a half hours. So that's maybe 1815, and the six bogeys are supposed to be back around then, potentially even before."

"Dammit! How about Hossein?"

"He'll probably be passed out starting from around 1600 until about 1730 or so, given all of the, uh, physical exertion," Jack said euphemistically as the rest of the team chuckled, "and energy that he's using now. We were quite frankly worried more about their not being knocked out long enough rather than knocked out for too long."

"And the women?"

"Should be out for a time period similar to their male counterparts. Candy will be out longer than Erika we think, but Erika and Hossein should be awakening at roughly the same time. You know, of course, that it's not an exact science here. People react differently to Ro based on their individual characteristics, including, but not limited to, their weight and age, in addition to the dosage strength. We're going to have to enact contingency plan Doublestall."

"Agreed," said David. "Make it so."

The two couples' lovemaking continued for a little while longer on their video feeds and afterwards, spent, the couples lay in each other's embrace, just about asleep. At about 1551 hours, it was clear to the Safety Screen team that the four of them were fast asleep and David called the entry team into action. The cable company van drove up to the curb next to Samir's home and a number of "repairmen" exited and approached the front door of the house. Using a copy of the key that Samir had provided, six repairmen entered the home and began the operation.

Two of those repairmen were Ben and Sri, escorted by their buddy Johnny G. Immediately prior to entering the home, they had all taken off their shoes and donned blue foot covers to mask their footprints within the house. Underneath their uniforms, they had donned some hazmat-like suits to protect them from any (unlikely) material RA-115 radiation. After they got into the home, Ben, Sir and Johnny G quickly made for the master bedroom closet and the safe room. Samir's copy of the safe room key worked perfectly so the three were able to get into the safe room literally within a minute of entering the home.

"Come on, baby," Sri said. "Where are you, Mr. Nuke? We're here to take you home with us." And then they all saw it at the same time, a lead composite-lined crate that was closed and padlocked. On top of the crate was a Geiger counter and some other miscellaneous instrumentation. Clearly the lid had been opened recently, probably to test that the radiation level was still at appropriate levels, but also probably accounting for the ability for their equipment to trace the RA-115's radiation signature.

"Piece of cake," Johnny G said quietly, as he pulled out some lockpicking tools and proceeded to open the padlock. "I bet you E(ye)-in-steins can't do this," he smiled, as he popped the lock open. Gently removing it, Johnny opened the lid and presto! there it was, a GRU "version 3" RA-115 staring back at them.

"What do you think, Ben?" asked Sri. "Looks like it's closest to #8 to me."

"Yeah, either #7 or #8, but you're right, the wear marks on the right side of the backpack line up with #8 better," Ben noted, as he flipped through their deck of fake RA-115 pictures. Hey Steven," he called out on the com mike to their NEST colleague still in the truck, can you bring #8 in now? That's number eight, octo, ocho, 4 + 4 equals eight. "

"Roger that, Ben," Steven replied, "number eight is on the way."

This was going way smoother that they had thought. Mark Childress' assault team was primed and ready to go, but it looked like they wouldn't be needed. Inside the U-Haul truck, Rick Columbia was twiddling his thumbs, key in the ignition of the Cannon 1 Humvee. Rick had Zen-like abilities to stay calm in the moment; he didn't care whether he was used or not, just that the mission was completed successfully.

Back at the Nellis command center, David Smithline and K2 were actually smiling and nodding their heads in amazement. This part of the plan was working out nicely, with no glitches so far. The software code breaker was placed on the device so that they could figure out the 20-35 digit alphanumeric code. NSA guaranteed that the code could be found within 40 minutes so all that they could do was wait. Meanwhile, the fake RA-115 was transported into the safe room and examined closely by the NEST team and the FBI agents.

"Pretty exactimundo, guys," Sri said excitedly. "Maybe an extra scuff mark here," he added, pointing to an area near one of the straps.

"And here too," Ben called out. Ben and Sri replicated the keylock for the titanium key as another critical step. It was around 1610 hours when Ben and Sri were finally satisfied that the fake RA-115 matched the real one as much as possible. At exactly 1635 hours, the alphanumeric code was cracked and the team had transferred all of the software information over to the fake nuke.

Gently taking the real RA-115 nuke out of the crate, a member of Jim Broussard's EOD Unit moved it out of the safe room and into another lead composite-lined crate that they had placed just outside the front door. The real nuke thus was quickly moved into a small van that had pulled up to the house and immediately took off after its precious cargo got safely loaded.

They had done it! A cheer erupted from the Nellis command center, and a signal was quickly transmitted to the President, Vice President and all others who were not already viewing the event live by video and/or audio feed. The message was simple and just said this: "Switchblade Complete." President Besselman just breathed a deep sigh of relief, shook his head appreciatively, and lit a cigar. *God, I love those Special Operations teams,* the President thought to himself.

During this whole time, the other "repairmen" in the home had successfully placed a large number of hidden video cameras and audio bugs in the house. The Safety Screen team would have 24x7 coverage of every room in the house, together with the van that had originally transported the RA-115 to Las Vegas. Tracking devices were also placed in the van as it was pretty clear to the FBI agents that the bomb would be loaded inside and driven to or near the Strip for detonation.

The fake RA-115 was loaded inside the crate and the padlock returned to its original locked position. Ben and Sri also had switched out some components of the Geiger counter and other instrumentation so that, if used, their readings would falsely indicate conformity with the radiation signature of the real nuke.

It was now only 1641 hours and they were done. Triple-checking that everything was exactly in the place that it was before, the team meticulously exited the safe room and house, leaving it in the same condition as when they had entered. It was as if the team was never there.

Clear on the other side of town, Amir was about as happy as he had been his entire life. Here he was, in the heart of the corruption in the hated American nation, the seat of all of the values that Islam stood against: gambling, intoxication and debauchery. But he had resisted these temptations, and in a few short days, would act against the US city which most encouraged these vices. He would act as a purifier of sorts, and more importantly, he would strike a blow at America and gain favor for his family with Rahimi and with Al Qods generally. Or so Amir thought, but of course even in this he was deluded as the ayatollahs and the leaders of Al Qods had no idea about this plan.

To Amir, it was altogether fitting that, a mere few days before the nuke would be set off, he would be praying at one of the finest mosques in the city, one that was comfortably 45 minutes away from the south end of the Strip. The festival of Mawlid there had started in the late morning and the mosque was festooned with bright colors and eager, excited worshippers who reveled in the celebration of their Prophet Muhammad's birthday. Food and music were in abundance, and a recitation of the Qasida-al-Burda Sharif was performed, together with numerous recitations of stories of the life of the Prophet.

The celebration had spilled over into the neighboring streets of the mosque, but no one had cared. Everyone seemed to be having a good time; the four terrorists certainly enjoyed this Mawlid celebration. Perhaps it was a niggling doubt, or a premonition that his brother Hossein was not fully trustworthy, that led Amir to want to leave early, but he had felt a twinge that something could be going on back at the house. So after finishing a prayer, Amir rounded up his colleagues and suggested that they go back to the house.

Javad and Karim nodded their assent to leave, but of course it would be the young guard Abdul who would ask to stay longer to enjoy the food and fun. Shaking his head no, Amir took hold of Abdul's shoulder and started pulling him away from the celebration. Amir herded the four of them back to the BMW X5 a full fifteen minutes early at 5:45pm.

"Hellfire," Sam Chalkias said, "we need to get into position faster for Doublestall," he told Kyle. Kyle gunned the engine and their Suburban roared to life and took off down the road.

Just as the four terrorists were approaching the BMW X5, an old Muslim woman fell down at the crossroads in front of their SUV. The Mawlid crowd quickly gathered around to try to help her get up. Abdul, Karim and Javad had also run to help the old woman, who seemed all right, but was bleeding a bit from her forehead.

One of the bystanders shouted, "Let me through, I am a doctor." The bystander parted the crowd to get to the woman. "I will need my bag," he said, summoning his son to run to their car to get the medical kit. A full fifteen people had now gathered around, seeking to help or just be involved in the action in some way. The son returned after a while and Amir, who had Abdul get a pillow from the X5 to make the woman more comfortable, could see the doctor taking out a large bandage from the kit. *Poor woman*, Amir thought to himself, *not too auspicious to fall at a Mawlid celebration*. After about five or so minutes, the doctor signaled that he was done bandaging and examining the woman.

An enterprising youth had gone to get a wheelchair for the woman. Abdul and Javad and a few other men helped place her gently in the chair. The old woman's daughter, a middle-aged woman in full niqab headscarf herself, bowed and scraped in appreciation, and profusely thanked everyone for their assistance. She slowly wheeled her the old woman away towards her own car a few blocks away, with Abdul and Javad and a number of other people assisting the daughter in loading her mother inside the car carefully.

By the time Abdul and Javad had returned, another five minutes had passed before they were able to all get into the SUV. Amir looked at his watch; it was 6:01pm. *Perhaps it was Allah's will that we stay at Mawlid until six*, Amir thought to himself. There was no fighting fate. Time to go home. He texted Hossein quickly that he was coming back, probably in 20 minutes, and was everything all right?

Hossein had only gotten up himself around 5:50pm in a daze. At first, he didn't exactly remember where he was, and then, just as suddenly, all of his memories rushed back to him. *Uh-oh, what time was it?* Hossein thought to himself, as he looked around. The clock said 5:51pm by that time, as he shook himself awake some more, brushing Erika's half-nude body in the process and speeding up her wake up process as well.

In a moment of panic he thought that Amir was coming up the walk to the front door, but then he realized that Amir wasn't scheduled to be back until about 6:15pm. "Erika," Hossein prodded her in the back, "you have to get up now. You have to go; remember, my brother is coming home and he can't see us like this."

Erika groaned in response, and then sat up straight in the bed. "Hey, you're right. Where's Candy and Hamid?" The two lovers hurriedly dressed, and Erika snatched up her makeup bag and other items in the room and dashed into the kitchen. In the family room, Hamid was still sound asleep, while Candy was groggily waking up. "What time is it?" Candy asked weakly.

"Never mind; we need to go," Erika implored.

"OK, OK, I get it, stop rushing me," Candy replied somewhat testily. Spying Hamid, Candy smiled and gave him a playful peck on the back. "Wake up, sleepyhead. Wow, that was fun. I must have been really tired because I don't remember much."

Erika and Hossein dashed around, picking up the items that the girls had brought. Erika put on her shoes and began putting stuff in Candy's car. Hossein was spraying around mint-scented air freshener, just as Amir's text came in.

"Thank Allah," Hossein said aloud, rolling his eyes upward to the heavens. "They're still twenty minutes away." It took another full sixteen minutes before Erika and Candy were packed off in the Toyota Celica and driving away.

Hossein surveyed the situation. The women and alcohol were gone, and all obvious signs that the two women were here had been removed. Hossein had brushed his teeth twice to get rid of the alcohol smell in his mouth. However, one big problem was that Hamid was barely awake. Hossein almost bodily threw Hamid into the shower to get ready and more awake for their friends' return. After taking care of Hamid, Hossein took stock of his own situation. He brushed his teeth a third time just to be sure that the alcohol smell was gone. Hossein further double-checked that everything in the house was put back in place. Just to be sure, Hossein opened up the safe room and breathed a sigh of relief when he saw the locked lead composite-lined case intact and present. *That was a close one, but I managed to pull it off*, Hossein thought to himself happily, as he shook the cobwebs out of his head.

Amir would turn out to be delayed another twenty minutes as a result of an accident on the I-215 beltway that resulted in all lanes stopping for twelve full minutes. Kyle and Sam had done their stall job too. Jack Smith smiled; the two delay tactics had delayed Amir's return by a total of over thirty minutes he noted in satisfaction. Not bad. Once Jack had gotten confirmation that Erika and Candy had driven away safely, the "accident" was slowly resolved and the lanes reopened carefully. When the BMW X5 reappeared in the garage at 6:47pm, he was greeted by Hossein with some feigned indignation. "Where have you been, brother?" Hossein asked. "I thought you were going to be back home over twenty minutes ago."

"Traffic," Amir replied, shrugging. "Wait, this is bizarre, you are chastising me for being late? You are playing the role of the paragon of virtue? It must be the Prophet's birthday indeed; this is not an ordinary occurrence, my brother. In fact, I find this rather unbelievable myself, if I had to tell the truth."

Hossein just smiled and hugged his brother. "No offense, dear brother. I'm just giving you a taste of your own medicine. I was just worried that something had happened to you and was about to text you back. I am just glad that you are home. I will go out and pick up our dinner now," he said, as he took the X5 keys from his brother and left the home. He winked at Hamid, who did not acknowledge him. Hamid rubbed his neck where it was still a bit sore from sleeping on it wrong. Hossein smiled some more. The Prophet's birthday was indeed a blessed day for the both of them.

CHAPTER 11

Following the confirmation that they had the real RA-115 nuke safely ensconced in Nellis and fully deactivated, it felt like a heavy weight had been lifted from the bodies of the Safety Screen team. Everyone was in a great mood. People were smiling, even beaming, when they were talking to each other. While the Safety Screen team's work was technically still not fully done, Ron and Marcia made the executive call to let most of the team stop working late that night and go to bed. That led to even more smiles and an even better sense of good feelings among the group.

A skeletal crew remained to ensure that they continued to monitor the situation at 1235 First Avenue. Ron insisted that David, K2 and Jim stop working that night. David for one did not have enough strength left to argue so he just nodded and took the opportunity offered. This was only the second night out of the last ten nights where David would get eight hours of continuous sleep. David was grateful for the opportunity to recharge his batteries.

K2 made Ben and Sri take the night off as well. She was so proud of them and the rest of the NEST team that she already started composing the words of her written report in her head, a report that would literally be glowing with praise for the NEST members who had helped them achieve this great result. Let's see how Proxmeier deals with this report, K2 couldn't help thinking to herself. It was going to be fun if Proxmeier tried to complain that the report was too effusive in its praise; K2 was going to lay it on thick and make Proxmeier squirm in discomfort. *Based on our resounding success, I don't think that we're going to be arguing about ridiculous funding cutbacks for a long time*, K2 thought happily to herself.

Two days later, the morning of December 30th mirrored the moods of the Safety Screen team. It was particularly clear and bright, and the sharpness of the morning was like the difference between high definition and regular television. Even the animals seemed to sense that it was going to be a good day. The birds, for example, were out in force in the morning, flitting this way and that in the almost cloudless sky. The fog had lifted.

Inside 1235 First Avenue, Amir was also feeling particularly happy. Having a moment of doubt about Hossein, Karim and Amir went into the safe room and opened the crate to confirm that the RA-115 was still there. It was, and the two, feeling comforted, and with the peace of mind coming from having seeing it there with their own eyes, locked up the crate and room carefully again. They went to the kitchen table with Javad to go over the detailed plans for tomorrow.

Karim opened up a large city map of Las Vegas and spread it out on the table. "Because this is a nuclear weapon, we don't need to be that close in order to have a lot of the Strip within the blast radius," Karim announced. "My belief is that some of the large casinos have some sort of radiation equipment monitoring the property. So we definitely don't want to drive too close to the biggest casinos. Instead, we can leave the van in an area with a bunch of industrial buildings near McCarran Airport, where the presence of a van won't be viewed as out of place. From there, it's a little less than two kilometers to the center of the Strip, which would be blocked off to cars anyway because of the New Year's Eve celebration. In fact, as I think about it, this is probably as close as we can reasonably get, given the circumstances."

"What will be the effect?"

"Hard to say exactly. The Americans have published a whole lot of studies estimating the number of fatalities from a nuclear blast. It depends on things like the population density (and here that density will be very high), the number of kilotons detonated and the vertical displacement, meaning how high the nuke is off the ground when it is detonated. Here the bomb is on the ground in the first place, which should be more optimal for us. But the initial blast is only part of the picture. It doesn't take into account the deaths from nuclear fallout. Fatalities will occur where the expected radiation dose is over the LD-50 of about 500 rem."

"You are speaking in Western scientific nonsense terms to me," Javad said to Karim. "Just speak plainly."

Karim sighed. Sometimes he wondered whether his colleagues understood anything about the difference between immutable scientific facts, which were not nonsense and not subject to the whims of religion, on the one hand, and culture and values, on the other hand, which Karim thought was where Westerners and Muslims could legitimately argue with each other all day. But he kept that personal distinction to himself. Karim would never share those personal thoughts with the others. "Look, LD-50 means the median lethal dose it will take ... never mind. How many people the nuke kills will depend on a lot of factors, Javad, my friend. Including how windy it is that day and whether people are outside or inside when the nuke explodes. If they are mostly inside, then they will be shielded more from the radiation, you see."

"That makes sense to me," Javad replied.

"So that is why I had suggested that we detonate the nuke at midnight, when most of the people will be out in the streets celebrating."

Amir spoke up. "This project is under my command Karim," he said to assert his control over the situation. "I have already accepted your proposal of midnight detonation per our earlier discussion. This is how we will do it. To avoid the chance that the van is discovered, we will drive the van to its detonation location only a few hours before midnight, say a little before 9:30pm. Hossein will caravan with us in his BMW, and after the detonation sequence is started by Karim, all of us will depart in the X5 and we will drive away from Las Vegas together. The city will be in chaos but we will be safely en route to Los Angeles, far away from the blast and the radiation fallout."

Hossein piped in: "Importantly, there shouldn't be any traffic, since we'll be one of the few people driving away from the Strip and out of Las Vegas. Most people, of course, will be trying to come in at that time. I don't think that we will be close to Las Vegas at all when the nuke explodes. As a matter of fact we should have driven into California by that time. We may even be past, let's see," he looked at the map carefully, "we may even be past Victorville, California at the moment of detonation."

The day went by quickly for the six men. Amir made Hossein go out and buy them all a special dinner costing twice as much as their normal meal. Amir let them all further celebrate by smoking from their hookah pipes, which he normally frowned upon. *Let them enjoy this last night in Las Vegas*, Amir thought to himself. *Tomorrow is the big day and everyone should be in a good frame of mind entering it.*

December 31st came suddenly for all of the people involved, the terrorists and the Safety Screen team alike. Once again it was a clear and bright day, only much colder this time, about fifteen degrees more chilly compared to the day before. The day passed uneventfully, but the four terrorists were still nervous throughout the day. At 5pm, Karim and Amir opened up the crate. Karim passed the Geiger counter over the device and nodded his head in satisfaction to Amir: the radiation readings were as expected. After dinner, the terrorist gassed up their vehicles in preparation for the trip, and the team then loaded the RA-115 into the payload bay of the van. They would leave at about 8:35pm in order to give themselves some extra time to get into the downtown Strip area. They would probably encounter some traffic on this part of their journey. Hossein's BMW would follow immediately behind the van.

"Bogey One and Bogey Two on the move," Rick called out to his team when the van left the garage.

"Roger that, Eagle One," came the reply. "We are ensuring a smooth, uneventful ride for Bogey One and Bogey Two. No accidents or police cars stopping them tonight, Eagle One."

At 9:25pm, the white van pulled up to a nondescript industrial warehouse near McCarran Airport. Amir parked it in between two other vans that were virtually indistinguishable from theirs. The BMW sport utility vehicle pulled up quickly behind them. As they opened the doors to their vehicles, the flashing lights of the nearby casinos and hotels in the distance hit them full on. The six men could partially hear the revelry beginning on the Strip, a low hum of people talking and milling about, sometimes punctuated by drunken shouts.

Karim was all business, though, as he sat inside the van, oblivious to the noise from outside. He gently opened the crate and began to type in his alphanumeric code to start the detonation sequence. Looking at his watch quickly, he carefully set the timer for two hours and thirty-two minutes so that the nuke would explode exactly at midnight for maximum effect. Karim inserted the titanium key and finished setting up the nuke to detonate. Finally, the RA-115 nuke was fully activated and began to beep gently. The countdown timer read 2:32:00, and then 2:31:59, 2:31:58 and 2:31:57 as Karim gently placed it back in the crate. Nodding to Amir that the RA-115 was activated, Karim quickly stuffed a blanket on top of the nuke to muffle the noise a bit. Then, Karim placed a sheet of thin, lead composite-lined foil on top of the bomb rather than replacing the thick lid of the crate. While ostensibly there was some risk of a radiation detector finding the bomb more easily this way, Karim believed that this was far outweighed by the increased fallout that would result if the crate lid was removed.

The six men slowly got into Hossein's BMW, each hugging Amir before entering the car. Their job was done. Hossein drove well within the speed limit all the way to the outskirts of Las Vegas before he started driving faster, but not too fast as to get caught by the highway patrol. Hossein was right; there was almost no traffic on the I-15 south out of Las Vegas. The terrorists left the city in their rear view mirror a little faster than Hossein anticipated. There was only about half a dozen cars going in their direction until they hit the border town of Primm, Nevada, right on the California-Nevada border.

Passing quickly through the border casinos and outlet shopping center there, the BMW gained speed as they raced through the sparsely populated desert. Hossein played some popular Iranian music that Abdul in particular liked as they drove. Amir, Karim and Javad didn't mind, and even slept most of the time. Amir had set his watch alarm to go off at 11:57pm.

Exactly at 11:57pm, Amir's watch alarm sounded and a faint hum of excitement permeated the vehicle, as the men anticipated the explosion that they had worked so hard to set up. The lights of Victorville could be seen beckoning to them in the distance, only a few miles away now.

"We are a part of history now," Javad said confidently to Amir. "We will have struck a blow to the Great Satan."

Amir smiled, "I know. It is a great honor to have struck this blow to the Americans. Hossein, please turn on the radio station broadcasting the New Year's Eve countdown."

"Yes, yes, brother," Hossein said a little testily. "I know. Can't you see that I am turning on the radio now?" He fiddled with the pre-set button and pressed it again.

"Good evening, Las Vegas!!!" the radio blared. "Are you having fun?" A loud cheer was the response by the crowd. "We are only one minute away!!!" An even louder cheer was the response. And then later, "Ten, nine, eight, seven," Hossein could not help but think of the irony. These people were counting down their own deaths, "six, five, four, ... THREE, TWO, ONE, HAPPY NEW YEAR!!!!!!" Bedlam ensued on the radio as horns went off and the shouts grew louder. Strains of the song "Auld Lang Syne" could be heard in the background. But no explosion.

Karim checked his watch, which he had synchronized down to the second with the countdown timer. The bomb should have gone off. Looking bewildered, he glanced over at Amir who was of course seething with rage.

"What happened, Karim?" Amir exploded.

"I don't know, Amir," Karim replied truthfully. Each of the other terrorists looked accusingly at Karim. "You saw me; I set the nuke correctly," he added defensively. Javad fidgeted in his seat, praying that there had been a simple mistake as to when the countdown timer would get to zero, and that the nuke would go off any second.

"Turn this car around NOW!" Amir shouted at Hossein.

Hossein protested, "We need gas first, Amir, so that we don't have to worry about running out on the return trip."

"Did you hear me, Hossein? Turn this car around NOW!" Amir shouted even louder.

Hossein had never seen his brother this angry before, so he instinctively obeyed. Soon the car was speeding back to Las Vegas like a bat out of hell.

"Bogey Two did a U-turn, and it's heading back to Bogey One," Rick informed David. They had bugged the X5 when it was at the mosque for Mawlid. "I would have given anything to have seen their faces when nothing happened," he cackled. "This operation was AWESOME." He high-fived Ben and Sri.

"Now, now," David admonished. "Let's not get too cocky. That's when we make mistakes. We have to play it out and let them return and then broadcast to their colleagues that the nuke was an epic fail."

It was a little after 2:25am in the morning when the X5 returned to the parking lot that they had so joyfully left around five hours ago. The mood in the car was darker than the night that they had driven through. Karim hopped out of the car and ran to the van, opening up the rear door. Sure enough, the nuke was still there, and the countdown timer had counted down to zero.

"You see, Amir?" Karim shouted. "It wasn't me. The Chechen dogs sold us a dud bomb." He turned on the Geiger counter which indicated that the radiation levels were still appropriate. "See, see? There must be a problem with the software or the hardware implosion system or something," Karim guessed. "I am not exactly going to be able to fix this," he moaned, "it's not like there's a "how to fix your nuke" troubleshooting guide, or any other special wiring diagrams provided."

Amir demanded Hossein's smartphone. Logging in to his alias email account, Amir sent an email to his Al Qods contact saying, "The transaction was not completed. CU Corporation," meaning Colonel Umarov, "gave us faulty equipment. Please terminate the arrangements fully." Umarov would regret his treachery, Amir promised to himself silently. It was not only the loss of the $100 million; there was honor at stake. Umarov and his men would repay the money first, with interest, and then they would pay with their lives. And their deaths would be made painful, extremely painful.

An email came back from the contact demanding an immediate conversation at a provided telephone number. "Hey, Hossein, this is a throwaway phone, right, that you paid for in cash? I can use it safely?"

Hossein glumly nodded; he would not be getting the second half of his promised $300,000 payment, Hossein suddenly realized. A rapid fire conversation between Amir and the Al Qods contact ensued. Lots of shouting back and forth, although code words were used to make it sound like just a busted business deal. "Here, he wants to talk to you, Karim," Amir said, tossing the phone to Karim. More shouting occurred, and the same shouting courtesy was later extended to Javad as well. After about five minutes of this, the Al Qods contact hung up in disgust and the six of them stood around in an eerie silence trying to plan their next move.

The crowds had long dispersed from the Strip. Mostly, only the trash and detritus of the raucous celebration remained. They could hear the hums of trash compacting machinery and sweepers doing their job, trying to make the roads clean again by the time people woke up the next morning, or the next afternoon.

Five minutes later, the six could hear the sounds of two helicopters in the night. Sirens blared too along the roads near their location. Amir shouted, "They must have traced us through our call. Maybe they were monitoring all conversations by our Al Qods contact." Amir anxiously texted the Al Qods contact, who was located in Algeria, that all of their covers were probably blown and that the contact should take evasive action immediately. The Al Qods contact acknowledged receipt, and signed off immediately. On a separate email system, he informed his leader, Rahimi, of what had happened quickly and then the contact took off, never to be heard from again.

The two guards had pulled out their weapons. These guards had both machine guns and pistols; the other four terrorists were relegated to only using handguns. Hamid and Abdul took a defensive position around some of the other vans in the parking lot. Amir, Javad, Karim, and Hossein got into the back of the van and tried to get the RA-115 working to no avail.

"What do you want to do now, David?" Mark Childress asked. He had reprised his two assault teams of ten FBI agents each, one led by Paul Antam and one by Artie M. These assault teams were getting positioned around the target area.

"Let's try and take them alive, Mark," David said. "Do the whole 'We've got your surrounded' schtick."

Mark nodded and barked the order to his ground troops. After the troops had gotten fully deployed, Artie got on a megaphone: "This is the FBI. Put your guns on the ground and come out with your hands up. We have got you surrounded."

This entreaty was met with a hail of gunfire, as the two guards emptied a few clips at the FBI agents. "Glow 1 Team," Richie Gutierrez hissed. "Who's got a shot?"

Ronnie Williams was the first to reply. "Glow 1 Leader, this is Glow 1 Beta. I got Target 3 painted."

"Take the shot, Glow 1 Beta," Riche said, and Ronnie's high-powered assault rifle shot hit Abdul squarely in the leg. He went down writhing in pain, dropping his gun in the process.

"Glow 1 Gamma's got Target 2 painted," Johnny G calmly announced, squeezing off the shot after approval was granted. So after Abdul had gone down only moments before, he was quickly followed in succession by Hamid, each taken out quickly by the Glow 1 team. Unfortunately, the guards refused to give up, and took our some pistols and continued to fire at the FBI agents. After a few more rounds of gunfire exchange, the FBI assault team decided that they had no choice but to go for the kill shots and the two guards lay dead. The main contingent of Artie's assault team got positioned offensively near the van.

Artie got on the megaphone again. "Those in the van, we have taken out your support team. Open up and surrender or we will open fire."

Amir glared at Karim as if the angry stare alone could make the nuclear specialist detonate the bomb. Amir could not believe that a mere few hours ago they were on top of the world, believing that they had just fulfilled their mission. Now they were about to be captured by the forces of the Great Satan. How could Allah let this happen to them?

With a resigned shrug, Amir hugged his brother Hossein and then opened the rear door of the van carefully, showing the

FBI that his hands were up and held no weapon. The four of them would have to live to fight again another day.

The FBI purposefully leaked a story to the press in the morning that six Middle Eastern terrorists had tried to bomb the Strip but had been thwarted. The FBI noted pointedly that some of the members were traced to various organizations, including Al Qods and Hezbollah. Of course, no mention was made of a nuclear bomb being present, and the media was told instead that the van was filled with conventional explosives that had failed to go off. This way they could let Rahimi and Al Qods know that they had apprehended Rahimi's agents. Rahimi would be running scared tonight, because he now knew that the FBI knew that Rahimi had tried to nuke America in its own backyard. Back in Iran, Rahimi would be on the hot seat and the US would find out soon enough as to whether Rahimi was acting on his own or with central authority backing.

Within a week the Iranians announced through a back channel to the American government that they had captured some rogue operatives who had been conducting an unauthorized operation. All of the rogue operatives, some fifteen individuals, had all been executed, including Rahimi. So now the FBI had their answer, which made a lot of sense. The high leaders of the Iranian government did not like America, but would never be so crazy as to set off a nuke in the US because of the retaliation that would follow.

Rahimi, though, was a madman who, before he was executed, claimed that he had had a dream in which God told him that the day of reckoning for Islam had come and that he was the chosen one to strike the first blow against the Great Satan of America. He had convinced a few of his compatriots that they too would be glorified in heaven for helping Rahimi strike that blow.

These compatriots believed that Rahimi was still a senior director of Al Qods, even though he was no longer a formal member of the organization. That was the problem often with cell-based terrorist networks with far flung operations. Since cells were self-contained units, cell members couldn't really verify whether their cell leaders still were in charge, or whether those leaders had been deposed by the central authority. Most cell members didn't even know how their supervisors fit into the intelligence hierarchy in the first place.

A group of moderate clerics would now be taking over the oversight of all of Al Qods and would institute changes to prevent this kind of thing from happening again. These clerics would also open a communication line with the US State Department. Relations between the two countries would certainly be less tense now with Rahimi's death, and the rhetoric would be, at least for the time being, a little more muted.

CHAPTER 12

"And, in summary, the assault team gained control of the situation and killed two of the terrorists after they refused to surrender. The assault team captured the remaining four terrorists. Right now, these four are undergoing interrogation so that we can ascertain what they know about how the RA-115 got here. We need to learn how to prevent any future repeat of these horrible circumstances. The Operation Safety Screen team," David waved his arms around to point out the team in attendance in the Joint Base Andrews conference room in DC, "deserves the highest accolades for their professionalism and attention to duty. It was a true team effort among countless team members: the FBI, NEST, Homeland Security, the Army, DIA and the rest of the military, including the National Guard, as well as NSA and CIA. Everyone had a part in preventing the RA-115 from going off," David said with a flourish as he finished his report on Operation Safety Screen to the large governmental audience. This meeting occurred exactly one week to the day following the New Year's Eve operation. Naturally the room erupted in applause after David finished speaking, and Marcia, Don, David, K2, Jim, Mark and the rest of the Safety Screen operations team got a prolonged standing ovation.

President Besselman cleared his throat on the video screen and the room became quiet. "Ladies and gentlemen of the Safety Screen team, the nation owes you a debt of eternal gratitude, more than what mere words can convey. Over the last few weeks, you have undergone a trying ordeal, working tirelessly, often away from your family in this holiday season. I don't think that it is an understatement when I say that you may have saved hundreds of thousands of lives. Indeed, you may have saved democracy itself in this country as we know it. Who knows what would have happened if the nuke had gone off? So I thank you, for myself and on behalf of the government and the American people. The nation owes you a debt of eternal gratitude." He signed off and the meeting ended just like that.

Everyone wanted to shake the ops team's hands and pat them on the back after the meeting. It was a full hour after the meeting before the crowd dispersed. Only Don, Marcia, David and K2 were left in the conference room.

"It's 1530 hours now; we still on for dinner and drinks tonight?"

Don yawned. "I'm kind of beat today. Why don't you three go tonight? I'll catch up some other day."

Marcia said, "Put me down as a maybe. Jeff had his Europe trip cancelled at the last second, and John and I were thinking of doing a parents-son night with him if Jeff can catch a flight out from Kennedy. We haven't seen him hardly at all over the holidays because of Safety Screen."

"Definitely see your son if you can, Marcia," Katherine said. "We can postpone the dinner for some other time."

"No, no," Marcia insisted. Ruminating a bit, she said, "There's only like a 10% chance Jeff can come tonight instead of tomorrow. Tell you what, David, since I drove Katherine here today, why don't you do me a favor and drive her? I'll make the reservation for three now, and I'll call you if I can't make it."

"No problem," David said coolly, although inside he was quite happy with this turn of events. He had been trying to figure out for a while how to be alone more with K2, in a non-awkward way, and this just drops in his lap. "You good with that, K2?"

"Oh, that would be really nice of you, David," K2 said, maybe a bit too nonchalantly. K2 had been thinking the same thing as David. "Tell you what, see you in the parking lot at, say, six?" K2 called out to David as she walked away back to her temporary office space.

"You got it," David said, also walking away.

Don winked at Marcia after the two had gotten out of earshot. "Nice. I was wondering when you might do something like that."

"Shut up, you old coot," Marcia teased. "They just needed an excuse. What they do with this is up to them; I'm out of it now."

David waited anxiously for 6pm to roll around. *What is wrong with me? Am I sixteen years old again?* David thought to himself. At 5:57pm, he went to the men's room, gave himself a once-over in the mirror, brushing back his hair a bit, and then took off for the parking lot. As a former military guy, he couldn't stand being late to anything.

K2 got to the parking lot about thirty seconds after David did, hair also brushed in place. They smiled politely at each other and started walking to David's car.

"Man, these last few weeks have been a blur," David said. "Glad it's over."

"Me too," Katherine agreed. "I'm not going to pretend to know what it's like going to war like you have, but for me it was like this: 95% of the time I felt exhausted, 4% of the time I felt bored, waiting around after we had finished preparing everything, and then, finally, 1% of the time I felt absolutely terrified when the critical part of the operation was happening, and the outcome was still uncertain."

"Yup, that's about the size of it." They fell into an easy conversation then, telling each other stories about their lives, which really is just a person's way of letting others know who they really are as a person. Moments of intimacy like this were what made people connect as friends. David found himself sharing with K2 how scared he was before his first Delta Force mission, thinking that he was going to die for sure, but even more afraid of letting his team down than dying.

K2 also found herself confiding in David about her private fears. K2 had her moments of sheer terror when she thought that she couldn't live up to what people believed that she could accomplish, like when she had to pass her orals for her PhD and they kept hammering her with harder and harder questions until she felt that her head was about to explode. Or her first assignment at NEST when she had to mediate a fight between two senior scientists who each were convinced that the other had completely botched a high-energy physics simulation experiment. Both turned in their resignation letters and Katherine was terrified that it was her fault that she would lose two almost irreplaceable giants in the field a mere few months after she got to her position. Fortunately, it turned out that both of them had made some small, subtle errors such that she could smooth over the ego issues and keep both of the valued people in place.

They were so engrossed in their conversation that, before they knew it, they were already at the restaurant, a French bistro near Dupont Circle. David had to hit the brakes suddenly to avoid passing a parking space just past the restaurant. He parked the car, and then Katherine and he went into the crowded and noisy restaurant together. They sat at the bar and ordered a few drinks first as they were going to wait for Marcia before sitting down at the table. Their reservations weren't until 7:15pm anyway so they had some time to kill. Once again, the two fell into an easy conversation, picking up right where they left off.

Marcia's text buzzed on David and K2's smartphones exactly at 7:15pm. Sorry, it said, Jeff did make it out here - just eat without me. The text further noted that Marcia had called the restaurant and took one person off the reservation. It would only be the two of them now. Secretly pleased, David shrugged to K2. "Oh well, she bailed on us. I'll have to do as company tonight."

"Hmm, I don't know. Marcia's got way better stories than you do," K2 teased. "And she does a way better imitation of Proxmeier than you do."

"What?" David replied with the most indignation that he could muster. "I beg your pardon? Jonathan Proxmeier and I are like so close that we can finish each other's sentences; people have mistaken my voice for his. Listen and learn, Katherine," David continued as he pretended to look down at a report and then looking up and scrunching up his face in mock disgust, he said, "Aren't these results just bull-----sheet?"

K2 busted out laughing.

David held up his hands. "No wait, there's more," David said with a straight face, paraphrasing one of Jonathan P's favorite phrases that he used all of the time, "So the bottom line is ... wait, what is the "bottom line" anyway. Oh yeah, the bottom line is that I am a horse's bottom, i.e., a butt, an ass even."

K2 laughed some more and flipped her hair back. "I don't know, David. For the "bull-----sheet" line, I'll give you a

10 out of 10. However, for the "bottom line" imitation, you only get a seven."

"Seven? That's 70%, that's a "C." C'mon, I deserve way better than a C. Oh, I was going to buy the next round of drinks, but now you're buying for the rest of the night K2," David said jokingly, "as I am totally offended."

"Hmm, I guess it's worth it to have taken you down a notch, Mr. Way-Above-Average Smithline," K2 said with a smile. "I bet you have never really gotten a C in your life. You have always been Mr. Perfect."

"Hey, look who's talking, Miss Perfect," David replied with a smile. "You are a goddess Katherine," (*why did you say that? don't go over the top, you idiot*, David thought to himself) "and I'm just a regular mere mortal here. So how about this for tonight: I buy you dinner, and you buy me drinks."

"Deal," K2 said, shaking on it. David escorted her up to the front of the restaurant to check in with the hostess for their table. The hostess looked quizzically at them and noted that the reservation had been cancelled, and that the wait was now an hour and a half for a table. David and K2 protested that the hostess had to have misunderstood: their friend Marcia meant to cancel her part of the reservation and not the whole thing. Unfortunately, the hostess said, there was nothing she could do about it at this time, as there was a huge wait in front of them. The hostess said that she could seat them in ninety minutes, but that was only if another couple ate quickly.

David and K2 were pretty mad at first, but calmed down quickly. David brightened as he thought of an idea: "Hey, I said that I owe you dinner tonight, Katherine. And I always keep my promises. What say you to an ad hoc home-cooked meal? We can go to the Trader Joes' grocery store near my condo, and then I can make you a true North Carolina clam fritter dish or something like that. We can get pre-made stuff too."

"OK, but then you have to let me make my mom's special recipe of special Chinese chicken salad, and then of course, as promised, I have to buy the wine."

"You're on," David smiled, as they walked out of the restaurant. "I'll even buy dessert," he added magnanimously. Briefly, they both considered whether Marcia had deviously planned this to happen or not, but by now they didn't care one bit. David's condo was in Alexandria, where a number of military personnel lived. It wasn't a super "hip" place for young professionals like Adams-Morgan was, but it had a great, comfortable vibe for thirtyish year old types like David and K2.

When they got to David's condo, David began to get a little anxious. "Just to warn you, my condo's a little, uh, spartan. I don't have a lot of stuff at all. And it's a little, umm, college dorm-like."

"No need to explain, David," K2 replied gently, "I have a brother who sounds like he has your similar decorating style and approach."

David opened the door and K2 smiled. "Yup, pretty much what I thought." She surveyed the condo. The main living room was fairly spacious, and contained a single couch with a "coffee table" in front of it. The "coffee table" consisted of a long plywood board sitting on top of two large milk crates. A flat screen TV rested on top of a wall unit. A cheap IKEA bookcase filled with history books and military biographies rounded out the furniture. The wall where a large window looked out on the streets of Old Town Alexandria, and was filled with neatly stacked plastic bottles of flavored water, about six bottles high and extending down most of the length of the wall. "Oh my god, you're right -- very dorm-like," she laughed. "Ooh, I love this brand of flavored water. Real natural and no added sugar."

"Yeah, I down this stuff like, well, like water," he said sheepishly. "Trying to lay off having too much sugar in my diet these days."

"Are you sure you're not Californian?" K2 said.

"Don't let my dad hear you say that," David said jokingly in mock horror. "We Smithlines are ten generations in North Carolina, mostly around Raleigh and the Outer Banks. For him, California is just the land of the fruits and nuts, and I mean like nutcases. Well, except for Orange County."

They bantered like this for the whole time as they were making their delicious dinner, which tasted ten times better, they both knew, because of the company. David moved to put away the dishes into the dishwasher but it was full already so he stacked the dishes and the serving plates into the sink. His face grimaced a little as he finished stacking the plates.

"Kind of bothers you, I see, that everything doesn't fit into the dishwasher. You have the All-Things-Must-Be-Clean-Neat-And-Orderly disease like I do. A little obsessive-compulsive, aren't we, Mr. OCD?"

"Agreed, Ms. OCD," David admitted. "However, the dishwasher is full and it will take thirty minutes to run a cycle."

"Haven't you ever heard of washing your dishes by hand, Mr. OCD?" K2 shot back. "You know, in my house, we never even ran the dishwasher. It was just used as a dish rack after we washed all of the dishes by hand. I do the same thing most of the time."

"Wow, for a tech girl like yourself, that's pretty shocking to me. Are you a Luddite or something?"

"Ha, ha. Just someone who saves water, David. Here, let me teach you some basic skills that you are clearly lacking," K2 continued as she moved behind David. Turning on the sink faucet, Katherine moved to stand right behind David and took a sponge, soaped it, and placed it and her hand into his. "So what you do is do a first pass and really get the soap all over the plate first," she said.

David's head was swimming from K2's warm breath next to his ear. He thought that he had never felt better in his whole life. He moved his hand, holding both the sponge and K2's hand, around the edge of the plate. "You mean, like this?"

"Exactly," K2 said breathlessly. "You know, I think you got it. I think ..." she started, but never finished her sentence as David had turned around slowly, inhaling K2's scent as he placed the plate carefully down in the bottom of the sink and turned off the water. Taking a drying cloth that was on the counter, he meticulously dried each of K2's fingers, caressing each other of them dry.

"I do think I have it," he said as he finished. A few strands of K2's hair had fallen down near the front of her face, and David gently brushed them back to their original position. "You know," he said, "I really think you are a wonderful person. I just wanted you to know that."

K2 blushed. "David, I think you are the finest, most amazing person that I have ever met," she said, taking the cloth and drying David's hands in return. She stroked the back of her hands along David's upper arms absently. David felt the heat rising at every touch by K2, and his arms felt a mini spark of electricity each time she touched him.

Slowly, treasuring the moment, David cupped K2's face with his hands, marveling at how the kitchen light sparkled in her lustrous skin. "Let me show you how wonderful I think you are," David said softly. His lips felt magnetically drawn then to her lips as they kissed for the first time. They both closed their eyes and reveled at the internal fireworks happening inside their brains. K2 sighed involuntarily and their lips hungrily sought each other's out again. Both of them by this time had closed their eyes, savoring the memory of this first kiss. When they both opened their eyes, somehow they had already unknowingly started to move over to the couch, where K2 ended up half-sitting on David's lap as David kissed her neck and lips and face again and again in uncontrollable succession.

"We have to wash dishes together more often," K2 cracked, as they both burst out laughing.

PART II

"Bad things come in groups of three."
-Ancient Superstition

CHAPTER 13

David and K2 quickly started dating formally after that night. They now had been a couple for around four months, settling into a comfortable routine. Since David was normally based in Washington, DC, and K2 in the Bay Area, one significant problem was figuring out how to handle a long-distance relationship. Fortunately, K2's boss, Don Llewes got wind of their situation from Marcia and was sympathetic to their predicament. He had arranged something that would work out for the benefit of NEST and them. John Van Dyke, the leader of NEST's East Coast Roosevelt Diamond Augmentation Team, was unfortunately now in the hospital and unable to fulfill his duties because of his cancer. Because of this, and for the good of the Roosevelt Diamond team, John announced his retirement soon thereafter. But this unfortunate situation allowed Don to make Katherine the temporary head of the Roosevelt Diamond. Ben Yang was forced to be the temporary head of Lincoln Diamond in the West Coast, until a suitable replacement could be found for John.

Ben was unhappy about this new situation, but when the rumors and finally truth spread about David and K2's relationship, Ben's displeasure at the temporary situation was blunted. "Ha, now I've got you, K2. You owe me one, after you come back to Lincoln Diamond," Ben said mischievously. "You know how much I hate doing all of this admin work."

K2 rented a place near David's so that they saw each other every day. It was still the dawn of their relationship, and the lovers enjoyed learning little secrets about the other. For example, who would have thought that they both enjoyed doing crossword puzzles? One of their great pleasures in their lives became lazing around together on Sunday morning at their neighborhood café finishing (or almost finishing) the New York Times Sunday crossword.

However, their idyllic life didn't last too long. Their work lives would be thrown back in turmoil again. This time, at least, they weren't woken up at 0445 hours in the morning by their pagers buzzing out a priority code alpha alert. Instead, this new priority code alpha alert happened during normal business hours on an otherwise unremarkable Thursday in mid-May. David and K2 drove together in David's car at warp speed to get to Joint Base Andrews.

Once again, the meeting occurred in the "war room" in Building Five. Pretty much the same cast of characters was present. At exactly 1430 hours ET, a visibly shaken President Besselman came on the videoconference and asked the HSA to initially address the gathering.

Jorgensen reprised his role as the messenger of bad news. "Ladies and Gentlemen, I cannot believe what I am about to tell you. We think that there two more RA-115s en route to the US." Cries of disbelief echoed through the room. "We're going to give you a quick background of why we think this. After Operation Safety Screen was completed, as you know, we had essentially started a major war between Al Qods, now run operationally by Ahmad Nazari for the moderate clerics, and the Chechens, run by Colonel Umarov. Nazari has always hated the Chechens and was infuriated that Umarov had sold Rahimi a nuke, let alone a defective nuke. Nazari thinks that the Chechens are always trying to make Iran look bad. So Nazari, through his organization's soldiers, and through other proxies, engaged in about a dozen assassination attempts against Umarov and the key officers in his group. We think that, altogether, each organization killed about one hundred to three hundred members of the other organization. It's been a bloodbath. Nazari blew up two ammunition depots of Umarov's as well. Nazari came really close to killing the Colonel, but Umarov seems to have nine lives like a cat. Jack Smith's DIA group will give you more information."

Jack Smith started the videoconference feed as he spoke. "As HSA Jorgensen noted, Nazari almost killed Umarov numerous times. Umarov saw that he was in deep trouble. Nazari is known as a particularly tenacious bastard, who would never give up trying to kill an enemy like Umarov. So the Colonel decided to take his money and run. Like all of these arms dealer kingpins, Umarov had a number of hidden bank accounts strewn across the world and a pre-set plan about how to disappear. Umarov went to the Caribbean, picking up a whole bunch of money in the Cayman Islands on the way to the island of St. Martin. But somehow, someone in his organization sold him out to Nazari once he saw that Umarov was leaving them. Probably gave him up for a couple of million dollars in payoff money, we think. So a group of assassins were sent by Nazari to the French side of the island, where Umarov owns a big mansion through a complex corporate arrangement. Another bloodbath ensued – note this happened only yesterday. Most of Umarov's inner circle of trusted advisors and bodyguards were killed this time, although Umarov yet again managed to survive. So Umarov now is in a major panic. His key advisors are dead, and he doesn't know who to trust. So last night he got in touch with our Caribbean CIA chief and offered up a deal. We help him truly disappear and he gives us some significant, actionable information that he says we really need to know immediately. D-95 will let us know about what Umarov told us;" he said as he pointed to have the participants look at the videoconference screen. An image of an Afro-Caribbean man with his face and voice distorted electronically showed up. "Please fill us in on the latest."

D-95 cleared his throat and spoke up in a lilting, Caribbean-accented English: "For the last six hours or so, we have been interrogating Colonel Umarov at our CIA safe house in the US Virgin Islands on St. Thomas. Umarov has told us how he got the RA-115 that Amir Abbasi was trying to detonate. Turns out that the Chechen mafiya group, of which Umarov is a senior leader, had gotten hold of the weapon from the GRU strategic arsenal through a series of sordid sex, murder and blackmail schemes. Originally, they had wanted the nuke as countervailing leverage against Putin's control. But now they've given up on that; Putin has too firm a grasp over Chechnya. So Umarov and his group's goal just became to monetize his cache of arms. If we take what Umarov has told us at face value, the total cost of acquiring the nuke was about $3.5 million, and he sold it to Al Qods for about $100 million. Together with some other arms sales shipments, Umarov is saying that he made about $200 million in profit from Rahimi over the past fifteen months alone."

Murmurs were heard throughout the audience; that was serious money. Jack held up his arms for silence, saying: "Look, Umarov is a genius arms dealer and a calculated risk taker. He realized that, for the level of risk he was taking to get one RA-115, he might as well double-down, or triple-down, in his bet to get a nuke. This was a once-in-a-lifetime opportunity with his insider GRU contact. So he didn't just go for one nuke. He risked about $10 million to try to get three nukes. He reasoned that he needed to buy more because he might not be successful in acquiring all of them. He ended up getting all three."

"Who bought the other RA-115s?" Vice President Branden demanded. "What did that bastard Umarov say about that?"

"That was the big question, Mr. Vice President, Jack replied. "Umarov wouldn't tell us unless we signed a full immunity and protection document. Presidential and Attorney General approval of that document happened two hours ago. Don't worry; he's going to live a crappy life looking over his shoulder all the time to see if someone's trying to kill him. Also, he's not getting any money from us taxpayers to live in any kind of luxury. After Umarov was satisfied with the paperwork, he told us that one of the nukes was sold around the beginning of September. The second nuke, the Iranian one that we defused, was sold in the beginning of October, while the other third nuke was sold recently, about a month and a half ago. He had planned to sell the last one for a higher price than the first two, but with Nazari after him, plans changed and he actually sold it for less money than the first and second nukes. Let me check my notes here. Yes, he sold the third nuke for only about $80 million. Umarov said that he just wanted to sell the last nuke as fast as he could in order to get out of town as soon as possible. This third, most recently sold, RA-115 went to a group that Umarov believes is affiliated with ISIS."

"Dammit!" roared Vice President Branden, who had been in a congressional meeting and had missed the Presidential and Attorney General meeting. He was fuming both at the situation and the fact that he hadn't been in the loop. "This is completely unacceptable."

"The first RA-115," D-95 now continued, ignoring the outburst as Jack Smith had instructed him to plow on, "meaning the one sold in early September last year, went to some kind of shadow organization that seems loosely affiliated with rogue elements of the North Korean intelligence agencies."

"Dammit!" Vice President Branden yelled out again together with others, punching the conference room table for added emphasis. Branden followed up with the fundamental question on everyone's mind: "Where does Umarov think that the nukes are going to be used?"

"Umarov doesn't know for sure," D-95 replied. "After the money changed hands with the ISIS buyer, one of his Chechen guards who speaks a little Iraqi Arabic thought he heard them murmur excitedly as they were leaving about how this would now allow them to exact "direct" revenge for Osama bin Laden's death. In the context of what was said, Umarov believes that "direct" revenge means that they are going after the people who killed bin Laden."

"You mean Seal Team Six?" K2 asked.

"Yes, exactly, that's exactly what we think" Jack Smith replied. "Like an "eye for an eye" kind of thing. We think that they want to literally take out Seal Team Six, or more formally DEVGRU, so they can say to the world that bin Laden was avenged. On paper, the best way to do that would be through taking out DEVGRU's headquarters. It would be symbolic, like bombing the World Trade Center was symbolic of hitting at Western capitalism. As you know, ISIS had pledged fealty to bin Laden originally, and we had referred to ISIS formerly as "al Qaeda in Iraq," or AQI, before the current ISIS designation. So it makes some kind of perverted sense that they would try to do this."

General McTighe reported dejectedly, "We've got the DEVGRU headquarters group in Virginia Beach on high alert for terrorist activity. Hell, they've been on high alert ever since it was published that they got bin Laden, but now they are on ultra-high alert. We need to quadruple the radiation detection runs. We're also in the process of moving the entire DEVGRU team elsewhere. And we're going to spread them out too, not just move them all to one place."

K2 nodded her head. "We already have a revised protocol that we have been developing for sweeps based on various target locations. We'll get right on the radiation detection plan, General. We can work with Mike, Jonathan, and your other assistant chiefs of staff on it." McTighe nodded his assent.

Jack pushed a button on the videoconference console and a few artist sketches of the main ISIS buyers popped up on the screen. D-95 noted to the group, "Here are the pictures of the ISIS buyers from what Umarov told us. The names are obviously fake, but Umarov said one was nicknamed the Camelmaster. Umarov had heard of him before. The Camelmaster is a lieutenant general in ISIS. We've heard of him too, and we're trying to put together a DIA profile on him, which will be ready tomorrow. One thing that Umarov mentioned is that the Camelmaster may have some Canadian connection. The transaction was done in English, as this was everyone's common second language. Umarov is well-traveled and the Camelmaster didn't exactly have a Canadian accent or anything, but maybe it was something about the English words he chose to say that made Umarov think Canada. A lot of this is sheer speculation and Umarov's gut feeling," D-95 admitted.

"Well, I think we can be pretty sure that they're not going to try to nuke Canada," David said, jumping into the conversation. ISIS has declared Canada one of its enemies, but nuking Toronto doesn't "directly" avenge bin Laden. So I agree that it's like 99% that they're going to try for Seal Team Six. Canada might be the entry point for the nuke, though."

FBI Director Edelman couldn't help but interrupt, "I'm aligned on what people are thinking about ISIS." "But," he added impatiently, "how about the North Korean buyer? What about the other nuke?"

D-95 shrugged. "That's harder. Umarov doesn't know much there. There were twelve people in the North Korean contingent, but from Umarov's perspective there was actually one main guy in charge, a rather distinguished-looking middle-aged man. There was someone else nominally in charge, an older man, but Umarov has a good sense of figuring out who the real power player is, despite appearances. Here's the sketch of the middle-aged guy." Jack flashed a sketch of a person onto the screen that no one knew at all.

"We are trying to build a profile on this guy. To be honest, though, I think that he hasn't ever been on the radar before. Since this is probably a rogue operation, he's probably some deep cover agent coming out of hiding, who has just been activated for this operation. We believe that we are much more likely to find info about the Camelmaster's group," Jack stated to the assembly.

D-95 added, "For the North Korean nuke, Umarov is racking his brain trying to remember any clue about where the nuke might be going. The middle-aged man was pretty well-spoken. Like he was educated in the West, at least for part of his life. He came across as very cultured, maybe some kind of diplomat or something. He enunciated his English very well."

"This is unbelievable," said the Vice President. "Hmm, a diplomat. Don't tell me they're going after Washington, DC."

"OK, ok, everyone, we're not going to play any guessing games. We'll be exploring all angles for both nukes, of course," Marcia said. "David, K2, we're going to need to meet almost right after this meeting to work with Jack and a subteam on the best operations plan."

"Yeah, and we've got a proposed operations name for this already," Jack piped in. "With three nukes being sold, it's only fitting that we call this something like 'Triple Play'. The evil guys are at bat, and we already got one out, and now we're just trying to get the other two."

"Operation 'Triple Play' it is, ladies and gentlemen," President Besselman said. "Now go get those other two nukes. Next general meeting is at 1800 hours Eastern Time tomorrow."

David and K2 prepared for another all-nighter. "I thought we were done with this nonsense," K2 said ruefully as they got into David's car. Marcia, Ron and Don had told them to go home, take a shower, and pack a bunch of clothes because they may be stuck in Joint Base Andrews and/or Joint Base Anacostia-Bolling for a long time. They couldn't rely on being able to go home, even if it was only an hour or so round-trip. "After saving the world, aren't we all supposed to have a happy ending where we all ride off in the sunset as the movie credits roll by?"

David gave K2 a long passionate kiss before they took off. "You are my happy ending," he said earnestly.

K2 gave him a long kiss back. "Good answer," she said. "You might be a keeper."

"This is déjà vu all over again," Mark Childress complained to no one in particular right before the subteam meeting had convened at Joint Base Anacostia-Bolling. "RA-115s all over the f-ing place, and no one knows where they are. Why does everyone want to kill us, and me in particular, man? I'm a lovable guy. I even shower every day," he said, sniffing his shirt, "yup, I'm clean and sweet-smelling. No need to nuke my ass."

"Settle down, Childress," Marcia complained. "It's only 1900 hours; you can get punchy when it's 0300 next morning."

"Yes ma'am," Mark saluted. "Just keeping it light."

Jack Smith started off the meeting abruptly. "Listen, folks. After talking with the President, Ron and Marcia, this subteam has been designated the core "finder" group for Triple Play. We will have two components of the finder group. The first component will be the "I" group. The "I" group will be charged with finding the nuke that we think is affiliated somehow with ISIS. The "K" group will be charged with finding the nuke that we think is affiliated with the North Koreans. Ron runs the whole thing nominally, but day-to-day, Marcia runs this core finder group, and David here is her ops leader. Kind of just like the old days," Jack said. "Oh wait," he said sarcastically, "that was just a few months ago."

"Did you work out anything yet with Mike and Jonathan on the fly-bys?" David asked K2 at the meeting.

"Yup, we already are implementing Phase I of the fly-by plan, everyone," K2 noted. "Think of it as quadrupling our number of radiation detection units and aircraft that we used during Safety Screen. It's necessary because we have much less of an idea where the "K" nuke might be coming in. So we're spread out more and need more planes and copters. For the "I" nuke, our superstar Sabrina McAllister had already been working on an idea that she has already been implementing to basically cover the entire US-Canada border with sensors. These sensors will be all over the place. We'll also surround all routes into and out of Virginia Beach with extra sensors, placing them in concentric circles around DEVGRU headquarters."

The core finder subteam discussed a bunch of various improvements to their plans. At 0200 ET, Katherine went to see Sabrina, who had settled in with her team at the Naval Research Labs, technically just outside the Joint Base.

"We're doing the final testing and deployment of our new sensor," Walter Van de Wiel said.

"What do you think Walt?" asked K2. Since Walt and K2 had been Stanford PhD classmates together, K2 knew about Walt's intellectual firepower, and completely trusted Walt's insights on these matters.

"It's brilliant as I told you before," he confirmed. "I'll let Sabrina take you through the math specifics, since it's her invention, which I had spared you from reviewing last time as we hadn't yet ironed out some minor technical flaws."

"I may have thought of the original idea, Walt, but, quite frankly, you solved the most important production issue we had, so let's call it what it really was, a group effort." Sabrina pointed to the whiteboard and began her presentation, whizzing through the maze of mathematical symbols like some sort of magician. "And in conclusion," she finished about fifteen minutes later, "that allows us to shrink the package to something basketball-sized. These spheres are networked via our military cellular system and the false-positives are reduced by at least two orders of magnitude."

"I think I have the nuances of it now," K2 said, nodding her head appreciatively. "It's mainly because of the narrowness of the radiation signature parameters, and your optimizing algorithm here," she continued, as she pointed to one block of equations. "That allows the sensor footprint to shrink by orders of magnitude."

"Yup," Sabrina replied. "that's it. We have a tool with a really specific purpose, and it'll be smaller and better than the general purpose sensor we're using now, with way better limits of detection, further helped by some new optimization formulas. Here's the analogy: Don has approved our placing 12,000 new basketballs from a helicopter in about equally spaced intervals to cover essentially the entire Canadian-US border. We have already starting implementing the plans, and have about 10,000 new basketball sensors in place there. These sensors help supplement our existing sensor network, which probably had a 50-70% chance to discover a nuke. Now I think we can bump that up to a 99% chance, unless it's being significantly shielded. We don't think that ISIS has the technological capability to understand how to make this shielding. We can do the final deployment within the next 24 to 48 hours."

"The key is that we couldn't do this before," Walt added. "Instead of dropping 12,000 basketball-sized objects, we would have had to drop 12,000 moving van-sized objects from helicopters to do the same thing. And it would have taken at least a few months to build each moving van on top of that. The sensor shrinkage is the brilliant part, of course."

"And how about Virginia Beach?"

"The plan is, concurrently with the Canada effort, to place about 50 basketball-sized sensors around Virginia Beach, and another 100 in concentric circles around the area, up to a 100 mile radius," Sabrina reported. "And we can always extend the radius as we desire or need."

"How many "basketballs" can we make a day?"

"Well, we're ramping up production. Right now, we can make about four to five thousand per day," Sabrina said. "The next part of the plan is to cover the US-Mexico border within 72 to 96 hours."

"Great work, guys," K2 said. "This is awesome!" she added enthusiastically. Ben and Sri had helped out a bit in the design and were equally excited. This was going to work.

CHAPTER 14

The Camelmaster, Ali al-Jamil, didn't feel like a master of anything. Ali just felt really hungry and tired. He and his three ISIS colleagues did not appreciate Western food that much, but it would do in a pinch, and it had had to do for the last few months. In the months of March and April, Ali al-Jamil and these three colleagues had taken a circuitous journey from Chechnya, through Russia all the way to the port of Vladivostok. From there, they had secured berths on various freighters, ultimately ending up in western Canada.

Canadian port security had been beefed up considerably since the September 11, 2001 terrorist attacks in the United States, and so, following a little bribery, Ali had arranged for a small boat to meet the freighter far before it was scheduled to dock near Vancouver. The four of them had been able to leave the freighter this way without detection, together with their treasured possession, the RA-115, which had been stored in a small crate off of the main cargo hold.

The small boat had docked in an out of the way marina near the outskirts of Vancouver, where a nondescript van, driven by his cousin Abu, also a Canadian citizen, had been waiting for them and their payload. The ISIS leadership had hotly debated what the best route would be to get the nuke into the United States. Most had preferred a southern route, through Mexico, but the most senior leaders rejected this as it would be expected. The leaders thought there would be a higher probability of success if they did the unexpected. Since Ali and Abu had Canadian citizenship, they would try to bring the RA-115 into the United States through western Canada.

Furthermore, after much discussion, Ali had convinced his ISIS handlers that Ali and Abu should go alone, without the other three ISIS colleagues, who were not Canadian and who did not speak English very well. Ali felt that the other three would draw unnecessary attention. So it was agreed that the other three ISIS members would stay in western Canada and wait for Ali to return. That way, if the two cousins were ever stopped along the way, either in Canada or the US, they would simply show their valid Canadian passports, arousing far less suspicion.

But Ali and Abu were not naïve enough to believe that, just because they were Canadian citizens, they could just drive up through a US-Canada customs checkpoint with a RA-115 in their trunk. In December 1999, even before checkpoint security was beefed up, Ahmed Ressam, an Algerian living in Montreal, Quebec, was caught by an alert customs official who thought that Ahmed was acting a little too nervously at the US-Canadian checkpoint. In the trunk of Ressam's car, customs officials found a significant number of explosives. Ahmed was planning to detonate these explosives and take out parts of the Los Angeles International Airport.

No, Ali had argued vociferously that the two of them would need to sneak over the border with the nuke in some remote area of Canada where they would not be detected. The ISIS handlers left the specific plan design up to Ali, who was more familiar with Canadian geography. Overall, the mission objective called for Ali to arrive at his ultimate destination of Naval Air Station Oceana, Seal Team Six's headquarters in Virginia Beach, Virginia, by the end of the summer.

Right about the time that Katherine and Sabrina McAllister were having their conversation about the new sensors, Ali and Abu were staying in a cabin that Ali had rented near Medicine Hat in Alberta, Canada. Only two nights before, they had been loading the van with the RA-115. While Ali had originally planned to leave tomorrow, if he felt that the coast was clear and they hadn't been traced; the weather was just not cooperating. The local weatherman had indicated that there was a 95% chance of a big rainstorm tomorrow; Ali didn't want to travel through this storm and risk an accident. They would be patient to avoid mistakes. The Camelmaster was getting close to his day of vengeance.

CHAPTER 15

The next day found a number of the FBI Glow team in helicopters placing additional radiation detection sensors in strategic points around the US-Canada border. Supposedly, these "basketballs" could withstand any amount of rain and snow, but after consultations with the technical team, the FBI agents were told to try to shield some of the most exposed sensors rather than just letting them remain open to the elements.

Johnny G could barely hear his team leader Richie Gutierrez over the wind and rain and the whirring of the helicopter blades. "Are you ready for deployment yet?" Richie was saying.

Rather than replying verbally, Johnny G simply gave Richie an unmistakable thumbs up sign. The helicopter hovered just above the top of a remote ridge in Montana as Johnny G and Ronnie Williams were lowered from the helicopter via a cable winch system. When they got to the ground, Richie sent out some wood and tarps. Johnny and Ronnie quickly built a little wooden platform that they nailed to the middle of a tree. Four feet above the platform, the two tied a thin tarp around some tree branches that allowed the platform itself to remain dry and sheltered from the wind. Finally, a box containing the "basketball" was lowered to the two and they carefully secured the sensor to the platform with some metal brackets. The sensor itself had markings on it denoting that the device was "US Government Property." It also was marked "National Weather Service Sensor – Civil and Criminal Penalties for Tampering and/or Removal" to deter hikers or other passers-by from touching the valuable pieces of equipment. Not that this was likely; most of these sensors were being placed in very remote, generally inaccessible areas.

"I feel like I'm building a treehouse again," Johnny said to Ronnie.

"I know; it's like I'm in my backyard again when I was ten," Ronnie replied. Ronnie flipped a switch on the basketball and it began the process of powering up. Five minutes later, the sensor had completed its diagnostic routines and was broadcasting a signal to the other sensor that had been placed about 25 miles away. A synchronization occurred, and one more sensor was added to the network. 11,350 sensors had now been fully deployed along the US-Canada border, with about 650 remaining to be deployed within the next 24 to 36 hours.

"Confirming that Balls A-11000 through A-11350 are up and running perfectly," Sabrina radioed to Richie. "Good job guys, keep it going."

"Man, I'm waterlogged," Johnny G said to Ronnie. "Rob Malo's team have got Mexico duty, lucky bastards. Billy's with them because they are a man short. Billy said they're going to finish most of Texas tomorrow and he's promised to get us some Tex-Mex at this sweet little dive near El Paso, as he's coming back to us the next day," he confided to Ronnie. "Even reheated, those burritos are the best."

"I'll pay for the burritos if you hammer the next three treehouses, bro," Ronnie replied. "The hammer slipped and I nailed my finger something awful."

"You've got a deal, bro," came the response, as the rain continued to pour down on the two. It was monotonous work, but oddly the anticipation of some good Tex-Mex food gave them the little psychological boost that they needed to keep going. The vast majority of the members of the FBI sharpshooter team were good that way, able to use any little thing to trick their own brains into higher performance.

CHAPTER 16

At the next all-hands meeting, Vice President Branden presided as the President was at a state dinner hosting the Prime Minister of Singapore. K2 and Sabrina took the team through the sensor deployment situation. A digital map showed the group where the detection equipment had been set up already throughout the US-Canada border. The entire group was actually quite impressed with how fast that NEST had set up its additional land-based sensor system. A series of fly-bys had also occurred and would continue on a daily basis, but nothing material had been found yet (just two false-positive readings). A member of Jack's team delivered a brief update to the team that they had so far found nothing material about the North Korean terrorists. The Vice President, learning his lesson from the last experience, kept his cool better this time with the lack of information, but exhorted the team to work harder to get a lead on the North Korean nuke.

Jack then personally delivered the report on the Camelmaster. "Unfortunately, we don't know the alias that the Camelmaster is using now. He was born Ali al-Jamil, a distant relative of the ISIS leader, Abu Bakr al-Baghdadi. He was partially educated in Montreal, Quebec and Toronto, Ontario, so he speaks fluent French as well as fluent English. We believe that he carries at least five different Canadian passports, obviously under very different names and occupations. He'll look a little different too for each of those aliases. Ali al-Jamil's been very effective as a behind-the-scenes operator for the group, both when it was known as AQI and now that it is known as ISIS or ISIL. His cover has often been as an importer of fine Middle Eastern goods, like Egyptian and Turkish ceramics, as well as all sorts of Middle Eastern rugs and blankets. That was when he used the passport with the name "Ken Deeb," a merchant allegedly from Cairo. However, he appears to have gone off the grid now, as Interpol and the Royal Canadian Mounted Police had started to scrutinize some of his businesses."

"Where in Canada do we think he is living now?" David asked.

"He's been in the wind," Jack admitted. "We don't really have any idea where he might be. Last known location was Montreal, but that was about a year ago. They've had an Interpol red notice out for 'Ken Deeb' for the last five months, although it's really unlikely that he's using that passport now and he's probably changed his appearance considerably. We at DIA, and our colleagues at CIA, all think that our best shot is for NEST to get a radiation signature on the nuke. We have another angle, though, that we are working on: Canadians are allowed to travel to the US for four to six months each year. So it is possible that the Camelmaster came through already within the last six months, and then snuck back across the border back to Canada. The thinking is that, since he's going to have to sneak back into the US, this would allow him to have a stamp showing that he previously validly entered within the last six months if he's ever stopped in the US."

"Wow, that sounds like a lot of records to comb through. Let me get this straight – you are going to look through all valid entrants by Canadian citizens or permanent residents from Canada to the US over the past six months?"

"Yup. We can eliminate the women and children, and then see what we get, and then hone in on candidates based on the pictures. Admittedly, he could probably just as easily forge a stamp to put on his fake passport. That would pass muster if all he wants to do is to look legit if he gets stopped by a US traffic cop. So it is possible that he hasn't come through within the last six months and we're just wasting our time. I'm also not saying that just knowing his current alias would necessarily be that helpful. We are assuming that he hasn't changed his appearance from that current alias. If we find a current alias, all we can do is put out an APB on that name and likeness. Like I said from the beginning, DIA thinks that the best bet is for NEST to find the nuke. Find the nuke, and then automatically we've found Ali al-Jamil."

"Agreed," K2 and Sabrina said concurrently. "NEST will find that nuke."

CHAPTER 17

The weather still hadn't cleared up, so Ali and Abu ended up having to stay in the Medicine Hat cabin for an extra two days. However, on the third day, on May 19, the rain stopped and the two were able to leave very early in the morning. They were about an eight hour drive away from their final Canadian destination. This was another cabin near Turtle Mountain Provincial Park, an idyllic park set among lakes in the southwestern part of Manitoba province, and adjacent to the state of North Dakota. Purposefully chosen as a remote border crossing area, Ali and Abu believed that this area would represent the best chance for them to enter the US without being detected. Unlike Mexico, where the border patrol is always on the guard against illegal immigrants, hardly any Americans ever thought about border security with respect to their neighbors to the north.

That was what Ali and Abu were betting on anyway. "You tired?" Abu asked, as he saw Ali yawn a few times as they continued eastward on Trans-Canada Highway 1. The day was turning out not only to be free of rain, but a gorgeously clear and fine mid-May day. There were scores of Canadian geese flying in formation in the sky. The ice had finally all melted in the lakes and it felt more like spring than it had a few weeks ago when the ice hadn't receded yet.

Ali yawned again. "I'm a little tired. But let's keep to the plan; we'll switch and you can drive when we get past Moose Jaw."

"You got it, cousin. Are you sure this plan is going to work?"

"No problem. We get to the Canadian side of Lake Metigoshe. Our contact has a small boat there, and it will transport us and the bomb over to the US side in the late evening. We boat over to the cabin that I've rented on that US side, so we can hide out there tonight. I bought a van a long time ago that our contact has retrofitted to store the nuke. I had our contact drive that van into the garage of the cabin. Then, tomorrow morning, we drive off in that van for the East Coast, just like that. So you see, this will be really easy. I've gone back and forth between Canada and the US twice this way already."

"Yes, but not with a 2 kiloton nuclear weapon in your vehicle, dear cousin."

"Granted, but there's a first time for everything," Ali smiled, as they kept at the speed limit on the highway. A road sign ahead said: Moose Jaw 25km, Turtle Mountain Provincial Park 500km. They would be there in around five hours.

CHAPTER 18

At the May 19th general meeting, David reported that the state of affairs was the same as for the last few days: nothing new had been found about the location of the two nukes. The mood was not overly glum, though. From a process standpoint, all of the "basketball" sensors had long been put into place by now. The Triple Play team would now likely have early warning of any nukes crossing the Canadian or Mexican borders, or nearing the Virginia Beach corridor. In addition, FBI sharpshooter teams had been stationed at various strategic US-Canada border locations so that they could respond quickly as needed.

So the detection plan had been fully implemented. The assault teams also had their tactical plans in place for what to do when a nuke was detected. Now all that the Triple Play team could do was to wait.

"What do you think, David?" HSA Jorgensen asked, closing out the meeting. "Do you think that there is any specific date that the ISIS or North Korean terrorists are targeting to detonate the nukes? Are we on some kind of imminent countdown?"

"Well, Pat, the intelligence folks have been analyzing this for us day and night," David replied. "We can never be 100% sure, but so far it doesn't feel like there is a specific date for these particular detonations. It's not like the New Year's Eve situation we just faced when the idea was to inflict the maximum number of casualties. If we are right about the ISIS terrorists, there is no focal date that they have to exact what they think is retribution for the SEALs killing bin Laden. It's already past May 2, the anniversary of Osama's death, so that seemingly "natural" date is not likely. I don't think they are going to wait almost a year to set off the nuke. The intelligence analysts looked at July 4th as a possibility. Remember, though, September 11 wasn't viewed as a natural, "focal" date either, and yet Al Qaeda chose that date for their 2001 attack."

"With respect to the North Korean nuke," Jack added on behalf of David, "it's even harder to say anything about potential detonation dates, since we don't even know the target. Let's assume that it's Washington, DC. Then July 4th does kind of make sense, but who knows? What's that Tom Clancy novel? Oh yeah, I remember now, it's called The Sum of All Fears. That's when some terrorists try to set off a bomb during the Super Bowl. Well, the Super Bowl is long over this year. But there's the Stanley Cup finals and the NBA finals around June; it's possible that they would target a sporting event, I guess. Sounds kind of farfetched, however. The point is that we don't really have any actionable information. Maybe they are going to try to do New York City and set off the bomb in the new One World Trade Center area. We just don't have enough data to do a meaningful analysis now."

The HSA nodded. "All right, I get it. What you are saying about each situation does make some sense. Keep me posted on any new intelligence." And just like that, after a few more minutes of discussion, that day's meeting was over.

Less than five hours later, a general alert buzzed as one of the "basketballs" had been activated. The reading was really high, so it immediately caught everyone's attention. The few false positives that had previously occurred didn't have nearly as high a signal reading. This was likely the real thing.

"Holy crap!" Don exclaimed. "I feel it; this is the 'I' nuke."

Sabrina McAllister punched a few buttons on the main equipment console. "Signal's coming from North Dakota. Near Turtle Mountain Provincial Park in Manitoba."

"Who's closest?" barked Edelman.

David answered quickly, after glancing at the log records, "Richie, Johnny G and Ronnie W are nearest, really close actually, as they're stationed at Minot AFB. Must be less than 100 miles or so away by air. They can scramble out there in their Black Hawk helicopter in about an hour or so."

"Get them ready to deploy in the morning," ordered Marcia. FBI Director Edelman nodded his approval.

"You got it Marcia," David replied.

K2 nodded. "Sri's there too with a small NEST team. We've got a 'Hot Spot Mobile' truck there already that they can deploy, and we can send up the Bell helicopter too. The King Air plane is about six hours away. We can do a zero-in from the satellite too. Quadruple verification at its best."

"Deploy the NEST folks tonight, and have them provide intel to the rest of the team, in coordination with Johnny and Ronnie, tau one protocol," Marcia said.

"Roger that. We're on it," David further replied. "Standard tau protocol is in motion."

The satellite image grew in intensity on the main screen, and after every click by Sabrina, it zoomed in even further. Turtle Mountain was a beautiful park, made even more pretty by the fact that the snow had just melted recently and the fact that there weren't a lot of people buzzing around the park. School was still in session and the summer crowds had not yet arrived.

A bright red dot indicated where the satellites and the "basketball" sensors estimated that the nuke was located. The dot had slowly moved across the lake from the Canadian side to the US side, and looked like it was now in a small cabin near the edge of Lake Metigoshe.

"Do you think that we should take out the nuke now?" asked the HSA.

Marcia replied, "Well, sir, our protocol is to wait for more troops to converge on the area and to assess the situation more fully. Only if we think that the nuke is going live would we act immediately. Since it's unlikely that they are going to detonate the nuke here in Lake Metigoshe, we'll probably stand down until the morning at least."

David concurred, "As Marcia noted, there are just no significant targets here that we are worried about. The location of the nuke is near the International Peace Garden, which is at the border over here," he pointed to a spot east of the lake less than 20 miles away, "but the Garden itself is hardly a likely target. Another reason not to go disable the nuke tonight is that it's also supposed to be a clear day tomorrow. It'll be way easier to take them down in the daytime when our sharpshooters will have better vision."

"How many people can we get over there by sunrise tomorrow morning?" Edelman demanded.

"Looks like maybe about twenty shooters. We only have one Humvee in the area, though, for now, but it looks like we will be able to get two more into Minot Air Force Base by, say, 0730 hours local time," David responded.

"Folks, here's Plan A for tomorrow," Marcia announced. "The nuke is probably going to be transported by van starting tomorrow morning. We gather our troops and assess the situation when they are all present tomorrow morning. My preference is to take out the nuke in an isolated area, far away from other people. Luckily, this is not high season, so there aren't a lot of tourists in the park yet. Works perfectly for us."

Now that the uncertainty was gone, the Triple Play team could let their professionalism take over as they prepared. Richie, Johnny G and Ronnie forced themselves to sleep earlier than usual so that they would be better rested for the next morning. Since they were there on-site already (and the others had to take red-eye flights over to the area), the Glow 1 team was designated as the primary sharpshooter group for the takedown. The sharpshooters would support the Black Hawk helicopter with the 30mm cannons.

CHAPTER 19

On the morning of May 20th, Ali al-Jamil got up at 7 am. The morning indeed was clear. Sunrise already had occurred about an hour before. He woke up his cousin and the two enjoyed the morning scenery. A few heron were around feeding on some fish in the lake. The morning sun was already making the lake's surface sparkle like a thousand candles had been lit in the water.

Ali and Abu had their breakfast, cleaning and putting away their breakfast dishes carefully. The kitchen had been previously stocked with road-friendly food that they liked, including granola bars, chicken jerky, fruit juices and water. This would allow them to travel in the van for long distances without stopping for food. After carefully packing these food items into the van, the two took a little walk around the lakefront to get some exercise in before getting into the van. The plan was to drive all the way to Omaha, Nebraska, about 700 miles away, before calling it quits for the day.

From there, they would play it by ear. Most likely, they would try to go through Kansas City and St. Louis, taking I-64 all the way to Virginia Beach. If they felt unsafe traveling that far on major highways, the backup plan was to take some smaller roads, especially through Western Virginia as they approached their destination. It would all depend on how they felt about things in the moment.

"Ready to go yet?" Abu pleaded to his friend. "We don't want to start too late."

"Let me enjoy the beginning of the last leg of our journey," Ali complained gently as he breathed in the clean lake air deeply. "You did not have to go through Grozny and eastern

Russia as I did, my cousin. Nor did you have to brave the Pacific on a freighter journey. This portion of the journey is the easy part."

"I am not complaining," Abu said to placate his cousin. "Our ISIS compatriots and I appreciate the suffering you have had to undergo for the cause. I am just eager to start, and we don't want to get there too late tonight."

Ali nodded. "I know, I know," he sighed. "I didn't mean to snap at you. I am as anxious about completing our mission as you are. Let's go. You drive first." And so they got into the van and began to drive away from their cabin.

Unbeknownst to them, NEST's "Hot Spot One" mobile van, disguised as a telephone company repair truck, was monitoring their every movement.

"Bogey is on the move," Sri reported. "Repeat, the "I" bogey is on the move."

"Roger that, Hot Spot One," came the reply. Richie Gutierrez, Johnny G and Ronnie Williams nodded to each other. The three checked and re-checked their weaponry. They were already airborne in a modified Black Hawk, Hawk One, ready to take out the van as needed to support the Terminator. The "Terminator" was the nickname for another Black Hawk helicopter that was armed to the teeth with 30mm cannons and air-to-surface missiles. The Terminator also had a foamer device that could envelop the van completely in foam before the cannons would shoot it up. Hawk One also had a sister copter, Hawk Two, that contained a backup sharpshooter team.

Four Humvees were ready to go, set up in groups of two. One group would cover the southern road and one would cover the eastern route. They would be deployed ahead of the van, pretending to be a slow-moving US Army convoy of military vehicles. When the van caught up to the convoy position, the helicopters and Humvees, working together, would vector in on the van and disable it.

Sri radioed in further information. "Watch out, guys. Here they come. Bogey is going the eastern route; just turning onto State Highway 43. Heading out to you, Cannon 2 and Cannon 4. Cannons 1 and 3, intercept will be in quadrant C4 in two minutes."

"Roger that, Hot Spot One," Steve Johnson from Cannon 2 and Joe Jacobsen from Cannon 4 replied.

"All right, E(ye)-in-steins, you did your job, now it's time for you to watch us do ours," Richie said.

Cannons 2 and 4 synchronized their speed to a slow fifteen miles per hour as they moved eastward on State Highway 43. Behind them was a covered jeep with a big sign on it saying "CAUTION! SLOW MOVING US GOVERNMENT MILITARY VEHICLES." The covered jeep also had the obligatory flashing yellow lights attached to its top. The convoy was a little over three miles ahead of Ali and Abu's van. Terminator was gearing up its 30mm cannons and Hawk One and Hawk Two were nearing ready position. Takedown was in one minute.

Back in DC, Triple Play headquarters was abuzz with adrenaline. Marcia and David were pacing around expectantly, as Marcia would give the official order for the takedown. "We need to wait for the van to pass into the clearing," she instructed. "Will happen in t minus 50 seconds."

Perhaps a sixth sense tugged at Ali as he drove down the highway. Something felt wrong. Why was there a US Army convoy ahead of them? He quickly switched off the music in the van, which had been playing some Arabic music that he stored on his phone's playlist. He heard the faint whisper of rotor blades coming from above.

"Turn off on the service road here! Now!" Ali screamed to Abu, who, startled, involuntarily complied with a jerk of the wheel. The van bumped along the dirt road, swerving left to right as Abu struggled to regain control of the vehicle.

"Dammit!" David exclaimed. "They must have gotten spooked."

"Instructions? Do I take the shot?" yelled the gunner on the Terminator.

"Take the shot, Terminator! You are cleared to take the shot!" Marcia shouted.

The 30mm cannon roared from the Terminator chopper, with only one of the shots hitting the van which was still careening wildly. Hawk One dove down to get into a closer position, but safely away from the hail of fire emanating from the Terminator. Another shot from the 30mm cannon took out the left front wheel of the van, and the van slammed into a copse of trees, bouncing off one of the trees, and finally coming to rest next to another, near to a denser growth of trees that was part of a forested area. The Terminator confirmed that the bogey was stopped, and it fired another set of 30mm cannon rounds at the vehicle, which blew out the driver's side of the van. Then the Terminator reported that it was engaging the foamer cycle. Swooping down, the Terminator shot forth a billowing and growing plume of foam onto the van.

Inside the van, Abu lay dead, parts of his body slumped over the steering wheel and the other parts nowhere to be found. Ali shook himself out of his pain, as he had made his way to the back of the van as the chaos was unfolding. He had made it to the back seat where the nuke was stored before the shooting had started. Fortunately for him, he had been able to put a seat belt on, or else he would have been dead already, ejected out of the rear window in all likelihood. Now he unfastened his seat belt with a groan. Looking over at where Abu once was, he let out a cry in grief for his cousin and friend. Ali then resolutely yanked himself out of his seat and opened the compartment containing the RA-115. Putting it on his back, and grabbing a machine gun that was stashed nearby, the Camelmaster opened the rear door and rolled out of the van quickly. A thick viscous white foam covered just about every part of the outside of the van and was all over the ground in a radius of fifty feet around the vehicle. Finally succeeding in fighting through the foam, he grunted and took off running towards the forest, trying to remain shielded by the cover of the trees.

As soon as the Terminator had finished its last blast of foam, Hawk One and Hawk Two swooped down again, looking for any survivors.

"There," shouted Jim, pointing at a spot on the big screen back in the conference room at Joint Base Anacostia-Bolling, "quadrant M4. Moving towards the deeper tree cover."

"On it!" screamed Richie Gutierrez, as Hawk One sped towards the quadrant. Ronnie Williams prepared to fire his machine gun, ready to shoot as soon as he saw the target. The scene was chaotic in the extreme. Humvees could be heard converging on the area and Hawk Two was buzzing above using its infrared sensors to pinpoint Ali's location. A dozen FBI assault team members were running into the forest chasing Ali.

Richie and Johnny G were fast-winched down by Hawk One ahead of these colleagues, into perfect position right next to the forest. Richie and Johnny G landed and simultaneously ran towards Ali's broadcasted location, sniper rifles in hand.

Ronnie unloaded a torrent of machine gun fire into quadrant M4 from inside the helicopter, barely missing Ali who was running out of energy from running and dodging between trees and rocks in the area.

Hiding behind a large tree and boulder outcropping, Ali realized that this was his last stand. He wriggled out of the backpack and opened up the monitor console. *Oh well*, he thought to himself, *while I can't take out SEAL Team Six, at least I can set off a nuke inside the United States.* Ronnie Williams unloaded a second blast of machine gun fire at Ali, pinning him down behind the tree and rock outcropping.

But Richie had taken a different angle and was on the other side of the rock, about fifteen feet higher than Ali and only fifty yards away, unobserved by Ali. He saw Ali taking off the backpack and preparing to activate the nuke.

This is what all my training has been for, Richie thought to himself. He aimed his sniper rifle at Ali, took a short breath, let it out, and then blasted a perfect kill shot at Ali, right as Ali was concentrating on opening the console. Time stood still for everyone as Ali's chest exploded in a sea of crimson red.

Richie Gutierrez's second and third shots weren't necessary, but he took them anyway, of course, just to ensure that the Camelmaster was truly dead.

"Bogey down," Richie screamed as he took off running towards Ali's corpse to ensure that Ali hadn't activated the nuke. *No way the nuke is active*, Richie prayed to himself, *no way the nuke is active.* Johnny G breathed a sigh of relief as he finally got to where the RA-115 was. "Nuke is secure and inactive. Repeat nuke is not active," he reported.

A cheer erupted from the Triple Play headquarters that could be heard all the way to Lake Metigoshe it seemed. About ten seconds later, Johnny G ran into the picture, nodding in satisfaction at what Richie had done. Two minutes later, Sri ran breathlessly up to the scene. Seeing the carnage and Richie sitting there casually, like nothing had happened, Sri stopped abruptly, out of breath from his unaccustomed physical exertion.

"See?" Richie said, pointing at Ali. "Sometimes you E(ye)-in-steins need us warriors to get the job finished all proper like."

"Never thought otherwise, buddy. You da man," Sri smiled appreciatively, giving Richie a grateful fist bump. Sri took another deep breath and repeated, "You da man" as he sat down exhausted next to where Richie and Johnny G stood. Richie and Johnny G were amused at how exhausted Sri was, as the two were only slightly winded.

Similar accolades poured forth from Operation Triple Play headquarters. "Way to go, Richie," David said. "Nice job," Marcia echoed her congratulations.

"Oo-rah, Richie and Johnny G," Mark Childress yelled out from the field nearby, "great job. Great job, team," he said as he congratulated the rest of the group that was gathering around securing the RA-115.

Two days later, a highly jazzed Triple Play team finished their verbal report of the capture of the second RA-115 at headquarters. The team members were exhausted, but exulted in the moment. It was exciting to talk about and relive their extraordinary success. When they had finished with their report, HSA Jorgensen thanked the entire group. Jorgensen reminded them, however, that there was still one nuke out there that was unaccounted for. President Besselman came on at the end, and after thanking them as well on behalf of the country, exhorted the team to work even harder: "Two down, and one to go, folks.

But, just like in baseball, turning the double play is hard, but it's not that hard. It's the third out that's the hardest. Let's go get that triple play."

PART III

"Audentes fortuna iuvat (Fortune favors the brave)"
-Virgil, <u>Aeneid</u>

CHAPTER 20

"Any news yet on the last nuke?" Vice President Branden demanded of the team a week later on May 27th. It was Memorial Day weekend, and the group was extremely concerned that the "K" nuke would be detonated over the weekend, or on Memorial Day itself.

"No," David confirmed, "we just don't seem to have any credible leads on the "K" nuke."

"It's very strange to me," HSA Jorgensen said ruefully. "We got an almost immediate hit on the ISIS nuke, but the North Korean nuke is proving elusive."

"Well, we were pretty lucky on the ISIS nuke," K2 responded.

"Agreed," David chimed in. "Pat, as you know, unfortunately, life just isn't that simple or linear. I wish it were like a TV show where every issue gets resolved quickly in a neat package. Maybe the terrorists are having some problems transporting the nuke over here. Maybe it was already here by the time we got the additional sensors in place. We just don't know."

"While we don't know much, what we have done," K2 said, "is to add a lot more sensors around the major metropolitan areas. Now there are not only sensors at the borders, but we also have them almost everywhere else too. At last count," K2 consulted her report, "we have added 92,000 of Sabrina's new sensors to complement the approximately 20,000 original sensors that had previously existed. So you would think that even if the last nuke was in the US, we would have found something by now. Obviously, however, it hasn't been detonated yet, so we're a little bit at a loss to explain what's going on."

Jack Smith from DIA posited a thought: "My theory is that it's not here yet. Maybe it's less a theory and more just wishful thinking. Maybe the North Korean terrorists are waiting for a specific opportune time to try to sneak the bomb into the US. We have everyone on high alert now for Memorial Day, but there's been no chatter. Maybe it's set for July 4th? In any event, they'll need some time to transport the nuke to its final intended destination once it gets to the US. That means that, if they are shooting for July 4th, they need to get the RA-115 here soon, perhaps within the next few weeks or so."

"We'll redouble our efforts, of course, but mostly we're just standing by in ready mode," David said. Hopefully, one of the new sensors will be activated in a remote border area so that we can do what we did last time for the second nuke. Something tells me that it won't be as easy this time, however," he confessed.

"No vacations for anyone this weekend," the Vice President said petulantly. "Everyone not only doubles, but everyone triples their efforts today and throughout this weekend to find something."

"Yes, sir," David responded, "we're all going to be here. But we have no leads, Mr. Vice President. We're mostly just waiting around to see if we get any chatter."

"I just can't stand waiting around," HSA Jorgensen complained. "Jack, don't we have anything at all in terms of intelligence leads or approaches? Even if you think it's a ridiculous lead, there's got to be something. What have we been doing to find out about the Korean buyer?"

"We've gone through all of our leads twice," Jack replied. "No one has heard of this guy. We have reached out again to one of my Chinese intelligence counterparts. His name is Robert

Li. We agreed to have a meeting in about two weeks. It's the earliest that the Chinese can do it because of travel schedules; that's when Robert gets back into the country. I don't want to have this meeting earlier with his lower-level subordinates. I need to have the meeting with Robert Li himself. You know, we did reach out to the Chinese before, but we decided to be coy and not tell them anything too specific last time. Now we're going to just straight out show them the drawing that we have from Umarov. Since you are now authorizing me to say that we think that the guy in the drawing is from North Korea, and is part of some plot to conduct a terrorist operation within the US, maybe we'll get some help. We're not beating around the bush so much anymore. Of course, we're not going to tell them about the nuke yet; we'll tell them everything but that. It's possible that Li will be able to give us something from their moles in North Korean intelligence. Stay tuned."

"We're all staying tuned for sure. With that, our meeting's a wrap. Marcia and David, I want at least part of your team to take part of Sunday off this weekend. Your team is no good to us if they are burned out," FBI Director Edelman said, looking at the Vice President pointedly to see if he would object. The Vice President didn't. "Most of the Triple Play team has been working six and seven days a week for too long."

"OK boss, we'll let some people get a rest," Marcia and David replied together. Some of his team did need a break after the adrenaline rush of stopping the "I" nuke had worn off over the week. Well, the entire team actually needed the break. However, they knew that they had one more important job, the "K" nuke, to complete before they could truly relax.

Fortunately, nothing happened on Memorial Day weekend, so the team breathed a sigh of relief. After the next full week went by, and the team was getting really burnt out, FBI Director Edelman then proclaimed that the rest of the team, the ones that didn't get Memorial Day weekend off, including David and K2, needed to take some time off to recharge their batteries. They had been all working without a break for far too long.

So two weekends following Memorial Day weekend, on Sunday, June 12th, David and K2 finally got some much needed rest. They both slept until about noon. David and K2 tried to re-establish their normal weekend routine a little bit by going out to brunch together. Instead of doing the Sunday crossword puzzle at their neighborhood café, however, this time they decided to take a walk in Founders Park in Old Town Alexandria. It was a gorgeous day, and the popular park was filled with people walking their pets, playing volleyball, and strolling along the shore.

They walked hand in hand down one of the park paths, enjoying the great weather and breathing in the scents of late spring. A light breeze blew in from the river and helped avoid the day from becoming too hot and humid.

"Penny for your thoughts, David," Katherine playfully asked.

"Me? Right now, I'm living in the moment, Katherine. Just enjoying the time here in DC and with you, and realizing how lucky I am."

"Yeah, I'm feeling the same about now. It's obviously been stressful over the last six months, but it's felt more," K2 struggled a bit to search for the right word, "I don't know, felt more meaningful I guess since we've been together." She blushed. "Sorry, don't want to get too heavy here."

"No, it's all right," David said. "I know what you mean; I am feeling the same thing, but not expressing it as well as you are," he somewhat stammered back in response. "Look, I'm way better at bonding with the guys. My Special Forces buddies and I just do things together, like go on operations. Then we go out drinking together. If we talk, we only talk about sports, cars and women. So it's really easy for me because I know what to do."

"And with me you don't?"

"You know what I mean. It's different. Except for my mother and sister, I didn't really hang around women that much growing up, and certainly not while I was in Special Forces."

"What, the studly David Smithline is saying that he's not a ladies' man? I thought we talked about this, and that you told me about your hot girlfriends before."

"Yeah, yeah, twist my words around and kick a guy when he's opening up. As I told you, I did have a girlfriend, Karen, when I was a senior in high school, but that, honestly, was mostly fooling around with a girl that had a crush on me since elementary school. At college, Karen and I still technically were going out during my freshman year there even though we were apart for most of the time, so that really sucked. By the end, though, we were only seeing each other on every other weekend or so because she was going to NYU. After we broke up (just to be clear, she broke up with me, since I refused to go see her every weekend), I went out with another girl, Christina, for sophomore year and part of junior year, but it ended quickly after the first semester of junior year. After them, I only casually dated, hmm, maybe three or four women, and then it was off to the Army and then Special Forces, which is hardly a great place to meet one's future wife. Wow, I don't think that I've opened up that much to a woman about my ex-girlfriends for a long time. How about you?"

"Well, I'm honored that you are deigning to share here," Katherine teased. "As for me, I was way too intense in high school to have a true boyfriend; I dated a couple of guys off and on, mostly off. I told you about Bill before, I think. When I got to Stanford as an undergrad, I had a boyfriend, Carl, that I told you about. That was when I was a sophomore, but he was a senior already so that didn't work out when he went to the East Coast for graduate school. And then, when I got my PhD, let's just say, like the Army for you, that wasn't a great time and place for me to have a boyfriend. When I graduated, I was already 27 years old, and getting my butt kicked as a newbie at the Lawrence Livermore lab. The lab wanted to fast track me to work as a NEST senior staffer, and I kind of fell into a routine of work, work, work for the last four years."

"Hello, fellow workaholic. At least we are serving our country."

Katherine slowed down her pace and gave David a quick peck on the cheek. "Yes, I don't want to sound like I'm complaining. It's a real privilege to do what I do, to be able to serve, and to do what I think is important and cool work."

"OK, so we've established that we've had fairly similarly blah dating lives and that we work too much. My mom tells me that all the time."

"Your mom is wise beyond words."

"I think that's also fairly well established in the Smithline household. Say, you know what, after we find the third nuke and conclude Operation Triple Play, we should take a trip together down to North Carolina." David started to get a little more animated. "I could show you the Outer Banks, where I spent many a summer when I was growing up. The clan has a summer home out there."

Katherine smiled. "That would be nice."

David stammered again a bit, "Uh, and then we could maybe even do a dinner with my family. They are out there sometimes."

"Hmm, meeting your folks. I might be able to go that next step. But, and this is a big but, you have to give me the all of the details about your parents and your sister so I can be prepared. What do they like to talk about? What bothers them about people? I don't want to look like an idiot and say stuff that offends them the first time they meet me."

David smiled, "I think, for fairness, you'd have to tell me about your family then."

"Deal," K2 said, shaking David's hand to seal the arrangement. "I'll even go first. My dad is pretty easy; he's the strong and silent type. First generation Chinese immigrant; he's an electrical engineering professor over at UC Berkeley. He's actually pretty athletic, so he breaks the stereotype of the Asian nerd. He loves playing both basketball and tennis. So you can do the guy sports bonding thing with him; just don't say anything bad about Steph Curry, Kevin Durant or Roger Federer."

"No problem, I love Steph and KD. Roger too. So your dad's easy. How about mom?"

"Mom's definitely tougher; she's from Hong Kong originally. No matter what, you have to compliment her cooking, and keep on asking for seconds. But not in a fake way; she can see right through that. Talk a lot about how you are so lucky to have been born in this generation, and how your relatives had it harder in the olden days. And no public displays of affection, please; she'll freak out."

"And your brother, Mike, and sister, Jennifer? Give me the inside scoop on them. Mike's in Hong Kong, right?"

"Yeah, he is actually coming back to the States soon; he was supposed to be in Hong Kong only for a three year stint with GE Power that is going almost into year five now. His wife Connie is so glad to be going back to Connecticut where she grew up. He's a little overprotective of me as a big brother, so you'll have to endure some grilling from him, even more than from my dad. I think he'll like you, though. Now my little sister Jennifer is the artist in the family."

"Lives in New York City, right? Works on Broadway or something?"

"Wow, nice memory. Yeah, she lives in Chelsea. Does a wide variety of stuff, including set design for some Broadway shows and some interior design work. Not exactly a big fan of the military, so maybe we'll go slow on introducing you to her. Look, my family doesn't even know what I do exactly. They think that I'm working on the nuclear fusion project in LLNL, since I'm not allowed to tell them anything else. OK, your turn now."

"Let's see. In a lot of ways, my family's pretty similar to yours, although I only have one sister instead of two siblings. Mom is key. The whole family revolves around her. She's kind of like the sun in a little solar system. She's a big stickler on making sure everyone feels welcome in her home. It's the whole Southern hospitality thing, I guess. She grew up in a military family, so that helped when she married my dad as she was used to the life already."

"How about dad?"

"My father is like your dad in that he's strong, but he's certainly not the silent type. We always have lively conversations as he is really opinionated about everything. You do realize that we are fourth generation Duke people, right? So you are not allowed to say anything bad about Duke, and especially not about Duke basketball. Remember, Coach Krzyzewski is like a god at our home. Dad retired as a full colonel in the Army ten years ago, and is now keeping busy by teaching military history at Duke as an adjunct professor. He's really athletic. I joined wrestling because he was a wrestler, but he likes a lot of sports, including basketball, tennis and golf."

"Great, I love tennis. Maybe I can play him when we meet."

"That would be a way to get into his good graces."

"And your sister? Her name is Jennifer too, like my sister, right?"

"Yes, but she's always gone by Jenni. Jenni will be the toughest on you. Mom is too gracious a host to ask you any tough questions. My sister, however, will grill you on everything."

"So she's the designated enforcer of the family."

"Yeah, Jenni's tough on people she doesn't like. She didn't like Karen, my high school girlfriend at all, even though we have known their family forever. Thought that Karen was a little stuck-up or something. Jenni would always try to deflate Karen's ego whenever they were around each other and Karen started to avoid Jenni whenever she could."

"Wow, what kind of stuff did she say?"

"Oh, nothing really bad. Karen would always talk about how she had the best parties, and went on the best vacations and stuff, and Jenni would always try to counter with how she had heard that people thought that someone else's party was better. Silly things like that. Karen always wanted to be considered really cosmopolitan. For example, she knew about all of the latest fashions and trends. And she just loved to talk about New York

City. Jenni just believed that Karen tried too hard to be cool. Don't worry; I think that Jenni will love you. But, in addition to asking about how we met, she will ask you tough questions about who your friends are, who you voted for in the last election, and when you're alone with her, she may even ask about whether you want a big family when you get married, etc. Just don't answer any questions you don't feel comfortable answering."

"Don't worry, David," Katherine said smilingly as she gave him a little hug, "I can handle this. Sounds like she's just a normal sister trying to be protective of big brother. Glad that we both have families that care about us."

"They're great. But we've had our issues. When I was thirteen, I couldn't stand my parents; I was always fighting with them about how late I could stay out with my friends. It got so bad that I stayed with my uncle and aunt for a month over the summer. Jenni was even worse; she fought with mom during the entire time that she was in high school. She never really fought with dad much, but that was because she mostly ignored him to focus on fighting with mom. But now Jenni and mom are best friends, thick as thieves. Of course, it doesn't hurt that Jenni still lives in North Carolina and is engaged to a man that my parents just adore."

"Hmm, sounds like a little jealousy there maybe? A little sibling rivalry?" K2 teased.

"No, I don't think so," David said, a little defensively. "I just chose a different life. And here I am, walking with you on a warm day in beautiful Alexandria. Why should I be jealous?"

"Good answer. You know, we really are fortunate to be here in Washington, DC together. I really am worried that DC is the target for the third nuke. It's a high value political target. But look around," K2 said pointing to the families enjoying the park with them, "all of these folks are just ordinary people living their lives. It's just crazy that they would be victims of a sick terrorist plot."

"Don't worry, we'll find the nuke and disarm it. Yes, it's all the regular, ordinary people, and I count our families and ourselves in that category, who we are fighting for here. We can't let them down."

They continued to walk down the park path back towards where they had started. "Maybe we're looking at this wrong," Katherine mused. Maybe there's another way to smuggle in the nuke that we aren't thinking about yet."

"Your NEST geniuses have come up with a thousand scenarios. So far, nothing."

"I know, I know. I've tasked Ben and Sabrina to try to figure out what kind of shielding it would take to prevent our detection of the nuke. There are some fairly new layered materials that had been commercially developed a few years ago, new specialized shielding. It's called "Graded Z+" shielding, and it can fool the detectors without being too thick."

"Meaning that maybe the nuke is already hidden somewhere inside the US?"

"Possibly. We can't rule it out. But it wouldn't explain why it hasn't been used if it's here already."

"Keep trying. Come up with craziest ideas that you can and test them out. We'll also see what Chinese intelligence has to say to us next week if we haven't found anything else by then."

CHAPTER 21

Li Luo-Bai, or Robert Li as he was known in English, was a major in the Ministry of State Security (MSS), the Chinese equivalent of the CIA. In fact, he was the station chief of the Chinese intelligence agency in Washington DC and this was not a secret. Like his American counterpart in Beijing, the countries believed that it was good form to let the other know who their intelligence chiefs were in each other's major cities so that they could engage in backchannel discussions when needed.

Of course, Robert Li's title was not MSS station chief for Washington, DC. His official day job title, printed neatly on the business cards he carried, was "special attaché for economic affairs" in the Chinese consulate, concentrating on promoting imports of American agricultural goods. Jack Smith and his CIA counterpart, Jamie Forrest, also had business cards noting that they were directors of business development at various agricultural companies that were really front companies funded by the US intelligence community.

One of those front companies, Worldwide Foodstuffs, was the host for the Friday, June 17th meeting. Worldwide Foodstuffs had a small office on the third floor of a nondescript office building in Chantilly, Virginia, near Dulles International Airport. At exactly 10:30am, Robert walked into the company's conference room with a few of his colleagues and shook hands with Jack and Jamie.

"Thanks for meeting with us," Jack said enthusiastically. "We trust that you had a good trip out here. Would you like any coffee or tea?"

"No thank you," Robert replied easily. "And our trip was fine out here. There wasn't any traffic and, as you know, that makes all of the difference in DC. These are my colleagues, James Liu and Natalie Wang. We had received your inquiry, which sounded urgent, and we actually have some interesting information for you. We hope that it will be helpful. But first things first. As we had told you earlier, we would like to talk about our soybean oil import business proposal that we discussed with you last week."

"Wonderful," Jamie said. "Let me close the door here and we can discuss this at your leisure." Jamie loved the back and forth of the coded dialogue among the intelligence professionals. It was a civilized game of quid pro quos and clever repartees that Jamie thoroughly enjoyed. He had played the other side of this game when the Chinese had a need for information, and the US was able to extract a favorable corn-related trade concession that time. Now the shoe was on the other foot.

Ninety minutes later, the group had concluded their negotiations on the soybean oil project to everyone's satisfaction. They took a quick break and reconvened in the conference room, and this time everyone had a cup of coffee or tea in their hands.

"Now," Robert continued, "about your inquiry. Where did you get this drawing again?" he asked as he took out a copy from his briefcase.

"We received it from one of Jack's colleagues," Jamie smoothly replied. "We believe that it came from a meeting in the Caucasus sometime last September or October."

"Very interesting. We are not 100% sure, mind you, because the drawing is not very good, but our sources indicate that this gentleman is the son of a formerly very prominent curator in the North Korean art institute scene from the 1980s.

The curator's name was Young-ji Kim. He was able to travel clandestinely during that time and apparently had a mistress in France. That mistress, Hyun-sook Park, a South Korean national, bore him a son, Sung-jin Park, who is the person in the drawing. His last name is Park, of course, because he took his mother's last name, since she never told him that his dad was Young-ji Kim. Our belief is that Young-ji himself didn't even know he had a son until much later."

"How do you spell the son's name?" Jamie asked.

"S-u-n-g, hyphen, j-i-n," Robert said politely. "Don't worry, you don't need to write this information down. We've decided to help you, and so we are going to provide you with a whole file on Sung-jin and Young-ji, together with some other information that you will hopefully find useful."

"Great," Jack nodded appreciatively. "Please do continue."

Robert gestured to James Liu, who took a thick folder out of his briefcase and passed it to Jamie, who accepted it gratefully. "Sung-jin grew up in his youth in Paris not knowing who his father was. Hyun-sook brought him up very well, and the son flourished in school, learning French and English, as well as Korean at home from his mom. When Sung-jin was fourteen, Hyun-sook took him back to Korea, where he finished off his education at a boarding school near Incheon, South Korea."

Jamie flipped through Sung-jin's dossier. "Says here that he majored in art history at Seoul National University."

"Indeed he did. The apple did not fall far from the tree, as you Americans say. Perhaps because of his parent's genes (his mom also majored in fine arts), or some other natural proclivity towards the fine arts, Sung-jin became a scholar of Asian art, specializing in Asian sculptures and paintings."

"When did he find out about his dad?" Jack asked.

"We don't know for sure. Our sources in North Korean intelligence tell us that at some time after Sung-jin graduated from college, Hyun-sook managed to get in touch with Young-ji and told him that he had a son. You can imagine Young-ji's surprise at this revelation after all of these years. Young-ji was not in the good graces with the North Korean government regime at the time, so he told North Korean intelligence, the State Security Department, immediately about this in order to curry favor."

"The State Security Department must have gotten really excited."

"Absolutely. Here was a potential deep cover asset that had dropped into their laps. Of course, the State Security Department was a little skeptical, fearing that this was some kind of trick by the South Koreans. So they used some pretense to get some of Sung-jin's DNA, from a blood donation I think. Then they matched Sung-jin's DNA to Young-ji and Hyun-sook's DNA. It verified beyond a doubt that Sung-jin was Young-ji's natural son."

"Then what did they do?"

"The record is not wholly complete here. Our sources don't have the full master file, which has been compartmentalized for confidentiality purposes. However, we do know that Young-ji later went surreptitiously to Romania and met with Sung-jin. This was at a time when Sung-jin was particularly vulnerable, as he had just broken up with his girlfriend, his job wasn't going well, and he was looking for more meaning in his life, including understanding who his natural father was."

"Makes sense, I guess. How long ago was this?"

"Again, not fully clear from the record. However, that record does indicate that Sung-jin technically was considered a North Korean asset as early as about five years ago. We know this because some cash was transferred to him in a roundabout way around that time that we can trace to North Korea. Not a huge sum of money, but enough money that it made Sung-jin's life a little more comfortable. We think it was basically a fake art transaction so that the cash looked like it was received legitimately."

"What activities did they pay him for? Does your record indicate anything related to terrorist activities?"

"This is where we are trying to compare what you are telling us with our profile of Sung-jin. He was never trained as a terrorist, according to our records. No combat training at all, from what we understand, as a matter of fact. After all, he was an art student. While South Korea has mandatory military service, Sung-jin got out of it with a medical exemption, claiming asthma or something like that, so he fulfilled his obligation by doing some civil service work. Most of what he was paid for over the past five years was to curry favor with some important people in the South Korean arts community. For example, Sung-jin had a classmate at Seoul National University who was a filmmaker, mostly a director and producer of documentary films. They were pretty good friends in college. That classmate made films sharply critical of North Korea. Sung-jin's job was to use his influence to moderate that filmmaker's future output. Not too overtly so it would be obvious he was being influenced. It was a longer-term project. A public relations effort, if you will."

"Any other examples?"

Robert gestured for another colleague, Natalie Wang, to give him the extra copy of the Sung-jin file that he had given over to Jamie. "If you look at page 17, you'll see that Sung-jin became fairly influential in the arts community. One of his best friends in college became the director of the National Museum of Korea. As a matter of fact, Sung-jin worked for this director for a couple of years as the head of acquisitions for Korean sculpture for the museum before he left for the private sector. Another friend became an influential art critic for one of the main South Korean newspapers. It's a small arts community in Korea, and Sung-jin knows a lot of the people in that circle."

"Why would he be in the Caucasus then?" Jamie asked innocently. "Do your records show any art acquisition activity over there?"

Robert shrugged. "None that our records show. Remember, though, that he is in the private sector now. We show him as working for a private art dealer in Seoul, the Park Oh Gallery, so maybe the trip was either as a buyer for the gallery, or maybe as a seller to a rich industrialist there. Can you tell me what country this picture was taken in? Perhaps Georgia or Chechnya or Azerbaijan?"

"Our source said probably Georgia or Chechnya," Jamie lied a bit here, in order not to give away too much information about Colonel Umarov. "Do you have any basis to think that Sung-jin went there to buy some arms or finance some terrorist activities?"

"No," Robert shrugged. "As I said, if it was Chechnya where he was, there are a number of really rich, well-connected families living there who have a lot of money and who buy art. But you know that. We think that it's likely he was selling some artwork there. Unless you're not telling us something, I don't understand why you think Sung-jin was there buying arms or financing terrorists. He seems more like a public relations asset."

Jack chimed in here. "OK, we'll let you on a piece of information. Our source is a person whose cover," some more strategic lying and misdirection here by the DIA, "let's just say, brings him or her close to these kinds of illicit activities. So we know he was there buying arms, or at least engaged in a related transaction, because our source was, let's just say, connected to that industry in some way."

"It must have been an important buy for you to be this concerned," Robert pried. "What was it? Anti-aircraft missiles? Anti-tank weapons? Explosive ordnance? Chemical weapons?"

"Our source didn't see the exact buy," Jack said smoothly, "but it was a large purchase as you might imagine. With all of the stuff going on in the Middle East, we just don't need this large a cache of arms floating around. And if Sung-jin is a new player on the scene, we want to know where he is going with the arms."

"Here's where we can provide you with something that may be of interest," Robert noted. "We believe that Sung-jin's father saw Sung-jin again in Romania, around the first week of September of last year. The information is in the file. Maybe they visited Georgia or Chechnya right after they initially met in Romania, although I'm just guessing here. Young-ji was traveling on a fake passport that we know about. Young-ji probably brought a suitcase of money with him, because Sung-jin's bank account grew by a reasonable amount in the following few weeks. One of our, ahem, agents in Seoul also saw that Sung-jin was hanging around a lot with one of his best friends, the National Museum of Korea director. We think that he was consulting for the museum on an exhibit of sculptures that is coming in from Thailand to Korea in the next month."

"Is Sung-jin traveling anywhere in the near future?" Jack asked.

"I don't think so. The museum's got a few big exhibits that it is preparing for in Seoul, including the Thai sculptures. And Sung-jin hasn't applied for any travel visas or anything. We actually checked after we found out about your inquiry and identified Sung-jin from the picture," Robert said.

"How about the museum director?" Jack continued.

"No, he's not going anywhere either," Robert replied. "We checked that too. He has a high profile trip coming up in a few months to China, but that's it."

"OK, this is still useful information. We appreciate it. Anything else of note in the dossier?"

"Hard to tell since we don't know what you're looking for precisely. Young-ji did leave Romania in late September, traveling by a circuitous route back to North Korea. One of our sources doesn't think this was government-sanctioned trip, so we were initially thinking that Young-ji had gone rogue or something. But we have no concrete evidence of that. We have an agent still monitoring Sung-jin; perhaps we could assist you in your monitoring by combining our efforts. You have us curious as to what Sung-jin is up to. We hope that he is not planning to support any terrorist groups that would hit at China. For example, what if all of the weapons are not going to the Middle East or the US to strike at your interests? What if a portion of that arms cache instead is going to Xinjiang? We need to know."

"Understood. We will coordinate our monitoring efforts with you as much as we can. In fact, we'll send an agent to rendezvous with your agent so that they can compare notes.

Your agent probably can assist us in getting up to speed with the situation on the ground much faster."

"Fine." Robert gestured to Natalie. "Please work with Jack's team to make this happen." Natalie nodded her assent. "As always, a pleasure to meet with you, Jack and Jamie."

"The pleasure is ours," Jamie replied effusively. "We don't always see eye to eye on everything, obviously, but it is wonderful to work together on these items of mutual benefit where our interests align."

The Chinese contingent shook hands with the American intelligence agents and then left to return to the consulate. After they left, Jack and Jamie pored over the dossier that Chinese had given to them.

Two hours later, they took a break to compare notes.

"You got anything new?" Jamie yawned.

"Nah, I finished two cups of coffee, though," Jack replied. "I've just been trying to get a sense of the guy. Who is Sung-jin Park (Kim)? Funny how our South Korean intelligence friends couldn't identify this guy from our picture, don't you think?"

"Well, to be fair to them, Jack, we did a whole bunch of misdirection when we gave them the drawing. The drawing's not that clear, and they couldn't connect the dots for us because, to them, Sung-jin Kim is an upstanding South Korean, not an agent in any spy database. On the other hand, North Korean intelligence has got a special file on precisely this guy, which the Chinese have partial access to, so naturally there's more of a chance of a hit, again even though the drawing is pretty bad."

"Well, then, back to my question, who is Sung-jin Park? He's a guy who speaks fluent Korean, French, and English. And he went to Seoul U, so he's smart. He's a fixture in the art scene who is well-connected, but he's not a big shot, like a museum director or anything. In fact, he left a job at the main Korean museum working for a big shot. He's a guy who grew up without a father, and then has his father enter his life at a late age. That had to be traumatic."

"Yeah, I don't know exactly what to think. I'll send the dossier to the National Counterterrorism Center and let the rest of the Triple Play team help us try to figure out something. Let's say that, as a wheeler dealer in art for a gallery, he probably has a lot of smuggling connections. Maybe he has used or is using those connections to smuggle the nuke into the US."

"That's what I was thinking. I'm trying to figure out their game plan overall. Let's start with Romania? Why did they meet in Romania? My theory is this: he is introduced to dad in Bucharest the first time and they establish that place as the future location for meetings. Maybe North Korea has a special safe house there or something, although that's pure conjecture. Maybe that's why they met there again last September. Now my theory is that, after Romania, they both went to Chechnya right after that, with the dad serving as the money man and the son responsible for transportation logistics. Let's get the pictures in the Chinese intelligence dossier over to Colonel Umarov to confirm our theory. It would verify that Sung-jin is involved."

"Makes sense so far to me. We'll do that. But then what?"

"That's the part where we still need more facts. Let's see, Young-ji provides the money and then goes back to North Korea. Sung-jin works his smuggling magic and gets the RA-115 nuke moved to where? Back to South Korea? Somewhere else?" Jack looked at the dossier again to review the chronology of Sung-jin's movements during September of the previous year.

"There's just no information in the dossier about Sung-jin's whereabouts from October through January. That's probably because of the compartmentalization of the intelligence data. However, at least it's consistent with some other years where there are also huge gaps of time where Sung-jin is not talked about. And I'm worried about how Robert thinks that Young-ji may have gone rogue."

"Clearly, Robert's mole inside North Korean intelligence didn't have authorization to see much about Sung-jin's information recently," Jamie ruminated. "The first time when Sung-jin's trail is talked about again this year is at the end of January when he is working on the Thai exhibit again. Let's take this to our buddies in South Korea intelligence and do a trace on Sung-jin's travel visas for this time."

"Of course," Jack agreed. "But I'll bet that it will turn up nothing. Sung-jin likely travelled on a fake passport from South Korea to Romania to Chechnya, and then from there to wherever he needed to go. Then he would return to South Korea on that fake passport."

"All right, then we'll do a search on all men that went from South Korea with a destination of Romania somewhere in their itinerary."

"Better. I bet, though, that Sung-jin still went there indirectly through a whole bunch of countries on a slew of fake passports."

"I know, I know, I'm just talking us through the process. Hmm, last best chance then is to hack the Romanian visa entry system, and look for any Asian man entering the country during that timeframe and see if we can trace through any breadcrumbs of information that Sung-jin may have left for us."

"Bingo. Yes, that's probably our only hope here of finding anything. Still, I'm not too optimistic, but we might get lucky. I can't help but think that we're missing something critical."

"OK, let's start with what we just outlined, report this progress to the Triple Play team, and go from there."

And that is what they did.

CHAPTER 22

Vice President Branden was getting testy again. He was highly frustrated by the lack of concrete progress on the "K" nuke. This time he tried to hide it better, and to not yell as much at everyone. But his agitation was clear to the rest of the Triple Play team in any event. The Vice President continued to make people more and more uncomfortable at every briefing meeting without even saying anything.

When Jack Smith had finished his discussion about Sung-jin, however, the Vice President was a little bit more happy than usual. At least they had a lead that they could follow up on. K2 and Sabrina listened with especial interest. They were trying to work out the equations for avoiding radiation detection. While the North Koreans couldn't have known about Sabrina's advances, perhaps they had built in a buffer in their shielding. Sabrina was explaining her findings at the meeting.

"The RA-115 'version 3' nuke's backpack dimensions are about three feet by a little over one and a half feet by one foot. There have been some significant advances in specialized shielding over the last decade or so, what the industry calls 'Graded Z shielding.' There is even a new technology, appropriately called 'Graded Z+ shielding,' that is out there, invented mostly by the Germans over the past few years. The Germans have figured out how to get the radiation halving thicknesses down in aggregate by over an order of magnitude, as compared to the pre-Graded Z+ shielding days. That's amazing when you think about it. If you used to need a foot of shielding, which is really heavy, now you can get the same effectiveness with only an inch or so of shielding. That's just an amazing level of improvement, and a lot of it is due to nanotechnology fabrication techniques."

"Wow, that's pretty impressive," Jim Broussard said admiringly, quickly adding, "although it is pretty unfortunate for us."

"Yeah, tell me about it," Sabrina said, continuing with her presentation. "We have this 'Graded Z+' technology ourselves, but it's been pretty expensive and we had never believed that any terrorists would be sophisticated enough to use it. When we only had our old detection equipment in place, i.e., the 20,000 sensors we had last year, we think that they still would have needed about 2 inches of shielding of Graded Z+ shielding to avoid detection at normal distances. With our new better detection technology, now they would need about ten inches of Graded Z+ shielding to avoid detection."

K2 added her perspective to the mix. "Sabrina and I have discussed what we would do if we were terrorists and trying to avoid radiation detectors. If we were somewhat sophisticated, we would build a Graded Z+-"castle shield" structure around the backpack of at least three inches and then add another lead composite layer of at least one inch around that structure. That would have confounded the original 20,000 sensors we had in place, unless the nuke was within 25 yards of the sensor. Now, with Sabrina's better basketball sensors, the sensors can detect any nuke within 500 yards of the sensor with that shielding. Again, this is with Graded Z+ castle plus lead shielding of four inches total."

"Importantly, that castle would still weigh a lot, maybe five or six hundred pounds, i.e., about a quarter of a ton," Sabrina said. "It would weigh even more, if they are super-conservative and make the Graded Z+ castle even thicker. So we're not talking about a lightweight system here. This isn't something that would be shipped with a painting, for example."

"Any theories about how they would transport such a package into the US?" David asked.

"Not really," Sabrina commented. "The materials for a Graded Z+ castle aren't that easy to get, but it's not that extraordinarily difficult either. The North Koreans are much more sophisticated than ISIS and the Iranians in this regard. And the Graded Z+ castle could take any number of forms. It could be built into a truck; it could be put into a boat or a plane. Since it's relatively small, the castle could show up in any number of configurations. The only special feature about the Graded Z+ castle that helps us is the weight."

"Can we try to detect the existence of a Graded Z+ castle shield system?" David asked. "If there are some unique materials involved, even if we can't detect the nuke itself, maybe we can focus on those unique materials instead. Detect the anti-detection device as it were."

"Not a bad idea for a layman," Sabrina smiled, "but the answer to your question is no. The point is that it is way easier to detect the nuke since it's throwing off all of that gamma radiation and the like. A Graded Z+ castle is pretty inert and would be hard to independently detect I think. And there is a lead composite structure around it, as you remember my saying, that helps mask the detection of those other, more exotic elements. We have lead detectors, but there are so many things that are made out of lead that we'd have false positives all over the place. There are lead pipes, lead acid batteries, lead power cables, etc."

"Just keep trying. Please keep working on this, and let us know what will work as soon as possible. As you've heard, we've gotten a lead on the human intelligence side. Now we need a technical breakthrough to complement that," Vice President Branden said.

"Working on it, Mr. Vice President," K2 said protectively towards Sabrina. "She's a wunderkind, not a miracle worker. We do have our technical limitations."

"Sorry," Vice President Branden said, even though he wasn't sorry at all, "we are just used to NEST doing some amazing things that no other folks can do. You brainiacs helped us successfully figure out the Switchblade plan to take care of the first nuke, and you helped discover where the second nuke was coming in so that our military guys could take it out. To me, all of this stuff was a miracle – we just need you to do it again," he said, hoping to appeal to the NEST team's vanity to do the impossible.

"We're on it; we're on it, Mr. Vice President," K2 replied, a little exasperated, but trying to keep her cool as much as possible. "We'll do the best that we can as always."

The meeting went out for another 35 minutes, and then broke up. Sabrina and K2 scheduled a four-hour meeting with Ben and Sri for the next day to brainstorm other detection methods. It was now near the end of the second full week of June, a little over a month since they had found out that there was a third nuke, and they still didn't have any concrete idea about where this last RA-115 was. They needed a big break to find the "K" nuke and disarm it before it could be set off.

CHAPTER 23

The four-hour meeting the following day started with an admission that they had no clue at all why the RA-115 nuke hadn't been detected or hadn't been detonated already.

"Let's try a different angle. Put yourself in Sung-jin's shoes. If you were he, how would you get a RA-115 nuke into the United States?" This was K2 trying to start off the conversation with a broader question.

"To be honest, K2," Ben said, "I would do the same thing that Amir Abbasi did – bring it through Mexico. But if the bomb was bought in the beginning of October, then it should have gotten inside the US already long ago. If that happened, quite frankly, it should already have been detonated, or else it should have been detected. Sabrina's new sensors are in place, so the probability of getting a hit should be really high now."

"And what does that make you conclude?"

"You want me to say that this means that the bomb isn't in the US yet, I think," Ben ruminated. "Yet I'm not so sure about that either. Let's say that Sung-jin was able to get the bomb into the US. If they are waiting for some special time to detonate it, like July 4th, then it would make sense that they are simply hiding it until then. And maybe they're smart enough to use a really thick Graded Z+ castle."

"Do you agree with that assessment, Sabrina?" asked K2.

"I'm not sure. On the one hand, I do think that it's more likely than not that the bomb is in the US, given when it was sold. I don't know why they wouldn't have detonated it already or where it might be now, however," Sabrina replied, "and that makes me question whether it really is here. It seems like we are just going round and round with the same basic analysis and questions. We need more data and I don't know where to get it except from Sung-jin."

"Yes, I think that this is our best bet," Sri said. "The DIA and the CIA are monitoring his movements together with South Korean/Chinese intelligence, but at some point, if the surveillance doesn't yield anything, the decision is going to have to be made to bring him in for questioning."

K2 nodded her head. "Since the surveillance is just starting, Jack is going to give it at least a few days or maybe a week or so before hauling him in for questioning. Do we have the new sensors around every major metropolitan area?"

"Almost, but not quite," Sabrina replied. "As you know, we concentrated on what we are calling the "tier one" risk areas. So Washington, DC, New York City, Los Angeles, San Francisco, Las Vegas, Chicago, Boston, and Philadelphia have been inundated with sensors. Per my last report, we are currently working on blanketing most of all of the "tier two" risk cities with sensors beyond the ones they originally had. We are about 90% done. Dallas, Miami, Houston and Atlanta are examples of "tier two" risk cities. Finally, after we finish the top two tiers, there are plans to put a lot more sensors into "tier three" risk cities like Detroit, Seattle, Phoenix, Minneapolis or Denver."

"I thought we were supposed to be done with "tier two" by the end of today," Sri said.

"Yeah, we had a manufacturing glitch on two of the sensor production lines, so it will be 4-5 days actually until the "tier two" coverage is complete," Sabrina admitted.

"And the "tier three" and "tier four" cities are at least a week from being completed," Ben added glumly. "The manufacturing glitch has required us to slow the production time in half, and we've had to replace a bunch of previously deployed sensors that turned out to be defective. We also have added a longer stability testing period for each production batch on top of that. It's on page 12 of today's report, K2."

"OK, I got it. Everyone wants us to come up with some super-brilliant technical answer to something that probably doesn't have a technical answer. Then we are all of the same mind it seems: Sung-jin is the key to all of this."

CHAPTER 24

Sung-jin Park was in a good mood. He had a great new girlfriend, and had the equivalent of about eight hundred thousand US dollars in the bank. He also had a nice apartment, a nice car, and was able to travel a fair bit around the world doing what he loved: dealing with art sculptures. His cellphone rang; it was his girlfriend Mina Cho, making sure that they were still on for dinner at 9pm.

"Yes, see you then," Sung-jin replied to her. "Remember that we are going to the East Village Restaurant tonight instead of the galbi place. And we'll go out afterwards to a club in the same area."

"Sounds great," Mina gushed. "Club Octagon's pretty close. We need to go there again as I promised Ji-hye that I would meet her there tonight to hang out a bit."

Sung-jin groaned a bit. He was getting a little old at 33 to be going clubbing as much as Mina liked. He just was less energetic than she was. This was one of the few disadvantages of dating someone nine years younger than he was. *But of course there were advantages as well*, he thought to himself and smiled.

Dinner at East Village was excellent, of course, and they feasted on fresh local fish and an exquisite short rib preparation. Sung-jin had already downed three bottles of soju by the time that dinner ended. Soju literally means "fire alcohol" and was a particularly potent liquor; currently, soju was the most widely consumed alcoholic drink in the world. With three bottles in him, Sung-jin was really drunk already as they made their way to the Seoul clubbing scene in a cab.

Little did Sung-jin know that they were being followed closely by Chinese and US intelligence agents. Mike Smith was born in South Korea to a Korean mother and US Army officer, and spoke fluent Korean. Mike had grown up near Seoul for the first twelve years of his life before his dad got transferred back to the United States, working in California. His Chinese intelligence counterpart, Ming Li, also spoke fluent Korean; she was the product of a Korean mother and Chinese father.

Ming yawned. "Sung-jin doesn't look like any kind of arms dealer I'm used to," she said absently to Mike. "But he certainly knows how to live the high life. His girlfriend is really pretty too. Are you sure your spymasters back in the US have got the right guy?"

"That's what I'm here to find out," Mike replied. "Frankly, I don't think that Sung-jin is exactly an arms dealer type myself, but I do what I'm told. Besides, I've had lots of worse assignments. We've gotten to eat at some nice restaurants and hang around some cool nightclubs. Nothing wrong with that from my point of view."

"Yeah, but it gets old after a while," Ming said. "Don't forget that my team has been surveilling Sung-jin off and on for about two years already. You just started less than a week ago, so this stuff looks exciting and fun. Believe me, after another few months, you will get bored of this."

Mike thought to himself that this was certainly not going to happen. His superiors gave him no uncertain orders that Mike needed to find something and report back within a few weeks. If Mike didn't find anything by then, it was likely that they would need to take Sung-jin in for questioning soon thereafter. Mike was running out of time. Of course, he couldn't tell Ming this, but he was feeling the pressure.

They followed Sung-jin and Mina to the Gangnam district, an area of Seoul made famous worldwide by the singer

Psy's song "Gangnam Style." When the two entered Club Octagon, Mike and Ming were only three minutes behind the targets when they entered. The enormous club wasn't yet filled with people since it was so early, only about 11:30pm on Saturday night. The crowds wouldn't really start coming until well after midnight, though when they did, the whole place would be filled to capacity and would really be rocking.

Mike spotted Mina talking with a friend at the bar, motioning to Ming when he saw Mina. The two agents sidled over to the bar area and got drinks themselves. Sung-jin was sitting behind Mina so the two agents hadn't spotted him at first. He was basically seated by himself and drinking as the two women were laughing and chatting with each other. Mike surreptitiously snapped some pictures of Mina's friend so that they could figure out who she was later.

At about 12:15am, a new DJ came on and began to play some particularly deep electronic dance music that got the girls grooving. Mina pulled Sung-jin to the dance floor and the three of them began to dance. Ming shrugged and pulled Mike out to the dance floor as well so they wouldn't look too out of place. After a while, Mina and her group stopped dancing and they went back to the bar. A number of guys tried to hit on Mina's friend, but she rebuffed them, preferring to continue to hang out with Mina and Sung-jin. Well, mostly Mina really, as the girls just grew progressively chattier and sillier by the hour. Sung-jin just passed the time by drinking even more soju until he looked really hammered. At 2:30am, the place was pretty much filled to maximum capacity and had gotten very loud, actually uncomfortably loud and boisterous. Well, uncomfortably loud from Mike's standpoint.

At 4am, Sung-jin gave Mina the clear "we have to go now" signal for the fourth time, but this time made it even more emphatic. Mina clearly wanted to stay for a while longer, but Sung-jin gave her one of those looks and Mina acquiesced this time. Hugging her friend Ji-hye one more time, Mina and the rest of the trio began to wind their way through the now completely overfilled club towards the exit.

Ming and Mike rushed out of the club just as Sung-jin and Mina disappeared into a cab. They had radioed that their targets were departing so another team was on them. Another night had passed and, while Mike had had a fair bit of fun, unless Mina's friend proved a breakthrough, he was fundamentally no closer in obtaining his objective than when the night had commenced.

Unfortunately, as Mike expected quite frankly, Mina's friend – determined quickly by the CIA and Chinese intelligence to be one Ji-hye Park – turned out to be a dead end. She was just a close friend of Mina's since junior high school who pretty clearly didn't have anything to do with arms sales or terrorist activities.

CHAPTER 25

Jamie Forrest had a sour expression on his face the entire time he delivered his report to Jack Smith. Jamie had found nothing concrete about Sung-jin's museum tour history that would link him to the RA-115, or to any shows in the United States in the upcoming six months. Sung-jin's consulting work for the Thai exhibit coming into Korea proved a dead-end as well. None of those Thai sculptures were coming into the United States. Jamie had even considered the possibility that the RA-115 would be detonated in South Korea, e.g., in Seoul, whether at the National Museum or at locations near where a few US soldiers had been quietly stationed at the capital. Maybe they would detonate the nuke at Camp Humphreys around Pyeongtaek, South Korea, where the US military was in the process of consolidating its forces. But a careful examination of those sculptures (they were all too small to contain a RA-115), and even the bases on which the sculptures were mounted, indicated no presence of any RA-115 devices, although continued monitoring would occur, just in case.

"We looked at every museum tour coming out of South Korea into the United States. First, there is no current art exhibition that Sung-jin has done any consulting work for. There is a painting exhibit from South Korea touring in Los Angeles currently that we checked out anyway, even though Sung-jin didn't do any work related to the exhibit. That exhibit turned out totally clean. And we really looked at each exhibition item under a microscope and found nothing. The problem is that there have been and are about 300 traveling art exhibits of various sorts going on in the US since October, with another 20 coming in the next few months, and I don't think that we have the manpower to go through each of those exhibits like we did the one in LA. That one took two days alone."

"So what do we do now?" Jack asked plaintively. "Take him in, or wait?"

"We're at an impasse, Jack," Jamie replied. "I can't figure out either the where the RA-115 might be, or the how, as in how it might have been transported. Zero for two as it were. We have to take him in soon for questioning."

"OK, but it's Saturday mid-morning in South Korea now. Sung-jin could be meeting someone this weekend that leads us somewhere. I think we need to wait until Friday, July 1st, after he gets off work to grab him."

"Deal. I'll set it up and call the team on it. We'll put him in the safehouse."

"By the way, no excuses about not checking out each of the 300 exhibits," Jack continued. "Get some help from the FBI and the National Guard; we need some teams on it immediately. We don't have to do as thorough a review of each exhibit as we did in LA, but I want people to look at each museum exhibit you just mentioned."

"Got it," Jamie muttered. He knew that he was not going to be very popular with the FBI and National Guard over the next few days.

CHAPTER 26

Around Seven Months Earlier ...

Ji-eun Lee yawned contentedly as she looked down at her baby, finally sleeping, resting in her arms as she sat in her rocking chair. It had been a long night to get to this point as her son, Min-jun, barely one month old, had been extremely fussy in the early evening. Ji-eun's husband, Min-ho Lee, had been laying on their bed snoring for the past fifteen minutes, finally oblivious to Min-jun's crying after suffering through it like Ji-eun did for the previous ninety minutes.

Ji-eun could never understand how her husband could sleep through Min-jun's crying, but knew that she couldn't simply because she was Min-jun's mother. As the one who carried Min-jun inside her for nine months, she simply had more attachment to the child than Min-ho. This stereotype was probably statistically true for most mothers as compared to most fathers. That biological attachment also made her worry more about their espionage assignment.

Like her husband, Ji-eun was trained as a deep-cover spy for North Korean intelligence, in their cases, the Reconnaissance General Bureau. The bureau is tasked with infiltrating North Korean intelligence agents into other countries, mostly South Korea. Ji-eun and Min-ho, who were brought up in North Korea until they were six, were indoctrinated into North Korean ideology there, and then were secretly smuggled into South Korea, where they were assimilated into South Korean culture. By a series of machinations, they were then directed to emigrate from South Korea over to the United States when they were university-age to become "sleeper agents," ready to be activated as necessary. They had been in the US for many years already, successfully taking over the identities of a couple of Korean-Americans who had been killed in a car accident.

Ji-eun and Min-ho weren't sure, but they estimated that there were about six other "sleeper agents" in the United States, although she had heard rumors that two of them had defected after coming to America. In Ji-eun's case, that was not a possibility, as her parents and family were living in North Korea and she couldn't let them suffer if she defected. Her family in fact, would certainly be killed in the most brutal way possible, just to punish her if she sold out. She was not really political, truth be told, but just wanted to live a good life with Min-ho and her newborn son; she certainly had never wanted to be activated.

On the other hand, Min-ho was still very much a North Korea patriot. He had been told that both his grandfather and his father had been killed by American soldiers, his father a martyr after being shot while spying at a US military installation in South Korea. His father had made it back to North Korea, where he had died from his gunshot wounds while Min-ho was just a few months old. At least that is what Min-ho had been told. Ji-eun had always wondered whether it was true or not, or whether it had been a lie to get him to hate Americans more.

Whatever the truth was, it was clear that Min-ho hated America. Unlike Ji-eun, he was ready to be fully activated and do the most damage he could to the United States at a moment's notice. Meanwhile, they prepared. Preparation consisted of working in the nuclear energy field, Min-ho as a nuclear systems design engineer at the main power company in Baltimore, Maryland, and Ji-eun as a nuclear engineer specializing in radiation shielding at the same company and location. Both had masters degrees in physics, with Ji-eun, who was on maternity leave, recently staying at home so that she could focus on taking care of Min-jun.

The two sleeper spies had received a message from their handler in the beginning of last October. A nuke would be smuggled into the US and it would be their job to activate it. The nuke would be something called a "version 3" of a GRU RA-115 backpack bomb. The handler had provided some very detailed technical information that they were supposed to study so that they were familiar with the device.

Min-ho didn't study the technical information that carefully, except for the parts involving the detonation sequence. He saw no need to dive deeply into the specifications when all that he wanted to do was to ensure that he knew how to set off the bomb. Ji-eun, on the other hand, carefully read every page of the technical information that she had been given. The more and more that she read about the nuke, the more and more she appreciated its intricacy.

The Russian engineers who designed this thing really knew what they were doing, Ji-eun thought to herself. They were exceedingly thorough in their design and documentation. After decryption, the electronic file containing the technical manual itself ran to something like 1,500 pages. Fully 200 pages of the manual contained the diagnostic testing components for the GRU RA-115 bomb. The diagnostic program allowed the user to simulate the arming and timer countdown of the bomb to make sure that all of the nuke's hardware and software components were working, without of course setting off the bomb itself.

Since Ji-eun had more time due to her maternity leave, even though she had to take care of the baby (they had hired an older Korean woman as a nanny to give Ji-eun a little more help), they had agreed that Ji-eun would be the one that would be the expert with respect to the RA-115 diagnostics testing. The couple needed to make sure that the nuke was still operational when they got it, and wasn't damaged in transit.

The RA-115 had come to the US around the end of the first week of November via a complicated and circuitous route through Greenland. The couple had to drive almost two hours to get to the nuclear backpack device, which had come by boat to a secluded beach area near Bombay Hook National Wildlife Refuge in coastal Delaware. The nuke had been encased in Graded-Z+ shielding for the trip, and had been transferred to another Graded-Z+ castle installed in a van that Min-Ho and Ji-eun had custom fitted out for the occasion. This Graded Z+ castle system was fully ten inches thick, as Min-ho had been concerned about detection, and he wanted to go way overboard and be ridiculously conservative with the shielding.

Over the course of the next few weeks that November, Ji-eun had conducted exhaustive diagnostics testing on the RA-115 at their suburban Baltimore home and proudly announced to her husband that the RA-115 had not been damaged in transit. All was in order. Afterwards, following instructions from their handler, Min-ho and Ji-eun had taken the van carrying the RA-115 to Washington, DC one late afternoon, where a scaffolding was covering a large Buddha sculpture that had been sitting in the northeast lawn area of a major building in downtown Washington near the Potomac River. Min-jun was at that time a much better sleeper than when he was first born, so the baby slept comfortably in the van while the two were doing their work. They were dressed in construction crew clothing, together with hard hats; their handler had arranged it so that the other construction crew members would not be present at the time.

The large Buddha sculpture was a gift from the country of Japan and had been placed in its present location in Washington, DC for the last year and a half. The Buddha, in seated position, was made of bronze and was about fifteen feet tall. A separate base was attached to the sculpture that itself was a cube with a width of approximately nine feet. Min-ho had driven the van onto the lawn right next to the statue, as the lawn had been covered by a large tarp near the statue. He had scrutinized the statue carefully as instructed, looking for the panel at the bottom of the base where the key that he had been provided would fit.

Twisting the key into the lock opened the panel, which exposed a lever that electronically opened up the base of the statue, where a cavity had been hollowed out. The statue base was a well-designed Graded Z+ castle itself, Ji-eun noted. Min-ho grunted in satisfaction at how cleverly manufactured the apparatus was. They were most impressed with how thick the walls of the base of the statue were, about twenty-one inches thick, with an additional three inch lead composite shield at the outside. This meant that the cavity itself was only about a five foot by five foot by five foot cube. The RA-115 nuke, however, could still easily fit into the structure with plenty of space to spare, even inside the separate four inch thick Graded Z+ castle box in which it sat within the van.

For the next hour, Min-ho and Ji-eun prepared the RA-115 Graded Z+ castle box in their van for loading into the cavity. They had installed an electronic winch that could lift the box, and slide it down a ramp directly into the cavity. The work took some painstaking effort on their part, but the nuclear engineers were particularly adept at this kind of painstakingly precise work.

"Ready?" Min-ho asked, after they had checked and double-checked that the winch cables were securely fastened to the Graded Z+ castle sitting in their van.

Ji-eun nodded her assent. "Ok to go."

"Hold the button down then," her husband instructed, "but be ready to let go if it's moving too fast."

Their payload slowly was lowered down into the statue cavity after another ten minutes of tiny micro-adjustments. Min-ho and Ji-eun wanted to be extremely careful with their payload, understandable given the circumstances. Finally, the RA-115 had been successfully loaded inside the statue.

"We did it!" Min-ho exclaimed, as he locked up the panel and the couple had loaded the ramp back into the van. Ji-eun shushed Min-ho, pointing to the quietly sleeping Min-jun who was still nestled comfortably in some blankets within his baby carrier seat inside the van.

"Let me do the final test before you celebrate," Ji-eun replied.

"OK, OK," Min-ho said. "Please do the honors."

Ji-eun took out her Geiger counter and looked for a reading. Nothing. They had done it. On November 22nd, they had successfully placed a 2 kiloton bomb right inside the heart of Washington, DC.

She gave Min-ho the thumbs up sign, and the two quietly finished fully repacking the van. Min-ho looked around to make sure that the area looked roughly similar to how it had looked when they had first arrived.

It was a fairly short drive back to suburban Baltimore since they were leaving after the evening commute had mostly ended. Min-ho drove, and could barely contain his euphoria on the drive back home, Ji-eun noticed. She smiled at her husband, but was much more pensive about what they had done than he was. She wondered to herself what the future would bring them as she gave her sleeping baby son a quick kiss on the forehead.

CHAPTER 27

Back in the present time ...

Joo Cheon contemplated his next move on the go board. *Life was a delicious blend of strategy and tactics*, he thought to himself. The pieces were already in place nicely, and he was the puppetmaster, pulling the strings invisibly from above, with other people completely oblivious to what was going on.

Joo, now in his mid-fifties, was within the core of North Korea's leadership, one of the elite under the current Supreme Leader. North Korea, formally known as the Democratic People's Republic of Korea (DPRK), had a number of competing core leaders, some in the political sector, some in the business sector, and of course, some in the military sector. Perhaps up to twenty thousand people could be thought of as comprising the totality of this core group, individuals who essentially were the main leaders of the country of 25 million people. Indeed, Joo knew that he was within the inner circle of this core group, perhaps one of the top 200 military leaders of the country, and within the military intelligence establishment, certainly one of the top fifty.

Importantly, Joo wanted to make sure that he was not too high up in the intelligence establishment, for that might attract the undue attention of the Supreme Leader, one of the long line of autocrats from the Kim family that started with Kim Il-Sung in 1948. For while being in the core conferred tremendous advantages to an individual, the truth was that the Supreme Leader had more power than the rest of the core group combined. He had personally seen two of his superior officers executed by Kim Il-Sung when he was a junior officer, as those superior officers were viewed as a threat to Kim's authority. Joo was formally, at least, only the fifteenth highest-ranking officer of the military intelligence arm of the DPRK, the Reconnaissance General Bureau (RGB). As an Assistant to the Deputy Associate Director of Clandestine Operations, however, Joo had access to significant RGB slush funds and a degree of personal autonomy. This resulted because part of his duties required him to travel abroad from time to time in order to manage some of his operations.

While these operations mostly involved trying to place individuals inside South Korea to influence that country's stance towards their neighbor to the north, ever since the October 2006 nuclear test where North Korea had detonated its first nuclear bomb near the village of P'unggye, North Korea had been feverishly trying to obtain technology that would miniaturize its nuclear capacity.

All of the Supreme Leaders had spent countless amounts of money trying to unsuccessfully obtain a tactical field nuclear weapon, like an RA-115, from the Russians for years. The Russians, though, simply would not sell any nuclear weapons to the volatile North Koreans. For one thing, they believed that the sale might be traced back to the Russians by the Americans or the Europeans, and lead to a serious political crisis. Secondly, they weren't so sure that the weapons might not be later used against one of Russia's allies or Russia itself. So a policy decision had been made by the Kremlin to continue to provide oil and natural gas, as well as food supplies, to the DPRK, and to offer some conventional military support like combat fighter aircraft, but to clearly avoid supporting the DPRK with respect to its nuclear arms program.

The ruling Kim family, of course, was infuriated by this stance. They thought it was hypocritical of the Russians to support them in these other ways but to refuse to help the DPRK obtain the most important deterrent against American interference in the DPRK's domestic affairs. So the DPRK tried other methods to get their hands on nuclear technology. However, the Chinese similarly refused to assist North Korea in obtaining what they wanted, basically having the same reasons as the Russians for not supplying any nukes, or miniaturization technology, for the DPRK nuclear program.

So the Supreme Leaders' efforts had languished for decades in this regard. Meanwhile, though, the North Koreans had made surprising advances in their internal strategic nuclear efforts to produce plutonium and enriched uranium. After the 2006 nuclear test, two additional tests had been conducted, the second in 2009 and the third in 2013, showing that the country had the capacity to detonate a nuclear bomb. And some progress had been made with respect to the DPRK's ballistic missile and rocketry program. But these ballistic missiles, part of the country's strategic arsenal, were error-prone, and, Joo had to admit to himself, extremely unreliable in battlefield conditions. On top of that reliability issue, the US and Europe had significant anti-missile defense programs in place that further reduced the chance of a successful launch of a ballistic missile.

Joo knew that the real prize to the Supreme Leader was to miniaturize the country's experience with nuclear technology enough to obtain tactical nuclear weaponry, weapons that could not be shot down because they were detonated at the target in the first place. However, he also knew that the Supreme Leader was a little bit worried about the effort, as he believed that the Western powers would seek to overthrow him if he ever demonstrated the capacity to wield such tactical nuclear weaponry.

For Joo, this fact was his driving motivator. While he hated America, and had no qualms about taking out one of its cities and killing hundreds of thousands, or even millions, of its people, Joo also hated the ruling Kim family with a passion, and hoped that the Kims would be overthrown. Ironically, Joo had idolized the Kim family for the first thirty some years of his life.

His hatred had started when one of Joo's mentors, General Byung-chul Moon, who also happened to be the father of his best friend, had inadvertently offended Kim Il-Sung at a military review. General Moon was the head of the RGB at the time, and normally was a favorite of the leader. Kim Il-Sung had flown into a rage when one of General Moon's chiefs of staff had accidentally tripped the leader, and General Moon had come to his aide's defense. That infuriated Kim Il-Sung even more, which still wouldn't have led to General Moon's execution, if he had just let the leader's anger blow over.

Instead, he made the mistake of telling his aide, in an aside afterwards where he thought no one could hear him, to profusely apologize to Kim Il-Sung even though "obviously it was Kim Il-Sung's fault." That remark got relayed by, of all people, the very aide that had tripped the leader, who was desperately trying to avoid getting executed, and corroborated by another general who had overheard the exchange.

Still, General Moon was looked at in such high regard by the Kims that they may not have executed him had General Moon simply denied ever saying those words. But Moon was a man of honor, and would not lie to save his own skin. General Moon admitted that he said those words, and said that the Supreme Leader could have his resignation immediately and even execute him if the leader wished, only requesting that his family be spared any punishment, in light of his many years of loyal service.

Kim Il-Sung was therefore put in a delicate situation. He had made up his mind already that he would have to execute General Moon for insubordination. General Moon would be made an example of what would happen if you disrespected the leader. The leader, though, was conflicted about whether to kill off the man's entire family. He genuinely liked General Moon's son, Colonel Byung-ho Moon; nevertheless, the leader was also afraid that the son would seek vengeance. So the leader compromised and decided to execute General Moon by placing him, his wife, and his son in front of an anti-aircraft gun and then obliterating them. However, he would respect General Moon's wishes with respect to the general's daughter, Soo-hee, who was only sixteen at the time.

Joo was devastated by the loss. He didn't even have a chance to say goodbye to his friend or his mentor, as they were kept away from everyone until the date of execution. Joo wondered whether, even if he had been allowed to see them, he would have had the guts to do so, since anyone who would have visited them might be branded as an enemy of the state. It was bad for him, but Joo knew that it was a thousand times worse for Soo-hee.

He didn't see Soo-hee for over six years following the execution. When he saw her, he almost didn't recognize the gaunt, beaten-down woman that arrived at his door late one night bearing a satchel that she carried with her, holding on to it as if her life itself depended upon safeguarding its contents.

Joo quickly ushered Soo-hee into his home, checking around to make sure that he wasn't being watched. After getting Soo-hee some water, he listened quietly as she told him her story. Following her family's execution, Soo-hee was allowed to continue to live, but at her family's country house, which was now shared by three other military families. She became the maid and servant for those families, preparing their meals, washing their clothes, and otherwise keeping the home clean. There were also farm animals to tend to, about a dozen chickens in all, and a few cows and goats. The days were filled with endless labor.

It was a difficult life, but Soo-hee bore it stoically. She was a favorite of her father, when he was alive, and was a close confidante of his activities. She knew about many of the RGB's intelligence operations, knew where most of the slush funds were held, and knew about the different operatives that were already in foreign countries. He had made sure that she had a lot of information about his life, and had trained her well as to how to stay alive in North Korea. Soo-hee realized that she would be under constant surveillance for quite some time following her family's execution. When executions take place, her father had told her, the RGB was instructed to monitor the surviving family of the executed for at least three years to see if they exhibited any suspicious behavior against the state. So Soo-hee had played it safe and had laid low for well over six years. Then an opportunity had presented itself. She was asked by one of the families living with her to accompany the family's patriarch, an eighty-eight year old man diagnosed with terminal lung cancer, to the city so that he could visit his place of birth one last time.

The patriarch's place of birth happened to be in an apartment on the same floor of the building where Soo-hee knew that Joo had continued to live, so she took this as a sign that she was meant to visit Joo at that time. Taking her father's secret papers that he had hidden in the country house, including some documents containing embedded microdots full of Swiss bank account numbers and codes and details of historical intelligence operations, Soo-hee had put the secret papers in a false bottom in her suitcase as she traveled with the eighty-eight year old man.

Then Soo-hee just waited for the right moment. It was almost midnight and most of the tenants were sleeping. The patriarch had been sleeping since 9:30pm, but Soo-hee thought it was too early given the hustle and bustle of the other apartment dwellers. When she thought the timing was right, Soo-hee had quietly knocked on Joo's door, taking the calculated risk that he would remember her and open the door for her.

Joo did, and there they were, kindred spirits recollecting their past memories of General Moon and his son Byung-ho. They wept together openly as Soo-hee showed Joo a few pictures of her family together, taken in the good old days long before the execution. Soo-hee made Joo promise that he would avenge her family somehow, the time and manner by which she would leave up to him.

Joo made his solemn pledge to do just that, and in the eleven years since that meeting, he had essentially dedicated his life to just that one task.

The information that Soo-hee had provided had helped tremendously. At the time, he was a mid-level functionary in the RGB, originally tasked with some strategic assignments partly because of his relationship with General Moon, although Joo was smart enough to realize that he shouldn't depend on just one person and had a number of other mentors. When Moon was executed, Joo worried that he was going to be blacklisted. Fortunately, however, others had the same insecurity, so there was a tacit understanding developed by the former protégés of

General Moon that they would not speak out against the others so that they could each survive being purged.

Moon's mentees, and there were a sizeable number of them, were also helped by the fact that their jobs at the RGB were still deemed incredibly valuable and important to the DPRK and to the Kim family by extension. Their training and expertise also made it hard to replace them quickly. The Kim family dynasty shrewdly recognized that if it purged too many of Moon's friends, that it would have lost an enormous amount of intelligence capabilities all at once. This would have been devastating to the RGB's ability to function. Moon's execution served as a check and balance on the ambitions of the RGB senior staff, though, and a reality check as to who was really in control of the DPRK overall.

Over time, as Joo read in full the documents given to him by Soo-hee, he began to fully appreciate the genius of General Moon. Moon had constructed a complex intelligence apparatus that had compartmentalized all of the departments and operations. Only the top two intelligence commanders, together with the ruling Kim family members, really had insight into most of the intelligence operations. And Moon had even managed to hide some of his bank accounts from the Kim family members through a very arcane system of slush accounts that were adjacent to, but not part of, the other official slush accounts that existed in Mauritius, Switzerland, the Cayman Islands, the Turks and Caicos islands, and the other offshore financial centers that held a large part of the money. Joo figured that Moon had secreted about $150 million into these special adjacent slush accounts; this was on top of the $6.5 billion in aggregate hidden offshore accounts that the RGB managed officially for the DPRK. Not bad considering that North Korea's annual GDP was estimated to be only about $40 billion.

It was from this $150 million in funds that Joo used to pay Colonel Umarov the $100 million it cost to obtain the RA-115. Getting the RA-115 to the United States cost another $10 million. The $150 million also paid for the Graded Z+ castle that sat in Washington, DC too; that operation separately cost a cool $30 million to pull off. Moon's special slush fund in fact was almost fully depleted after these and other costs. But it didn't matter, Joo reassured himself confidently, the operation was almost fully completed. A little over a week from now, on Independence Day in the US, Joo would fulfill his promise to Soo-hee to avenge her family's deaths. And his actions would take out the hated Americans' capital to boot. While it would be a shame that Pyongyang would be leveled in retaliation, Joo would make sure that he was safely away when it happened. *That must be what is meant by the English phrase "killing two birds with one stone,"* Joo mused to himself.

CHAPTER 28

Mike Smith got the final, official go-ahead on the morning of Tuesday, June 28th, to take in Sung-jin for questioning on Friday evening, July 1st (Korea time). They had hoped that Sung-jin would lead them to his DPRK contact without the need of any interrogation, but that hadn't panned out. On balance, the Triple Play leadership determined that the risk that taking Sung-jin in would cause the terrorists to set off the nuke was outweighed by the chance that the nuke was going to be set off relatively soon if they didn't take Sung-jin in. For one thing, July 4th was coming up in only a few days, and they wanted to find out if anything was going to happen on that focal date. Also, the team had learned that Sung-jin was taking off Monday and Tuesday of the following week for a short vacation, so taking him on that Friday late afternoon or evening meant that he wouldn't be missed at work until Wednesday, July 6th. As a result of listening in on Sung-jin's phone conversations, they also had figured out that his girlfriend Mina was out of town visiting her grandparents and would be out of town until July 9th as well.

The timing for the takedown would be therefore pretty auspicious. Jack Smith himself had called Mike and personally had given him the instructions on how the operation would play out. They would inform Chinese intelligence about the takedown, but for obvious reasons, no Chinese agent would be allowed in the interrogation of Sung-jin. Sung-jin would be moved to a special joint DIA and CIA safe house, where he would be questioned about what he knew about the "K" bomb.

On Friday afternoon, Sung-jin went downtown for a set of meetings, presumably some consulting work at the National

Museum. When Friday evening came and Sung-jin had wrapped up his meetings, the operation was able to begin, starting precisely at 6:57pm. "Target is acquired," Ming said to Mike as she looked through her high-powered binoculars at the street below. "Target is leaving the National Museum of Korea now."

"Got it," Mike replied. "Do you copy that?" he asked his team, nicknamed the K-Pops as a joking reference to the music genre.

"Roger that," said K-Pop One. "We see him walking east out of his office building. Looks like he is going back home. He's entering the subway now."

Sung-jin disappeared down into the maze of Seoul's metro subway system at the Ichon station, quickly followed by the agents known as K-Pop Two, K-Pop Three, and K-Pop Four. While in the subway, Sung-jin called Mina to see how her grandparents were doing; Mina immediately picked up the call and noted that she was just about to go out to dinner with them, chatting away with Sung-jin about how she was so excited to be able to go see them and just wished that he could have come too.

They talked a few minutes while the agents jostled around for better position on the crowded subway. K-Pop Three managed to stand right behind Sung-jin, who was oblivious to his presence as he was engrossed in his conversation with Mina. K-Pop Two stood right by one of the subway doors so that Sung-jin would not be able to exit without his being able to follow. K-Pop Four guarded the other subway door exit. K-Pop One, the leader of the group, stayed on his cell phone connected with Mike and the rest of the operational command people.

Basically, K-Pop One did this just by pretending to be on a conversation with his wife during the trip: "Hi, honey," he said. "Yes, I'm on the subway and confirm that everything's OK. My people are, umm, ready for their assignments at work."

"What's he doing now?" Mike's boss, John Kim asked.

"Talking on the phone, of course," K-Pop One replied smoothly. He made a show of looking at his watch. "Look, nothing's changed from the original plan. I'm about to exit now to switch subway lines. Should be at the, umm, restaurant near Insa-dong very shortly. Will call you if there is a delay."

The subway stopped and, still talking, Sung-jin exited the subway and made a beeline for the other subway line with four agents following closely behind.

This time two of the agents went in a different car when the subway train arrived. K-Pop One and K-Pop Four, on the other hand, got into the same subway car as Sung-jin.

"Only a few more stops to Jonggak Station," reported K-Pop One. "All is good, and looking forward to seeing you soon."

"Roger that," John Kim said. "We are set for the takedown half a block away from his home."

"Understood," K-Pop One responded. "No problem."

By the time that Sung-jin had gotten off the train at Jonggak Station, he had hung up with Mina, but still did not suspect that he was being tailed. Sung-jin stretched his arms out a bit as it had been crowded on the subway; he had gotten a little sore from carrying his briefcase in an awkward position. He ambled out of the station and into the street. Jonggak Station was extremely busy at this time of day, and it was easy for the K-Pop surveillance team to remain unspotted.

As Sung-jin got to within a block of his home, K-Pop One radioed it in and the next phase of the operation began. An old man with a map, looking lost, stopped Sung-jin as he was walking by, performed a perfunctory bow, and politely asked

Sung-jin for directions to a local art gallery. Sung-jin smiled and was happy to oblige; he was very familiar with that particular art gallery and had enjoyed looking at a few pieces there just about a month ago. As Sung-jin was pointing out the location to the old man on the map, another man dressed in a suit walked by Sung-jin and dropped his briefcase between Sung-jin and the old man. As Sung-jin bent over to help the man pick up his briefcase, the man quickly brushed his hand near Sung-jin's head, sticking him with a needle. This caused Sung-jin to instantaneously grab the part of his neck where he had been pricked.

Confused and dazed, Sung-jin was feeling woozy within seconds. He grabbed his heart and staggered to the ground.

"Help!" the old man and the suited man shouted together, "This man is having a heart attack!"

Bystanders gathered around to assist. The suited man made a show of calling on his cell phone for an ambulance. Another man noted that he was a doctor and came over to try to help. The doctor quickly loosened Sung-jin's tie and unbuttoned the top buttons of Sung-jin's shirt.

"Ambulance is coming soon!" the suited man announced.

The doctor nodded and tried to make Sung-jin more comfortable by having him sit down on the ground. "Are you comfortable?" the doctor asked gently.

Sung-jin could barely speak, saying something like "ugghh," but he nodded his head to note that he was as comfortable as he was going to get.

"Do you take any medicines? Have you had any heart problems before?" the doctor continued.

Sung-jin shook his head no. He really couldn't talk now, and he was about to pass out.

Within six minutes, an ambulance had arrived and the paramedics began to carefully load Sung-jin into the emergency vehicle by placing him first into a gurney. The doctor had made everyone else stay away, and the medical professionals were the only ones allowed to touch Sung-jin. The suited man gave Sung-jin's briefcase to one of the paramedics, who loaded it into the ambulance where Sung-jin was lying down in a gurney, but now completely unconscious.

"What happened?" a curious pedestrian who had just arrived asked the old man.

"No one knows," the old man shrugged. "I was asking him for directions, and all of a sudden, he just passed out. They are saying that it was a heart attack."

"Wow, that's too bad," the pedestrian mused. "My mother had a heart attack last year. I hope that he's all right."

"Yes, me too," the old man replied. "He's pretty young and it looks like he will get to the hospital quickly. Hopefully, they can fix him up," he continued as they looked at the paramedics finishing up.

Finally, the ambulance doors were shut quickly after all of their gear was loaded inside. The ambulance screeched off.

Sung-jin woke up, groggy, about a few hours later. He had been transported not to a hospital, but to a special safe house located in the Seoul suburbs. "What? Where am I?" Sung-jin said as he woke up in a bed in a nondescript room. He tried to move around, but couldn't. His leg had an ankle ring placed on it that was chained to the bedpost so he had very limited mobility.

Less than fifteen minutes later, John Kim and Mike Smith entered the room. Mike had an attaché case with him that he left near the door. "What's going on here? I demand to be released!" Sung-jin protested. John and Mike didn't say a word, but Mike unceremoniously handcuffed Sung-jin's hands together behind him, then unchained his ankle from the bedpost and forced Sung-jin to get up. They were moving to the interrogation room.

The interrogation room was exactly what you would expect such a room to look like. There was only one door leading into and out of the room and there was a single table in the middle of it. It was here that Sung-jin was pushed into the chair on one side of the table that faced a large one-way mirror. The metal ring that had been attached to his ankle was re-chained to a post on the floor underneath the table. John and Mike sat in the two chairs placed on the other side of the table.

"Want some water?" Mike asked.

Sung-jin nodded warily but affirmatively. Mike pulled a plastic water bottle from his pocket, unscrewed the top off and placed it on the table. Sung-jin, his hands now cuffed in front of him, picked up the water bottle and began drinking greedily. One of the K-Pop agents had intravenously given Sung-jin some truth serum when he was unconscious. While truth serum is notoriously not that reliable, the agents thought it nevertheless might be useful to lower Sung-Jin's inhibitions against speaking. After three big gulps of water, Sung-jin put down the bottle and resumed his indignation at his treatment. "You still haven't answered me; what's going on? I demand to be released. Am I being arrested? And if so, why? I've done nothing wrong."

John Kim spoke: "We'll be the ones asking the questions here. Let's begin with an easy one: what's your name?"

Sung-jin at first thought about remaining silent, although he then thought better of it. His mind was a little hazy from the truth serum. "My name is Sung-jin Park. But somehow I think you knew that already," he smirked.

"OK, thanks. And what do you do for a living, Mr. Park?"

"I am an art agent, for sellers mostly, but sometimes buyers, and I'm an art consultant too."

"Agent and consultant for who?"

"Well, I freelance a lot, but mostly work as a seller's agent and consultant for The Park Oh Gallery. I have cards from the gallery in my wallet, which is in my briefcase. But it looks like you stole that from me so I can't show you."

"Oh, we have your briefcase, Mr. Park. And we will give it back to you when we are done here."

Sung-jin jerked his head up at this. The implication that he could get out of this and leave was not lost on him.

"Yes, Mr. Park, we are not murderers or kidnappers, so you can expect to leave here, quite soon as a matter of fact. But only, of course, after you answer our questions." John Kim chose his words carefully here. He was a good interrogator, trained to probe his subject's weaknesses and get them to talk.

"So what do you really want to know?" asked Sung-jin.

"What we really want to know is what you've been doing since, say, last August or so until now."

"That's it?" Sung-jin replied incredulously.

"Yup, that's it," John responded.

"Well, then, that's easy. Last July and August, I was stuck in Seoul for just about the entire two month period, as the Park Oh Gallery had a big showing. We sold a huge number of paintings and sculptures. The market was really hot then, although it's still pretty good now too. I got a big commission near the end of August since several of the pieces that I had helped originally buy had gotten sold. I also was able to facilitate a few of the sales transactions from a number of wealthy buyers. It was a great month," Sung-jin boasted.

"And then what?"

"Well, then I took a vacation at the end of August," he continued. "To celebrate."

"Where did you go?"

"Oh, a bunch of places," he said evasively. "Let's see. I went to Europe on vacation, with a little bit of a side business development action as always. There's a good Bulgarian client of mine in Sofia, so I went there first. He's bought a few pieces from me over the years, although not at our big showing the month before. He's more of a quiet buyer, and I show him special stuff from time to time."

"How long did you stay in Sofia?"

"I don't exactly remember, but it was at least four days. And then I went over to Varna, on the coast. It's one of my favorite beach cities in Europe because it's still relatively unknown."

"Varna's great. Been there only once though. How long did you stay in Varna?"

"I had rented an apartment there on Airbnb for a month. It's a place I had rented before so I knew how great it was. It was my base as I took some day trips along the Bulgarian coast from there."

"You vacationed for an entire month?"

"Look – hey, I don't even know your name ..."

"Just call me Mr. Kim."

"OK, Mr. Kim, look, I'm not an office worker. While my card says Park Oh Gallery, I'm really their agent and consultant, and not their employee. That means I pretty much determine my own hours, except when the gallery needs me present for a particular showing. It's one of the perks of being a free-lancer."

"Keep going. You stayed in Varna for a month. Then what?"

"Then nothing. I had to go back to Seoul as I also consult for the National Museum of Korea. There is an exhibit that is coming in from Thailand next month. Part of that exhibit showcases a number of sculptures, which is my specialty, as I somehow also think that you are aware. My job back then was to help figure out which sculptures to show, and then to help curate the sculptural part of the exhibition. You know, help draft the narrative that goes along with the exhibit, to make it more meaningful to the museum visitor. It's a great deal of work actually, and I'm still not done with it entirely. As a matter of fact, that's what I was doing most of today, meeting with the folks in the National Museum. And ..."

John cut him off with a wave of his hand. He shook his head and rubbed his eyes a bit, motioning for Mike to get and give him the briefcase, which Mike did, sliding it onto the table. Sung-jin watched this with bemused interest. John opened the case and pulled out a few manila folders. "So let's stay with the time that you were in Varna, shall we? Want to make sure that we have that part of your trip straight."

"I'm telling you the truth."

"No doubt, no doubt," John continued. "You're giving us the overview, but not the details we need."

"Details?"

"Yes, details. Can you provide us more about the month that you were in and around Varna?" John said carefully. The folders remained closed on the table, a silent warning to Sung-jin to make doubly sure that he was providing each and every pertinent detail.

"There is not much to tell," Sung-jin protested, looking a little uneasier now, and stealing some glances at the folder. The truth serum was making him feel light-headed and woozy. "Have you been tailing me or something? What's with the folders? Who do you work for anyway? Are you with the government? Is this a tax thing; are you with the National Tax Service or something? I've paid all my taxes on my art earnings, you know."

"Not much to tell? That means that there is something to tell. So tell us and don't leave out any details."

"Come on," Sung-jin protested, "this was almost a year ago. I don't remember everything that I did. Let's see. I went to the beach on the first day, and ate at this great seafood restaurant, Captain something, I think Captain Cook. It's right near the water, and the fish is fantastic. On the second day, I went north a bit, past the university. Is that detailed enough for you?"

"Did you see anyone? Clients or others?" John prodded.

"No, not in the beginning," Sung-jin said. "I had already seen my big client in Sofia, and had met with another client at the end of the month. It was just a rest-and-relaxation trip for me mostly. I mean, my girlfriend Mina wasn't there until the end, but I was mostly decompressing. Reading some art history stuff, some novels, going to the beach, some bars, you know what I mean."

"Actually I do. Did you go to any other countries during that month?"

Sung-jin's mind was spinning. "Uhh," Sung-jin said calmly. "Hey, my passport shows that I didn't go anywhere; go look at it if you want. It shows that I was in Bulgaria the whole time."

"Really now," John chided. "Is that your story?" He glanced over at the folder.

Sung-jin licked his lips a little nervously. "Like I said, look at my passport."

"Oh, I believe that part of your story, Sung-jin. You wouldn't lie about something that can be so easily verified. But you could have traveled under a bogus passport or something. Have you heard of that before?"

"I guess. This seems too James Bond-like for me. Are you with the National Intelligence Service then or something?" he ventured. "I have no idea why you would be interested in me. Is this some sort of art forgery thing?"

"No, not an art forgery thing, for sure." John fixed a steely eyed gaze on Sung-jin. "Did you ever go to Romania during this time?"

"Umm, I don't remember exactly," Sung-jin said weakly. "Like I said, that was a long time ago."

"I think that you would remember going to a different country," Mike snapped. John held up his hand to quiet his subordinate. They had rehearsed this, so John wasn't really mad at Mike. Mike was playing the bad cop today.

"Let's say we kind of know that you went to Romania," John said amiably. "Can you tell us what you were doing there?"

"OK, OK," Sung-jin started, flustered and a little unsure of how to play this. How much did these people know? The truth serum was basically just making his head hurt. He tried one more gambit to test out his theory that they were pretty clueless, and just fishing for information. "Art is a funny business. Let me put it this way; some of my clients aren't exactly pillars of society. And it's a cutthroat business too, where you don't want your competitors to know what you are doing. I have a customer in Romania that's a little shady, and quite frankly, I don't want to be seen to know him, and he doesn't want to be seen as knowing me, for that matter. So he got me a fake passport, and when I want to visit him, then I use that passport to meet him in Romania."

"I see," John said noncommittally. "Anything else you want to share?"

"What do you mean?"

"Like I said, we're testing you a bit to confirm what we know. So when you didn't tell us the whole truth in the first place about being in Romania, it makes us wonder what else you are hiding."

"Are you toying with me then? Tell me what you know about my own travels then."

Mike took the cue. "Listen, you don't know how much trouble you're in, Sung-jin. Start talking about the details, and tell us everything," he screamed in Sung-jin's face.

"Look, I was in Bucharest only for a day I think."

"Come on!" Mike screamed. He smacked Sung-jin on the head hard with one of the folders that had been lying on the table. "Stop hiding the truth from us! We know that you were in Constanta. Tell us about Constanta."

Sung-jin went pale. *They really did know a lot. But how could they?* he thought to himself. He had been so careful. "Umm," Sung-jin started to stammer, "right, I did go to Constanta. At a condo near the beach on the Strada Caiuti."

"Yes, go on," John said calmly, restraining Mike and pushing him back into his seat. The good cop-bad cop act was being played to perfection here. "Don't shade the truth to us like this. We are going to need to put you on the polygraph at this time." John made a signal to the one-way mirror and K-Pop Three came into the room bearing a polygraph machine which they hooked up to Sung-jin and another chair for K-Pop Three to sit in. After the device was set up, John continued with the interrogation. "See, now look what you made us do. We are going to need to start all over again, and it just means more time before we can let you go. First, what is your name?"

Sung-jin was feeling really tired now. "Sung-jin Park. As you know."

"And what do you do for a living and where do you work?"

"Come on, I'm feeling exhausted. Can we get a break here? Like I said before, I'm a free-lance art agent and art consultant. I work for the Park Oh Gallery mostly, although I do work for the National Museum too."

K-Pop Three nodded his head. They now had the baseline polygraph results for some known truths. John continued his relentless questioning. Sung-jin's head was spinning. "You'll get a break soon once you tell us the whole truth. Tell us about Constanta. When did you go there and who did you meet?"

"Hmm, let's see. I'm a little foggy on the dates. Oh yeah, I remember now. I was in Varna the last week of August, and had gone to Constanta on August 31. I spent a couple of days there."

The payoff questions were coming. "And who did you meet?"

"I met with a couple of people," Sung-jin said. "The key for my job was that I renewed my contact with an important Romanian industrialist who is a big art buyer of mine. He has bought a total of $5 million of art works in the last year from me. You know what my commission is on that? After expenses, I get like two percent, so that's about one hundred thousand US dollars! God, I love that guy," he said dreamily. "One of my favorite customers; I think he's worth a couple billion dollars."

"Forget that guy for a moment," John pressed. "Who else did you meet with in Constanta?"

"Oh, just some people," Sung-jin said, demurring from providing any additional color to his interrogators.

"I think you're just being difficult, Sung-jin," John said gently. "You're not going to get to leave this way. You have to be more forthright with us. Who else exactly did you meet?"

"Uhh, no one that you would know," Sung-jin protested. It was getting harder and harder to concentrate.

"Oh, don't be so sure," Mike said. Mike pulled out a picture of Young-ji Kim from one of the folders on the table. "Did you meet with this guy?"

Sung-jin's vision was blurry, but he focused intently on the picture. *They had a picture of his father! How did they know all of this?* he thought frantically to himself. They seem to know everything! "Yes! Yes! He is one of the people I met with in Constanta!" he found himself saying.

"And who is he?" John demanded.

Sung-jin hung his head. "He is my father," he said quietly. "My dad that I never knew growing up."

John nodded to Mike; they were making some progress now. "And what is his name?"

"His name is Young-ji, Young-ji Kim," Sung-jin found himself saying. "He's from North Korea."

"Thank you, Sung-jin. We knew that, but appreciate your candor with us. You're doing great; stay with us, as we only have a little bit more to go."

Sung-jin looked dreamily at the picture and held it in his hands. Getting to meet his dad was one of the best things in his life that had ever happened to him. It was such an opportune meeting, as he was really unhappy at that time of his life immediately before the meeting. Everything seemed to work out really well after they had met. His dad helped him get on his feet financially. He had even met Mina shortly after that. His circle of customers had shot up dramatically, and he felt like he was a real player now in the art community, way more so than before.

"And what did you do with your dad in Constanta?"

"We just got caught up. You know, he's a real art connoisseur like me, and he has amazing knowledge of early Korean art, even more than me."

"Did you go anywhere with him?"

Sung-jin hesitated. "Yes, we took a trip across the Black Sea, ending up near Poti, in Georgia."

John and Mike's ears perked up at this. They were getting some information about how the father and son had gotten to Chechnya. "Why Poti? Where did you go after that?"

"We went to Chechnya. It was a long drive. We had a meeting in an area outside Grozny with an, umm, art customer."

"When was this?"

"Oh, it was the first weekend in September, I think. I think that it was Saturday night if I remember correctly." That would have been September 5th.

"What kind of meeting was this?"

"We were looking to buy some … stuff. You know, something that my dad wanted to buy."

"And what was this stuff?"

"Oh, I can't really say."

"You can and you will," Mike screamed, leaping up to get into Sung-jin's face. "What were you buying?"

Sung-jin started to weep a bit. "Can't talk about this."

Mike started pushing Sung-jin around, shaking him hard. "You've got to tell us, Sung-jin."

Sung-jin violently began to shake his hand to the negative. Mike kept up with the verbal abuse, while John tempted him with soothing words that they were almost done, and just needed these last vital pieces of information. They continued to press him from all of these angles. Interrogation was indeed an art, as John and Mike played off on each other, not daring to press too hard as they were making progress. For now, though, it was to no avail as Sung-jin was growing more difficult to deal with and was on the verge of passing out. And then he did, becoming unconscious.

John and Mike discussed their options. They believed that they were running out of time, but feared pressing too hard, or else their subject would either remain unconscious or become completely incoherent. After discussion among the team, they decided to let Sung-jin rest for a few more hours, but they would wake him up again in the middle of one of his deep sleep cycles so that they could disorient him even further.

About two and a half hours later, at around 12:35am on Saturday morning, Mike splashed Sung-jin with some water and got him up again. Sung-jin was still in the interrogation room, and had been re-chained back to where he had been two and a half hours ago. John and Mike were exhausted as it had already been a long week just in preparing for this operation.

"Wakey, wakey," Mike said sarcastically. "Time for some more questions, Sung-jin."

Sung-jin had been dreaming wildly over the past few hours. The dreams were not coherent, but he vaguely recalled thinking about the first time that he had met his dad some six years ago. He had also dreamed, strangely enough, about the time that he was five years old, when he had vivid memories of his first time that he had recalled going to the beach with his mom and a childhood friend. Interspersed between these dreams were dreams about Mina and his previous girlfriends. It was all a jumble.

"We are in Chechnya now with you," John intoned. He nodded and Colonel Umarov's voice was piped into the room.

"Good morning," Colonel Umarov said. "Муха ду гӀуллакхаш? (*mookh doo ghool-lah-qash*) (How are you?)" When they had met last, the language that they had used primarily was English as it was the only common language that the Chechens and North Koreans had among them.

Sung-jin couldn't believe it at first. Was he back in Chechnya? He tried to open his eyes, but his vision was completely dark. He moved his arms and legs around, but seemed rooted in place. He figured that he was still dreaming, although he definitely recognized the voice of Colonel Umarov. Where was his father, though? "Дика ду, баркалла. (*deek doo, bar-kahl*) (Fine, thank you)" he found himself saying in Chechen, which he had been instructed to do by his father. Those were pretty much the only words that he knew in Chechen, other than "hello" (Салам (*sa-lam*)) and "good night" (Буьйса декъал йогӀийла (*boos dek-kal yo-gh*)).

"Do you have the money?" Colonel Umarov continued.

Sung-jin remained silent as it had been his father who, after the pleasantries had been exchanged, had dealt with the Colonel. But his father didn't say anything, and Sung-jin was confused. "Father?" he said.

"Your father is looking to you to consummate the transaction," Colonel Umarov said emotionlessly. "He is waiting outside for you."

"Father? Father?" Sung-jin went on, disregarding what the Colonel was saying. He was now on the verge of panic as he didn't know what to do.

"OK, calm down," Colonel Umarov went on, "your father has delivered the money to me. We are counting that money now. Please go inside with your father to discuss the transportation logistics."

Sung-jin visibly relaxed and he let his mind wander a bit. The operation was going smoothly again. A voice that was not his father's broke the silence.

"Where do we go with the arms, Sung-jin? Where do your father and you want the nuclear weapon to go?" John whispered into Sung-jin's ear, through the blindfold that had been placed to disorient Sung-jin further.

"What? What are you talking to me for?" Sung-jin said confusedly. "And what do you mean by nuclear weapon? I thought my father was just buying some rocket launchers. My father Young-ji, you should know, is dealing with the transportation of the arms anyway, not me. And I was supposed to wait outside. Who are you again?"

John ignored the question. "Then why are you here in Chechnya? Where are the weapons going?"

"I don't know!" Sung-jin shouted. "It was always implied that it would be somewhere in the United States, of course," he admitted, "but I don't know where exactly."

"When will the weapons be used?" John persisted.

"I said I don't know!" Sung-jin shouted again. "I think soon, though. I overheard father talking to one of his colleagues. Something about "independence night" being part of the operation. Figured that he meant the American's Independence Day fireworks celebration. Father also wanted me to make sure that I was not traveling to the United States until this fall."

John, Mike and K-Pop Three looked at each other worriedly. Mike left the room hurriedly to make a call to the Triple Play team in the US. It was about 12:55am in the morning in South Korea on Saturday, July 2nd, so that meant it was around 11:55am on Friday, July 1st at Triple Play headquarters in Washington, DC. They were going to get a terrible morning newsflash in DC. It would be sure to cause a lot of pre-lunch indigestion. And, of course, it was at the worst possible time, right before a major holiday weekend. No rest for the weary.

"We need to know where the nuke is going to be set off and how," John said, resuming the interrogation.

"I'm just an art agent and consultant," Sung-jin wailed. "I don't know about these things; I just wanted to see my father and to have some money to live a good life with Mina." John could see that Sung-jin was breaking down now and beginning to babble. John had to get Sung-jin more focused on the issues at hand.

"OK, Sung-jin, you are doing great. You're almost done and home-free. What else do you know? Can you give us any more information?"

Sung-jin was still groggy, but now more awake and cognizant of where he was. "Hey, you tricked me. I'm done talking. I'm not saying anything more. I want a lawyer. You with the police? You haven't told me anything about who you are. I'm supposed to be on vacation now. Hey, my car service was supposed to take me to Ggotji Beach near Anmyeon-eup tonight where I was supposed to meet a friend. You know, people are going to miss me from this kidnapping of yours."

John sat back down dejectedly. This wasn't really going well at all. They needed some answers fast. "Look, we took your cell phone, and replied to the texts that your car service and friend had sent asking where you were. We just texted that you were sick and needed to cancel for now. Let's try a different tack now. You just admitted basically that there is a nuke on US soil, that it's going to go off on the night of July 4th, and that you are responsible for this, or at least that you are part of the conspiracy."

"Why do you keep talking about a nuclear bomb? I have no idea what you are talking about!" protested Sung-jin.

John assiduously ignored Sung-jin's complaints. "Do you know how much trouble you are in?" John flashed his credentials. "I am with the United States government. I'm part of military intelligence with the Defense Department. If a nuke goes off in the US and we know you're responsible, do you realize what we're going to do in retaliation? We are going to nuke North Korea and kill your father. Your own South Korean government is going to disavow you, and we are going to take away all the money that you have, and then you are going to be publicly executed by your own government. Your girlfriend Mina will probably get swept into this and executed as well, even if she had nothing to do with this." John was reaching for anything now; he had no idea about what would happen to Mina, but he had to scare Sung-jin into talking at any cost. "Do you want to die a slow, painful death, and be known to your family and friends as the person who destroyed both North and South Korea? Is that what you want?"

Stubbornly, Sung-jin still refused to talk, especially when John told him that he was an American intelligence agent. John's threats fell on deaf ears from that point on. However, Sung-jin was beginning to get very scared. He didn't realize that his father and he were buying a nuclear bomb, although he did think that his dad was doing an arms purchase. While he had been introduced to Colonel Umarov, his father had arranged it so that they had met outside the facility. Sung-jin had never gone into the warehouse where the actual nuke-for-money exchange had taken place.

Really, his father had bought a nuke in Chechnya? Sung-jin thought to himself. This was all of course assuming that the American was telling the truth. What if there was no nuclear weapon at all, and they were just lying to get him to screw his father? Who knew what in the hell was really going on? Sung-jin resolved to himself to just shut up for now until he could think this through some more. The "friend" that he was supposed to have met last night was his father. His dad was the one who had set up the car service for him to get to Anmyeon-eup tonight; they were supposed to have some father-son time at Ggotji Beach tomorrow. Sung-jin wondered whether his father was looking for him now. He wished he could contact his father and figure out what his father would want him to say to these guys.

Meanwhile, back in DC, Mike's emergency call had indeed caused considerable consternation. Yet another all-hands emergency meeting had been called that was scheduled to start around 1pm DC time. Lunch was definitely going to be ruined for a whole lot of people.

CHAPTER 29

"These all-hands emergency meetings are getting out of hand," Jim Broussard complained to no one in particular before the meeting started in the Joint Base Andrews war room. "What, isn't this like our fourth or fifth one in the last year? It's ridiculous. We've got to find this "K" nuke and be done with this insanity. Uh-oh, people are looking pretty somber. Something big must be up," he muttered to himself. "This doesn't look good. Shoot, and I was hoping that I could sleep in this weekend."

President Besselman opened up the meeting, which started at 1305 hours ET on Friday afternoon on July 1st. "Ladies and gentlemen, we have a crisis. And this one is worse than the Iranian nuke crisis. I have moved all US armed forces in Asia into DEFCON 2 status." Chaos erupted as everyone started talking in disbelief. The US had not been in DEFCON 2 status since Operation Desert Storm in 1991, and before that, during the Cuban Missile Crisis in 1962. The President raised his hands for silence. "This status is only for our forces in Asia. The rest of the country will be in DEFCON 3 status, just like when we had the Iranian nuke situation. God, that was such a short time ago! In addition, we have currently broadcast a NTAS alert, but only so far at the "Elevated" level -- again, just like before in the Iranian nuke situation. The difference is this: at 1300 hours Eastern Time tomorrow, Saturday, July 2nd, I will move the NTAS alert to "Imminent" if we haven't figured out what the hell is going on with the "K" nuke. At that time, I will also move the entire country into DEFCON 2 status. That means we have 24 hours to find and disarm the "K" nuke before we go public."

Once again, people started talking all at once, and it took a full ten seconds before order could be restored. "This is bad, folks. I'm not going to sugarcoat this. We have a strong belief that a nuke will be set off on the night of July 4th. Pat Jorgensen will fill you in on the details. Here we go again, everyone; the country is once more depending on you to save the day. We need to get this 'third out' now – we must complete the triple play," the President stressed with all of his might.

Pat Jorgensen took over from the President. "Thank you, Mr. President. Lots of safety protocols are being enacted, most of which you are familiar with. Thankfully, Congress isn't in session so many people aren't in DC now. However, the President was scheduled to be present at this year's July 4th fireworks celebration. Obviously, that's not going to happen now. In fact, right after this meeting, as a precautionary matter, we are going to put the President on Air Force One and get him and his family away from DC. Certain other government people are going to be evacuated now too. My staffers will be in touch with each of your staffers on this."

The HSA took a breath before continuing. "Here's the background on the reason for the evacuation. Our DIA operatives in Korea have been interrogating Sung-jin Park (Kim) for the last few hours. Many of you know that Sung-jin is a South Korean art agent and consultant. He has provided credible intelligence that his father, one Young-ji Kim, a North Korean who was only known by Sung-jin recently to be his birth father, purchased the third nuke, the so-called "K" nuke, from Colonel Umarov in September of last year. As an additional confirmation, Colonel Umarov has gotten pictures and video of Sung-jin and has confirmed that this was one of the people that he had met when the purchase occurred. However, an interesting sidenote on this situation is that Sung-jin says that he did not realize that the transaction involved a nuke. He just thought it was a regular arms sale of some sort. We are inclined to believe him for now. Separately, Sung-jin has also provided credible intelligence that the nuke was transported to the United States and is intended to be detonated on the evening of July 4th, literally three and a half days from now. Jack, any more info to give here?"

Jack Smith was speaking softly on the phone to Mike and John while the HSA had been talking. He put his hand over the phone, and vigorously shook his head no and to keep going.

"OK, so we know the what (it's the "K" nuke for sure) and the when (likely the evening of July 4th). I have to say, though, we are worried that, if we announce NTAS 'Imminent' status on Saturday afternoon, then the nuke detonation schedule will be moved up too. We'll discuss that later. More importantly, however, we don't even know the where. We are guessing that it has to be a major target: we think that it's going to either be (1) Washington, DC; or (2) New York City. As I said before, Sung-jin continues to protest that he does not know about the where. We are searching his apartment for clues, anything that would give us a hint. I think that it's DC for sure, personally."

"Have the North Koreans gone mad?" Jonathan Proxmeier exclaimed, saying what everyone was thinking. "They've got to know that we're going to nuke them in retaliation. We just can't stand here and let them take out DC or any other major US city!"

"As I told you, Jonathan, we have no idea what the North Koreans are thinking. Maybe they thought we couldn't figure out it was them, since it's a Russian tactical nuke. I have no idea what's in their mind. It's almost 0145 in the morning in

North Korea right now. The plan is to call them at 0800 in their morning on the crisis phone, and start a dialogue with them, letting them pointedly know that we know it's them. Hopefully, that makes them back down. Since we want to stress diplomacy here, it will be Secretary of State Walker and her assistant talking to her counterparts there. If we sense it's needed, we'll have the President immediately available to talk to their Supreme Leader if necessary. Don't forget, the North Koreans will wake up to the US and South Korean forces being on DEFCON 2 status. Hopefully, that alone will give them pause. We are going to rattle the sword for sure."

General McTighe spoke up, "Oh, we'll rattle our sword for damn sure, sir. We are going to rattle the hell out of all of our swords."

Pat Jorgensen went on: "And starting tonight, immediately before we talk to the North Koreans, we're going to think about restricting access in and out of DC, New York and all of the major cities. It's going to cause havoc on the freeways, but we are going to have checkpoints on all of the major arteries into and out of likely target cities. As I understand it, the timer on the RA-115 nuke can only be set up to a max of 24 hours before it detonates. Therefore, many of us are generally thinking," he looked over at Jack Smith, "that it is more likely than not that the nuke still needs to be brought into the city where it is going to be detonated, since it hasn't been detected yet. By that logic, our checkpoints may prevent the nuke from even getting where it's supposed to detonate."

K2 whispered to David, "Oh my god, checkpoints all around each major US city? It's going to be a zoo tonight."

David whispered back, "Yeah, I know; and with the rain that is expected this afternoon here in the city, there's going to be a whole lot of angry people in the Washington DC metro area tonight. Not that you or I will be affected," he said sourly, "as we'll be basically living at Andrews here for the next 96 hours."

The meeting formally ended at 1345 ET, but it almost didn't matter as everyone had follow-up meetings that they had to immediately attend.

CHAPTER 30

Marcia hugged K2 before they started their next meeting. "This is so terrible; I can't stand it. Luckily, John and Jeff are at John's parents' home in Charlottesville. Without telling them any details about why, I told them to stay there no matter what, and that I'd try to be there as soon as I could. Do you think it's DC too?" she stated anxiously.

"Yes," K2 admitted, "unfortunately, I do."

"Me too," David said. "So let's stop this bomb. OK, Jack, what's the news?"

Jack Smith had just gotten off the phone. "We've got agents swarming all over Sung-jin's place. We're examining every consulting invoice he's ever done in the last five years to see where the nuke might be. Maybe he consulted off-record and there is no document linkage to the site, but we have to try. We've got a few leads so far, and are checking them out, but Sung-jin's still not talking. There's a good chance he's not lying. He probably didn't know the purchase was for a nuke. That's my belief anyway."

"OK, let's talk deployment. Don, you good with how your NEST folks are split up?"

"Well," Don replied on the videophone, "K2, Ben and I got into a big argument on this one. I also think that DC is the likely target, so Ben and I wanted to switch locations with K2. She convinced me, though, that we just have to play it where people are, for logistical efficiency. I couldn't convince her otherwise."

"You've got that right!" K2 exclaimed.

Don continued, "So, since I am in New York City anyway because of an IAEA thing, I'm just staying here to cover it and Boston. K2 will continue to cover DC with you from Andrews. Ben's covering the West Coast from LA/Nellis, and Sri's covering the Midwest from near Chicago. We're spread a little thin, but you play the cards you're dealt. About three-fourths of the Roosevelt Diamond Augmentation Team are with K2 there at Andrews, including Sabrina McAllister. The other fourth are on the way to me in New York City."

Jim Broussard chimed in, "David, I'm really spread thin too, and I have way fewer people than Don. For my Humvees, Rick and Steve are here in DC as Cannon 1 and Cannon 2. I have Mark in LA as Cannon 3. The only thing that's probably new to you is that I have Joe and Nick both in New York City as Cannon 4 and Cannon 5, with JJ being the backup now in Boston as Cannon 6."

David turned to Mark Childress next. "What's the final word on the assault troops?"

"At the risk of sounding like a broken record, we are spread too thin like Don and Jim. As you know, David, we had to split up our "A" team quite a bit. Artie M is covering New York City and the New England area with his team of ten, and Paul A is in LA with his guys. With respect to the sharpshooters, Richie is here with a small crew. However, we had to move Rob over to Boston and Rocky over to Chicago. Part of Richie's team was sent over in LA, where Ronnie Williams is leading them. He's hating life."

"Too bad. He'll deal with it like we all are, Mark," David replied testily. "Are all of the command centers up and running?"

"For the last thirty minutes," came the reply from one of his senior communications officer. "The gun, so to speak, is loaded and cocked. We just need something to point it at."

"How's the weather affecting our air support?" asked David.

Jimmy Robbson, the liaison between the WMD Directorate and the Air Force, answered succinctly, "Well, David, it sucks. We've got only 60 Black Hawks, three Black Hawks to cover each of the top 20 major metropolitan area, one carrying the shooters, one carrying the NEST guys, and one for everything else. The plan is to keep at least one Black Hawk in the air at all times, but the weather will make that tough. Other air support is better. We've got regular F-16 patrols coming out of the 121st Fighter Squadron of the 113th Wing here at Andrews. A few of them also got dispatched to New York, where they are running out of Joint Base McGuire. Chicago's being protected from Wright-Patterson. F-16s and F-22s are being flown from the 57th Wing at Nellis."

"Sounds pretty good to me."

"It's the best I can do for now."

"And the National Guard?" David continued.

"The NGB is pissed at us again, since we're asking for another all-out major deployment on a major holiday weekend. McTighe reamed the hell out of the NGB Chief, though, and they are being nicer to us now. Again, we're not telling them everything, but starting tomorrow at around 1000 hours Eastern Time, there are going to be 50,000 National Guardsmen at our disposal. The NGB is activating the phone call tree now to get hold of everyone. The guardsmen will know they are being activated because of a possible terrorist attack, but once again, they won't know it's because of a suspected nuke. Once the President goes to NTAS 'Imminent,' however, tomorrow at 1pm, I think most of them are going to suspect something big is happening, like a potential nuke attack."

For the next three hours, the team prepared various scenarios and contingencies and got pretty comfortable with where they stood. It was now almost 1700 ET in the afternoon with no quitting time in sight. Furthermore, it was already raining lightly in DC, with the forecast calling for heavy showers within the hour until past midnight. *It was going to be one of those crappy weekends*, David thought to himself.

CHAPTER 31

Joo Cheon was getting panicky. His clandestine projects director for this situation, Joon-ho Lee, who was stationed in Seoul, had told him that Young-ji Kim had called Joon-ho around 1am local time from Anmyeon-eup. Young-ji had informed Joon-ho on the call that something had happened to Sung-jin. Sung-jin had not shown up at their intended rendezvous point, and had not responded with the right code words to Young-ji's urgent texts from Young-ji's burner cell phone. They were only a few days away from detonating the nuke and this development was unnerving.

Originally, as the price of Young-ji's participation, Young-ji had insisted that Joo guarantee Young-ji that Young-ji and his son would be outside Seoul after the nuke was set off. This was in case the US figured out it was North Korea who set off the nuke and there was an armed confrontation between the two countries. In that circumstance, Young-ji had figured, it would be prudent for the both of them to be as far away from the capital city of South Korea as reasonably possible.

And so Joon-ho had arranged for a car service to take Sung-jin to Anmyeon-eup, where Young-ji was now, and where Young-ji had wanted to explain to his son what was going down on July 4th. As the saying goes, however, the best-laid plans of mice and men often go awry.

Joo's plans were certainly going awry. He was scheduled to leave North Korea late in the afternoon today, Saturday, July 2nd, where he had planned to smuggle himself into Seoul, and then to leave Seoul on a fake passport from Seoul-Incheon Airport to Frankfurt on the afternoon of Sunday, July 3rd. Now he had to figure out whether to change those plans. Joo decided that he needed a little more information. Therefore, Joo directed Joon-ho to drop by Sung-jin's apartment to see if he could make contact with Sung-jin. Maybe Sung-jin was very sick, and had screwed up the codes because he was simply too ill to think straight. It could be a false alarm, although deep in his heart, Joo didn't think so.

Joon-ho called Joo back breathlessly two and a half hours later. "It's bad, boss. Looks like there are all sorts of people crawling around the place." Joon-ho and Joo were careful not to use names in case someone was listening on the cell line. "What do you want to do? He didn't really know anything about the project."

Joo thought long and hard. "Initiate the Z protocol," he finally said simply.

"Understood, Z protocol," came the reply. It was about 4:30am in the morning in South Korea, and about 4am in North Korea.

Z protocol meant that Joon-ho, in a roundabout way and through a number of intermediaries, would get in touch with Min-ho and Ji-eun and instruct them to start the nuke detonation timer as soon as possible. It would not be a suicide mission; they were to set it to whatever lead time they believed necessary in order to allow them to escape successfully, with the default being a few hours.

CHAPTER 32

Min-ho's and Ji-eun's beepers went off at the same time at 3:28pm ET on Friday, July 1st, in the US. Min-ho was scheduled to present last in a technical meeting that would end at 6pm; he decided that he would not leave the meeting early, so that he would not attract undue suspicion. Ji-eun was home with the baby when her beeper went off. The message just said "Z Protocol." When she turned it off, as per protocol, in five minutes it went off again and a duplicate message saying "Z Protocol" showed up. That just meant that the message was confirmed and not a mistake. She started packing immediately, aware that Min-ho would be arriving home by approximately 6:30pm, depending on traffic.

In her mind, the family would need to drive all the way to Chicago starting tonight, instead of leaving on Sunday night, July 3rd, as they had originally planned. Min-ho had said that there they could start a new life in Chicago among the local Korean population, far away from the nuclear fallout. Fortunately, the prevailing westerlies meant that the wind would blow the nuclear fallout eastward, towards the Atlantic Ocean and away from Chicago. Ji-eun finished packing as many of Min-jun's favorite clothes and toys as she could stuff into their Honda Odyssey. She had already done most of the packing in anticipation of their weekend departure. She also went to the bank to take out a large amount of the cash that they had stashed in their accounts.

Min-ho came back around 6:20pm. Traffic had been light on this holiday weekend. They ate in grim silence as they realized the magnitude of what lay before them.

"So we're going to Chicago tonight?" Ji-eun asked.

"Yes, that's the plan," Min-ho confirmed. "We need to clear out of town as far as we reasonably can tonight. Looks like we'll able to leave around 7:20pm from here. Let's be conservative and say that, with the rain, we can get to DC and be done within two hours at max. That's around 9 o'clock, or maybe 9:15 or 9:30pm at worst. Then if we drive at a normal pace," he looked on Google Maps on his laptop, "I'm guessing we can get to Pittsburgh around 1am or maybe 1:15am in the morning. We get our same hotel there, just two nights early, and then we take off for Chicago after we get some sleep so we'll be far away when the nuke goes off. I'm going to set it for the maximum time of 24 hours so it'll go off in the evening of July 2nd. It won't cause as much damage as under the original plan of setting it off on July 4th, but it's the best we can do now. It'll still cause a huge amount of damage."

"Sounds about right," Ji-eun said, nodding in assent. They went on the internet to change their original reservations for two days earlier. The price turned out to be about the same. The couple smiled and let out some breaths of relief when all of the reservations were finally successfully updated and the confirmations emailed to them. They were ready to go. With that, they bundled Min-jun in warm clothes, put him into the minivan car seat and prepared to drive off.

"Hmm, seems like there's a lot of traffic getting into DC tonight. And the rain's only going get worse tonight. Well, it's not like we have a choice. Here we go," Min-ho said as they drove off towards Washington, DC.

CHAPTER 33

The call occurred at 1900 hours ET. Secretary of State Walker didn't mince any words. She blasted her North Korean counterpart in no uncertain terms. She went through the litany of evidence that they had that North Korea was planning to bomb Washington, DC, despite her counterpart's protestations to the contrary. The Secretary of State also noted that they would be emailing North Korea this evidence, including pictures of the North Korean agents (Young-ji and Sung-jin) that had purchased the nuclear weapon. She also noted that the United States had moved its Asian forces to DEFCON 2 status. In light of the seriousness of the situation, the plan was to have State deliver this message, and then follow it by a call between the President and their Supreme Leader in thirty minutes to let the North Koreans think about their response.

The high command in North Korea was in chaos. The Supreme Leader immediately called for an emergency meeting of all of his military advisors, and pointedly demanded that all intelligence officers would have to report in at that meeting. The Supreme Leader was furious; he wanted to know every detail about the alleged operation that he wasn't even aware of. Nothing was supposed to happen without his say so!

The head of military intelligence, Sang-chul Ahn, was sweating profusely in his office in Pyongyang. He had no idea what was going on, or how he had gotten himself into this predicament. He knew that he was close to being executed and he hadn't done anything wrong.

Ahn was trying to piece together the puzzle. He knew about Young-ji Kim. Young-ji was being run by Joo Cheon, one of the three Assistants to the Deputy Associate Director of

Clandestine Operations. After the call with the US Secretary of State, Joo Cheon had been forcibly brought to the military installation in Kaesong, where he had been stationed for an operation. Kaesong was near the border with South Korea, and Ahn knew that Joo was supposed to secretly slip into South Korea in only a few hours and fly off to Europe the following day. *Too coincidental*, Ahn thought to himself, *that Joo Cheon was leaving the country in light of what was going on.* Now there was no danger of Joo's departure. Joo would be held in Kaesong and questioned about this messy situation. Ahn would be personally leading the interrogation.

Because Joo was so senior, Ahn wanted to tread delicately. Unfortunately, this was balanced by the need for speed, as he only would be able to talk to Joo separately for ten minutes before the Supreme Leader got onto the call.

"What in the hell is going on, Joo? What do you know about this?" Ahn exploded at Joo when his subordinate appeared on the screen.

"I don't know what you are talking about, sir," Joo replied calmly.

"The Americans are claiming that we are going to set off a nuclear bomb in Washington on July 4th!" Ahn exclaimed. "They also have sworn testimony from a Colonel Umarov that Young-ji Kim and Sung-jin Park were the buyers in a Chechnyan arms transaction back in last September or something like that."

"Well, I don't know why they saying this," Joo replied defensively. "As you know, I was in Pyongyang the entire month last September. I think that the Americans are just trying to trick us. Where would Young-ji and Sung-jin have gotten the money to pay for this nuke anyway?"

"I don't know," Ahn said plaintively. "I was hoping that you could tell me."

"Let's put out a communication to Young-ji then, and just ask him directly," Joo said disingenuously. Joo already knew that Young-ji was told to stay incommunicado until the nuke was detonated as part of the Z protocol. He knew Young-ji was at a beachfront resort in South Korea to boot. It would be impossible for his North Korean comrades to bring in Young-ji for questioning in time.

"Where is Young-ji?" came the next question from the military intelligence chief.

"I don't know," Joo lied, "but I know that he's not engaged directly in an operation according to my logs. I think that he should be in Pyongyang. Don't you think so? You know his cell number; give him a ring. Or I'll call him."

"We tried to call him twenty times already," Sang-chul explained patiently. "Don't you think that is the first thing that we'd do? No answer, of course."

"Could he have gone rogue?" Joo questioned, trying to sound alarmed.

"I have no idea," Sang-chul said, wiping the sweat off his brow. This was bad; Joo didn't know what was going on either. "He's an art expert, not a weapons expert! What would he know about buying and setting off a nuclear bomb? This just makes no sense," Ahn complained. "Let me ask you a more delicate question, but I need to do this confidentially." He signaled to the two military officers in the room with Joo Cheon, "Leave us now; I must speak to Joo on matters of the highest national security."

When the two officers left the room, Ahn continued speaking. "I, I don't know how to say this, so I will just be forthright with you, Joo. You know how much I value and respect you. You don't need to tell me any details, but is this a special operation sanctioned by the Supreme Leader that I don't know about?"

"You know I couldn't tell you any details if it was, General Ahn, sir," Joo replied. "However, rest assured, the Supreme Leader did not instruct me to have Young-ji buy a nuclear bomb. I swear to you, sir, that this is the truth."

General Ahn breathed a small sign of relief. At least he wasn't being shut out by the Supreme Leader on this one. That didn't change the fact, however, that Sang-chul and Joo were going to have to do a great deal of explaining to the Supreme Leader.

The emergency meeting of the North Korean military leadership happened five minutes later in the main conference room of the central military headquarters. All of the military leadership was there in person, including the Supreme Leader and General Ahn. Joo Cheon, of course, was in attendance via videoconference.

After the background of the crisis had been explained to those who had heretofore been out of the loop, all eyes turned to the Supreme Leader. As expected, he was livid.

"What is going on here, General Ahn? Is it true that, without my permission, we have purchased a Russian tactical nuclear weapon, a RA-115, from the Chechens?"

"No, Supreme Leader sir, I am not aware of any such purchase."

"Joo, what do you have to say for yourself?" the Supreme Leader said, as he turned his attention to the figure on the video screen.

"No, Supreme Leader sir, I am also unaware of such purchase."

"Do not tell me what you are unaware of!" screamed the Supreme Leader. "Tell me what you are aware of."

"We are trying to figure out what is going on, Supreme Leader," Ahn continued, trying to pacify his commander. "We have not yet been able to reach Young-ji Kim, although we are still trying. It seems like he has turned off his cell phone, and we are unable to trace his whereabouts at present," he ended nervously. "We believe that he either is in Pyongyang or he has fled to South Korea, but are not sure of his exact whereabouts."

"That's ridiculous," the Supreme Leader scoffed. "Find him now. Who was running Young-ji again?"

"I was," Joo gulped.

"Then you have thirty minutes to put us in touch with Young-ji. After that, I may consider you an enemy of the state," he said menacingly to the video screen. The screen went ominously blank after that.

The President of the United States and the Supreme Leader had a very uncomfortable conversation. President Besselman methodically explained the evidence that the US had that Young-ji had purchased a nuclear weapon. The Supreme Leader methodically explained in reply that he and the North Korea government had nothing to do with this. The Supreme Leader did note to the President that they were looking for Young-ji at present to prove that he had not purchased the RA-115 nuke, but that they could not ascertain where he was. The two promised to follow up on matters to keep the communications lines open. They scheduled another call between their State Department heads which would take place in two more hours.

President Besselman got off the phone in an exasperated mood. "It's possible that this Young-ji has gone rogue," he told General McTighe, who had been sitting next to him, "because I can't see for the life of me how North Korea would think that they could get away with this. Nevertheless, we are all in an untenable situation. If Young-ji is acting under the authority of the North Korean regime, then our conversations will definitely make them stop the operation. But if Young-ji is not acting under the sponsorship of the government, then we are all screwed, since we are going to have to retaliate based on the evidence."

"Yes sir, I know. This is the only way that I thought we'd ever have a nuclear catastrophe – it would be when a non-traditional nation-state actor got hold of a nuke. Look at what's happened so far. We've had a rogue Iranian splinter faction try to take out Las Vegas. We've had ISIS, which is hardly a traditional nation-state, try to take out Seal Team Six. And now we probably have a North Korean rogue operative trying to take out DC. The pattern is there, sir."

"Unfortunately, I have to agree with General McTighe, sir," chimed in Jack Smith. "At this point, I'm inclined to believe it's more likely than not that Young-ji is rogue. We may never know the full truth, however, and we will be still right to retaliate given the solid evidence. If North Korea didn't directly plan this, then they are still culpable by letting Young-ji siphon off the money to buy the nuke. That money had to come from North Korea in some way, shape or manner. How else does Young-ji get hold of $100 million to pay for the nuke? The lesson here for these regimes is to control their operatives – rogue or not, the regime is going to be held accountable."

"Have to agree with you there, Jack," replied McTighe. "There's no way in hell we're not retaliating based on the evidence we have."

"Gentlemen, let's stop talking about retaliation and focus on stopping the nuke from going off in the first place," the President cut in. "What's the situation on the roadblocks?"

"Well sir," this was now the HSA talking, "we have been implementing the roadblocks. Most of the major freeway arteries are now stopping cars, and our police have been equipped with some handheld Geiger counters and the like. They're being instructed to open up all car trunks, and to look especially carefully inside vans and trucks. Tonight's going to really suck to be a motorist coming into any major metro area, particularly here in DC where the rain's just getting heavier and heavier."

Meanwhile, back in North Korea, Joo was being carefully watched by a cadre of armed military guards as he sat in a conference room on the phone, ostensibly trying to reach his team, who were futilely trying to figure out where Young-ji Park was located. His lieutenant, Dong-hyun No, was on the phone with Joo and Joon-ho; the three of them were going over Young-ji's last communication with them. Dong-hyun was beyond nervous. Dong-hyun's life was on the line here, and he was merely a lieutenant of Joo's who had no idea what was going on. *Life is totally unfair*, Dong-hyun thought to himself morosely.

Joo calmly noted that it was probably Dong-hyun himself who had the last conversation with Young-ji. "Wasn't it about a week and a half or two weeks ago? Remember when you were trying to figure out what we were going to do about the new movie out in South Korea about the Korean War? You were going to try to have Young-ji tell Sung-jin to influence his friends to make North Korea look a little better in the movie."

"Yes, I remember that conversation," Dong-hyun admitted ruefully. "It was almost exactly a week and a half ago. But it was a routine conversation, and Young-ji said that he would get on it right away. There was no indication anything else was going on. I swear it! This is just unbelievable!"

When the thirty minutes had passed, Joo was again summoned to get on the phone with the Supreme Leader. "Well," the leader asked, "have you found Young-ji?"

"No sir," Joo replied. "My operations group cannot find him at present."

The Supreme Leader grew visibly agitated. "Then you are indeed an enemy of the state. Perhaps you will be able to find him right before you are executed by being placed in front of an anti-aircraft gun in the next thirty minutes. Take him away!" he shouted.

The guards grabbed Joo, who now seemed resigned to his fate after hearing this pronouncement. "Hold on," he told the guards, "I have something to say to the Supreme Leader." The guards were confused, and looked for direction from the video screen. In the confusion, Joo continued. "This is for General Moon," he said plainly. "Plans are in motion to hit the US with a nuke. You can't stop it. For what it's worth, no one else on my team knew about this plan – it was all me." And with that, he chewed a suicide pill that he had concealed with his other medicines. The suicide pill made foam come out of Joo's mouth almost immediately. Joo fell dead on the floor to the horror of the others within five seconds of chewing the pill.

An uneasy and shocked silence permeated the videoconference call. No one knew what to say. Then the Supreme Leader simply said, "Find Young-ji now, along with everyone in the US who is a part of Joo's agent network. We need to stop whatever is going on." Unfortunately, the Z protocol had been enacted by Joo with respect to Min-ho and Ji-eun. No one would be able to contact them before the nuke was detonated.

CHAPTER 34

Min-ho's and Ji-eun's Honda Odyssey was filled to the brim with Min-jun's stuff. There was a travel crib, diapers, baby clothes, baby formula, toys, books, etc., together with two large suitcases for the parents. So when they were stopped by the police at the highway roadblock into Washington, DC, the Korean couple looked like what they were, harried parents trying to get into DC on a wet Friday night. After the police conducted a cursory check of their vehicle, a police officer quickly waved the family through and that was that. The time was 8:53pm on their car clock.

"What do you think that was about?" Ji-eun whispered to Min-ho as they passed the checkpoint.

"Not sure," Min-ho admitted. "Looks like the Americans have some inkling about what is going on. Either that, or they are just flailing around against some potential vague random terrorist threat. Who knows? Anyway, we're through."

"Yeah, but I wonder what's waiting for us ahead," Ji-eun continued nervously. "Maybe they will be on the alert for us in DC."

"I doubt it, but it's possible," Min-ho conceded. "We'll just have to be careful. I'll take the gun I have in the hidden compartment. Don't worry, I can open up the Graded Z+ castle, arm the bomb and we can get out of town, all within fifteen minutes. Just like the original plan, but two days earlier. Don't worry," he said again, to assure his wife.

"Can't help it," she replied, as they sat in the continued traffic on the way to DC. "I will remain worried until we safely get to Pittsburgh." The rain had grown a little heavier and Ji-eun was lost in her thoughts as she watched the rhythmic thump-

thump-thump of the car's wipers across the windshield. She just wanted to be far away from the city of Washington, DC, with her family intact and happy.

As Ji-eun was contemplating her family's future, the Triple Play team headquarters was a beehive of activity. They had amassed almost thirty terabytes of data on Sung-jin's agent and consulting activities, pulled from a variety of sources including tax records, phone records, invoices, conversations with his co-workers and friends, etc. Marcia had tweaked David's deployment of the various field units all around Washington DC and the other major metropolitan areas, but had pretty much left the rest of the plan intact.

Almost an hour before Min-ho and Ji-eun had gotten to the roadblock, at around 7:57pm, the Triple Play team had gotten an excited call from one of the DIA analysts. An invoice of Sung-jin's with Hwangsong Enterprises had been found with respect to the delivery of a large statue that was being stored at a warehouse in the DC metropolitan area, near Dulles Airport.

This was it! every member of the team thought to himself or herself simultaneously. David nodded to Marcia. "Recommending that we send both Cannon 1 and Cannon 2 to Dulles; it'll take them about 50 minutes to get there from where they are in downtown DC. Richie's in Black Hawk One with his sharpshooter team; K2 will lead the NEST team from Black Hawk Two; I will be in Black Hawk Three as backup, with the 30mm cannons ready to blast the nuke if necessary."

"Make it happen, David," Marcia said, nodding in assent. "This is the last nuke, David; let's get this done." HSA Jorgensen and FBI Director Edelman piped in as well: "Go get them, David. Let's get this triple play."

The team set 2058 hours ET as the time for the start of the operation. K2 was doing a last minute check of the NEST equipment on Black Hawk Two to make sure that all of the gear was in working order. She wished dearly that Ben and Sri were here, but she would have to make do. *Play the cards you're dealt*, she admonished herself in her mind. Sabrina was a big help, but she was way better at analytical work than she was at this operational stuff. Nonetheless, along with three other NEST technicians, the NEST team methodically and efficiently completed running through the diagnostics tests for their gear. Tonight, they had a new beta piece of equipment, a specially pressurized portable tank that contained liquid nitrogen and other proprietary ingredients. The tank emitted a stream of liquid that literally would freeze the electronics of any device it touched, thereby preventing the RA-115's countdown timer from working and detonating the bomb. The beta equipment was the size of a large external frame backpack and weighed about twenty-eight pounds; it was meant to be worn like a camping backpack by an FBI agent. Sabrina gave K2 and the other techs the thumbs-up signal after testing out the liquid nitrogen tank and the foamer. They were set to go.

Black Hawk Two took off into the rainy night only a few minutes after the NEST equipment had been checked. Onboard were K2, Sabrina, three other NEST techs, two FBI agents (one of whom would carry the liquid nitrogen tank) and two Black Hawk pilots. Rain, more than a drizzle now, but far less than a torrential downpour, was coming down on them in sheets. Black Hawk One had already taken off by that time, filled with Richie Gutierrez and his team of snipers.

David's role was to serve as a backup to Black Hawks One and Two. In his helicopter, Black Hawk Three, he had one

NEST technician, two sharpshooters, and a member of Jim Broussard's EOD team, in addition to two pilots. Black Hawk Three, however, was like the "Terminator" helicopter that they used for the "I" nuke, in that the chopper carried two mounted 30mm cannons to blast the nuke to smithereens if necessary. Black Hawk Three took off two minutes after Black Hawk Two did.

Marcia directed the operation from Andrews. "Everyone in place?" she asked at 2055 hours.

"Roger that," came the replies. The plan was simple and comparable to the Reno simulation, except that they wouldn't be using the foamer from the warehouse rooftop. Fortunately, the "Hot Spot Mobile" truck, which was originally running late, had made up time getting to Dulles as it had picked up a police escort. Unfortunately, the truck could not pick up any radiation signatures within the warehouse so far.

"What's the situation on the ground, David?" Marcia asked anxiously.

"Hard to say," David admitted. "We don't have any suspicious bogeys on our screen. The advance reconnaissance team picked up two night watchmen on their rounds outside the target warehouse and the neighboring one, but they've been talked to, and replaced by our agents. We think that the crate is somewhere in the middle of the warehouse. Rick in Cannon One will be coming in from the front entrance and Mark in Cannon Two will be coming in from the back. Richie's on the roof with a few shooters. We've divided the rest of the team up in half and they are going to infiltrate the warehouse now."

"How about terrorist guards inside the warehouse? Did the owners call back yet?"

"No, we just left a message, but it is July 4th weekend and it's not surprising that no one has gotten back to us yet. We have heat signature readings showing four people inside the warehouse office off to the west side, as you know. They're probably just innocent security staff, and not terrorists, but we're taking no chances since we haven't been able to verify it yet with the owners."

"What's your call? Does this feel right?"

"I'm getting less sure now. At this point, let's just take it slow. We'll neutralize the four remaining people and open the crate. We have all sorts of radiation detection machinery, the foamer, and the liquid nitrogen freezer device."

At precisely 2058 hours, the front and back hangar doors of the warehouse were opened and Cannon 1 and Cannon 2 zoomed into the warehouse. A loudspeaker horn blared out that this was an FBI raid and the four men were told to get down on the ground. In less than three minutes, the warehouse was secured and the crate that they were looking for had been located. K2 nodded to her NEST techs and the FBI man wearing the liquid nitrogen tank. Josephine Rachmaninoff, the NEST tech with the radiation detection equipment, shrugged her shoulders. There were no radiation readings coming from the crate. Even if the crate were fully Graded Z+ shielded with ten inches of shielding, there should be some reading from the detectors now, since the detector was literally only a few inches away. One of the FBI tactical team members took a crowbar to the crate, and jimmied it open quickly. A slew of foam packing peanuts spilled all over the floor and an interior metal box was revealed. That metal box was immediately further pried open, yielding a bronze statue. Josephine thrust her radiation detector at the statue, but there was still no radiation reading. Nada.

Johnny G took a sledgehammer to the statue to confirm nothing was in there. There was no RA-115 anywhere in the statue, the box, or in the crate. The team, which of course up to this time was in battlefield readiness, took a collective deep breath. To be safe, they checked and re-checked their readings and looked around the rest of the warehouse, including in adjacent crates. Still nothing. No sign of the RA-115.

"So what's the scoop, K2?" Marcia asked nervously into K2's headset.

"Looks like we're clear," K2 replied. "Nothing here."

"Dammit!" Marcia cursed over the communications line. Then she remarked, "I don't know whether to be alarmed or relieved. I'll pick being alarmed for now, since we still don't know where the "K" nuke is. Is it possible that there is no nuke in DC? Maybe it's not going off on July 4th?"

"I don't know if we are that lucky," David said in reply. Almost as if mocking his statement, a few seconds later a klaxon started sounding at Triple Play headquarters. One of the many basketball sensors that now blanketed Washington had detected what could be the "K" nuke!

"Dammit!" David said. "I think that I just jinxed us."

"Where is it?" Marcia demanded of the team. "Where's the signal coming from?"

"We've got a reading near the west end of the Mall. Hold it, it's a little north of that, at the Kennedy Center! We have reports of an agent in trouble!" one of the technicians shouted.

"Who else do we have there?"

"Well, there are two other FBI agents, and fifty police officers stationed all around the mall area, but no NEST people or other heavy equipment."

"Then get them there, for god's sake!" Marcia shouted. "Now!" she added for emphasis needlessly. The team looked at the clock – it read 2119 hours.

David signaled to the pilot of Black Hawk Three and the pilot immediately took off for the Kennedy Center. The rest of the Dulles warehouse team were also scrambling to get back onboard their choppers. It was a short eight to nine minute or so flight back to downtown DC. They were going to make it! They had to make it in time!

David knew, however, that they would be handicapped in their response. Cannon 1 and 2 were too far away from the Kennedy Center to get back to downtown DC in time, so they would not be able to help. A large number of the FBI's ground troops also would not be available. Many of the troops had gotten to Dulles via ground vehicles, since they couldn't all fit on the Black Hawks. Those ground troops also would not be able to get to the Kennedy Center in time to help.

As the Black Hawks screamed through the air in the rainy night, the Triple Play team tried to get more intel on what had happened. How did the bomb get to downtown DC? They had thousands of people stationed on the outskirts of DC, thinking that the bomb hadn't gotten there yet. These people were stationed too far away and would not be able to assist either. The Black Hawk's short flight unfortunately felt like the longest minutes of David's life.

About twelve minutes before Black Hawk Three was taking off back to downtown DC, Min-ho had pulled up the Odyssey at one of the Kennedy Center curbs, at a place nearest to the statue where they had placed the RA-115 over seven months ago.

The Kennedy Center was full to capacity tonight. The National Youth Orchestra, together with three other state and regional youth orchestras, were performing there as part of a July 4th weekend music festival. The performance had started at 7pm, and the audience had already long ago returned to its seats following the intermission. As a result, there weren't any people milling around within the Kennedy Center building; they were all seated inside the main concert hall watching the final part of the performance.

Leaving the minivan running to keep the air circulating for his wife and child, Min-ho had gotten out and walked over to the statue. He took the handgun that he had hidden in a panel within the Odyssey, along with a bunch of extra ammunition clips. Inserting the key into the bottom of the statue to open it up, Min-ho carefully began the process of activating the nuke. Once the statue base was open, he was able to see and access the separate Graded Z+ castle inside. It was hard to see the keyhole of the interior Graded Z+ castle with the rain dripping down off of the umbrella he held, but he eventually turned the key and threw the lid of the castle open. The RA-115 backpack that looked back at him was in fairly pristine condition, exactly like it was when they had sealed the nuke inside the statue so many months ago.

Min-ho dug the codebook out of his pocket as he gave a thumbs up signal to Ji-eun. She was patiently waiting for him in the minivan about fifty yards away. Ji-eun smiled at the signal; they were almost ready to start their new life. And then she froze as she saw a man walk up about ten yards away from Min-ho.

"Hey, sir, what are you doing there?" This was an FBI agent who had noticed Min-ho squatting near the base of the statute. Min-ho looked up to see the agent, clearly from the FBI as the letters were emblazoned in yellow on his windbreaker, walking towards him. "Step away from that statue!" the agent ordered. It looked like he was going to call it in on the radio, so Min-ho quickly took out his gun with attached silencer from his pocket. He shot the agent three times point blank in the abdomen. The agent went down with a thud.

Ji-eun tensed in the car as she saw the FBI agent go down. This was not good; they were supposed to get out of there unnoticed. The FBI agent's radio was squawking, asking what was going on. Ji-eun jumped out of the car and started running towards Min-ho. "We've got to go," she screamed to her husband. "Just forget about the bomb. Think about Min-jun."

Min-ho evaluated the situation. He went over to the fallen agent, who was writhing in pain, even though he had been wearing a bulletproof vest. Min-ho quickly hit him on the head with his gun, rendering the agent unconscious immediately. The radio was still squawking so Min-ho turned it off. "This man is not a normal police officer; he's with the FBI," he shouted at Ji-eun who was still running, but getting closer to him. "They know something is up. I don't know how, but it seems like they do. We have to set off the bomb now."

Ji-eun was flabbergasted. "Are you crazy?" Ji-eun shouted as she got to where her husband was. "You'd really try to kill all of us with the bomb! Listen, forget about the nuke," she pleaded with her husband. "Take care of your family. We can escape to fight another day. There's no one coming for a little while at least; let's just run away now."

"No," Min-ho said solemnly. "I am sorry. We must do our duty even at the expense of our own lives. I need to set the bomb now for the minimum time." Min-ho started walking back to the RA-115.

Ji-eun looked icily at her husband as she followed his movements. "Don't do this Min-ho. Let's leave now," she said to him. Together. Set it for longer. Either way, I'm going. And I'm going with your son." She walked towards him to try to pull him away from the nuke.

Min-ho ignored her and began programming the RA-115. He then reflected for a moment, and paused his programming. "OK, for you and Min-jun, I am setting the bomb now for thirty minutes," he announced. "I'll lock the bomb back into the castle, and then back into the statue. They won't be able to figure out what's going on for at least thirty minutes. We'll then take off with Min-jun, and get out of the blast radius at least. I don't think we're necessarily going to live, but that's the most I'll do."

In the distance, Ji-eun began to hear the wail of sirens coming closer. "Deal," Ji-eun said quickly. "Now hurry up! Make it happen. We need to get out of here." She squeezed Min-ho's shoulder gently and started to walk towards the minivan.

As Min-ho continued with setting the detonation sequence, there was a disturbance in the rainy night as two Black Hawk helicopters were rushing down towards the ground at the northeast section of the building where Min-ho and Ji-eun were located. The semi-silent whirring of the helicopter blades cut through the falling rain. Min-ho looked up to see the silhouettes of two Black Hawk helicopters coming down from the sky. Soon, Min-ho immediately realized, armed men would be rappelling down on ropes from the Black Hawks.

"No!" Min-ho screamed, as he punched in the final code numbers to finish with the detonation sequence. No time now for a thirty minute lead time. *Oh well, I am going to be a martyr*, Min-ho thought to himself. He finalized the sequence, setting the time to the minimum of three minutes instead of thirty minutes. Then he turned the titanium key and finished the process by pressing the two fail-safe buttons simultaneously. The nuke was fully activated. He put on the backpack and started running towards the main Kennedy Center Building a short distance away. He fired his gun blindly back at the Black Hawks. Just as Min-ho had feared, a few FBI agents had already started rappelling down from ropes dangling from the Black Hawk helicopters.

Ji-eun heard the shots and stopped moving towards the Odyssey as she saw her husband take off at a full sprint the other way. She turned around and ran after him quickly. "Leave the nuke! We need to … " Ji-eun cried. Her next words was cut off as she was hit by gunfire by one of the FBI agents shooting from inside Black Hawk Two. The agent was aiming at Min-ho, but Ji-eun had gotten in the way right as he was shooting. She went down and stayed down. Black Hawk Three was now swooping down from the sky from behind the other two Black Hawks and began to prepare to fire its 30mm cannons after it could get a clear shot.

"Stay with Min-jun in the car, Ji-eun!" Min-ho called out as he continued to run. He had made it to the first set of plaza doors. Min-ho flung open the doors and entered the interior of the building, taking the backpack off his back in one smooth motion onto the floor just inside the Family Theater. Black Hawk Three was five seconds late in getting into shooting position; there was no target for the 30mm cannons to get a shot at now.

The Black Hawk Three pilot shouted, "I don't have a shot! No shot! Ground troops continue to engage!" Min-ho looked up to see two FBI tactical sharpshooters coming at him full bore inside the first set of doors at the plaza entrance. He started shooting at the men and the glass doors, hitting the first one in the torso and in the arm, causing that agent to drop his machine gun in anguish. Some of the glass doors began to shatter from the gunfire. It looked like the FBI agents were wearing some sort of body armor so Min-ho began to aim alternately at their helmets and their arms. The other FBI agent dove on the ground, but maintained his forward momentum.

From a slightly different angle, Min-ho saw out of the corner of his eye that another FBI agent was coming towards him from the other side of the Kennedy Center building. This one looked like he had a tank of some sort on his back so Min-ho started shooting at the tank and agent, fully emptying his magazine at the target. Quickly reloading with a different magazine, Min-ho continued his firing until the man went down.

By that time, Richie and the remaining FBI sharpshooter from the first helicopter were running towards the plaza doors at full speed, zigzagging in their course so as to make it harder to hit them.

"Is the nuke armed?" Marcia shouted at her tactical team.

"Can't tell, can't tell," came the response from both Richie and David. David had also just hit the ground running just outside the plaza as Black Hawk Three bounced onto the slick ground.

Having discharged its personnel, Black Hawk Three was now back in the air trying to maneuver outside the center to get a clear shot at Min-Ho. Black Hawk Three was itching to let loose with its 30mm cannons. Unfortunately, by this time, Min-ho had picked up the RA-115 nuclear backpack again, rapidly running deep into the interior of the Family Theater where he hid behind the front of the rear section's row of seats. The Black Hawk Three pilot couldn't see anything to aim at now, and didn't have any shot.

In the night sky, three F-16 fighters also screamed overhead, but they also had no target. It would be useless to fire a missile at the building because it would just bury the nuke in rubble and not disarm it.

"We need actionable information," Marcia shouted. Edelman shouted, "Give us eyes! Tell us what you see!"

"We're on it," David shouted back. "Nothing yet. Almost at the door." K2 ran over to the downed agent carrying the liquid nitrogen setup, and helped to remove it from his back, putting it on herself. After she had strapped on the equipment, she started to run towards the Family Theater. However, it was clear to K2 as she was running that the device had been hit by bullets from Min-ho's gun. It wasn't clear if the device would work, as the pressure was swiftly dropping. Cursing from the weight of the equipment, K2 almost fell over a few times as she was running, but she righted herself each time and finally got near to the front door of the Family Theater.

David was ahead of her by five strides. Ahead of David, and inside the Family Theater already, Richie and three other FBI tactical snipers were exchanging gunfire with Min-ho. K2 could see that this was going to be a dicey situation as she entered the Family Theater.

Sounds of gunfire reverberated through the theater as K2 positioned herself just inside the entrance right behind

David. She stole a look at the pressure gauge; it was down to 18% of its intended normal reading and still falling.

The four sharpshooters had positioned themselves behind the last seats of the rear section, two on each side, and were spraying the theater with gunfire. Min-ho sporadically fired from his hidden position at the front of the rear section of seats. He glanced over at the timer – only 38 seconds to go.

"Is the nuke activated?" David asked Richie, as he joined his friend on one side of the rear section.

"Don't know," came the reply from Richie. "I think I hear some beeping. Could be the timer. Only one bad guy, though, and we know where he is, so let's just get this done." David assessed the situation. It was pretty bleak. They were going to have to assume that the terrorist was activating the nuke now, meaning that they would have to rush him, no matter what the consequences. David motioned to have two of the sharpshooters make a rush down the left side of the rear section, while the other two would rush down the right side. David indicated that he would provide cover fire from the middle of the rear section. The snipers grimly re-checked their ammos and magazines and nodded to David that they were ready; they would rush Min-ho in three seconds.

"What's the call, David?" Marcia asked from the headquarters.

"Go time," David said as he leapt up from behind the middle seats of the back of the rear section and sprayed the theater with bullets from his machine gun. K2 fed him magazine after magazine, after David had emptied out the previous one. David continued to fire to provide cover for the advancing troops.

The four FBI sharpshooters rushed the front of the rear section where Min-ho had been patiently waiting. Min-ho let one of the sharpshooters have it with two shots to the torso as he couldn't lift the gun high enough for a head shot. Then he swung the gun around the other way to fire his remaining bullets into the sharpshooters coming from the other direction. Richie by this time had gotten a bead on Min-ho and took him out. The fight was over; Min-ho lay dead in a pool of his own blood.

The four sharpshooters signaled to David that they had killed Min-ho. David and K2 quickly ran down to where the nuclear backpack lay at the front of the rear section, with David helping K2 with the weight of the equipment. "Can you disarm this?" he asked K2 anxiously.

"I'm sure going to try," K2 replied. K2 surveyed the situation. The RA-115 timer was in its countdown mode and said 14 seconds. She would only have one chance at this. David helped her remove the backpack and she placed the sprayer hoses directly onto the areas on the RA-115 where the sprayers could perform the most freezing action on the electronics. The nozzles were activated at the correct setting. She directed David and Richie to hold the nozzles firmly. K2 worriedly looked at the pressure reading on the device. It had dropped to 6% of normal; this wasn't good at all.

Nodding at David and Richie, K2 depressed the start button that would activate the maximum flow of the freezing agents. A hissing sound ensued and some of the freezing agent sputtered out, foaming a bit on the surface of the RA-115. The countdown clock on the nuke kept going, unaffected by the liquid nitrogen. K2 depressed the start button again and again. Some more freezing agent sputtered out. Then, after a few seconds, nothing more came out. The countdown clock was now down to seven seconds and still going.

"No!!!" K2, David and Richie exclaimed together. There was no time to do anything; they couldn't get the RA-115 out of the building in time to blast it with the 30mm cannons from a Black Hawk. Even that may not have stopped the detonation sequence, but it would have likely at least diminished the impact of the blast.

Meanwhile, in the main concert hall, one of the youth orchestras was nearing the end of the fourth movement of Shostakovich's Tenth Symphony. Unfortunately, the time remaining was such that the nuke would go off a little before the last measure would be reached. *How pathetic*, K2 thought to herself, *given the history of this particular symphony.* She turned to look at David.

"I love you," K2 said to David simply.

"I love you too," David replied back.

"Well, I love you guys too, just not in that way," Richie chimed in.

David and K2 could not help but smile at this as they kissed each other passionately. Richie was a joker until the end. Three … two … one. David and K2 felt everything and nothing as they continued to kiss for what seemed like an eternity. Zero. The nuke's timer buzzed and David and K2 melted together into infinity.

Strangely, though, K2 could swear that she heard the final measures of the Shostakovich symphony, followed by rapturous applause from the audience. Was she dreaming? What was happening? Richie, of course, shook them out of their dreamlike trance. "Uh, guys, while it would have been really romantic for you to die in each other's arms, not looking like that is going to happen tonight. I hate to break it to you, but we're still alive. The nuke didn't go off."

David and K2 opened their eyes. The RA-115 just sat there, incessantly blinking and buzzing at "0:00:00." No detonation. No explosion.

Richie couldn't help himself. He had to keep on talking. "Hey, David, can I start my vacation now, since the nuke's a dud? Wait, speaking of duds, do they sell Milk Duds in this theater? I love Milk Duds. And I'm really hungry." Richie smiled at the two of them. David just shook his head at Richie's humor, fist-bumped him, and gave K2 an extra kiss for the road. Then the three of them wearily got up and called it in to headquarters.

Triple Play headquarters burst out into spontaneous applause when they heard the news. It was just like at the Kennedy Center after the orchestra performance had ended, but this applause felt ten times louder. The President traded high-fives with HSA Jorgensen and FBI colleagues Marcia Brown and Ron Edelman gave each other a congratulatory hug. They had done it - they had completed the Triple Play!

Back at the Kennedy Center, the performance had concluded and the concertgoers were noisily beginning to stream out of the main concert hall. K2 and the NEST team took control over the nuke, carefully loading it into a Black Hawk to get it away from the nation's capital as they were trying to figure out why it didn't go off. An elite group of technicians would analyze the bomb carefully over the next few hours to ensure that it was actually fully disarmed. The scene was chaotic as the DC police and other FBI agents had arrived en masse. The concertgoers by now had begun to file out of the building into the rainy night. They were quite bewildered at the number of FBI agents, policemen and ambulances around the Kennedy

Center, as well as all of the broken glass and detritus around. The concertgoers had been fairly oblivious to the goings-on since the main concert hall was pretty far away from the Family Theater. Moreover, most of the gunfire had been relatively silent, as everyone had been using sound suppressors on their weapons.

David had gone over to Ji-eun, who was carefully being lifted onto a stretcher. She was bloodsoaked as the bullets that had hit her had clearly done considerable internal damage. Unlike the FBI sharpshooters, Ji-eun had not been wearing a bulletproof vest or body armor. She stopped the emergency techs as she saw David with his "FBI Special Agent in Charge" windbreaker come near her. "My son," she implored. She labored to continue speaking. "In the Honda Odyssey. Take care of him. Safe deposit key in the left zipper pocket of my purse in the minivan. Explains everything." And then she died as the rain continued to fall on the team. The rain seemed like it would go on forever.

EPILOGUE

During the week following July 4th, the Triple Play team felt like they were floating on air. They were asked to participate in meeting after meeting where they debriefed rapturous audiences who could not be more delighted to hear again and again about the team's exploits.

NEST had of course by then carefully and permanently disabled the third RA-115. Ji-eun's safe deposit key had led the team to a bank in Baltimore, where they had found Ji-eun's journal. The journal had explained at length her reasons for sabotaging the nuke. Indeed, in their debriefings, the team's report about the "K" nuke proved the most interesting part to their audiences, who were incredulous that the only reason that a 2 kiloton nuclear bomb had not been detonated in Washington DC was that a female terrorist simply believed that it was wrong to use any nuke to kill so many innocent people, no matter which country it was used against.

The original journal would be stored safely, as a classified document, within the archives at FBI headquarters, part of the nation's historical record. David and K2, however, had been allowed to make a copy of it, which they had taken to David's condo at the end of the week.

***

Katherine and David sat entwined on the couch in David's living room. Next to them, Min-jun was finally asleep, rocked gently by the nanny that the WMD Directorate had provided to them to help take care of the baby. The FBI was trying to figure out how to take care of Min-jun for the long-term. Outside, the nighttime rain was coming down hard. It was raining just as hard as when they were at the Kennedy Center on that fateful night one week ago. Don, Marcia and Sabrina were also there. Even Ben and Sri had flown in, and the two were milling around inside David's place. Sri was amazed by how many used water bottles that David had stacked up against his wall. They had all read and re-read Ji-eun's journal, continuing to be fascinated by it.

"I can't believe that we're still alive, David," K2 said.

"Me neither," David confessed.

"She was a remarkable woman," K2 continued, as she perused the journal. The journal started this way: "My name is Ji-eun Lee and I was sent from North Korean to America as a deep cover agent many years ago. My husband, Min-ho Lee, is also a deep cover agent, and we were sent to America to be what you would call 'sleeper' spies."

"Wow, deep cover for years and years," K2 muttered to no one in particular. "That's a long time."

"Yeah, Sri's never done anything secretly every day for years, well, except eat double-stuffed Oreos," Ben joked.

"Shh," Sri said, putting his finger over his mouth. "You weren't supposed to tell anyone, remember?"

K2 kept on reading the document, with David reading over her shoulder: "I was brought up to hate America, and truthfully I did for a long time. However, perhaps I am not genetically made up to continue to hate forever. Part of my change in heart occurred shortly following my arrival in the US. It didn't escape me how well my neighbors treated us when we moved in, even though we were "foreigners." I believe that was when I first started thinking that I couldn't and shouldn't kill these people. Then, during Min-jun's birth, when he had some medical issues and the doctors and nurses at the hospital took incredible care of him and me, that also made me think twice about my completing my mission. I think that Min-jun's birth itself was the thing that put me over the edge and made me realize how precious all life was. Perhaps there were other subconscious factors that made me change my mind. Anyway, the more and more I thought about it, the more and more it was apparent to me that I couldn't go through with detonating the RA-115."

K2 glanced at the bassinet where the eight month old Min-jun was sleeping peacefully. He looked like his mother, especially his eyes. David seemed to have the identical thought, saying "He really does look like Ji-eun, doesn't he?" K2 looked over at David and smiled. Marcia went over and tucked Min-jun in a little bit more.

"Such a brave little boy," Marcia remarked. "It must have been a brutal first few days to adjust to not having his parents around, but since then he's been getting a little better every day with the separation anxiety. What a trooper! I can't imagine what he's going through. It must have been quite a shock to just have strangers around to take care of you."

K2 and David both nodded in assent at this. Neither could or wanted to imagine what it would be like as a baby not to have your parents around. K2 pointed to a section of the journal. "This is the part that gets me the most," she announced to the group, reading aloud the passage. "Since I was at home on my maternity leave when Min-ho was at work, I had much more time than Min-ho to read the manual for the RA-115. After reading it, I decided that I could try to manipulate the detonation software." She stopped reading and looked around at her friends. "Imagine that! She just decides one day that, you know what, I can change this nuke's software so it can't go off! Amazing!"

"Yeah, who does she think she is? Ben or Sabrina or something? That's a legendary amount of self-confidence," Sri said, smiling at Ben and Sabrina when he said it, so they knew he was just making good-natured fun of their extraordinary abilities.

Katherine continued reading Ji-eun's writing. "It was hard since the manual was written originally only in Cyrillic. The English translation was a little spotty, but I finally managed to figure out how to access the test diagnostic mode. It took me a while to make it such that my husband Min-ho could not tell that the nuke was perpetually in diagnostics mode. By that method, I could ensure that the detonation sequence could never actually set off the bomb."

"This woman was a genius," Don said admiringly. "In my book, she's an honorary NEST member."

"Hear, hear," K2, Ben and Sri said together.

"I'll drink to that!" Ben exclaimed.

"Yeah, well you'll drink to anything, so long as I'm buying," Sri ribbed Ben, getting him back a bit about the Oreo comment.

K2 went on: "The key is to let my husband think that we were setting off the bomb. The plan of course is to make Min-ho use the maximum 24 hour delay in the timer setting. Then Min-ho would leave with me and we would be too far away from the nuke to come back. My plan is to start the timer on the night of Sunday, July 3rd. Then we would leave Washington, DC, and the nuke would "detonate" on the night of July 4th when a lot of people would be watching the fireworks show near the National Mall."

K2 stopped reading and David broke in. "When we took in Sung-jin to interrogate him, it must have spooked his handlers. Ji-eun had scratched in a hastily written addendum here: 'Change in plans. Z protocol: revised directive to set the nuke off as soon as possible. Will convince Min-ho to still set for 24 hours, to "detonate" on July 2nd. Basically, just moving up the timetable by two days.' Wow, they really knew how to improvise."

K2 continued reading from the journal: "When the nuke doesn't go off as Min-ho expects, I would just tell my husband that this was a sign from God that we should forget about the nuke. It was not meant to be. God is telling us we should give up our spy mission and just live like a regular family. I will tell Min-ho that we should simply send a final message to our handler noting that we did what you told us to do, but the nuke failed to go off. It's not our fault, but because of you, we are on the run. We won't be able to communicate with you any longer. We'd really just be a normal family then."

"Hmm, speaking of normal families," David said, "hold on." He got up off the couch and went over to one of the kitchen drawers and started rummaging around. K2 looked confusedly at Marcia, who just shrugged her shoulders. Finding what he was looking for, David came back to the couch and kneeled before Katherine. "So, Katherine, after all that we've been through, I just wanted to say something. Every day that I have known you has been the best day of my life. Ji-eun's devotion to her family was amazing, and makes me want to devote my life to you, and I hope our bigger family. I'll still need to clear it with your parents and all that of course. What I'm trying to say is, umm, will you consider possibly marrying me?" As he finished, he took out the box that he had fished out of the drawer and opened it, showing Katherine the engagement ring that had been in the Smithline family for three generations.

K2 was floored; she hadn't seen this coming at this time. Maybe later, much later, when the excitement of the Triple Play operation died down, after they had visited North Carolina together, but not now. And then K2 thought to herself, why not now? Why not associate her engagement with the pinnacle of her professional life? "Well, David," she said, as the others looked on expectantly, "I think that I can only say one thing …." David was getting nervous with anticipation now. She decided to make him squirm a little bit. "You know you are kind of surprising me here, which isn't that fair. As a result, I'm not sure how to respond, except to say …" David's heart almost stopped. "… an absolutely unequivocal yes."

Everyone in the room clapped and hugged the two friends. They were all smiling, David and K2 the most of all, of course. The baby Min-jun stirred, but remained asleep as the nanny started to rock the bassinet. Min-jun would have stayed asleep except that the final lightning bolt and corresponding thunderclap of the rainstorm occurred just then, startling the baby awake. Min-jun started bawling and Katherine quickly went over and picked him up; she started to rock him gently in her arms.

The baby calmed down only after a couple minutes of being cradled by Katherine and being fussed over. Katherine moved over to the window where they could see the rain still falling on the city. "You know, we're going to also need to make our own babies too, David," she teased.

"Ready to report for duty whenever you need me," David saluted and smiled. They just stood there, then, David hugging Katherine from behind, both of them transfixed by the rain.

This is it; it's the last of the rain, someone behind them said. It had been the heaviest rainfall of the year, but it looked like reasonably clear skies going forward.

LIST OF ABBREVIATIONS

AQI	Al Qaeda in Iraq, predecessor of ISIS
CIA	Central Intelligence Agency
DC	District of Columbia (Washington, DC)
DEA	Drug Enforcement Administration
Delta	Delta Force, Army 1st Special Forces Operational Detachment-Delta unit
DEFCON	Defense Readiness Condition, alert state used by US military
DEVGRU	US Special Naval Warfare Development Group, also known as SEAL Team Six
DHS	Department of Homeland Security
DIA	Defense Intelligence Agency
DoD	Defense Department
DoE	Department of Energy
DPRK	Democratic People's Republic of Korea; North Korea
EOD	Explosive Ordnance Disposal, part of US Army
ET	Eastern Time
FAA	Federal Aviation Administration
FBI	Federal Bureau of Investigation
FISA	Foreign Intelligence Surveillance Act
G7	Group of 7 organization (US, Canada, UK, Germany, France, Italy, Japan + EU)
GCF	Global Consolidated Foods
GRU	Glavnoye razvedyvatel'noye upravleniye, Russian foreign military intelligence directorate
HSA	Homeland Security Advisor
HSC	Homeland Security Council

IACC	Iranian-American Chamber of Commerce
IND	Improvised Nuclear Device
ISIL	Islamic State of Iraq and the Levant, also more commonly known as ISIS
ISIS	Islamic State of Iraq and Syria
JCTF	Joint Counterterrorism Task Force
K2	Katherine Kung (nickname)
LANL	Los Alamos National Laboratory
LLNL	Lawrence Livermore National Laboratory
NCTC	National Counterterrorism Center
NEST	Nuclear Emergency Support Team
NGB	National Guard Bureau
NNSA	National Nuclear Security Administration
NRAT	Nuclear Radiological Advisory Team
NSA	National Security Agency
NSS	National Security Staff
NTAS	National Terrorism Advisory System
OCD	Obsessive-Compulsive Disorder
PT	Pacific Time
RDD	Radiological Dispersion Device
RV	Recreational Vehicle (camping vehicle)
SAIC	Special Agent in Charge (FBI)
SEAL	Sea, Air and Land Team; US Navy Special Forces
TSA	Transportation Security Administration
UNLV	University of Nevada, Las Vegas
VP	Vice President
WMD	Weapon(s) of Mass Destruction

ACKNOWLEDGMENTS

Thanks to all of the wonderful people who helped me write this novel – you know who you are. Without each of you, this book could never have been written. Special thanks to my family, and also to, among others, Hun-seng C, David C, Ted L and Steven Y for their review and edits. Of course, any remaining errors and/or omissions in this book are solely my responsibility and not theirs.

ABOUT THE AUTHOR

Maverick Lee is the pseudonym for a first-time author who has always been fascinated by technothrillers. Maverick lives in the San Francisco Bay Area.

www.ingramcontent.com/pod-product-compliance
Lightning Source LLC
Chambersburg PA
CBHW060155260626
47160CB00001B/280

9 780692 670361